*Someone to Blame* is as convicting as it is moving. Lakin deftly explores the complexities of family relationships and their consequences, and reminds us what happens when we judge those we know nothing about. Readers will enjoy this rising new talent.

Terri Blackstock, *author of*
Intervention *and* Predator

C. S. Lakin's captivating writing and well-drawn characters immediately drew me into this story. I loved it!

Cindy Martinusen Coloma, *bestselling author of*
Orchid House *and* Beautiful

Lakin's is a welcome voice bringing fresh emotion to a story that doesn't shy away from difficult issues. I knew Lakin was special from the first chapter. I kept thinking, "I hope people think this when they read my stuff."

Harry Kraus, *bestselling author of* The Six-Liter
Club *and* Salty Like Blood

Beautifully written by C. S. Lakin, this deeply moving story of grace in hard places will linger with you long after the last page.

James Scott Bell, *author of* Sins of the Fathers

Lakin is a skilled wordsmith with a unique, compelling voice. In Someone to Blame, she spins the story of a family in chaos while digging deeper into what it means to be a scapegoat. A surprising, great read.

*Mary DeMuth, author of The Defiance Texas*
*Trilogy*

A poignant and relevant story of redemption and renewal, wonderfully written and powerfully paced. C. S. Lakin deftly explores the heart's desperate struggle to make sense of loss. Well done.

*Susan Meissner, author of* The Shape of Mercy

# SOMEONE TO BLAME

*A novel*

C. S. LAKIN

**ZONDERVAN**®

**ZONDERVAN**.com/
**AUTHORTRACKER**
*follow your favorite authors*

ZONDERVAN

*Someone to Blame*
Copyright © 2010 by Susanne Lakin

This title is also available as a Zondervan ebook. Visit www.zondervan.com/ebooks.

This title is also available in a Zondervan audio edition. Visit www.zondervan.fm.

Requests for information should be addressed to:
Zondervan, *Grand Rapids, Michigan* 49530

---

Library of Congress Cataloging-in-Publication Data

Lakin, C. S., 1956 –
    Someone to Blame: a novel / C.S. Lakin.
      p.  cm.
    ISBN 978-0-310-32739-4 (pbk.)
      1. Domestic fiction. 2. Suicide victims—Family relationships—Fiction.
    3. California—Fiction. I. Title.
    PS3612.A54S66  2010
    813'.6—dc22
                                                2010016482

---

*Cover design: Laura Maitner-Mason*
*Cover photography: Andy & Michelle Kerry / Trevillion Images*
*Interior design: Beth Shagene*

*Printed in the United States of America*

---

10 11 12 13 14 15 /DCI/ 22 21 20 19 18 17 16 15 14 13 12 11 10 9 8 7 6 5 4 3 2 1

*To Leebears*
*For your steadfast encouragement and love.*

# Chapter 1

IRENE ONCE HEARD THAT IF YOU FELL OFF A CLIFF IN YOUR dream, you would always wake before smacking the ground.

If only real life were that merciful.

She pulled her damp cheek away from the warm glass of the truck window and gazed at the Trinity River meandering hundreds of feet below, gloomy green water snaking through a precipitous canyon. Narrow curves hugged the steep sides of cliff with only a short retaining wall of stacked rocks separating them from disaster—many of the stones chipped, some ominously missing from the ledge.

Irene imagined the fear a driver would feel straining to discern the gray road on a foggy night. Stunned as the stone wall came up too fast, too close, jerking the steering wheel, hearing the chilling screech of tires spinning out on loose gravel. And she could almost taste the desperate panic contained in the freefall, the driver trapped in the confines of the car as the vehicle plunged to the rocks and icy water below.

*Freefalling.*

Maybe that word came closest to defining this indefinable sensation of pain. No other words quite fit, and Irene desperately needed one that would. For months she had tested adjectives, placing them alongside the events that punctured their lives, yearning for a match.

*Raw. Horrific. Suffocating. Tragic. Debilitating.*

Impotent, feeble words.

After you fell for a while, you'd reach a constant speed— terminal velocity. Irene remembered reading that a skydiver in freefall leveled out at two hundred miles per hour. Had the person who invented that term realized the implied double meaning? How a fall at that great a speed could only be terminal?

Haunting images flooded her mind. Desperate people leaping from skyscraper windows in a futile attempt to escape a fire. A plane exploding at high altitude, spilling people out of their seats thousands of feet above the polar ice caps.

Yet, those tragic victims suffered only a merciful few seconds of horror before death.

When you lose a child, you tumble in freefall continually, without acquittal. The ground rushes up at you, your mind frantic and disbelieving. Impending doom pulls you toward impact at dizzying speeds.

But you never hit bottom.

Never a reprieve from panic. Never startling awake before the moment of contact. Never breathing that sigh of relief as the wisp of nightmare dissolves and you learn you are safe, tangled in bedcovers, your husband sleeping undisturbed at your side.

You are always falling.

Irene wrenched her eyes from the river and turned to Matt. He had barely spoken all day, but she was growing accustomed to his long stretches of silence. She watched him shift his weight and hunker down over the steering wheel, eyeing the rental trailer in the side-view mirror as it dragged behind them like an albatross.

They had sold most of their furniture with the house, shed it all, along with as many memories as possible. Crammed all the tangible remnants of their past into that twelve-foot box dragging behind them. How was it so easy to fit the pieces of their lives into such a small container?

The strain etched in Matt's face was telltale: his red, tired eyes; the pallor across his features; a grimace that annihilated any former trace of joy. Even the way he gripped the wheel evidenced the weeks of sleepless nights that eroded his concentration.

Exhaustion—plain and simple.

Irene knew she looked just as haggard. She adjusted the small vanity mirror attached to the sun visor so she could see into the backseat. Behind her, Casey's eyes were closed. Indecipherable strains of music filtered out of her daughter's headphones. Irene wished she could smother her own inner monologue that easily.

They had left the Motel 6 in Redding at dawn with the air already sweltering and shimmering across the highway. Matt had made one trip north the week before to relocate his work trailer and other equipment. Irene knew he had disposed of most of his tools, given them away or thrown them out. An inconceivable act. But then, nearly every choice they made these days seemed incongruous.

"Where are we now?" she asked.

"Almost to Willow Creek." He glanced at her, his eyes vacant. "Do you need to stop?"

Irene shook her head.

Casey leaned forward, raw impatience in her voice. "How much longer?"

"About an hour," Matt said.

"You hungry?" Irene turned and touched Casey's shoulder, felt a barely perceptible flinch. "We could get a bite."

Casey flopped back against her seat. "Let's just get there."

"There" meant the coastal town of Breakers—their new home. Most people would visit a place before making such a big decision, but theirs had been an act of hasty desperation. Irene had accepted the first job offered; she'd had no energy to think beyond that. She left all the moving details to Matt.

As they rounded another treacherous curve, her eyes caught a makeshift cross half buried in the weeds alongside the road, faded plastic flowers stapled to the wood. The sight snagged her heart, like hide on barbed wire.

There she was again. Falling.

In the town they'd left behind, a poorly banked curve two miles below their home was called the "Trap." Driving down the mountain grade into Running Springs was trying enough— all tight hairpin curves, compounded by three seasons of fog, ice, and sleet. No wonder the fatalities racked up. On more than one occasion, Matt had ushered Jesse and Daniel out in front of the station wagon with a flashlight while he inched the car behind them, locking sight on their waving hands, which looked like disembodied limbs. The road would materialize like an apparition, a foot at a time, out of nowhere. Eventually, there'd be a break in the fog and the boys would stomp the cold from their feet and tumble back into the car, blowing on their hands, wishing for hot chocolate.

The Trap had claimed countless victims over the years, accidents caused by mats of slick maple leaves rotting along the edges of the asphalt and the eerie way the fog gathered and pooled along that stretch of two-lane road. Yet in all those years, Irene never imagined her own family would be added to the grim statistics.

When had it all started to fall apart? That tragic day Daniel got his driver's license? Or earlier—the first time he was summoned to the principal's office in third grade? Or perhaps it traced even further back, to the day she'd met Matt and seen a man so carefully in control of his life.

Irene squeezed her eyes shut. Why hadn't warning bells gone off in her head that night? Why hadn't God stepped in and prevented the accident? Friends at church meant to be consoling, but their platitudes only stoked her anger. The "nonanswers."

We don't know why.

Why God allows some to live and some to die.

Why we can pray for him to protect our children and yet he lets things like this happen. Maybe for a greater glory and purpose.

So the town would now install warning lights and guard rails, and future lives would be spared—Jesse's life not lost in vain, et cetera, et cetera.

Irene clenched her teeth. She'd been over and over this for more than a year now—a tireless barrage of questions that yielded no answers.

She glanced at Matt and saw his blank expression, the stone wall he erected alongside his own raging river chasm. Who was she fooling? Did she think she could salvage a family out of the ashes of disaster? She knew she had to try—for Casey. At least she kept telling herself that, willing herself to believe it.

WHEN THEY ARRIVED AT BREAKERS, MATT SLOWED THE truck and eased up to a stop sign. Casey leaned forward and smoothed her cropped black hair.

"Are we here? Is this it?"

Matt nodded.

Irene looked at the small shopping center across the street and lowered the window. A strong breeze of salt air rushed in, cool and startling. Seagulls winged on the updraft above her, and she even heard the sea. Across the street a clapboard-sided market, post office, police station, and a few mismatched shops lined a parking lot. Casey leaned forward to peek out the windshield, then retreated to her seat with a disapproving sigh.

They drove the last five miles in silence, passing one rundown motel after another, dark wooden structures backed up against pockets of giant redwood trees. The road sank and tipped at the mercy of eroding cliffs, cliffs slowly dissolving at the insouciance of an unforgiving sea, while below them a turbulent metal-gray ocean slammed against the rocky shoreline, spray erupting high into the air.

Irene felt a kinship with the restless shifting of elements.

The rental house sat at the end of a dirt lane, close to the state park. Irene got out and eyed the small weathered cottage with its rotting plank siding and peeling brown paint. She had little doubt that, in no time, Matt would have it spruced up, with plumbing and lights working to his satisfaction. Matt would never have picked a house in perfect condition. She knew he needed something to fix ... since there was so much he couldn't fix in his own life.

Casey got out of the truck and stopped beside her mother, evaluating her new home. "You gotta be kidding," she mumbled, then trudged through the front door.

Matt busied himself detaching the trailer and setting chocks behind the tires. Irene closed her eyes and let the crisp wind whip her hair. Off in the distance waves pounded the shore, a low thrumming, like an advancing army.

She hesitated at the sagging threshold of the front door. Maybe this would be a good move. She would start teaching at Breakers Elementary. Casey would begin eighth grade with a whole new set of classmates—students who wouldn't stare at her with pity or back away, afraid her bad luck was contagious. Matt would pour his frustrated energy into repairing the cottage. They could begin a new life, one unmarred by pain and disaster. Allow some semblance of normalcy to seep back into their lives.

At least that was what Irene had hoped for, had prayed for.

She turned, about to say something to Jesse.

Her dead son.

At the edge of a crumbling cliff, Irene felt her feet give way. As the ground rushed up to meet her, she clutched the word in her fist.

*Freefalling.*

# Chapter 2

JERRY HUBBLE CAUGHT A GLIMPSE OF THE OLD FORD TRUCK as it veered into the market parking lot. He was midway to loading the last bag of groceries into his glossy red Corvette when the thing chugged to a stop. Even though tourist season had officially ended, travelers often made a pit stop in Breakers—the only small town for more than thirty miles going north or south on 101. Jerry was keen on noticing who showed up in his town and what business they had, especially if they looked like they sought lodging. His motel was just down the way and he sure needed some ready cash.

He looked back at his own car. Never once had he allowed himself to regret his new purchase. His ex might have stripped him of all but his dignity, but he sure wasn't going to keep driving that old Neon like a dog with his tail between his legs. So what if the payments on the 'Vette were killing him? He was fifty-two years old and had never had a nice car. A *nice* car.

Jerry gave his ride an affectionate pat while he watched the truck door swing open on a stubborn set of hinges. The truck bed, built up with two-by-twelves, contained a hefty load of firewood. Oak and madrone, from the looks of it. A sloppily painted "Firewood 4 Sale" spelled out the owner's business in black letters across the side of the truck.

Jerry expected to see someone as old and weathered as his vehicle step down from the running board, so the kid who hopped out was a surprise. In some other life, this young man might have been considered handsome, even winsome, with his deep green eyes and dusty blond hair. But those eyes carried a meanness Jerry could sense even yards away, which raised his hackles.

Jerry took in the lumberjack-style clothes: the worn flannel shirt, the scuffed jeans and boots, the wool cap on his head. He pegged the kid for twenty, maybe twenty-two, with a whole world of trouble trailing behind him. In all his years as a fire-fighter, Jerry had seen few faces as hardened on one so young, and doubted he'd find anything pretty underneath.

With a tender push, Jerry closed the trunk of his car and walked over to the post office to check his mail. He hated to turn the key in the lock; he still cringed, months after the divorce had been finalized. If he got one more stinking letter from that lawyer he would ... bust something, that's for sure.

But not today. With relief, he thumbed through the small assortment of bills, pocketed his disability check, and on his way out tossed the junk mail into the metal trash can.

He paused. Across the way, his neighbor, Mrs. Waverly, was speaking to the kid. The runt wasn't very tall; she could look him in the eye, even that bent over. Jerry could see her palsy-stricken legs tremble from where he stood. She clutched her drop-kick dog—same silvery color as her hair—close to her chest. The stupid dog was like an appendage or something; he never saw her without it pinned between her drab smock and her scarf. More nights than he could count, Jerry had nearly leapt out of bed to cross the street and strangle the yipping mutt. Well, one of these days ...

She pointed north and the kid nodded. Jerry grunted. Seems the boy had scored his first sale.

As Mrs. Waverly hobbled toward the market in as straight a line as her feet could see fit, Jerry traversed the parking lot to his Corvette and marveled again at how the car door miraculously unlocked on its own, just by sensing his keys in his pocket. *This* was a car.

He looked up and the grin melted from his face. The kid was studying his Corvette, letting his eyes drift over the shiny surface of paint, the chrome wheels, and come to rest on Jerry's features. Jerry watched him take in his unkempt hair, the formidable heftiness of his body, the extra tire of fat bulging over his belted jeans, the stained white T-shirt. The kid met Jerry's befuddled expression, and with a cock of his head, smiled a smile that was anything but friendly, then got into his Ford and drove north on Seawood Lane.

Jerry felt like someone had knocked the wind out of him. The feeling gave him the creeps. This kid was trouble; there was no mistaking it. And he didn't like the way he had eyed his car.

Jerry snorted and opened his car door, his attention fixed on the chug of smoke coming from the Ford truck's tailpipe as it disappeared around a bend. Yep, the sooner that strange kid left Breakers, the better.

# Chapter 3

Irene looked up from her desk and saw Casey standing at the door to the classroom. Sometimes she didn't recognize her daughter. She let her eyes roam over Casey's ink-black hair—which used to be some shade of dusty brown—and down to the faded gray shirt and tan cords that had once been Jesse's. That in itself unsettled her—seeing a distortion of Jesse in female form, down to the cross-trainers he used to wear. Casey had worn something of his each day for the last year and a half, even if just his buck knife in her pocket or the chain of old shoe laces she had woven into a choker. Irene had given up nagging, and Matt, after the first startled glance, acted like he never noticed, like it didn't tear his heart to shreds.

Casey scrunched her face in impatience. Irene stopped fussing with the stacks of papers and cut-out orange pumpkins piled on the desk and picked up her shoulder bag.

"I'm coming." She looked at the clock. The bell had rung only four minutes ago. "Don't you want to hang out with some of your classmates for a while, get to know them better?"

Casey's mouth dropped open before she obviously changed her mind about saying anything. Irene silently came up with the retorts: *"Mom, I don't need to make friends. I'm the out-sider; can't you see how different I am? I don't fit in. These kids are dumb, anyway."* Irene had heard every variation over the last few weeks.

*Give her time*, she chided herself. She imagined how hard it was for Casey to leave her middle school of three hundred kids and come to this backwater town where she had to rub elbows with the same twelve students each day. There were only four other girls in her eighth-grade class and Casey liked none of them.

Casey trailed Irene to the parking lot. Mr. Reese, her teacher, gave a friendly wave as he opened his car door. Wind whipped his thinning hair, revealing a large bald spot on the top of his head. A few papers blew out of his hand and headed her way. She picked them up and handed them to him. The metal clips on the flagpole out in the field clanged wildly, like a fire alarm, as raindrops splattered the asphalt.

"Thanks, Casey. Some wind," he said, heading back to his car. Over his shoulder he added, "Don't forget to work on your science fair ideas this weekend!"

Irene and Casey got into the Camry. Casey smoothed out her hair. "I hate the wind."

"So you're going to be doing a science project. Do you have a topic in mind?" Irene knew her voice sounded too eager.

"Mom. Please. Stop trying to be my best buddy, okay?"

Irene nodded and drove down First Street toward home.

"Can you stop at the market? I need to get something."

"Okay." She turned into the lot and parked. Pulling some bills from her purse, she said, "Pick up a carton of eggs and a small milk while you're in there."

Casey took the money and left while Irene sat in the car, watching students walk down the street, hefting their back-packs and joking around. Was it helping—immersing herself in the simple energies of third-graders? The problems they encountered were easily remedied: a stuck glue-stick cap, a milk carton spilled over the lunch table, trying to make the cursive letters fit inside the lines. And don't forget long division.

By third grade, Daniel's behavior problems had taken front stage in their family. Doctors threw acronyms around—ADD, ADHD, BPD—and also the names of drugs: Ritalin, Concerta, Synaptol. Matt refused to medicate Daniel. He recited label warnings to her. "Could cause possible brain damage, psychotic behavior, heart attacks, strokes, sudden death." How could any parent in his right mind take a chance administering this kind of death cocktail to his child? Daniel could weather this, tough it out, beat it on his own. And if Daniel refused to try, Matt would battle for him. It was just a matter of persistent determination.

Maybe the drugs would have helped. Maybe they could have prevented all their heartache, if only they had given Daniel something early on.

If only Irene had spoken more forcefully.

*If only.*

Casey startled Irene by tossing the bag of groceries onto the backseat. She slid into the front and stared out the window. For the rest of the ride down Seawood Lane she said nothing.

As they neared a long stretch of tall pine trees, Irene noticed Casey's attention snag. She glanced to the road's edge and saw a young man dumping an armful of split firewood alongside a light blue cottage with white trim. He turned to walk back to his truck, his body facing the road. She watched him wipe his forehead with the back of his hand, pushing soft blond hair from his eyes. His stance reeked of masculinity. As he tipped his head and watched them go by, she wondered at the intense expression on his face.

Irene felt a shift in Casey's mood, but by the time she looked over at her daughter, the blank stare had returned. If she touched Casey's arm at that moment, she suspected her daughter would have jumped; she seemed that wound up.

Irene narrowed her eyes in concern. She felt as if someone had grabbed her shoulders and shaken her awake.

# Chapter 4

Tim Brody looked up from reading his newspaper as Matt pushed open the front door and let in the crisp fall air. He had taken a liking to Matt Moore from the first moment he saw him. Maybe it was because he resembled his own son at that age, before Larry lost all his hair to chemo. That wavy dark hair falling over his forehead. And the way he brushed it out of his face with a swipe of his hand. He liked the thoughtful deliberation of Matt's eyes and his clean manner. Yes, he much resembled his son, God rest his soul.

Tim waved hello, then turned back to his reading. Dottie, Tim's petite wife, came from behind the ponderous counter and shuffled up to Matt in faded pink bunny slippers. At some point in the day, Dottie would go back to their house behind the store and put on some sneakers. Tim chuckled. Getting dressed, she called it.

"Whacha looking for today, hon?" Her bouffant white hair stood stiff on her head.

Matt smiled at Dottie and mumbled something, turning away to browse the rows of packaged screws and bolts hanging from their silver hooks.

Tim studied his customer. Dottie had a gift of understanding, Tim had learned long ago. After Matt had left their store the first time, back in August, she pointed out, "That man's in a heap of pain, I can tell, poor thing." After that, Tim paid closer attention, trying to suss out what Dottie had garnered from that unreadable face. Well, whatever secret messages Matt transmitted in his demeanor, Tim figured the man guarded his privacy—no good prying it out of him with a crowbar. He had to admit, sometimes Dottie was a bit nosy and tended to irritate the customers. But he paid it no mind; his was the only hardware store around, and when things needed fixing, everyone and their mother came to Breakers Hardware.

Matt deposited an armful of odds and ends on the glass countertop and Dottie rang him up, chattering on. "I hear you're trying to lick that old Salmonberry house into shape. No one's lived there for such a long time. I'm s'prised that realtor bothered to buy the dump. Shoulda been tore down."

Tim looked up from his newspaper. "Which place is that?"

Dottie didn't give Matt a chance to answer. "Why, you know, dear—the red one near the corner. Where the Elwells lived once upon a time."

Tim shrugged and shifted on the hard stool. The arthritis in his hips was killing him. His doctor had insisted he was due for an operation, but no way was he going to let anyone cut into him. Never had an operation in his eighty-some years and didn't plan to start the habit now.

Dottie bagged up the purchases and handed them to Matt. "You know that expression 'lick into shape'? Comes from bears."

Matt and Tim stared at her. She continued. "They say baby bears have no real shape when they're born; the mom has to lick 'em into shape, to turn 'em into little bears."

Tim chuckled. "Well, that's the dumbest thing I've heard today."

Dottie playfully punched him. "Day's not over yet."

Tim gave Dottie a peck on the cheek for being so clever.

MATT SAID HIS GOOD-BYES WITH A HEAVINESS IN HIS GUT. Was it that long ago he'd imagined easing into a fine old age with Irene, joking with each other that carelessly, like the world spun just fine on its axis, season after season, with little complaint? Was it only his assessment, or didn't the world tilt a little too much, stab a little too painfully, promise, and then renege? Once more he felt he'd been singled out, picked on.

He snorted as he started up his truck. He would *not* feel sorry for himself. Self-pity was unacceptable. And he refused to blame himself for all the rotten things that'd happened to him. He knew he'd done nothing wrong. *Nothing.*

Maybe Pastor Terry was right, that God was testing him. Well, if that was so, then he'd failed the test, hadn't he? He felt like Job, scratching his sores while his wife chided him. *Curse God*, she'd taunted him. Well, unlike Job, he *did* curse God. He blamed God for giving and taking away, and he didn't care. Let God strike him down with a lightning bolt; what did it matter?

His throat constricted as he pulled out of the lot and drove back through town. His mind returned to that night almost two years ago. The memory smashed against his will, an unrelenting battering ram. How easy to fling the gates open and let the pain assault him.

Only five-thirty and the sky had been pitch dark that December. Such a dreary season for a birthday, an inauspicious time of year. He had done a double take, driving up from the job site, his eyes tired and his body trashed from hanging drywall for nine straight hours.

The slump in the person's walk—a shape barely visible under the canopy of trees—drew his attention away from the slick road. He slowed as a barrage of hail pelted the roof. He still remembered the noise, harsh and stinging.

He watched the lone figure for almost a minute before it registered. And then he jammed the stick shift into Park and threw open the door, the wet ice spattering his face. He buried his chin into his coat and ran downhill, grabbing Daniel and spinning him around, unable to see his eyes in the dark, but smelling something: dirt, leaves, rain. Blood. A displaced and alarming scent.

Matt shook Daniel like a rag doll, trying to bring his son back from whatever evil held him in such a death grip. Daniel's eyes wandered, searching past Matt, searching for a clarity that couldn't be found in this world. Matt wrapped an arm around him, drawing him close, questions burning like acid on the tip of his tongue. He sheltered him under his coat as he reached the door of the truck.

In the harsh overhead light of the truck cab, Matt looked at the blood soaking Daniel's shirt, streaking down his arms, then studied his son's stricken face.

A sense of doom pierced his heart when, after frantic inspection, he understood the blood was not Daniel's.


THE BELLS OVER THE FRONT DOOR JINGLED. DOTTIE STOPPED unpacking the carton of tape rolls to look down the long aisle. She studied the scruffy young man who pushed the door open, his hand twitching nervously at his side, but got only a glimpse of his face tucked down in a woolen coat. As he turned a corner, she watched the man's back, the way he moved with deliberation down the aisle without so much as a nod, the way his head darted in jerky motions, looking up and down the walls of merchandise.

Tim glanced up from his newspaper. The expression on his face set off Dottie's antennae. She stopped what she was doing and came around the corner to find the man withdrawing his hand from an inside coat pocket.

*Thief*, she concluded. Over the man's shoulder she saw Tim straining his neck to see to the back of the store, adjusting his bifocals on his face. Dottie indulged in a bit of self-congratulation. She could always tell the type, but wasn't one for cornering a shoplifter. Most times all she could do was herd them out of the store and cut her losses. What small items fit in a coat were rarely costly, except for the few expensive things they kept in the locked case at the counter, like those hand-engraved pocketknives—and camera batteries, of course.

If she had any kind of smug expression on her face, it disappeared quickly when the young man's challenging green eyes met hers.

His voice came out acerbic and taut. "What're you staring at?"

Dottie felt a claw travel up her spine and fumbled for words that seemed to scurry away. She could swear the man was feeding on her fear, like he was some kind of zombie or vampire from those old black-and-white movies Tim loved to watch on rainy nights while stuffing popcorn into his mouth. His gaze held hers captive and she froze—a deer in the headlights. Her inner patter of words fell silent; her arms slacked to her sides. By the time Tim reached her, the man had spun around and headed for the door, knocking him into the light bulb display so neatly arranged at the corner of the aisle.

At least Tim was able to find words. As he reached down to restack the tumbled boxes he called out, "Can I help you find something?" Dottie wondered at the shakiness in his voice.

With one hand on the door, the man hesitated. "You don't have what I need," was what he said. What Dottie sensed was, "Don't even think of messing with me."

Tim touched Dottie's arm and broke the spell. She released a long, pent-up breath and followed him to the counter, pulling her cable-knit pink sweater tighter around her shoulders. She tipped her head to see out the window as the Ford, loaded with firewood, turned north out of the lot. "Who was that?"

Tim shrugged. He motioned to her and she came to his side, wrapping thin, bony arms around him, feeling they had escaped some kind of danger. Through her arms she felt the pounding of Tim's heart, beating a little too fast.

# Chapter 5

JERRY WAS GLAD FOR A BREAK IN THE WIND, BUT NO WAY WAS he going to climb roofs to brush off the mats of redwood and Douglas fir needles. He'd find some neighborhood kid to do it for cheap.

He surveyed the parking lot, buried under two inches of fluffy needles. Well, now was as good a time as any, although a short snooze on the sofa sounded so much better. The doctor had told him to go easy on his back, not strain himself with heavy exercise. Hah! Like he had any choice. *There are only three people around to keep that motel up to snuff,* Jerry told himself: *me, myself, and I.* Maybe his rich doctor could afford a gardener, maintenance man, and housekeeper. Jerry grunted. *Let's see him get his hands dirty scrubbing toilets.*

Jerry grumbled as he raked, starting at one end of the row of identical rooms and working his way down the driveway. His tiny box of a house sat at the back, in the dark, dank stand of trees. He thought of his ex enjoying the bay view from their Eureka Victorian—an 1880s three-story relic Jerry had renovated over a six-year period. A labor of love wasted on her. She didn't even like the house, never had. He knew she kept it to spite him. And after that lawyer had gotten through with him, all he could afford to invest in was this dump—The Riptide Motel.

Wasn't that just an ironic name? He pictured all his belongings being sucked out to sea, ripped out of his hands. The name sure was fitting.

Jerry raked hard, working up a sweat, clenching his teeth all the while. He let the anger flow through his arms, replayed every screaming argument he could dig up, every snippy criticism that spewed from his ex's mouth. And then he pictured that smug lawyer sitting next to her, patting her hand in that conspiratorial way. He knew he'd been wrong to lunge at the guy; it would only make matters worse ... He smiled. Yeah, well, it was worth it to see him scared out of his wits, knocking the chair over and trembling like a little girl.

Jerry stopped to catch his breath. Movement drew his eye, and he put his hand up to shield the sun's glare. Across the street Mrs. Waverly was acting strange, bent over and wandering in small circles. She caught sight of Jerry, then summoned him with a frantic wave of her hand. Jerry grunted, set the rake down, and crossed the road.

Her dog had its nose pressed against the window from inside the house, yipping so hard its eyeballs bulged from its sockets. Jerry made a face at it and the dog barked even louder. He came up close to Mrs. Waverley to be able to hear her over the riotous barking.

"What's the problem? Are you sick?" he asked.

The old woman looked perturbed, her eyes flitting around. "Oh, Mr. Hubble, my goodness, I am quite fine, thank you. I seem to have lost my necklace, you see. My heirloom from my grandmother. I always have it on and just now, when I felt at my throat, why, it's not there." Her shaky hand reached for her neck, checking again. "I was thinking maybe the clasp broke and it slipped off when I took my walk with Doodles."

"Maybe you should retrace your steps." Jerry backed away, unwilling to waste his time helping her find a stupid piece of sentimental jewelry.

"I've already done that. I just keep thinking how, when I came back from my walk yesterday—you remember how windy it was—the back door was blown open. I never unlock that door. And that young man was here, with the firewood. Billy. Billy Thurber, he said."

Jerry's eyes widened. It would take a dummy not to put two and two together. How easy it would have been for that kid to sneak into her house while she was out with her dog, pinch a few things, then go back to stacking wood. Jerry shook his head. He wasn't one bit surprised. Didn't he have that kid pegged from the get-go?

"You missing anything else, Mrs. Waverly?"

"Not that I noticed." Her voice lowered, as if the trees had ears. "Should I check? Do you think I had a break-in? Oh, my, never in all these years ..."

"It wouldn't hurt to look around. And maybe give Joe Huff a ring, tell him about it, in case other incidents crop up."

At the mention of the sheriff, her face went pale and her breath quickened. "Oh, I don't know ... I don't think I should make that big a fuss." Her eyes implored him, but he turned to leave. He wasn't getting involved in this.

He mumbled some consolation and crossed back to his motel. A spattering of rain, smelling of dust and asphalt, fell as he resumed his raking, making mounds of needles. When he looked up, his neighbor was retreating back into her house—just as a squall let loose. A downpour of water fell on the shingled roofs, a droning symphony. Now the sofa and a hot drink seemed just the thing. A hot whiskey, with lemon and sugar.

Jerry's palms started sweating at the thought of a drink. He deliberated for only a few seconds before he put down the rake and abandoned his chore. A warning went off in his head, but he squelched it quickly and efficiently. Without another thought, he bee-lined back to his house, stripped off his soaked coat and mud boots, and went straight to the kitchen cupboard, where a bottle of amber liquid beckoned.

A well-deserved reward for all his hard work.

# Chapter 6

BILLY THURBER SWUNG THE DOOR OPEN, LETTING A SPRAY OF rain blow into the humid, stuffy diner. The aroma of Mexican food hung heavy in the air as he scanned the room, searching for an empty seat. No one paid him any mind. The restaurant was packed, all eyes on the TV screen mounted on the rafters. As he removed his hooded sweatshirt, he glimpsed a man with a thick head of red hair and a bushy moustache pull at his beer and snicker as a team scored on the screen. The table in front of the redhead resembled the aftermath of a food war, with salsa, broken chips, and sour cream smeared on plates and table alike.

Loud moans erupted across the room. A few irate fans yelled out profanities and insults to the players. Billy wended his way around furniture and bodies to a vacant chair, catching the redheaded man's attention with a polite tap.

"This seat taken?"

The man shook his head and gestured. "It's yours, man." A voice deep and gruff. Billy guessed him around twenty-five. Through the heavy aroma of salsa and beer, he detected another. Weed.

Billy reached out his hand. "Name's Thurber. Billy."

"Zack." The man offered a brusque handshake. "This here's Randy." Zack nudged his friend.

"Hey," was all his buddy said.

When the waitress came around, Billy ordered a beer and, as an afterthought, leaned over the table. "Want another? I'll buy."

That caught Zack's attention. He raised his eyebrows. "Hey, that's good of you, man. Sure."

Randy and Zack scooted over to let Billy join them at their table. For the rest of the hour they sat and watched the game, working their way through two more pitchers, Zack yelling at the TV when his favored team missed a field goal. Billy drank little, paying more attention to the diners than to the game.

At the last goal attempt, grumblings broke out and swelled across the room like a tide. Chairs shuffled and men gathered coats and put them on. A few women laughed and followed their men out. The door opened and closed as the room emptied.

Zack rested his chin in his hand, his eyes glassed over. Randy tapped the table with a spoon. He straightened and poked at Zack. "We should get back to the boat."

Billy cocked his head. "You guys fish?" Zack grunted, looked around, and found his jacket. Billy continued. "Hard work, fishing. I don't know how you do that, rough seas and all. Would scare the daylights out of me."

Randy stood and stretched. He ran a hand through his long dark hair and scratched at the neat beard on his face. "Been doing it most of our lives. It's what we're used to."

Billy nodded. They found their belongings and opened the door to a blast of wet wind.

"Whoa, if that doesn't wake a guy up." Zack pulled his jacket hood over his head, managing to stuff most of his wild hair beneath it. He turned to Billy. "Haven't seen you before. Live around here?"

"I've been in town unloading firewood. Staying at a place up in Fairhaven."

"Oh."

"I take it you probably don't need any firewood. Living on a boat."

Randy laughed and tripped over something. "No, guess we don't." He looked to balance himself, the way a person might on his boat in a heavy swell. Billy wondered: sea legs or too much brew?

Billy stopped in the middle of the lot. "You guys are probably just going down to the harbor, but don't you think you've had a bit much to drink? I can give you a ride."

Zack looked at Randy, then scanned the vehicles parked in the lot, confusion in his eyes. Billy figured Zack had forgotten where he parked.

"Hey, that'd be great," Randy said.

"My pleasure. Over here." Billy led them to his truck and opened the passenger door. "It'll be a little cozy." He laughed.

He started the engine and it kicked into a steady rumble. When he cranked the heater, cold air blew at his face. In a quiet, almost apologetic voice, he asked, "I don't mean to put you on the spot or anything, but do you fellas have any weed you can spare?"

The terse exchange of glances between the two passengers was not lost on Billy. He waited a moment, then started down Seawood. "Just looking for a joint, that's all."

He heard Zack exhale next to him and it got him wondering. "Never mind," he added.

Warm air now blew from the vents. Zack rubbed his hands in the heat, getting the chill out.

Randy fumbled inside his coat. "No, man, I think I've got something stashed away in a pocket somewhere." Billy kept driving while Randy found what he was searching for. "Need a light?" Randy asked.

Billy glanced over at Randy's outstretched hand. He nodded and Randy lit the joint, then passed it over.

Zack pointed. "You can just drop us off at the pier. We have a dinghy there."

Billy took a large toke off the joint. He offered it back to Randy, then Zack. They shook their heads. Billy scrunched his eyebrows in concern. "You need me to row you out there, so you don't get lost and drift out to sea?"

Zack and Randy laughed heartily as the smoke filled the cab. Billy stopped the truck and the two tumbled out. Randy waved to Billy, still chuckling. "No, man. We can manage."

Billy raised the joint in thanks. Zack pounded the hood of the truck once with his fist. "Thanks for the brew."

Billy caught Randy's attention. "Next Monday, same time?"

"Yeah, see ya," Randy answered with another wave.

Billy watched the two men stumble down the gravel road to the pier. After finishing the joint, he shut off his engine and cut the headlights, then got out of his truck. Rain splattered lightly as he ambled toward the water. A couple dozen small crafts rocked at their slips in the sheltered harbor. Indian Rock loomed high, a few feet off the pier, like a sentinel for sailors. He kept back from the mounted floodlights, which illuminated the black water lapping against the pilings. He made out the small skiff moving across the surface of the water like a ghost ship.

The skiff knocked against a trawler, the noise barely discernable in the whistling wind. As Randy and Zack rocked around, climbing aboard and tying off the dinghy, Billy made out the name of the boat: *The Merry Lynn*. He repeated the name aloud, his tongue thick in his mouth, then pulled his cap tightly over his ears and returned to his truck.

*Next Monday, fellas.*

# *Chapter 7*

MORNINGS HAD TURNED COLDER AND WINDIER. WORKING two blocks from the beach with gusts blowing down from Alaska gave new meaning to the word *chilly.* Usually Matt didn't mind weather. Up in the mountains he'd often shoveled snow to uncover his trenches or stacks of lumber. But that was a dry cold, not like this damp and biting wind that chewed voraciously through every layer of clothing.

Digging out a walkway and driveway in stubborn rocky ground was becoming more of a chore than he liked. A hazy October sun tried hard to penetrate the cloud layer but failed to warm the air. After two hours of slow going, Matt rubbed his hands and wondered where his fingers had gone. Sweat cooled instantly on his neck, sending a chill down his back. He put down the pickaxe and zipped up his jacket.

Irene was the one who'd chosen this town. He hadn't cared where they went — the farther the better — and Breakers was about as far away as they could get from Running Springs and still stay in California, where Irene could teach with her state certificate and not have to submit to special training and classes required by some other states. She seemed set on taking a full-time job, and he understood her need. Working helped take his mind off the rest of his miserable life. Nothing like pounding a hammer or attacking the ground with a pick.

If only he could hack away at memories and break them up into harmless pieces.

He reached through the window of his truck cab and grabbed his travel mug, then walked the three blocks to the row of tourist shops lined up along First Street. Shorelines, a tiny coffee shop Matt frequented lately, sat at the end with a small outside patio that he doubted was used much, considering the weather. As he pushed open the front door, a rush of warmth enveloped him, and the aroma of coffee and pastries set his mouth watering.

Celia looked up from her work table and brushed her floury hands across her apron, her round face and full cheeks glowing from the heat of the oven beside her. She came to the counter and reached into the display case.

"Here, Señor Moore, *pruebela*." She broke off a piece of scone and handed it to him, watching eagerly as he chewed. "Not bad, eh?"

"Delicious, Celia." He set his mug on the counter and Celia poured coffee out of a silver thermos. "I'll take a couple of whatever those are."

A loud crash came from the back room. Celia set down the thermos and hurried toward the noise. "*Ay*, Miguel! Now what?"

Matt took his mug and sat at one of the small café tables, overhearing a hushed barrage of Spanish and a boy's muffled whining. Celia came back with the resisting boy in tow — a skinny child with black hair and tearful eyes.

"Now sit, *acá*, read your book." Her eyes bored into Miguel's, and he lowered his head, burying himself in his big picture book.

Celia's stern expression disappeared and the wide grin returned. She placed two scones on a plate and brought them over to Matt. "So sorry. My grandson. I can't leave him out of my sight for three minutes. Always into something." She shrugged.

The last time he'd been in the coffee shop, she'd told him how her family had moved to Breakers to get away from the San Jose smog—which greatly aggravated her grandson's asthma—and the gangs encroaching on their neighborhood. "Not a safe place to raise a child," she had told him.

Was any place safe?

Matt heard the door open and turned to see a large, bulky man enter the shop. He recognized Joe Huff, the local sheriff, who thundered in like an elephant, his big boots thumping the floor as he walked to the counter. He pulled off brown deerskin gloves and set them on the glass, nodding a friendly hello to Matt. His broad face had the dark gleam of Yurok Indian, with ebony eyes and thick brows overpowering his features. He had streaks of gray in his hair, a few laugh lines alongside his eyes, but Matt could only guess his age. Celia poured him a cup of coffee and took his change.

"Good to see you today, Señor Huff ..."

"Joe. Like the coffee." He chuckled and sat on the stool across from Matt.

Celia shrugged, confusion in her eyes. She knew he had made a joke, but did not understand. "Okay, Joe. O-kay Do-kay. Something to eat?" she added.

The sheriff shook his head, took off his hat, and offered his hand to Matt. Matt felt his amiable eyes assessing him. "Joe Huff."

"Matt Moore."

The sheriff caught a glimpse of the boy staring shyly at him through the glass, between the pastries. He waved at Miguel and the boy giggled. After a moment, the sheriff sipped his coffee thoughtfully and returned his attention to Matt.

"You're working on the house down the way? I've noticed you there for a couple of weeks. My place is on the next block, on Huckleberry."

Matt nodded. "I've seen your cruiser go by."

Joe smiled. "Glad to see someone's putting money into fixing that heap up. It's been an eyesore for years and then some."

Matt ate his scones, not really tasting them as he and the sheriff talked. Matt gave a brief history of his relocation, then made some comments about the idyllic community of Breakers, which caused Joe to chuckle. Celia disappeared into the back with Miguel; a steady stream of Spanish phrases followed. More lecturing, Matt gathered.

Joe reached for the jar on the table and pulled out two sugar packets. He opened them and dumped the sugar into his cup. "You see, people look at this beautiful, picturesque town and think, 'Oh, what a nice, quiet little place to live. No trouble, far away from big city problems.' They have no clue what goes on here. Especially the seasonal tourists."

"How long have you lived here, Sheriff?"

"Joe. Please." A big grin full of teeth. "Some forty years. Wanda and I were spending half the year up on the reservation, near Weitchpec, until our former chief of police here got relieved for, let's say, excessive behavior on the job. Now I'm covering until the city council can get a new one. Let's see, that's been going on for nearly two years now. If you just moved up here, then you missed all the brouhaha over the last twelve months. The city treasurer got nine years for embezzlement. The school bus driver's serving a year in jail for lewd conduct with minors. That's *minors*, plural. The mayor went on a drunken binge and slammed his car into his neighbor's house. Busted right through the plate-glass window. He's been removed from office and is in rehab in Fortuna. Lots of excitement for a quiet little town, you see?"

Matt nodded. He didn't have any idealistic fantasies about Breakers. The world was full of trouble, and troublesome people were everywhere. Maybe just more noticeable in a small town.

For the next ten minutes, Joe finished his coffee and told him about Breakers—places to hike and fish, the fugitives hiding in the hills that Joe picked up from time to time. Wanted for some crime or other—drugs, theft, you name it. The sheriff bided his time on the ones he couldn't find. Eventually all the cockroaches came out of the woodwork, he said.

Joe then rambled on about life on the reservation, salmon fishing, and tribal rights. And his rock collection. He was a member of some lapidary society, big on gem and mineral shows. Matt's attention wandered as Joe went on about something called cabochons; he started making a supply list in his head.

The sheriff tapped Matt on the shoulder. "Sorry, I get a bit carried away when it comes to rocks. Wanda gets that same glazed expression on her face too. Makes jokes about my having rocks in my head." The tap turned into a manly pat. "Well, Matt, glad to know you. I hope you enjoy our *quiet* little town." The sarcasm was not lost on Matt.

He shook Joe's thick warm hand. "I'd like to get someone to help me on these forms I'm digging. Know anyone in town needing some work?"

Joe shrugged. "You can put up a card at the market, on the bulletin board. That should do it."

"Okay, thanks."

Matt rallied up determination to return to work. He set four dollars on the counter and said good-bye to Celia, then stepped outside. Wind ruffled his hair and he pulled up the collar on his jacket. On a whim, he walked across the street and down to Bayview Drive. Expansive homes with redwood siding and massive glass windows lined the street, facing the pristine harbor. Most were two storied, with cathedral ceilings and Trex decks. Little landscaping seemed to survive the elements there. Scraggly shrubs—ceanothus, pampas grass, and Scotch broom—pressed against the houses, as if seeking shelter from the battering wind.

As Matt walked along, he studied the quality of the construction, guessing the age of the houses and which ones needed work. Rust was a problem, eating at the old-style metal-wrapped windows and rain gutters. Not as many cars were parked on the street as in summer. He guessed most of these were second homes; not a few had vacation rental signs posted beside the front door.

As he ascended the hill from the harbor, he passed a white van where two men were unloading a large carpet shampooer. He watched them haul the machine up a rickety set of steps, wondering if their feet would break through the rotted fir. Maybe he would contact the home owner and see if they'd be interested in a new staircase before someone sued them for injury.

At the top of the hill, before he turned the block, he stood at the bluff and looked out at the harbor. Like something out of a wall calendar or *Sunset* magazine, the crescent-shaped bay wrapped the coast in huge, jagged pinnacles of shoreline, with waves crashing onto sandy beaches. Sea lions and gray spotted harbor seals stretched out across the rocks. A mist lingered on the surface of the water, enhancing the surreal tableau.

Any other year the sight would have taken his breath away. He would have snapped dozens of photographs to develop and frame. He stared at the view, hoping to stir some passion, anything, but the only sensation accessible to him was anger. It lay sleeping at the bottom of his heart, easily stirred and disturbed.

A snarling beast that lunged and eviscerated him any chance it got. Nature was meant to help heal, to soothe, but the equation had changed: beauty prompted pain, not solace. Beauty now mocked him, excluded him.

He turned and walked briskly away, the wind at his back, memories assailing him.

After he had seen the blood on Daniel's arms and face, ripped open the boy's shirt, and felt along his cold ribs and stomach, Matt had cranked the heater in the truck and sat there. He'd felt angry then too. When his words came out, they were accusatory, and Daniel cried. Great racking sobs and gushes of tears. Matt sat stunned; he had rarely seen Daniel cry, not since he was a baby. He rammed questions at him, one after another, but all Daniel could do was sob. In frustration, Matt gunned the engine and started back up the winding mountain road toward home, hail flinging across the windshield as the wipers swished back and forth.

He saw the flashing red lights before he rounded the Trap. In the dark, he didn't recognize the flipped-over car, its wheels upended like some massive turtle stuck on its back. Two police cars flanked the wreck. A handful of people in rain slickers milled about, giant buzzards gathered around carrion. Matt slowed and almost drove by when, out of the corner of his eye, he saw Daniel's finger pointing. He turned to Daniel, who looked past him, shell-shocked.

"What?" Matt demanded. "What in God's name are you trying to say?"

In that one second, all the seemingly disjointed elements came together in a rush, holding the moment together in acute suspension. His heart stopped and he began to choke. He sucked air.

Daniel's bloody finger — a finger that hung in the air, that haunted Matt's nightmares in the subsequent months — reached across Matt's lap, to the window, to the police, the overturned car ... and a shape on the ground ...

When Matt got back to his job site, he leaned his forehead against the cold metal of the truck, feeling the chill press into his skull, numbing his brain. He stood there for a minute, then grabbed his pickaxe and resumed his attack on the hard, unresponsive ground.

# Chapter 8

EVEN THOUGH A FIRE BLAZED IN THE WOODSTOVE, IRENE felt cold. She had been cold from the moment they arrived in Breakers, and no matter how many sweaters she layered or how many cups of hot tea she drank, nothing chased the chill out of her bones. An ice age had settled at the very core of her being and she could only guess at the years it would take to melt those glaciers down to manageable size.

The house was quiet with Casey and Matt gone off to school and work. She had hoped her cold would ease but had awakened this morning congested and achy. With a hot mug of Echinacea tea in her hand, she stood in the living room and looked around at her home: dark walls, dark carpeting, drafty windows that whistled from the incursion of wind, a few pieces of derelict furniture. Matt had made apologies; they wouldn't have to live there forever, he'd get things buttoned up before winter. When they were ready, if they chose to stay in Breakers, they could look to buy a house. Irene recalled Matt's string of assurances, their hollow ring, his flat and detached tone.

She refilled the kettle and picked up the sponge. As she scrubbed the pots and dishes, she lectured herself about getting some rest, but her words fell on her own deaf ears. What started as a simple kitchen cleanup grew into a frenzied attack on every reachable surface. After all the counters, stove, and cabinets had been scoured clean, Irene stood on a chair and worked her way through the cabinet shelves, taking down glasses and plates and vases, losing herself in the mindlessness of the task. Her head pounded mercilessly despite the two aspirin she had taken. Her nose ran and she wiped it with her shirtsleeve. Sweat trickled down her face, the front of her shirt, matted her hair.

As worked up and heated as she was, the cold in her bones sat heavy and unaffected. When the room spun and her vision fuzzed, she wobbled down from the chair and collapsed on the floor. While she waited for the room to settle, she felt the weight of her displacement bear down in looming judgment.

She had caused this, all of it.

Matt had been against Daniel getting his license from the first. He was reckless and unfocused, Matt had argued. Hadn't she seen the way he lacked attention when he drove the car? Rather than concede, Irene fell into her role as champion and defender of Daniel—a role that had been hers from the start.

Force of habit.

Irene pondered those words. *Force* of habit.

She had been swept up in that force unaware, her responses automatic and set.

Irene had always been soft on her son. She'd had to be, to counteract Matt's harsh response to Daniel's nature. What Matt yearned for in a son and found lacking in Daniel, he discovered joyously in Jesse—a quiet, thoughtful boy who could sit and build with his Erector Set for hours, unmoving in his focused concentration. Didn't everyone know the fatal flaw of a parent was to show preference to one child and disappointment in another? How many times had she argued with Matt about this? As much as he denied his preferential treatment of Jesse, his actions contradicted himself. Even Casey and Jesse had cringed at the continual denigration of Daniel, rallying their wagons of support around him.

Irene knew all about criticism, its sensation of stabbing needles. As an only child of overly ambitious parents, she had borne the brunt of endless silent recriminations of failure. She knew the pressure of sitting at a school desk, taking a test and feeling the swooping terror when an answer would not come, when the math made no sense. Knowing that when the report card arrived in the mail there would be lectures and candid looks of disappointment. Failure, somehow, meant letting her parents down, implying *they* had failed, and how could she do that to them?

After graduating high school, when she moved to San Diego and started college, she thought she had found a way to insulate herself by sheer distance. But she didn't notice the invisible chain around her neck, a chain that dragged an iron ball of judgment behind her everywhere she went.

She married Matt, a builder, but he was below her; she could have done better.

She got her teaching certification, but why did she settle for such a low-paying career when she could have been a doctor or a lawyer?

She gave birth to three beautiful children, but oh, how she spoiled them, failing to teach them the important things — whatever those were.

Matt was the one who got fed up, unable to tolerate his in-laws' carefully worded snide comments, their running interference with "suggestions" that Matt repeatedly ignored. He saw the damage wreaked on the children as well, how nervous they were around their grandparents, how sullen and on edge. Daniel especially. Matt would cringe when Irene's father challenged Daniel's moodiness, told him to stop sulking and straighten up.

It began with the hastily canceled flights to visit her parents one Christmas break, Matt apologizing for the unexpected flu ravaging the household—a bit of exaggeration on his part. Polite thank-you cards were sent for the mountain of presents shipped in consolation. A different excuse accompanied each subsequent holiday vacation. Jesse broke his leg, Casey was going on a school campout, this summer they planned a road trip to the Grand Canyon. Irene watched as her parents tried to insert themselves in between those carefully laid plans but found no ingress. Phone calls grew sporadic; volumes were said in less, but more potent, words.

The chain was eventually severed, although Irene felt little relief. She knew her actions were cruel, denying her parents the joy of their grandchildren. Yet it had become a matter of survival. *Emotional* survival.

What Matt failed to see, though, was the similarity of his own parenting tactics. You'd think he, of all people, would notice.

Irene shivered and stood abruptly. She put on her rain boots and parka and stormed out the front door. In the garage, she rummaged through a large cardboard box, removing folded curtains and bedspreads until she found the electric blanket. She went back into the kitchen and made another cup of scalding hot tea.

Casey had set up a shrine in her bedroom. While Irene and Matt could barely stand to glance at the family photo on the mantle, Casey spent hours at her altar rearranging photos, trinkets, candles. A small bulletin board covered in pictures and poems stood as a backdrop to the altar, portraying a summation of both her brothers' lives—what could be contained in so small a space.

Since moving to Breakers, Irene had cleaned Casey's room many times, picking up dirty clothes and straightening papers.

She never gave more than a cursory glance at the shrine in the corner, however much it called to her. Casey accused her and Matt of forgetting her brothers, but Casey did not understand. Daniel and Jesse were so etched in her soul that she could not take even one breath without them hovering, incriminating and unforgiving.

Rain fell lightly on the roof. Casey's bedside clock ticked quietly. The moment grew thick and muddled. Irene plugged in the electric blanket and set the dial to high. She lowered herself onto the rug and sat before the shrine, wrapping the blanket tightly around her. Her eyes slowly focused on the photographs.

She studied the one of the three kids in their blanket jungle on the back patio. They must have been between six and ten years old. They had taken every blanket from the house and draped them from the rafters, then positioned all their stuffed animals in the crevices of blanket mountains—dinosaurs, alligators, frogs, and hippos. When Irene brought out the camera, they made her wait while they dressed up in their "safari" attire, made up of an odd combination of cowboy boots, belts, Irene's nightgown, and the requisite toy rifles. In the picture, Daniel held one of his stuffed serpents by the tail—the intrepid hunter. Casey and Jesse were laughing, their arms around each other's waist. They were trying to put on a serious face but it wasn't happening.

Irene looked over at the bed, where Jesse's red stuffed dinosaur rested against Casey's pillow. Casey slept with the threadbare toy clutched in her arms every night.

An ache started up in Irene's heart.

How empty her arms felt—arms that used to be full of laughing, wiggling children. Arms that enfolded, comforted, and reassured that no harm would touch them, that they were safe. Arms with the power to ward off each bad dream as it invaded. Wasn't that the divine gift of motherhood, those arms? When had they become impotent?

The day Daniel had gotten his driver's license, Irene let him drive the car home. She sat next to him, up front, glad to see him happy. His face beamed with pride and attainment of manhood. Matt had finally given up his tirade, sick of the nagging. Two against one, again.

On the way home, not a mile from the DMV, a woman pulled out from the curb without looking. Daniel veered left—a reflex response—and stomped on his brakes. When he smashed into the car in the left lane, Irene's head cracked against the windshield. The car behind them skidded and did a one-eighty. The driver suffered a broken collarbone and arm when the car following him rammed into his front end. Three cars had been damaged. Fortunately, no one else had been hurt.

Irene never for one moment felt Daniel was at fault or could have responded any better. But when Matt heard what happened, he went ballistic. Irene couldn't stand to watch Matt's attack on Daniel; she'd had to go outside and cover her ears.

On that day, Irene recalled, the dynamics changed between Daniel and Matt. Where they had been at war up till then, a much worse silence now ensued. Daniel lost all driving privileges, but Irene knew he didn't care. The accident had terrified him; she had seen the skittish look in his eyes. The restriction was a reprieve and a welcome punishment. Only Irene noticed how Daniel suffered, saw through his bravado and outward aloofness.

It was Daniel's haunted, self-condemning look that made Irene cross the line. Why, three weeks later, on Matt's birthday, when they realized they'd forgotten the ice cream and Daniel offered to go, she let him. He hadn't asked because he yearned for a chance to drive. Irene could see her son wanted the birthday celebration to be perfect, a reconciliatory effort that Irene was grateful for.

Casey was busy squirting icing on the cake while Irene stirred spaghetti sauce on the stove. Go, she told Daniel, take Jesse and hurry back.

Did she add the words: be careful?

*Did I?* she asked the photos on the altar. Surely she would have. And in her heart she believed he had been careful.

Irene let the tears run down her face. Was Casey right? Was Daniel like King Lear, "a man more sinned against than sinning" as she claimed? A victim of expected failure? Maybe not at that moment, Irene thought. But surely later, as the months of silent accusations piled on Daniel's shoulders, growing heavy and unbearable, making him collapse under their weight.

Irene sobbed and reached to touch a photograph of the two boys hamming it up for the camera. *What else could I have done?* she asked them. All her subsequent attempts to talk with Daniel, to comfort him, had been spurned. The loving outstretched arms had held no magic any longer, and that was all she had left to offer him.

It hadn't been enough.

# Chapter 9

As Matt pounded a wooden stake into the ground, he sensed someone behind him. He turned and met a pair of green eyes and wondered how long the young man had been standing there watching him work. The boy nodded hello and introduced himself, offering his hand. Matt shook it and noted the strong, confident grip.

"I saw your card posted on the board. They told me over at the market where you were working. You still need some help?"

Matt took in the kid's demeanor. He could tell by Thurber's build that he was accustomed to hard labor. His hands were rough and felt like worker's hands. "You have any construction experience, Billy?"

"Some. Helped build a cabin once. Basic tools and carpentry, I guess."

For now Matt just needed a grunt and that required more back strength than geometry skills. "I can pay you fifteen an hour, but you have to show up on time and work hard."

"No problem."

Matt sensed a nervousness about the young man, noticed his hands twitching and his attention flitting. Not unlike how

Daniel had been. Matt clamped down his thoughts and focused on Thurber. "Did you walk here from somewhere? You have a car?"

"Clutch went out on my truck. It's getting fixed, but I'm short of cash. Kinda hard to work without a truck."

Matt nodded. "So you live here in town?"

"Fairhaven."

Fairhaven was an adjacent community a few miles south and east. The road that led under the freeway wound up into the forest that flanked the coast, circling back on itself farther south. Matt had taken the old road once and ended up at Pelican Beach, south of Breakers. Homes weren't visible as you drove along, but there were lots of rutted dirt lanes taking off into the hills. Someone had told him it used to be part of the old highway linking Eureka to Crescent City.

Thurber added, "I can get to town easy enough. I only need a couple weeks' work, to pay for repairs on my truck."

"I think that'd work. You want to start now?"

Thurber nodded and pulled ratty cotton gloves from his coat pocket. Matt pointed to the gravel pile and instructed him to fill the wheelbarrow and start moving gravel to the driveway, to spread it out in preparation for compacting. He figured that alone would take up a good part of the day.

Matt went back to pounding stakes and fitting in the two-by-fours for the sidewalk. Clouds drifted overhead, casting shadows that flowed like liquid across the ground. When the wind died down, the morning sun warmed the air, and Matt stripped off his jacket and sweatshirt. He watched Thurber work, the kid shoveling gravel with a steady, quick thrust. He was glad for the help; loading and pushing a wheelbarrow up a hill was not his favorite part of construction. Back south he had made a good living building custom homes in Lake Arrowhead. Fancy, expensive homes — many of them destroyed in that fire a few years back. Homes he had spent nearly a year building, scrolling intricate railings and posts, laying Italian tile, and hand oiling pine tongue-and-groove—all up in smoke in a matter of hours.

Wasn't that just like life? Spend years raising a family, putting your heart and blood into the effort, and in minutes their lives are erased. Gone. Over.

Matt went over to his truck and opened one of the tool chests, then ducked his head under the metal lid. He took deep breaths, willing his heart to stop pounding. He wanted to pray, needed to, but he'd determined a while back that no one was listening.

And what if God did listen and answer him, just what would he tell him?

"What?" he whispered in challenge. "What on earth could you say that would make it all better? Give it meaning?"

Matt closed the box and grabbed the landscape comb from the back of the truck. He walked to the top of the driveway and started knocking down and spreading out the piles of gravel Thurber had dumped out. They spoke little over the next few hours. Matt broke for lunch, sat on his tailgate and ate a sandwich while Thurber went for a walk. The trail Thurber took was a footpath that started behind the Mexican restaurant and meandered through town until it turned into steps leading down to Drifter's Cove.

Matt watched the kid head toward the beach and wondered where Daniel would be today, if he were here. Irene had often talked to Daniel about college, brought him brochures to read, tried to get his interest up. Matt assumed his kids would all go to college and thought it odd how Daniel resisted Irene's urgings to apply to schools. What did his son think—that he'd get to stay home and lay around on the couch watching TV forever?

That last summer, before Daniel entered his senior year, Matt had made him come to work with him, his son acting like it was a prison sentence. Daniel was plenty adept with his hands, and he had the brains too. He just lacked motivation. Sure, he wanted money to buy toys—iPods and computer games—and he had worked on occasion doing odd jobs for neighbors. The problem was, and *always* was, that Matt and Daniel never meshed. Irene accused Matt of impatience; Matt accused Daniel of attitude. Daniel called his dad plain-out mean. Said he was a perfectionist and nothing Daniel did was ever good enough. Why they had never been able to find a compromise, a midway point of mutual respect, Matt didn't know. Daniel had been so sensitive, so defensive and quick to strike back. He couldn't take criticism from anyone, and, hey, you had to get used to that if you were going to survive in this world.

Matt never considered that surviving could be a choice, that you could refuse it.

He thought back to the day his useless father had stormed out of the house—leaving his mother to raise all four children on her own. And she'd done just fine—working hard to support them. Matt had watched the way she sacrificed for them, giving up her own dreams of finishing nursing school and taking a job as a bookkeeper with a construction firm. She did what she had to. And as Matt grew up, he did what he had to as well—became the man of the house and took odd jobs after school, fixed what needed fixing. Became the strong one everyone could count on. Wasn't that expected of men? He never *got* why Daniel couldn't toughen up and take responsibility.

Matt snorted. It surely wasn't from a lack of admonishing on his part.

At the end of the third day, with Thurber's help, Matt was ready for a concrete pour. He called the plant and scheduled it for the following morning. He looked at his watch—three-thirty. Thurber loaded tools into the truck, then rinsed out the wheelbarrow and set it beside the house. He stood a few feet away from Matt, who was on the phone. While he waited for the dispatcher to confirm the time, Matt scrutinized Thurber's face, wondering at the keen, hungry expression that came over his features.

Matt turned his head in the direction of Thurber's gaze. Thurber was watching a girl walk down the street. She had just rounded the corner and was walking down the lane toward them. Thurber studied her and his eyes narrowed. Matt wasn't sure if he heard it right, what Thurber muttered. Something so disgusting that Matt cringed. The dispatcher spoke to him but he didn't hear a word.

Matt watched Casey come toward him. She wore a bulky sweater—Jesse's hunter green wool one that Irene had bought him his last Christmas. He flicked his cell phone shut and studied the way his daughter walked. Her short, black skirt exposed two pale, shapely legs that walked in a womanly fashion. He realized in that moment three things.

That his little girl was not so little anymore; she looked older than fourteen and she knew it.

That she took an interest in the young man who stood near him. Matt saw how self-conscious she was, how *self-aware*. Her walk bespoke volumes, and Matt didn't need to decipher the message to know its portent.

That this creep was drooling over his daughter, his baby.

All of this stark realization led to one strong urge: to plant his fist in Thurber's face.

Instead, Matt turned to Thurber and said in an even voice, "We're done here. You can leave now."

Matt felt hot eyes on him as he walked down the driveway to the street, where Casey gave him a little wave. He wrapped his arms around her in a hug—a gesture she resisted—hoping that, when he turned back, Thurber would be gone. He had no intention of introducing Casey to Billy Thurber.

But it was already too late.

When he took her hand to walk her up to the truck, he saw it in her eyes. Thurber quickly looked away and put on his coat and walked across the lawn as soon as Matt caught his gaze. Matt had seen his face, though, for just a second, and what he saw sent a surge of electricity through every pore in his body. What he would have given to wipe that smug smile off Thurber's face. Even when Thurber clearly understood Casey was Matt's daughter, it seemed he didn't care. He leered even more, smiling at her in a way that Matt found disgusting.

The word *defiant* came to mind.

Some odd piece of verse floated into his awareness, a childhood rhyme: *Step into my parlor, said the spider to the fly . . .*

As he drove home with Casey quiet beside him, he took his attention off the road for a moment and glanced at her face.

He saw Billy Thurber written all over it.

Tomorrow he would tell the young man he didn't need his help any longer.

He could leave.

# *Chapter 10*

CASEY WATCHED MR. REESE WRITE NAMES ON THE chalkboard. "This," he said, his commanding voice causing heads to look up from their desks, "will tell you who your science partner will be, based on the subject interests you specified. I've grouped seventh and eighth together. Be sure to seek out your partner and start putting your heads together. The preliminary hypothesis is due next Wednesday."

Casey returned to her essay. One thing she could say in favor of Mr. Reese—he appreciated Shakespeare, even if none of the kids in her class had a clue. She had seen a dozen or more productions of various plays over the years back in Los Angeles; surely, no one else in the room had even heard of Hamlet, let alone the Duke of Gloucester. When Casey had discussed her theme with him—comparing tragic figures in Shakespeare's three greatest tragedies—his eyes lit up. She could only guess what stupid topics Molly and Debby were going to write about. Probably something on dumb Harry Potter and Hogwarts.

Casey snorted and pushed her bangs out of her eyes. She reread the last sentence she'd written.

*The calamities of tragedy are no accident; they proceed from the actions of men. A true tragic hero falls from his own mistakes, contributing in some measure to his own downfall.*

She looked up the word *calamity* in her pocket dictionary to see if it would spark more ideas. "A great misfortune or disaster, grievous affliction, cataclysm, mishap, mischance." *A missed chance.* She thought about Hamlet and how he'd hesitated to kill Claudius while the king knelt in remorse and prayer. His missed chance, thus his error.

She shuffled through her notes and found the passage she had written yesterday.

*We feel the hero could have been a great man, that his death is a waste, this ruin. His fatal flaw is what causes his downfall, and the tragic recognition comes when he knows he alone is to blame, and it is too late to correct the error.*

Her mind sifted through scenes with Othello and Macbeth. She thought of Edgar and Kent, blaming Fortune for the disastrous turn of events, but Gloucester had said "the gods kill us for their sport."

Had Daniel displayed a fatal flaw, or was he the victim of outrageous Fortune's slings and arrows? Jesse had been the hapless victim, but hadn't Daniel been one as well? Was his flaw his resistance to be molded into some pliant caricature of their father's whim? That he refused to bend, so, in the end, he could only break? Was his error like Hamlet's—could he have acted in some way to prevent his demise? Had he hesitated somehow—hesitated to speak up—as Hamlet had when he held back from killing Claudius?

Casey tapped her pencil on the desk—until she caught Molly's disapproving glare out of the corner of her eye. She sighed in irritation and got up from her seat, then walked over to Mr. Reese and told him she needed to go to "the little girl's room."

Since lunch break was only five minutes away, Casey pushed open the hall doors and headed down the street toward the harbor, figuring no one would notice. The light breeze smelled of the sea, of fish and salt and sand. The sky was a petulant gray, a color she was still unused to.

She needed to stretch her cramped legs; a walk on the beach would feel good. As she followed the footpath through town, a face intruded in her thoughts.

What was it about that guy that intrigued her, pulled her in like a magnet? Well, besides the fact that he was all-out gorgeous. Just thinking about him stirred her up, hastened her step. She pictured running her hand through his hair, looking into those deep, troubled eyes. There was something troubling about him, wasn't there? He had the same aura about him that Daniel'd had. His face appeared confident, but there was a disturbance underneath, some struggle or pain that couldn't help but seep out of those bottomless green eyes. Casey, of all people, could see it.

Halfway down the steps to the beach, she tripped and fell. As she berated herself for her carelessness, a man called out to her. He had loping shears in his hand and looked at her over a hedge.

"Hi, there," he said, setting down his trimmers. "Are you okay?"

Casey sat up and rubbed her ankle. "Yeah, just tweaked it a little, that's all."

She watched as the man came over; he was a little taller than she, with a broad Hispanic face, small black moustache, and big friendly eyes. Maybe about the age of her dad. "Really, I'm okay."

The man squatted alongside Casey and offered his hand. "I'm Luis Muñez—I pastor over at the community church. I haven't met you before, have I?"

Casey shook his hand and stood. Her ankle pained her, but she could put pressure on it. Luis smiled. "Well, that doesn't appear to be too bad. Do you want an ice pack?"

"No, thanks. Are you Celia's husband?"

He chuckled. "Everyone in town knows my wife. What is your favorite? Mine is the cheese tart."

Casey smiled. "I like the sugar cookies. They're deadly." She added, "Your wife is nice. Sometimes she gives me the broken cookies for free."

Luis grew quiet and Casey fidgeted. She knew that sympathetic look was due to turn into a sermon at any moment. With the shrubs sheltering the trail from the wind, the sun warmed her limbs. "This is a nice spot." She pointed. "That your house?"

Luis nodded. "We moved here a few years ago from San Jose. Are you new in town? I thought I knew everyone in Breakers."

"We came here a couple of months ago. From around Los Angeles." She stopped talking but felt words pressing to come out. She clamped her lips together.

Luis had questions in his eyes. "Tell me—I'm sorry, what is your name?"

"Casey. Casey Moore."

His voice was soft and quiet. Something about him made Casey feel safe. "Tell me, Casey, are you in school here? And your family?"

As Casey stood by the path in the warm afternoon sun, she tried to hold back the torrent of words aching to be released. "It's just my mom and dad and me. I had two brothers …" The words lodged in her throat. "I really … I can't say anything. My parents feel it's nobody's business. That's why we moved away …"

"Casey, I'm a pastor. Nothing you tell me would ever be repeated." He sat atop a low wall next to her and rested his hands in his lap. "Do you know where the church is?"

Casey nodded. She had walked by the old yellow building with the tall spire many times.

"My office is in the back of the church and I am always there every day after school until about five. We have a youth group that meets on Mondays and you are welcome to come."

"I used to go to a church back home. We stopped going after … well …" Casey took a breath and wiped her face. "I should be getting back to school. Lunch is probably over by now."

"Casey," Luis said, resting a hand on her shoulder. "Come by and see me, anytime." He stared into her eyes. "You need someone to talk with, to confide in. You've been bottling up a lot of emotion for a long time, yes?"

All Casey could do was nod.

Luis patted her on the shoulder. "I spent thirty years working with teens in the inner city, running a halfway house and listening to their problems. And they had plenty. Casey, this is not an easy life, and God knows it. You think he doesn't? He is there and he cares about you and your family. This is not the life he intended for any of us, *verdad*? He has better plans; just remember that, okay?"

Normally, Casey would have responded with an acerbic reply, some catchy retort about God's concern with her life. But for some reason Luis's words gave her a touch of comfort and reassurance. Maybe they were empty, meaningless sentiments, but Luis believed them. He seemed to understand something about God that Casey couldn't fathom. What if she was wrong about God, and maybe Luis knew better than she did—that God wasn't mean and heartless after all?

She clenched her teeth. She doubted this pastor had seen the kind of horror she had seen … and lost as much as she had lost. Easy for him to think God cared.

Casey walked back to school, her heart heavy and pained. Thinking about her brothers opened wounds she didn't want to face right now. Now a fresh gash bled inside. Jesse's sweet face intruded, his big puppy-brown eyes, the way he'd giggled when he tickled her. His childhood friends had probably forgotten him by now, and her parents rarely spoke of him, as if the mention of his name would conjure up more disaster. He was disappearing from their daily vocabulary. It was up to Casey to keep his memory alive, a weighty and exhausting burden.

And then there was Daniel.

When she had finished icing her dad's birthday cake that December night, she set about making him a card. She could see it now—a swirl of rainbow colors, flowers drawn with pink and orange markers. She had been sitting on the stool at the bar counter, writing the word *happy* at the top of the card, when the door blew open and cold winter air assailed the warmth of the kitchen.

The bowl of spaghetti that her mother held in her hands crashed to the floor; red sauce like blood flung across the room, splattering the cupboards, table, and refrigerator. Casey looked at the mess, then turned to the front door, where her father stumbled in, his arm draped around Daniel's shoulder. Daniel's head hung down, his disheveled hair wet and stringy over his face. Casey could not see his expression. What she thought was dark paint streaked his clothes. She was twelve; she didn't understand why her mother became hysterical, clawing at her dad and Daniel and crying Jesse's name.

Time had screeched to a halt. In a daze of horror, Casey grasped bits of the story from innuendo and the roiling emotion around her. In the mayhem and flurry of the accident's aftermath, with strange men in uniforms traipsing through the kitchen and hushed voices speaking into phones, Casey sat on the stool, ignored and invisible. Her parents later refused her screaming demands to go to the scene of the accident, to the hospital. There was no point, her Dad told her in a voice that sounded weak and faraway. She banged on Daniel's door, but he had locked himself in. She felt her entire life slipping away, like a boat pulled from shore by some turbulent current, heading for the inevitable falls—and the sharp rocks waiting below.

Long past midnight, she looked down at the counter and saw the card she had been making for her dad, the word *happy* glaring at her like some mean joke. For the next half hour she tore the card into tiny little bits, making a mound of paper on the counter as the stream of strangers thinned and the house fell ominously silent. The cake she had decorated sat by the refrigerator, untouched.

After two days, when no one ate it, her mother threw it out—plate and all.

# Chapter 11

MATT STUFFED THE SANDWICH WRAPPER BACK INTO HIS
lunch bag and stood, then brushed off his pants. He picked
up a brisk pace as he trod along the dirt trail that wound
through groves of alders and ferns. The combination of the
cold weather, framing a laundry room in an unheated house,
and the penetrating fog had prompted him to spend his lunch
hour hiking along the bluff at the state park to work up a
sweat.

Since sending Thurber off the job, Matt had decided to
work by himself awhile. The labor was easy; two strong arms
were sufficient. He would sub out the flooring, electrical, and
drywall, so it didn't make sense to hire anyone else.

He gave a cursory glance at the pristine beach below, although he could see little through the drifting fog. Thinking
about Thurber stirred up all kinds of emotions—none of them
pleasant. After the way the kid had looked at Casey and Matt
had glared at him, he'd figured Thurber got the hint. Whether
Thurber was just stupid or confrontational, Matt didn't know,
but the last thing he expected on the following morning was
to see Thurber at the job site. And then he'd remembered he

hadn't paid him yet. As he counted out bills and handed them to Thurber—the kid standing there with a look in his eye that could fry an egg thirty feet away—his whole body shook.

Why did that kid rattle him so much? Thurber surged with meanness, like a tide ripping up the beach and tumbling whatever blocked its path.

Without even a word of thanks or a good-bye, Thurber had turned and left. At least he wasn't expecting more work. Matt watched Thurber get into an old Ford truck loaded with firewood and drive away, the engine chugging and blurting smoke from the tailpipe.

That had been a week ago. Good riddance.

As Matt came through the wooden stile at the parking lot, he stopped and stared at his truck. At first he thought he'd been stupid and forgotten to latch down the metal tool box attached to the side of the long bed. Then he saw the glitter on the ground. Chunks of safety glass by the passenger door led his gaze up to the shattered window. Matt hurried over to assess the damage, rage rumbling in his chest. A quick survey of the lot showed he hadn't been the only target. Two other cars at the southern end near a different trailhead had broken windows as well.

Apart from bird chatter, the parking lot was quiet and empty.

Matt pulled his cell phone from his pocket and called 911. While the dispatcher connected him to the local police office, he rummaged through the box and made a mental note of all the tools missing. It wasn't so much the cost of the stolen tools as the invasiveness of the act that infuriated him. And, after fingering the lock, he gritted his teeth. He'd have to fashion a new one, seeing how the perp had used something like a screwdriver to break the box open. Until he got it fixed, none of his tools would be secure.

The dispatcher came back on and instructed Matt to wait until the sheriff arrived. Matt patted his jacket to make sure his wallet was in the pocket. At least he hadn't left that in the cab.

He opened the door and looked inside. Nothing appeared damaged apart from the window. His travel mug sat in the cup holder. His sunglasses were still clipped to the visor. His old Swiss army knife was missing from the glove box, but the flashlight, car registration, and all his repair receipts were still in there.

His first thought was Thurber, but he dismissed that; Thurber would be the kind of guy to slash tires and take a tire iron to the side of the chassis if the mood suited him. But when Joe Huff questioned Matt fifteen minutes later, tapping his meaty fingers on the cover of his report book, Matt wondered if he should mention Thurber's name—just in case.

"These things happen on occasion, you see," Huff said. "But usually in the summer, when tourists are packing in the place. Some punk troublemakers see a golden opportunity with those cameras and Gameboys and such left in the backseats of the cars. Hence the sign." Huff pointed to the laminated warning posted on a billboard between a trail map and another sign encouraging the use of the bear-proof trashcans. *Don't leave valuables unattended in the car*, et cetera.

Huff popped something into his mouth and chewed. Matt waited while the sheriff took down the plate numbers of the two cars and scanned the premises for anything telltale. He scribbled on a form and handed a copy to Matt. "For your insurance company," he said.

Thurber's face reappeared in Matt's mind. Matt cleared his throat. "Don't you have to dust for prints or something?"

Huff cocked his head and the corners of his mouth lifted. "Probably wouldn't do any good. No doubt it's some local kids—and the county has plenty more serious crimes to throw taxpayer dollars at, between the meth dealers and gang wanna-bes in Eureka. Something like this, they'd just brush me off." He shrugged as if saying "My hands are tied."

HUFF WALKED AROUND THE WIDE GRAVEL PARKING LOT. Thievery seemed to be on the increase, he concluded. Besides the call from old Mrs. Waverly, which he partially dismissed due to the lady's possible dementia, reports had come in over the last two weeks from the Breakers Realty office that some of their vacation rentals were missing items. There had been no signs of forced entry. Huff figured that was part of the risk, renting your nice vacation home to strangers, but Julie had elaborated. They screened the renters. People paying three hundred and upwards a night didn't need to take artwork off the walls or CD players or telescopes. And besides, what were the odds that things like that would disappear from four different homes in the last two weeks? Had the renters gotten together and coordinated that little heist? Not likely.

Huff saw her point. Add those little items to today's incident and he thought he should start paying attention. Although petty crimes like these usually came and went in waves. Give it time and this too shall pass. What he'd rather be doing was net fishing up on the Klamath with Wanda. They had a big smoker in the backyard for all the salmon they caught, and Wanda's family recipe was second to none. And since there'd been a heavy rain over the weekend, the flow was perfect.

He'd lost count how many times he cursed himself for letting the city council pull him out of retirement for this thankless job. Sure, he liked his coastal neighbors well enough, but since Wanda preferred staying up on the Res, this job took him away from his wife and tribal commitments. Plus, his six wild grandkids were always clamoring to go rock hunting with

Paps. Which reminded him—he was late with his monthly column on rock collecting.

He was torn, to say the least, and clearly, no one was hurrying to fill the police chief position anytime soon.

He sighed and watched Matt move tools from the broken box to the one on the other side of his truck. He checked his watch. The school was putting on their Halloween parade in a half hour. He liked to watch the little squirts march around town in their costumes—not that anyone expected any trouble. Usually it required some traffic control, and making sure none of the kids wandered off down the wrong street. One year some drunken hippie had mooned the first-graders from his living room window, causing a lot of giggles and pointing but little permanent emotional damage to the kids.

He had just enough time to get back to town to catch the parade.


"You okay here, Matt?"

Matt nodded and waved the sheriff off. There was nothing Huff could do. Stuff happened. He brushed the remnants of broken glass off the passenger seat and got into his truck. Fog enveloped him as he left the parking lot, erased his surroundings. He leaned forward to find the road through his windshield. Gravel turned to asphalt; houses drifted by like ghosts.

As he drove back to town he searched his feelings, tried to assess whether he was upset, angry, or what. It wasn't the lack of feeling that set him on edge as much as the realization that he didn't care. His life had fallen into patterns of routine, of requisite conversation. Of measured responses and expected behaviors. He knew his heart was numb, all the nerve endings severed. He was sleepwalking through a different kind of fog. Somehow he couldn't see a way to connect the dots of his life.

He saw moments in time as isolated pixels—baby Casey in his arms in the hospital room; Jesse sprawled across the bed, chewing his pencil while working out a math problem; Daniel throwing the ball against his bedroom wall over and over; Irene bringing lunch to the job site, sitting with him and looking out at the lake on a spring day. You could take a million of these images and lay them all side by side, each tiny moment, and you'd have a picture to show for it all. Something you could point to and say, "Here, this is the sum total of my life."

For what it was worth.

"The creation was subjected to futility." Well, wasn't that the truest observation in the Scriptures? "Subjected not of its own will but by the will of the one who subjected it." For what reason? If he remembered his Bible correctly, it was for the sole purpose of inspiring hope—freedom from bondage to decay, from the whole painful process of mortality. Creation groaning in pain for release, waiting for rescue.

Matt grunted. The words came by rote, even though he hadn't picked up a Bible in nearly two years. He chalked it up to all those Sunday school classes he had attended throughout his childhood. He mouthed the words: "For in hope we were saved. Who hopes for what is seen? But if we hope for what we do not see, we wait for it with patience."

Matt drove up the newly poured driveway on Salmonberry Lane. He cut the engine and sat there. God sure had some warped sense of purpose. Live a life of futility, full of sound and fury, as Casey was wont to quote from Macbeth. How did it go—life was "a tale told by an idiot ... signifying nothing"? What was the logic in living out your years in futility, years meant to teach you to be patient in waiting for something better?

Voices drifted into the cab, overlapping, high-pitched, and excited. Matt adjusted the rearview mirror and saw a swath of color moving down the street at the base of the driveway. Adults gathered to line along the curb all the way to the corner. They waved and smiled to the witches, princesses, superheroes, and ghosts that tromped in a haphazard march down the center of the lane. Little people—happy, carefree, hopeful. What did their coffers of hope contain besides a bucket full of brightly wrapped candy? Was it right for their parents to offer them much more? Matt wondered, when all was said and done at the end of their earthly years, just what picture would form for them? Would they look back over a too-short, troubled life and say it had been worth it?

Matt stared vacantly at the small rectangular mirror mounted on his windshield. The ribbon of colorfully costumed children bisected the glass. They looked so tiny and unaware that life held dangers, that their shiny portrait of joy was actually fragile and brittle, and could break so easily.

He watched as a heavyset woman in a cowgirl dress herded the marchers along, keeping them on course.

He watched as a tall, thin man with a gray ponytail down his back stepped into the street and handed out candy to some of the children.

He watched as a little boy in a red cape, looking so much like Jesse, handed one of his candy bars to a pink mermaid who looked a lot like Casey.

He squeezed shut his eyes and watched as his son Daniel raised a gun to his head and blasted his brains out all over the auditorium stage.

# *Chapter 12*

LEE CHIN, THE OLD ASIAN FISHERMAN WHO RAN THE BAIT shop next to the pier, eyed the nervous young man in the dark wool coat. There the kid stood, same place as yesterday, waiting behind the wooden fence overgrown with blackberry brambles. Every day, the last week or so, at different times, just standing there, like he was waiting for someone to arrive. Sometimes he walked down the beach and then came back. Sometimes he smoked a cigarette. The shop owner had long spells of time on his hands. He spent his hours behind the counter reading small Chinese paperback books, their covers embellished with poorly drawn sketches of Asian girls with short skirts. The fishing season had dropped off, and until crabbing started in December, business would be slow. So, he tended to notice things.

Like the way the young fellow's hands twitched, as if he were typing or playing a piano. His daughter used to do that—practice her scales in the air. Another thing the young man did was mumble. He'd get in a heated fret, maybe thinking no one saw him. Surely this man had something up his sleeve, was up to no good. One could tell the type. At least Lee Chin could. He never spoke to the man, only nodded when their eyes chanced meeting. Chin did not like the man's beady eyes. They were too small for his face and held no depth. One had to wonder about a person with shallow eyes. They portended bad things, stagnant *chi*.

He put his thick glasses on and went back to reading his book, unaware that the young man had wandered off into the parking area. When he looked up a few minutes later, the man was gone, vanished into the fog.

ZACK KEPT CHECKING THE SPEEDOMETER AS HE DROVE DOWN First Street toward the pier. *Keep to the speed limit. Twenty-five steady.*

Randy's face reflected none of Zack's tension. Zack *so* did not want to be doing this in the middle of the day, but they had an impatient buyer in Point Arena. Rather than take the chance of losing a big sale, Randy had opened his big mouth and offered to get a delivery to him by nightfall. Zack almost punched him when he heard the deal go down over the phone.

He was really having second thoughts about taking on this venture with such a bozo. Randy spoke before he thought. Everyone was his good ol' buddy. *Chill*, was what he told Zack. Like that was the magic word to ward off disaster. *Chill*— right! *Chill* was going to get them busted if they weren't careful.

Zack peered through the thick fog and checked the cars in the lot. The usual boat trailers in their usual spots. The bait shop owner's old dented Rambler. Three nice-looking cars parked near the beach, and an old truck with firewood in it. That one looked vaguely familiar, but he couldn't place it.

Zack assumed the vehicles belonged to folks at the beach. Why they wanted to stroll on a day when you couldn't see your nose on your face was beyond Zack's understanding. Maybe some of these people had driven hundreds of miles to see the ocean, so a little fog wasn't going to stop them from enjoying their vacation. Well, let them enjoy—as long as they stayed *over there.*

Randy hopped out of the truck the moment Zack put it in Park. How they were going to cart these boxes to the skiff without attracting attention was Zack's main concern. Randy had argued that people took gear out to their boats all the time. What was the problem? You just loaded up like any other day. Zack wanted to rattle some sense into Randy. This was harvest season and the local law well knew it.

He cringed, thinking back to the night their truck had broken down on the freeway, a few weeks ago. When the highway patrol pulled up alongside them, Zack knew he was a goner. Rain poured in sheets as the guy propped his flashlight up against the window and scanned the cab. Randy's head was buried under the hood, reattaching a loose wire to some terminal. Three huge Hefty bags lay on the floor behind the front seat—filled with untrimmed plants. Zack figured the cop could smell the stuff all the way from his patrol car. But he only asked if they needed a tow truck, and when they told him no, the cop wished them well and went on his merry way. Randy called it good karma. Zack knew they had been lucky.

But you only got so many lucky coupons.

Now, as they started to unload boxes from the bed of the truck, Zack hoped they still had another coupon left. And hoped the fog would lift enough for them to find the cove for the drop-off.

As Randy stacked two of the cardboard boxes onto the dolly, Zack froze. He didn't realize he was holding his breath until he recognized that guy from the restaurant—Thurber, that was his name—walking down the side of the parking lot to the pier. He watched Thurber smile as he came toward them. Randy stopped and waved. Zack stiffened.

"Hey, it's you guys," Thurber said, his voice booming in the fog. Zack wanted to quiet him, but that would look plain obvious, wouldn't it?

"Hey, Thurber," Zack said in a hushed tone. "What's up?"

"Not much, man. I looked for you on Monday—at the bar. You missed a great game."

Zack nodded but said nothing. *We have no time for this.* He nudged Randy, to get him moving, but Randy wanted to shoot the breeze.

"Yeah, we were somewhere; I don't remember where. But we saw the game. Oh yeah, it was at Dave's Joint in Eureka. Great pizza—ever been there?"

Thurber shook his head and looked at the boxes.

Zack gritted his teeth. *Don't look at the boxes.* He nudged Randy a little harder this time. "Randy, let's get going, okay?"

Randy's look asked, "What's your rush?"

Zack took hold of the dolly and pushed Randy out of the way. "I don't mean to be rude, man," he said to Thurber in an apologetic voice, "but we have to make south a ways before dark. We're already getting a late start."

"Well, let me help you, then." As Thurber reached down to lift up a box, Zack stopped him with his hand.

"That's okay, we can manage." *Get the hint!*

Randy gave up the chatter and took the dolly from Zack. As he rolled it across the lot to the pier, Thurber leaned into Zack.

"Seems like more than fishing going on here, from what I can gather."

Zack's heart pounded like a hammer. *Oh great!* He unloaded another box from the truck. Time moved agonizingly slowly. "Just supplies, food and such. Gotta restock when you come to town."

"Oh, yeah, right." Thurber chuckled.

At the unmistakable cynicism, Zack looked into Thurber's face. He wished he hadn't. His voice came out in a whisper and he knew he couldn't mask his fear. "What do you want, Thurber?" He didn't know this guy from Adam—just a few beers at a bar. The guy could be an undercover for all he knew. This was bad, *real* bad.

Thurber studied Zack's expression. A smiled inched up his face. "Nothing, man. Just friendly talk. Just observing."

*Observing? Right!* Zack blurted the words, "Say, when we get back, we'll hang, okay? Next Monday for Mexican sound good?"

Thurber paused for a minute and turned his head. He watched Randy load the last of his boxes into the skiff and head back with the dolly. He chuckled. "Sure, man."

Zack felt sweat stream down his neck.

Thurber waved good-bye to Randy, then faced Zack. In a soft voice, he said, "Oh, and if it's not too much trouble, could you bring me a bag? I'd really appreciate it."

Zack nodded weakly. As he watched Thurber melt into the fog, Randy came up alongside him with the empty dolly. He had a big grin on his face as he thoughtfully stroked his beard.

"Hey, nice guy, huh? Not too many guys would give you a lift to your boat like he did."

Zack glared at Randy. Randy looked back at his partner with lifted eyebrows. "What? What is it?"

Zack held his tongue. *A total bozo.*

Randy patted his partner's shoulder. "Zack, my man," he said, chuckling. "You just need to chill."


A SURGE OF COLD WATER REFILLED THE TIDE POOLS, MAKING the sea grass waver around Casey's feet. The fog settled wet on her clothes and hair, but through the haze the sun warmed the salty air. Seagulls winged overhead, vanishing and reappearing out of the gray murk. She and Meredith were counting snails for their science project. Mr. Reese and Meredith's teacher, Mrs. Connolly, had let them miss the afternoon study period so they could go down to the beach.

Casey liked Meredith. Even though Meredith was only twelve, she was a lot more together than the dorks in Casey's grade who only cared about getting manicures and reading *Cosmo*. Meredith called herself a free spirit and had no qualms about prying into Casey's life and commenting on her work partner's "bizarre" wardrobe. Casey found her blatant honesty refreshing; it made Casey realize how smothered she was in her own silent judgment.

Judgment and blame, such weights people dragged around. She saw them every day in her parents' eyes. Her mom blamed herself; her dad blamed everyone *but* himself. Whom did she blame? She felt a twinge of guilt thinking about Daniel. She saw him as a catalyst, triggering reaction.

*It was* not *his fault*, she chided herself. *Don't even go there.*

Casey sighed and knelt on the sand. She knew Meredith squatted only a few yards away, but all Casey could see was the small enclosure of barnacled rocks around her.

Meredith came over to Casey, her tie-dyed shirtsleeves rolled up to the elbows.

"How's it going?" Casey said. "I think I'm finished here."

"Dang, my feet are frozen. Can we be done?" Meredith asked.

Casey chuckled. *Dang* was a Meredith word, along with *groovy* and *dyno*. Casey still hadn't figured out if *dyno* had something to do with dinosaurs or dynamite.

"Now *there's* a cute guy." Meredith tipped her head and Casey looked behind her. For a twelve-year-old, Meredith sure had boy radar. From what Casey gathered, Meredith lived alone with her new-agey mom who did Reiki attunements and burned incense all day long. While they explored the tide pools, Casey had learned more than she wanted to about Meredith's promiscuous mother.

Casey watched a man walk along the edge of the parking lot where the beach spilled over onto the gravel. It took a few seconds to register, but there was no mistaking the guy. Her heart pounded hard in her chest as he lifted his gaze from the ground to where the girls stood. His eyes locked onto hers.

Meredith whispered, "That is one totally groovy hunk." She elbowed Casey, then caught her friend's expression and laughed. "Okay, go talk to him—you can do it." She gave a little shove that threw Casey off balance. "Tell him how absolutely gorgeous he is," she added, perhaps thinking Casey could use a script. "Don't you just love his jeans?"

The last thing Casey needed was a cheering section—or an observer. She could tell her cheeks were flushed; the heat radiated off her face into the fog. She watched as Meredith wandered off down the beach, pretending to study more snails. Despite feeling flustered, how could she pass up this chance? She took a breath and pushed her bangs aside, then walked to the guy who stood there, looking her over.

Casey was glad for the fog as she stopped next to him. It enclosed them in a private world, erasing the beach and parking lot, reminding her of the witches in *Macbeth* who wove their spells and chanted about the fog and filthy air. Casey felt pulled into their spell, for she found herself speaking but heard nothing. She told him her name and he told her his. *Billy.* His voice was soft and deep, and his thoughtful face held mystery. She suddenly wished she hadn't worn such baggy shorts and Jesse's football shirt. Still, Billy eyed her like a cake in a bakery window.

He told her, "I saw you the other week, at your dad's job."

Casey was dumbstruck. How to respond to that? She asked him short questions that he seemed to find amusing. He told her he came down from the mountains, where he lived most of the year. That he cut and sold firewood in the fall to make a few bucks. No, he didn't have a girlfriend. He chuckled at that one. Once more, she felt her face flush hot, felt her tongue thick in her mouth.

Casey couldn't guess how long they stood there talking. The waves soughing behind her made her sleepy; Billy's attentions lulled her as well. When he reached over and touched her cheek, she knew she was under his spell, for she could not move, or barely even breathe. A wave of agitation surged through her like a tide. She heard herself gasp.

He let his hand drop. "Just how old are you, anyway?"

"Uh, seventeen ..." someone inside her replied, some voice not hers.

Billy smiled and let out a breath. He bit down on his lower lip, thinking. Casey couldn't take her eyes off his mouth.

"I think," Billy said, pushing Casey's bangs out of her eyes, "someone could use a kiss."

Before Billy's comment could sink in with all its nuances and potential, Casey felt warm lips on hers. A riptide swept her away as he held her arms gently with his hands as the kiss went on, her mouth and limbs afire.

Finally, he pulled back and studied her face, returning her to a familiar beach. With his eyes on her, she felt her face flush hot and, embarrassed, looked toward the shoreline. She heard Meredith calling in the distance, snapping her out of a reverie she thought she'd be trapped in forever.

"See ya, Casey Moore," was all he said, giving her a wink. He turned and went toward his truck, leaving Casey wrapped in fog.

Meredith found her, standing on the beach, lost in thought. As Meredith babbled on about boys and science projects, Casey tried to shake off the spell. Numb, she followed Meredith back to where they had left their things, swung her backpack onto her shoulder, and the two of them headed up the hill toward school.

Her thoughts returned to the passage in Macbeth she had reviewed just last night while working on her essay. She imagined an apparition appearing, perhaps in the fog. A ghost, a bloody child, assuring Macbeth: "No man that's born of woman shall e'er have power upon thee." The ghost had spoken truly, for Macbeth defeated Malcolm in battle and ruled unvanquished as king.

She heard Billy's voice again, saying her name, claiming it somehow. She could still feel his kiss on her lips. She was not Macbeth; *this* man, born of woman, had power over her. He had claimed her, and now what was to be done?

# Chapter 13

IRENE SCRAPED THE PLATES OVER THE TRASH CAN IN THE kitchen, glancing out the window as the wind buffeted the glass panes. With daylight saving time ended, the sky was now dark when Matt came home. Over dinner, they had engaged in polite conversation: Casey detailing the progress of her science project, and her impression of Meredith's mother, Sunny, who sounded a bit wild but seemed to garner some curious respect from her daughter; Matt listing the tasks completed to date at the Salmonberry house, the to-do list shrinking; Irene sharing a story about a boy with a lisp who struggled through reading a limerick. Irene recalled an expression: ignoring the elephant in the room. A big, ugly elephant that took a seat at every meal.

No wonder the small house seemed so crowded.

Casey retreated to her room. Matt got up and collected dirty silverware, showing solidarity in domestication. As she cleared more dishes off the table, Irene noticed her jeans barely stayed on her hips. She still hadn't gotten her appetite back and wondered if she ever would. How many years had she spent dieting, trying to lose those stubborn ten pounds of bulge? How many different diets? Well, she could now tell anyone the recipe for losing weight. Just lose a couple of kids—that'd do the trick. Plus, hard as she might, she couldn't get the image of the buffet at the side of the auditorium stage out of her mind whenever she saw food on a table. The way the red and brown slopped over the dainty sandwiches, lemon bars, and cupcakes.

At least she had stopped vomiting.

Irene scoured the frying pan. Matt came in and watched, hypnotized by her ardor. The windows steamed up from the hot sink water. Outside, rain banged on the roof and siding, a clamorous sound. A cup sat on the floor in the corner, catching an errant drip every few minutes. Matt still hadn't gotten around to fixing the roof.

Irene scrubbed harder, stacking dishes neatly in the dish drainer. Matt hovered by the counter. He used to hover like that, when they'd first met in San Diego, when she lived in her apartment while attending UCSD. Each morning she'd hurry down the sidewalk to the bus stop and pass the house he was building. While she sat on the wooden bench, studying for her classes, he would find a way to get her into view. Gradually, he worked his way over to talk with her some mornings. He was six years older, so comfortable speaking with her—having been raised by a single mother and hemmed in by three younger sisters. Irene had been amused and flattered by this handsome man's interest, but didn't take him seriously. Not at first. She had no idea that Matt Moore was a man who took everything seriously. That his quiet, thoughtful demeanor held an intensity she would never truly fathom.

Irene walked over to the fridge. This had been one hard day to get through.

She had thought twice at the store when she reached for the cake mix.

She'd thought twice in the kitchen after getting out the electric mixer.

She'd thought twice when she iced the cake and set it in the fridge.

Now she hesitated again, wondering what this cake meant. This cake was a symbol, and symbols held power. A layer cake that held layers of implications, layers of memories. She took her hand off the refrigerator door. Why had she baked the blasted thing?

"What are you doing?" Matt asked.

Irene turned. Matt stood in the middle of the steamy kitchen, a little-lost-boy look on his face. No, this look was more frightened. A visage she imagined on an old, disoriented man, wandering down the aisles of a supermarket, forgetting where he'd left his grocery basket. A tinge of panic showed through, a signal to Irene that she was not allowed to fall apart, that her job was to keep the dam from bursting, even if every finger was already plugging up some hole.

Irene backed away when Matt came over and opened the fridge. The cake seemed to stare at them. Chocolate icing with sprinkles, the way Daniel had always insisted. Every year the same cake, since forever.

"It's his birthday," Irene noted flatly. "I just—"

Matt turned to her and scrunched his face. His voice came out unexpectedly harsh. "Don't you think I know that? You think I'd forget?"

"No, Matt, of course not." Irene fumbled for something more to say but drew a blank.

Matt studied the cake that sat on the top shelf between the milk and the peanut butter. He suddenly grabbed the plate and took the cake out to the dining room, then set it on the table. "Then let's eat it," he said, anger spilling into the room. "Casey!"

Matt got plates and forks, found a long serrated knife. When he returned to the table, Casey was standing a few feet away, tears pooling in her eyes.

"What are you doing, Dad?" She watched her father move in a flurry of motion, pulling out chairs.

"Sit. It's your brother's birthday and your mom made a cake to remember him by."

Casey cowered as if his words were shrapnel from a bomb. "Not like this, Dad. You can't—"

"Can't what?" He took the knife and sliced the cake in half, in quarters, in eighths, with quick, deliberate strokes as if cutting up a batt of insulation. Irene watched him place three pieces on three plates. She eased into her seat, afraid something would break—if not the chair, then what was left of her spirit.

Casey sat next to her, annoyance evident in her face. "You're being disrespectful of the dead." Irene looked at her daughter's reddened complexion and saw anger in her eyes. "I want to say a prayer."

"Go ahead," Matt said with a hard edge. He started to say something else, but instead he strode across the room and threw open the front door, taking his plate outside, where the rain poured down with a vengeance.

Irene and Casey waited but Matt did not come back in. Casey shook her head, a mixture of disgust and disappointment flitting across her features. Irene ventured a touch, reaching over to place her hand on Casey's shoulder. Casey sighed, reminding Irene of when her little girl was a baby. How, right before she'd fall to sleep, she'd let out a sigh like that. Irene had read it as an expression of contentment, of peace. But this sigh had no similarity to those long-lost feelings.

Casey prayed while Irene bowed her head, listening. Her daughter's mumbled words came out between sobs. She asked God to take care of Jesse and Daniel. She thanked God for the short time they'd had with her brothers and wished there

had been more. She told God how much she missed them.
She didn't ask for answers or explanations or even help to get
through all this, and Irene knew why. There were no answers
or explanations. And if God had it in his heart to help them,
he would—if there was any possible way.

Maybe even that was beyond God's power.


THE NEXT MORNING, EARLY, MATT ANSWERED HIS PHONE
while he spooned coffee grounds into a paper filter. A motel
owner down the street needed a fast roof patch; one of his
motel rooms had an inch of water on the floor. Pressing his
cell phone to his ear, Matt opened the front door to a chilly
but dry morning. Yes, he told the owner, he could come now,
while there was a break in the weather. No, he couldn't tell the
man how much it was going to cost until he took a look. The
damage could be minimal, or it could be extensive. There was
no telling over the phone. He was glad Dottie at the hardware
store had recommended him.

Matt hung up and pressed the red button on the coffeemaker. Sounds of stirring drifted through the house—Casey
in the shower, Irene making the bed. He stuck his travel mug
under the stream of brown liquid, then put the glass pot in its
place. He put on his coat, zipped it up, and closed the door
behind him before he had to make pleasant conversation. He
was not in a good mood today and he had no interest in doing
anything about it. Surely he was entitled to indulge in a few
bad moods from time to time.

The first thing Matt noticed about the motel owner was
his sloppiness: stained gray T-shirt, ratty sweatpants, hair flying in all directions. The second impression came hard on the
heels of the first: alcohol on the man's breath at—what was

it?—not even eight a.m. The man introduced himself as "Jerry Hubble-like-the-telescope."

Standing at the door to the owner's tiny cottage, Matt swiveled slowly, taking in the old structures, already anticipating mold and mildew and dry rot. Really, the best remedy for a place like this was a bulldozer. With over two hundred days of rain a year, no wonder these ancient lodges and cabins were leaking. You had to be diligent to combat the weather here, before it overran your life.

Matt looked to his right. Parked next to the motel, in sharp contrast, was a red Corvette, waxed so perfectly it gleamed in the filtered sunlight. A car very much out of place.

Jerry gestured across the parking lot to an open door. Matt pulled on his muck boots and waded into the motel room. The carpeting squished underfoot. One look at the ceiling told Matt all he needed to know.

"You need a new roof here," he said.

"Can't you just patch it? At least for now?"

Matt pressed his lips together. "I'd have to get up there and start pulling shingles off. No telling just where the leak starts and what it looks like underneath."

Jerry stood outside the motel room, peering in. Matt asked, "Won't your insurance cover this?"

"I checked and I'm not sure. There's nothing in the policy I can see for flood or water damage. I have a call out to the insurance guy, but he's not in yet."

Matt stepped outside and looked at the sky. "This would be a good day to do this. Of course, if it needs a whole roof, that'd take more than a day. You have a shop vac you can use to suck the water out?"

Jerry nodded. "Well, that's going to be a whole lot of fun. This motel is starting to become a millstone around my neck."

Matt waited, listening to the motel owner complain.

"Sure, I got it for a song, but how much money will I have to pour into the trash heap just to keep it presentable? It's not like the tourists who stay here expect five-star accommodations, mind you. They want cheap; they get cheap. But they sure aren't going to stay in a room that requires wearing waders."

Matt couldn't think of any consoling words to calm Jerry down.

"Well," Jerry said, "why don't you go ahead and check out the roof. I have to fix it regardless. Let's see how bad she is."

While Matt got out a ladder and tools, Jerry went to fetch the shop vac. Matt noticed he walked with a limp, favoring one leg. He positioned the ladder and climbed up on the roof as Jerry returned, dragging the vacuum behind him like a stubborn horse. Jerry called up to him.

"I see you drive by. You live on Seawood?"

"Next to the state park, on Pelican Lane."

Jerry stood under the ladder so Matt could hear him. "You heard about the break-ins in town?" He pointed to the broken window on Matt's truck and the bent-up tool box. "How'd that happen?"

Matt told him.

"I *knew* it. Listen." He motioned Matt over to the edge of the roof. "Breakers is a small town, and when someone shows up looking for trouble, well, it's just plain obvious. I tried to talk to Huff about it, but he shines it on. Too busy with his stupid rocks. But, listen, there's been a whole lot of break-ins in town—rich folks' homes. It was in the paper. And then there's your truck, and across the street Mrs. Waverly had someone go into her house and steal some antique necklace." He balled his fist and shook it. "And all this bull-pucky started when that cocky kid came to town a few weeks ago—you get my point? You seen that kid? Blond, twenty-something, dressed like a logger. That kid delivered a load of wood to the old lady's house, probably cased her place while he was there."

Oh, Matt had seen him, all right. He let Jerry rant for a while about the lax law enforcement in town, how things were going to get worse unless someone did something. Matt heard every other word. He kept seeing Thurber's smug expression and the way he had salivated over Casey.

Jerry's sharp tone brought Matt's attention back. "Hey, here's something else I know—I've learned at least two people paid that punk for cords of firewood—in advance, can you believe being that gullible? He's never showed back up on their doorsteps. Whadda ya make of that?"

Jerry didn't wait for Matt to answer. He huffed and grabbed the handle on the vacuum, then disappeared into the swampy motel room.

Matt pulled sections of composite shingles from the roof, tore off tar paper, working outward from the area most likely to be the culprit. One section of roof sheeting, about three feet in diameter, was rotted through. Matt poked around with his screwdriver, delineating an area. It could be worse, way worse. A patch would work temporarily.

When he climbed down the ladder and looked into the motel room, Jerry was vacuuming the sodden carpet. Matt got his attention and gave him an assessment of the damage. Jerry had already worked up a sweat; his shirt was soaked through and his face was red, even more flushed than the trademark alcoholic's tint. Matt gave him an estimate of the repair cost and Jerry whistled.

"Well, just go ahead and do it. Glad I don't need a whole new roof."

Matt advised him to think about reroofing all the buildings before he suffered more flooded rooms.

Jerry grunted. "Well, make sure you give me all the receipts and I'll see what I can squeeze out of my insurance. And listen—" He leaned into Matt. A faint scent of liquor drifted on the air. "You keep your eyes on that punk. He's all over town, stirring up trouble. You hear what I'm saying?"

He shook a knowing finger at Matt. "Trouble, that's what he is."

# *Chapter 14*

AFTER A FINAL LOOK AROUND THE CHURCH TO MAKE SURE everything was put away, Luis turned off the lights and locked the door. He wished he had been able to speak with the woman sitting in the back, but by the time he had worked his way down the aisle, greeting his parishioners and praying with the Steens, she had left. He got a look at her, though, and she seemed distraught and sad. It was the first time she'd been in his church. A tourist or a local? Hard to tell. He said a silent prayer for her and hoped she'd return next Sunday.

The huge storm predicted to hit the north coast had passed Breakers by, allowing for a brisk, sunny day. Luis stood on the church's front lawn—a tiny patch of grass—and gazed out over the harbor. He breathed deeply, invigorated by the crisp air—such a contrast from the pollution in San Jose. Such a blessing to live in this *tranquilidad*. He remembered what old Mr. Collins had said to him when Luis called this place "God's country." He had chortled and answered, "Pastor Muñez, this isn't God's country; this is where God takes his vacations."

He thought about Celia, already home and probably cooking Sunday dinner. Enchilada casserole—his favorite. You'd think with baking six days a week she'd take time off from the kitchen, but not his wife. Even when they relaxed in the living room, reading the Bible or watching a movie, Celia would drift into the kitchen and start mixing something in a bowl. Thank God he had a fast metabolism. He and Celia were the perfect match—she smothered him with food and he loved to eat, but he never put on weight. *Bendiga su corazón.* Bless her heart! A match made in heaven.

Luis walked along the street toward home. After the hectic traffic of the summer—cars clogging the small lanes in town and people browsing the shops—he gratefully immersed himself in the quiet. He loved the way the waves broke one after another, and how the sound carried up the hill and washed over him. The apartment he had lived in down south was a block from the highway and only a few miles from the airport. *Mucho ruido.* Way too much noise. Here a person could think and pray without distraction.

Luis walked across the street to the memorial post erected for the souls lost at sea. The tall brass monument had names engraved in two columns, along with the dates of their demise. Sitting next to the monument was the woman he had seen in church.

*Gracias a Dios.* God always found a way.

The woman had her back to him and was looking out over the harbor. Her brown hair fell around her shoulders and waved in the breeze. As he came around to introduce himself, he saw she had her head buried in her hands. He didn't want to startle her, so he walked over to the bluff and asked God to give him words of comfort.

IRENE LET THE STREAM OF TEARS ROLL DOWN HER CHEEKS and onto her sweater. Already the knit collar was drenched.

How many tears could a person cry? Was there a limit; did you run out at some point? And what happened then—did the well of your heart run dry, leaving nothing but cracked, thirsty ground?

She lifted her eyes and noticed him—the pastor from the church. He must have felt her gaze, for he turned and nodded at her.

"Would you like to be left alone? Or do you want to talk?"

Irene sniffled and motioned him to sit beside her. Luis squeezed her hand and told her his name. She introduced herself in a broken voice. "I enjoyed the sermon this morning. About charity."

He sat beside her. "We forget sometimes how powerful a simple act of kindness can be. Even Jesus felt that giving a small cup of water to a stranger was worthy of great reward."

His words dissipated in the air. Irene could tell the pastor was a thoughtful man, comfortable with silence. She liked his eyes and the way he tipped his head while listening.

At that moment, it hit her—hard.

Four months had passed since Daniel's death and she had opened up to no one. Not even Matt. Forever skirting that topic, never facing it head on. How did you even begin to talk about a horror like that? That day was still unreal in Irene's mind: the immensity of Daniel's action, his choice of timing and location. Subjecting a thousand witnesses to his pain, and to graphic violence no one could ever erase from memory.

Irene cringed at the intrusion of images. The mood only moments earlier—joyous, excited, proud. So sharply contrasted with the horror to follow. Parents and grandparents and brothers and sisters and cousins filling the auditorium. Hurrying to kneel in the aisle when their student's name was called, snapping pictures from cameras that flashed like tiny firecrackers in the cavernous room. Casey elbowing Irene when Daniel walked up the steps to where the robed principal stood at the microphone, Casey's wide smile lighting up her whole face.

The last time Irene ever saw her joyous like that. Would she ever again?

Pastor Muñez was saying something. Irene shut her eyes, forcing the picture out of her head before the terrible scene unfolded. Replaying those next few minutes only tortured her, but those were the images that haunted her again and again, during the day while she stood at the chalkboard, and during the night, yanking her out of a troubled sleep. She didn't want to remember Daniel like that, but when he'd ended up lying there on the stage floor, blood spreading around him, half his head gone, the image had burned into her mind—a cattle brand of hot metal, searing flesh and leaving a permanent wound. Thinking such a wound could become an unfeeling scar was, well, unthinkable. She yearned to forget, but swore to remember. How could you do both?

"Irene," Luis said gently. "What can I do for you? How can I help?"

Her voice came out flat and unemotional. "I lost a son in June. Daniel was his name." She let the words linger on the air between the two of them. "I wanted to talk to someone, but—" Her throat choked up, making her gasp. Luis laid his hand on her shoulder and her breath unloosed. Irene wiped her eyes with the back of her hand. Luis reached into a pocket and pulled out a small packet of tissues.

"Always carry one. Goes with the job."

Irene attempted a smile as she used the tissue to blow her nose. She sighed and words came tumbling out.

The whole time she spoke, Luis listened. He listened for perhaps a half hour without saying a word. Then he cleared his throat and spoke. "You ever see *The Shawshank Redemption*? It's one of my favorite movies."

"Yes, mine too," Irene mumbled.

"While you were talking, for some reason that movie kept coming to mind. How we humans go through so much pain in our lives—some more than others, to be sure. Undeserved pain, oftentimes, yes? But how the human spirit is an indestructible thing. Do you remember the ending—when Red gets out of prison and he says, 'Get busy living or get busy dying'? He has the choice of hanging himself, like the fella in the room before him, or moving on. He can succumb to that weight of misery and give up, or he can embrace something else."

"What was that?" She remembered Red walking on the white sand beach of Mexico and reuniting with his friend Andy.

"I memorized the ending of that movie because it resonates so well with what the Bible tells us." Luis stood and looked over the ocean. " 'Remember, Red,' " he said in a dramatic voice laced with an Hispanic accent. " 'Hope is a good thing, maybe the best of things. And no good thing ever dies.' "

Luis stood there, letting the words sink in. He turned to Irene. "I always chuckle when I think about the apostle Paul. The guy went through floggings, beatings, shipwrecks, all kinds of attacks. And then he called all this we go through 'a slight affliction.' Do you remember that passage in Corinthians? He said this slight affliction—this mortal life of ours—'is momentary and light, working for us a far more exceeding and eternal weight of glory, while we keep our eyes, not on the things seen, but on the things unseen. For the things which are seen are temporary, but the things unseen are eternal.' "

Irene stood and straightened out her clothes. Her knees wobbled, as if all the life had drained out of her.

Luis took her arm. "It is no comfort, I know, to tell someone with such horrible loss as you have endured to focus on the next life. And that is not what I am saying. Paul is trying to put things in perspective. We live such a short life. Like the Bible says, our lives are like a little mist, a vapor that appears and then disappears. If this is all there is, life is pointless, devoid of meaning and purpose. Why bother? Yet, we are not supposed to just get this life over with so we can move on. We are here to learn some things, and I believe all the suffering we go through teaches us compassion, makes us more the kind of people God wants us to become in the end. Like him."

The pastor looked into Irene's eyes, and each word he said went straight to her heart. "Irene, you have lost your boys. I cannot even picture the pain you are going through. But I want to say one more thing: you cannot expect yourself, or your husband or Casey, to get past this, like it is a road block. You are in a place of choiceless pain and God is there alongside you. Trying to pretend you are not there, trying to live a normal life and handle all of your responsibilities just as before — you cannot do this. God does not expect you to do this. You need to give yourself, and your family, time. There will be healing, but not now. Now there is pain, and you need to hang onto hope, even if blindly. And you need to reach your arms around your family and love them, yes? Find a way to turn this pain into compassion, and ask God to help you. He will."

Irene nodded. She knew he was right; she was expecting so much from herself and Matt. She had hoped that by ignoring the pain she could get on with her life, but the pain debilitated her. Her heart ached as if from a literal wound.

"Look," Luis said. "Will you have lunch with me and my family? Do you have to get home soon?"

"Matt and Casey went hiking in the park today. Your offer is kind, Pastor Muñez, but I'm not really hungry."

"Oh, I think you will get an appetite once you smell all that good food. Come, Irene." He gestured up the street. "My house is a block away. My daughter, son-in-law, and grandson will all be there. A lot of noise and chaos, but maybe you'll find it refreshing." His smile was a warm lamp to her heart.

"All right. Thank you, Pastor Muñez—for listening too."

"Luis. Call me Luis."


AS THEY TURNED DOWN LUIS'S STREET, HE SAID A SILENT prayer. He hoped his words encouraged Irene, if only a little. He hoped God would make his presence known in her life. The words spoken in that movie were true: hope *was* a good thing, maybe the best of things. And no good thing ever died.

This he believed with all his heart.

# *Chapter 15*

DOTTIE TOOK THE DISH OUT OF THE MICROWAVE AND POURED the butter over the top of the popcorn. She looked at the clock, an old-style Swiss cuckoo she had ordered on the Shopping Channel last spring—a deal at $29.95. She liked the way the little plastic bird came out of the birdhouse on the hour and chirped. Ten more minutes and that little hatch would open again, announcing midnight.

She looked at the heart-shaped magnet on the fridge. "Today is the tomorrow you thought about yesterday." Well, it was almost tomorrow, and then it'd be today.

Dottie yawned. She tried to stay up and watch movies with Tim on Friday nights; they considered it their special time together. But tonight she was plum tuckered out. She shuffled into the living room, her long flannel nightgown trailing the floor as she walked. She'd bought this cute pink stripy thing on the Shopping Channel as well—just hadn't had the time to raise the hem. Being so short often required making adjustments to her wardrobe. Seems the clothing makers didn't figure there were any short people left in the world. All those fashion models in magazines were nearly six feet tall. What planet did they hail from?

As she handed Tim the metal bowl, he guffawed and pointed to the TV. Even when she sat beside him, he gave her a blow-by-blow account of every scene, forgetting she was watching the movie alongside him. And right now a herd of tarantulas was overrunning some town, with a bunch of scared folks holed up in a hotel. This spider movie was not one of her favorites. Spiders creeped her out, even those daddy longlegs that worked their way into the hardware store through the floor cracks. Tim had told her they were the good kind: they ate what he called "decomposing veg-etative matter" and even ate other spiders, including those nasty brown recluse ones. Just thinking about spiders made her skin crawl.

"Here, look," Tim said excitedly. "They're surrounding the hotel. Just watch—this dumb woman'll try to run out and the spiders are gonna get her." He stuffed a handful of popcorn in his mouth as giant furry spiders marched across the screen. The sound was way up. Dozens of spider legs crunched bodies underfoot. Bodies all covered with spider web goo.

Dottie patted Tim's head. "Hon, why don't you put in your hearing aid? The noise from the TV is probably scaring the neighbors."

"What?" Tim asked, his eyes never leaving the screen.

"Never mind, dear. I think I'll go to bed."

Tim glanced over at his wife. Even with her hair in curlers, he still smiled at her as if she were the cat's meow. He clicked the remote and the screaming of spider victims lowered to a manageable level. "It's almost over. Don't you want to see the ending? You know, where that brave fella—"

Dottie rested her hand on Tim's. "Hon, I've seen it. I know how it ends."

"Oh," Tim said, disappointment in his eyes. "S'pose you have." He pressed the button on the remote and the spiders vanished into black.

"I didn't mean for you to turn it off," Dottie said.

"That's okay. It's past my bedtime. Gotta open the store at seven."

"Well, when are you going to switch to winter hours? It's barely light at that time."

Tim got up and took the popcorn bowl into the kitchen. Dottie heard him pour a glass of water. "With the weather holding, people are still busy-busy. Next big storm, I'll move it to eight."

Dottie followed Tim into the bedroom and they went about their nighttime rituals. Tim brushed his teeth and ran a comb through the few strands of silver hair flopping across his scalp. Dottie rechecked her hairpins and fastened a scarf over the neat rows of curlers atop her head. As she picked up a pillow and pounded it, she heard something like a crash outside the bedroom window.

"You hear that?" she yelled to Tim, who was still in the bathroom.

Tim came out. "What?"

"I said, did you hear that noise?"

Another sound came from outside. This one sounded like the chain link gate smacking against the metal storage building. "There," she declared.

Tim stood quietly, waiting. "No wind tonight. Not sure what it could be. I'll go check."

"I'm coming too."

Tim laid a hand on her arm. "Last time it was just a bunch of raccoons. Probably some critter up to no good."

Dottie followed Tim into the front room. He opened a drawer to the hutch and pulled out a large flashlight.

"Take a metal bowl, so you can bang it. Here," she said, going into the kitchen and bringing one out. "Could be a bear, you know."

"I know. I'll be careful." Tim slipped his bare feet into a pair of loafers that he kept by the door. He peeked outside into darkness and waved his hand in the air. "That's odd. The security light's not coming on. Bet the bulb burned out. Remind me to replace that tomorrow."

"Okay," Dottie said, not liking the idea of Tim wandering out back in the dark. She tried to talk herself into going out with him, but that image of marching spiders came back to her in living Technicolor. As Tim ventured outside, she strained her head into the night, keeping her slippered feet inside the threshold. Black as pitch out there, with a thick mat of clouds blocking out the moon and stars.

Dottie listened as Tim kept up a monologue in a loud voice, working his way around toward the storage shed in the far corner of the lot. That's where they kept their rental equipment: chainsaws, tile cutters, plate compactors, and electric tree limbers.

"Don't see anything. I'll just keep talking real loud and maybe it'll scare something off." Dottie heard Tim banging on the bowl with the flashlight, making a sound plenty loud to frighten off a few raccoons.

"Well, that's odd," Dottie heard him say. "The gate's swung open."

She yelled out into the night. "Maybe the wind blew it."

"No," he yelled back. "Someone's been in here. The lock's been popped open and the shed door's ajar."

Dottie's stomach twisted in a knot. "Tim Brody, you come on back inside right now. Don't even think of going in that shed!" She held her breath, awaiting a reply. An open lock meant more trouble than a pack of raccoons or even a hungry bear. Worse even than a herd of marching tarantulas. "Tim!" After what seemed a lifetime, he answered her.

"I don't see anything. It's — "

Dottie held her breath and waited. She yelled again, but Tim didn't answer her. Fear crawled like tiny spiders over every inch of her body. "Tim," she said again, this time her voice barely a whisper.

IN THE DOORWAY OF THE STORAGE SHED, TIM FELT A SHARP smack to his forehead and in a flash found himself on the cold concrete floor. Before he blacked out, he was sure he heard footsteps, someone running. More than one someone. It sounded like the legs of a dozen spiders galloping across the gravel parking lot on their way to invade the next town.

DOTTIE PATTED TIM'S FOREHEAD WITH A DAMP CLOTH, BUT he pushed it aside. "Honey, I'm fine. Just a little bump."

The patrol car lights flashed red, casting strange patterns on Tim's face that reminded Dottie of the alien monster in the movie they'd watched last Friday. Tim sat in a chair that Sheriff Huff had brought out from the house. The sheriff had insisted Tim try not to walk for a while. He wanted to call for an ambulance, but Tim was adamant. No ambulances, no doctors. Dottie knew how stubborn Tim could be, but he did seem to be all right. He claimed he'd only blacked out for a moment, but Huff told her Tim could be suffering from a concussion.

"Are you feeling okay?" she asked Tim. "At all nauseous?" He shook his head.

As directed by the sheriff, Dottie picked up the big flashlight and shuffled slowly around inside the shed. Tim kept everything neatly in its place, and from what she could tell there was nothing missing. She told that to the sheriff. Two other policemen wandered around the grounds, searching the driveway, looking into bushes.

"Maybe you scared him off before he could take anything," Huff said.

Tim grunted. Dottie could tell Tim was trying to feel proud, having scared off some crook. Yet, she saw through his bravado. His hands shook so hard he couldn't hold onto the arms of the chair.

Dottie came to his side and looked him over. "Hon, I think I should drive you to Emergency. Your face is flushed. What if you're having a heart attack or something?"

Tim gave Dottie a reassuring smile. "Honey-pie, my ticker's working just fine. How 'bout you fetch some soda for the sheriff and his pals?"

Dottie studied the smile plastered on Tim's face. Stubborn to the last. Well, no sense standing in the way. She headed back to the house to fetch the drinks and a plate of cookies.

HUFF KNELT NEXT TO TIM, MAKING SURE HIS PUPILS WEREN'T dilated. The older man's shallow breathing concerned him.

"Did you see anyone? Any faces?"

Tim shook his head. "It was too dark and—I don't know. I was facing the shed, shining the light in there. No one was inside. Then ..." Tim squinted his eyes at a throb of pain. "I think someone hit me from the side."

"You think there was more than one?"

Tim paused. "I don't know. I thought I heard a bunch of footsteps, but the memory's a jumble in my mind. Sorry."

The two officers came up to Huff. "We found this," one man said. He handed something to the sheriff, wrapped in a cloth. Huff turned it over, careful not to touch it with his hands. A Swiss Army knife, an old one, with the short blade still extended. The tip was bent.

He examined the shed door. "Probably used this to jimmy the door open." He handed it back to the officer, who dropped the knife into a plastic bag.

The sheriff walked a ways out into the parking lot while an officer took Tim's statement. The night air hung damp and heavy, coating his jacket with a film of moisture. He ran one hand through wet hair and with the other fingered the agates he had in his pocket. He grinned. Those were the ones his little grandson had found last weekend at Drifter's Cove. Giving his little treasures to Paps. He had hoped to go up to Weitchpec and spend the weekend with those little rascals, but with all these "incidents" piling up, he had to go to Eureka on Saturday — he looked at his watch and snorted — today. The department felt some more manpower should be assigned to battle the shenanigans arising in his little town, and Huff had been asked to hold a powwow, as his white co-workers liked to call it.

Huff doubted anything would come of it. They'd send a couple of guys over for a week, snoop around. What else could they learn that Huff didn't already know? But he understood how the locals needed reassurance. To see a few uniforms posted around town.

Dottie came out the side door and walked over to offer molasses cookies from a plate. He took three and thanked her. As he watched her go over to the shed, he thought about the kind, decent folks who lived in this community. If there was someone up to no good, he owed it to them to get to the bottom of it. On the other hand, Tim Brody was a forgetful old man. Was it possible he'd just turned and hit his head on the metal shelving in the shed? Maybe his imagination had run away with him and he only *thought* he heard feet running. Huff studied the asphalt parking lot. Whatever damp footprints might have been left were no longer evident.

Well, the shed door *was* forced open, and there was the Swiss Army knife to consider. But, then again, that could have been dropped days ago in the parking lot, and maybe it was only a coincidence the tip was bent. He had shown Tim the padlock, that it hadn't been broken, just unsnapped. Maybe the last time Tim went to lock the gate, he didn't click the lock all the way in. So things weren't always as cut and dried as people supposed. They often let their fears get the best of them.

Huff looked across the parking lot and saw Mrs. Brody with her frail arms around her man. She sure loved Tim; it reminded Huff of Wanda and how he wished he was in her arms this late Friday night instead of snooping around looking for crooks.

A wave of irritation overtook him. After this winter, he would tell the city council he was done filling in. Two years was plenty of time to find a full-time police chief for this tiny town. They were just using him, keeping him on as long as possible. They trusted him—and after the scandal around the last police chief, he understood their thinking. But still, he wasn't getting any younger.

Huff made a promise to himself. He would stick it out until spring. And then move up to the Res, sell his house in town, and spend his days fishing and polishing rocks.

He carried the chair back into the house, then told the Brodys to lock up tight and not worry. He would be sure to do all he could to solve this mystery.

Tim and Dottie thanked the sheriff, gratitude spilling from their eyes. As he got into the patrol car, he wondered again if it was possible that all these crimes were somehow linked: the break-ins on Bayview, the vehicles vandalized at the state park trailhead, Mrs. Waverly's missing necklace, and now this—a likely break-in attempt at the hardware store. He couldn't recall an autumn where much of anything bad occurred. A quiet time of year. But not even a quaint little community like Breakers was immune to crime. In retrospect, looking at all the troubles plaguing Breakers over the last two years, he wondered if maybe this was a cursed town.

Yep, it was high time to get out of Dodge.

# Chapter 16

JERRY HUBBLE HURRIED PAST THE LIQUOR AISLE AND TURNED up the next one, which displayed rows of chips and snack foods. He reached for a large can of salted peanuts, and as he dropped it into his green plastic basket, he felt a tap on his shoulder. He startled, realizing he was edgy. Well, sure he was! That liquor aisle was beckoning him, and it took every ounce of determination not to heed that seductive call.

"How's that roof holding up?" Matt Moore asked him. The contractor looked bright eyed and bushy tailed, like he had that morning he'd come to repair the roof. How could anyone even see straight at eight o'clock in the morning? He would still be in bed himself if he hadn't noticed the coffee can was nearly empty. Without coffee to start his day, he was sunk. Coffee was his lifeline—from sunup to sundown, the stronger and muddier the better. Oh, and he was getting low on sugar too.

Jerry returned his attention to Matt. "Haven't seen any drips, so maybe we're good for now."

Matt nodded and wished him a good day.

On impulse, Jerry stuffed a couple of bags of potato chips in his basket and then tried to remember where the sugar aisle was. When he rounded the front of the store, his eye caught something outside the large picture windows facing the parking lot. Sure enough, it was that punk—the one who'd stolen his neighbor's necklace. The kid was walking away from his old truck—right toward the market.

Jerry's heart went into overdrive and blood throbbed in his ears. His skin crawled, giving meaning to the words "itching for a fight." He wiped his clammy palms on his sweatpants and fidgeted. If there was ever a time he needed a drink, it was now. He resisted the urge to go back to the liquor aisle, twist open a whiskey bottle, and chug down a few ounces—right there in the middle of the market. He knew the idea was outrageous, but he wrestled hard with it, forcing it to the back of his mind. Like whipping a snarling lion back into its cage.

He pondered what to do, standing there near the entrance to the store, as people walked around him, eyeing him curiously. Saturday mornings plenty of people came to do their shopping. The place was pretty crowded.

A plan came to him; he felt his face flush with excitement. He would confront this punk, expose his dirty dealings. If that didn't scare the kid and make him clean up his act, he'd be surprised.

He turned his gaze away from the front door where Billy Thurber was coming in. Keeping his head down, he hurried to the last aisle and studied the chickens and fish fillets. Salmon steaks were on sale: $8.99 a pound. The butcher came over and asked if he wanted anything. Jerry paced as the doddering man wrapped him up a pound of bacon. He glanced around, saw Moore picking out a block of cheese down the way. No sign of the punk, but he wouldn't be able to see him from there.

He snatched the package of bacon from the butcher's hand and hurried around the corner. Three registers were open. He chose the one where that high school student checked, then walked over and got in line with two people ahead of him. If only his heart would stop pounding so hard!

By the time Thurber strolled to the checkout line, basket in hand, Jerry could hardly contain his ire. Just seeing the punk up close—his twitchy manner and flitting eyes—Jerry knew beyond a doubt the kid was bad news. Everything about him screamed defiance and arrogance. Back when Jerry was a pudgy, short kid in school, the punks had pushed him around, thrown his lunch on the ground, and stomped on it. They never got in trouble, never got punished. Well, at some point your rotten dealings had to catch up with you. Jerry figured it was time for this lying cheat to taste his own medicine.

Thurber got into line the next register over. Jerry turned to him and made sure his voice carried across the store.

"You have a lot of nerve, Thurber."

The kid pulled back in a defensive stance. Jerry snorted.

Thurber's face showed disgust. "You talking to me? Just what is your problem, man?" He set his groceries on the conveyor belt as the checker rang up the items, watching with curiosity. People in line instinctively backed away a few feet.

"Nice little scam you got going, punk. Getting people to pay you for firewood in advance—and then ripping them off."

Thurber scowled and edged closer to Jerry, who planted his feet firmly where he stood. "No one's getting ripped off. I'm making another trip today to get more wood. You should mind your own business."

Jerry stepped out of line and let Moore go ahead of him. He was glad Moore was there; maybe he'd back him up. But Moore kept his eyes on the checker as she scanned his items, not saying a word.

"This town *is* my business. Why don't you go back under that rock you crawled out of."

Jerry waited, his teeth clenched so hard his jaw ached, while Thurber paid for his groceries and took the bag from the checker. Jerry spoke up again, even louder. "You think you're getting away with all the stuff you've been doing around town? The break-ins, robberies?" He gestured at Moore. "What'd you steal out of *his* truck?"

Thurber's face showed he'd had enough. The sounds in the store died down; people stopped whispering and barely moved. Even the checkers stopped ringing up items and watched as Thurber quickly pushed his way back through the line until he reached Jerry. In a quick motion, he gripped Jerry's shirt at the neck. Jerry's breath caught in his throat as the punk pulled him close. Jerry forced himself to meet the kid's beady eyes as Thurber snorted through his nostrils like a race horse straining at the gate.

Thurber's voice was condescending. "You're that motel guy, aren't you?" Jerry balled his hands into fists, aching to start swinging.

After a long moment, Thurber pushed him away, letting go of the shirt, and Jerry crashed against the candy rack. "You have that fancy Corvette. Wonder how you paid for that."

Jerry backed away, shaking. He felt his knees begin to buckle but refused to show any sign of weakness. "I don't like your tone, punk."

Thurber laughed and walked toward the front of the store. "Who are you—my homeroom teacher?"

Jerry felt eyes riveted on him. He looked around at the faces of his neighbors and saw what looked like pity. Hey, where was their support? Was he the only one brave enough to face this thief? How dare they look at him like that?

He turned back and saw Thurber pushing open the front glass door. Why wasn't anyone stopping him?

A rush of noise filled Jerry's ears as Thurber stopped and pointed back at him. Bile rose in his throat and he fought down nausea. Despite the coolness of the building, sweat streamed down his forehead, drenched his T-shirt.

Thurber's gaze drilled into him like a laser. Before he stepped outside, Thurber said in a calm, threatening voice, "I know where you live, jerk."

His words filled Jerry with terror.

Shoppers resumed their conversations and registers clicked and rang. Jerry moved back into line. He saw Moore head out without even turning or saying good-bye. So much for his support! Without a word, Jerry paid for his groceries and stormed out, a thousand volts of electricity coursing through his body. He put the bag in the trunk of his car, checking over the chassis, making sure Thurber hadn't scratched the paint job with his keys. When he was satisfied with his examination, he marched straight to the police station.

Enough was enough.


HUFF SAT BEHIND HIS DESK AND LISTENED TO HUBBLE'S COM-plaints. He offered the guy a Styrofoam cup full of coffee and that seemed to calm him down. He'd spoken with Hubble a few times since he'd bought that motel. Huff knew his type well. Just let the guy blow out some steam and in time he'd cool down. He assured Hubble that the department was well aware of all the incidents in town, and that even today they were meeting to discuss the problem.

What interested Huff, though, was Hubble's mention of this kid, Billy Thurber. Huff had seen the truck around town for a few weeks but had paid it no mind.

Hubble seemed adamant that Thurber was behind all the trouble.

"What makes you so sure?" Huff asked. "Have you seen him doing anything suspicious?"

Hubble paced in the small room. "Well, of course not. The punk's not an idiot. But think about it—all this stuff started when he showed up. And he was at Mrs. Waverly's just the day before she noticed her necklace was stolen." Jerry added, "You need to investigate this guy. Search his truck, check out his driver's license, stuff like that."

Huff nodded. "Okay, Hubble, I'll look. If he has a record, it'll come up." He stood and walked over to Hubble, then rested a hand on the agitated man's shoulder. "Listen, let me do my job, all right? That's what I get paid for. You stay away from that guy; you'll only aggravate things. You gotta do things by the book, and that way, if the kid is caught, the charges will stick. You see?"

Huff could tell Hubble was not mollified. His type—they were always trying to take the law into their own hands, vigilante justice. Making rash assumptions and convicting before there was any proof. He'd seen it too many times and it only resulted in disaster. Well, he had warned the man, and that was all he could do.

Huff grunted as his visitor slammed the door behind him. Patience, that's what Hubble needed, patience and trust. Huff doubted those were qualities Hubble was on familiar terms with.

JERRY SAT IN HIS CAR, FUMING. HE WAS SO MAD HE WOULDN'T be surprised if steam started coming out his ears, just like in those cartoons. On a whim, he popped open the trunk, then got out and rummaged through the grocery bag until he found the can of peanuts. Cars pulled in and out of the market lot, and Jerry felt more eyes on him. He ducked back into his car, his safe, cozy nest that smelled like new leather, like money. Thinking about Thurber generated some kind of combustion inside him. As he popped peanuts into his mouth, his nest started feeling like a cage; claustrophobia washed over him, giving him the jitters.

Speed would do the trick. Just open it up on the highway as fast as he could go, trees flying by, the wind whipping his hair through the open window. Better yet, the sound of squealing tires appealed more. He gunned the engine, crammed it into First, and tore out of the parking lot, scaring two old ladies about to cross the street. He screamed profanities at them, telling them to watch where they were going, but doubted they heard him over the roar of the engine. He was so tired of stuck-up rotten people getting their way all the time. Getting away with all kinds of stuff when they should be put in their place.

As he sped under the freeway overpass, he hunkered down to maneuver the curves along the old highway through Fairhaven. The narrow two-lane road snaked around trees that grew close to the blacktop, with ten-mile-per-hour warning signs posted every hundred yards or so. Jerry glanced down at his speedometer and saw he was pushing fifty.

He pressed all the window buttons and wind wailed through the car. Sweat evaporated from his head and neck, sending a chill down his back. With each curve he pictured his ex crossing the road, watching the terror grow in her eyes as she realized the driver bearing down on her was Jerry.

He gave a loud laugh. If only he had three wishes, that'd be one of them.

He came to a short straight stretch and slammed his foot all the way down on the gas. A car coming from the opposite direction pulled off onto the shoulder as his car flew by. He braked just enough to catch the next set of curves, but swung too wide, and the car nearly spun out. He exhaled and let off a little on the gas.

He thought of a second wish and imagined Lucy sitting beside him as he showed off the power of his car. She was his favorite exotic dancer at the topless club in Eureka; he'd passed plenty of bills to her over the last few months. What he wouldn't give to have her sit on his lap right now.

He picked up more speed and wove back and forth down the road. Now for a third wish. A wonderfully aged bottle of scotch would be the thing. Or maybe—

Jerry had almost passed the next wide gravel road when he caught a glimpse of a truck's tailgate through the kicked-up dust and gravel. He slammed the brakes and screeched to a stop a few yards beyond the unmarked road. By the time he swung the car around and positioned himself at the corner, he could barely make out the truck.

Well, forget the scotch—this was an even better wish come true! There was no mistaking the Ford with the wooden slat sides and the smoke that churned out the tailpipe.

*Gotcha.*

Jerry hesitated for a moment, thinking about his beautiful car covered in grimy dust. But what did it matter? He'd just wash and wax it when he got home. No way was he going to pass this opportunity by. The gods were smiling on him today; somebody up there appreciated him, even if no one on earth did.

Jerry hung back just far enough to catch the last bit of dust settling ahead of him. He knew Thurber would never be able to detect his tail. He stuffed more peanuts in his mouth as he strained to miss the potholes. There were some pretty nasty ones; the county didn't maintain private lanes, and in the winter the potholes turned into small lakes. How could anyone stand to navigate these obstacles every time they went to the store? Why, they'd have to wash their car twice a day!

After four miles Jerry tired of the jostling and bumping. Just when he started thinking this was a bad idea, the dust trail veered sharply left, up a narrow drive. Jerry pulled off under a cover of trees and let the air clear. He waited a few minutes and calmed himself, then quietly opened the door and closed it behind him. When he got to the bottom of the steep driveway, he saw the truck parked beside a small rundown camper, the kind with a sleeping compartment that fit over a pickup truck cab. This one sat on concrete blocks, next to a stone fire pit.

Jerry ducked behind a big boulder and studied the scene. Some trash lay strewn about, along with a couple of rusted car bodies, mostly buried in the tall weeds. The lot was overrun with blackberry brambles. Jerry couldn't see any power lines or evidence of a water source. No doubt Thurber was squatting on someone's property. Maybe someone should look up the parcel number and see whose place it was. Add trespassing to this punk's list of crimes.

Jerry watched as Thurber got out of his truck, holding his bag of groceries with one hand and sucking on a cigarette with the other. As Thurber ducked inside the small camper, Jerry smiled.

"Well, now I know where *you* live too. Jerk."

# *Chapter 17*

AGONY—THAT WAS THE WORD FOR IT. EVERY WAKING MIN-
ute of every day, Casey fought to concentrate, fought off depression. During class she'd keep looking through the window,
hoping foolishly she'd get a glimpse of Billy—as if he would
hang out on the school grounds looking for her. Still, she
couldn't help herself. For the last week and a half she stayed
after school on some pretense or another, at four o'clock catching the only public bus that went north. For that forty-five-
minute window of opportunity she roamed the streets of town
looking for signs of him. Nothing.

Today—same thing. Casey cringed at the prospect he might
have left town for good. Her stomach did flip-flops as she
turned down Third Street. She checked her watch and walked
faster. Her parents would go ballistic if they knew. Especially
her dad. He wanted her to stay his "little girl," trap her in
childhood forever. He wouldn't understand.

For the millionth time, Casey replayed that kiss in her mind.
An addiction, that's what he was. She had never thought much
about boys until that day she saw Billy. But Billy wasn't just a
dumb boy; he was mature, confident, sure of himself. Casey loved

the way his eyes searched hers. How, when he touched her with his fingers, a tingly current raced across the surface of her skin.

She took a deep breath and fought back tears. She couldn't, *wouldn't*, lose Billy too. It wasn't fair.

That too-familiar sense of doom and tragedy returned. She thought of Hamlet toying with Ophelia, then breaking her heart. Try as she might, she couldn't get the image of Ophelia out of her head—drowned in a stream, having taken her life, unable to live with Hamlet's insane rejection of her. She remembered the famous painting, with Ophelia floating downstream: her dead, vacant eyes open, her hands raised in supplication. Another tragic figure.

Casey replaced Ophelia's face with her own, saw her own black hair, now long and flowing around her face, her own glassy eyes struck with pain.

She looked at her watch and realized she'd lost track of the time. She chastised herself under her breath as she ran down the street. Her dad could give her a lift home; he was only working a few blocks away. But that meant facing his questions and hanging out until he was ready to leave for the day. She'd try for the bus.

She picked up her pace; her backpack banged hard against her shoulders as she rounded the last block. But before she could get the driver's attention, the bus pulled away from the curb and headed out of town. Casey collapsed onto the sidewalk and caught her breath.

Drips of water tapped her head. She looked up at the thick covering of murky clouds. Rain began to fall lightly on the sidewalk around her, darkening the concrete. She stood up, pulled her sweatshirt hood over her head, and hurried down First Street, past the school and across the street to Shorelines. A loud crack of thunder rattled the glass door as she pushed it open. With her bus money she bought a sugar cookie and a cup of coffee. Her parents didn't like her drinking coffee, said she was too young. Like coffee was a drug for adults only. She was practically grown up; why didn't they treat her that way? Not even Molly and Debby had as many restrictions placed on them, and they had no street smarts whatsoever. Their parents let them run loose all over Eureka late at night, something Casey would be afraid to do without a few big, strong guys flanking her.

Sure, she understood why her parents were overly cautious, setting curfews and grilling her each time she went out: "Who are you going with, where are you going, when will you be home? Call the minute you get there, call the minute you leave. No riding in cars with anyone under twenty-five." No riding in cars at all, for that matter, with anyone they didn't know. Casey sighed. Could she really blame them? She was the remaining child: two down, one to go.

Maybe it was normal for them to be paranoid. Maybe they thought if they just held on a little tighter, they could keep her safe, protect her from whatever calamity was out there with her name on it.

Fat lot of good that would do.

As the rain splattered against the store windows, Casey ignored the other students and patrons talking and eating and drinking. She looked over at Celia, who was refilling coffee thermoses, and recalled Luis's kind, confident face. How did anyone get to that place—where you were so sure God was there, watching your back, and knowing he had a special place in his heart for you? How could you know that someone so huge and incomprehensible actually loved you—not just you as a human, in general, but *you*, personally.

*"Do I not fill heaven and earth? says the Lord."* Casey tried to imagine God inhabiting every molecule, every inch of space, filling the universe. The thought boggled her mind. Did people just delude themselves into believing in this all-loving, all-knowing God? Or was there some trick to it?

When Jesse had died and Daniel locked himself in his room, Casey had spent the night on her knees praying to that God. After she had stared down at what was left of Daniel's face as he lay on the auditorium floor, she'd pleaded with God to show himself, to explain why and how her brother could do such a thing. Her youth pastor had said that God didn't yell out of the sky at you, but whispered in the silence of your heart. You just had to listen, was all.

Casey tried.

For months she'd tried to hear that whisper. Instead, she kept hearing the loud pop of the gun coming through the principal's microphone. The only sound she now heard in the silence of her heart was the echo of her own scream, trapped and ricocheting forever inside her chest.

Casey reached into her backpack and pulled out a worn copy of Shakespeare's sonnets. She flipped through the pages and found a favorite. *"What is your substance, whereof are you made, that millions of strange shadows on you tend? Since every one hath, every one, one shade, and you, but one, can every shadow lend."* Casey sighed as she closed her eyes and let herself drift off into the memory of that indelible kiss.

When the rain stopped, she'd go find her dad.

IRENE HAD FORGOTTEN ABOUT THE YOUNG MAN WITH THE firewood. As she drove up to the house, he was there, standing in his truck bed on a pile of split wood, throwing pieces onto the ground next to the house. He paused for a minute, gave a wave, and resumed his work. Irene had seen his truck at the gas station the other day and asked if he could bring her a cord. He said he would, on his next trip back from the mountains.

Irene went in the house and stoked the coals in the wood-stove, adding kindling and stuffing more logs inside the belly of the stove. A chill draped the house. She rubbed her hands and hurried into the kitchen to put up the kettle. By the time the pot whistled, rain beat on the roof. She opened the front door and looked at the man getting drenched as he hefted pieces from the pile and stacked them against the house.

"Do you want a rain slicker? You're getting soaked."

The young man raised his eyes at her but didn't interrupt his rhythm. "I have one in the truck."

Irene felt the rain soak into her hair and clothes, reawakening her ever-present chill. She retreated inside and put on a heavy fleece and a rain parka. Moments later, she approached the man with a mug of hot chocolate in her hand. "Here, this should warm you. I'll get your raincoat."

He took the mug from her and wiped dripping bangs out of his face, sipping while he watched her open the truck cab and search for his coat.

"Here, put it on." She handed him the yellow slicker. She studied the strange expression in his eyes as he gave her the mug to hold and then put his arms through the sleeves. After he zipped up, she offered him back the mug.

A crack of lightning startled her. A few seconds later thunder vibrated the ground. "That was close," she said.

The young man stared at the rain coming down. "You should get inside. You're getting all wet."

She backed under the porch awning and signaled for him to join her. When he hesitated, she waved him over again.

"What's your name?" she asked over the din of rain striking the metal roof. "Mine's Irene. I didn't expect you to remember from the other day."

"I remember." He came alongside her. "I'm Billy Thurber." They stood with their backs against the front door, watching the rain blow in sheets as the wind assaulted it. "Irene. That was my mother's name, actually." He fell quiet and stared at the rain, sipping his chocolate.

Irene couldn't believe the amount of water coming down. Cats and dogs. More like cows and polar bears. She chuckled at the image. "This is crazy. You know, I can just stack this wood another day; it's not in the way. Come inside. I'll get my checkbook and pay you."

She opened the door and ushered him in. As she went into the kitchen to get her purse, Billy took off the wet slicker and went to stand next to the stove. She thought about Casey sitting at the bus stop in this rain. The irony hit her — moving to a place where it rained so much. Had it been some kind of subconscious choice? A continual reminder of Jesse's accident? Well, maybe all this rain would purge something out of her soul, wash away the pain one drop at a time.

Billy stared at her. She realized she had stopped in the middle of the room, in midstride, the checkbook in one hand and her cup of tea in the other.

The fire blazed hot, crackling in the cast-iron stove. Billy waited while Irene wrote out a check and handed it to him. "I'll come back tomorrow, if the weather's better. Finish stacking," he said.

"If you like. You don't have to." Irene pointed to the sofa. "Sit. Finish your drink, at least."

Billy sank down into the cushions and looked around the room. Irene detected a nervousness about him. His hands shook and she wondered if he took drugs. He didn't appear wired, only hard, unbreakable, suspicious. She had yet to see him crack a smile. Another serious one, like Daniel. Trouble rolled across his face and her heart ached.

*"That was my mother's name."*

Was.

What caused this young man to look so lost behind his obvious tough-guy façade?

Billy finished his drink and stood. "Here." He handed her the mug.

He started to put on his coat, but Irene stopped him with her hand. A feeling grew inside her, something urgent and needy. Thurber glared into her eyes and she saw a trapped animal.

"What?" he said. "What do you want?" He yanked his arm away from her.

Irene backed off a step, sensing his need to flee.

*Cornered.*

Her voice came out quiet and pained. "What happened to you?" Even as she said the words, they sounded stupid to her ears. Why was she talking this way to a stranger?

He scowled and put on his raincoat. "Listen, lady ..." He started for the door.

"Your mother, did she die?"

Thurber spun around. "Who do you think you are, prying into my life? You want to feel sorry for me or something ..."

Irene brushed tears from her eyes. Billy froze on the spot, stared at her.

"My son Daniel was just a little younger than you are now. He put a gun to his head, on graduation day." Silence filled the room, thick and suffocating. "I don't get it."

"Get what?" Billy's hand dropped from the doorknob. "Why he killed himself?"

Irene pressed her lips together. "The anger."

She looked into Billy's eyes and pinned him there. She sensed him squirm. "It festered in him, year after year. Ate him up. I never knew if he was angry at his father, or just at life in general. He never fit into life, like forcing a square peg into a round hole."

Billy shifted his weight. "Yeah, well, life sucks." He gave a cynical laugh, and Irene could almost see the defensive wall rise up around him. "Maybe your son is better off."

The words cut into Irene, sharper than any knife. She lunged at Billy.

He jumped back, banged against the wall.

She leaned into his face, so close she felt heat radiating off his skin. "Why are you so mean? Make you feel important, better than others?" She didn't give him a chance to reply. She thought of all the questions she wished she could have asked Daniel. Her need grew in urgency as the questions gushed out.

"Who hurt you so badly that you need to hurt those around you? Was it your father? Your mother—"

Billy pushed her back, not hard, but she still stumbled and fell into the sofa. She sat there, tears falling down her face.

Billy's cheeks burned red. "I said, butt out!"

Weakly, she waved him away. Her breath grew shallow and faint. "Go. Just go."

As she buried her head in her hands, she heard the door quietly open and close. She lifted her eyes, and through the living room window saw Billy standing by his truck.

Outside, he seemed to struggle to calm his breathing as he uncurled his clenched fists and smoothed his hair. With a trembling hand, he felt around his shirt for his smokes. The rain had eased up; now only a light sprinkle dripped on him as he lit a match and drew hard on his cigarette.

Inside, Irene dropped her head into her hands.

Inside, she heard the truck door slam hard and the engine gun.

Inside, she slammed the door to her heart shut, and it was all she could do to barricade the painful flow straining to get out.

MATT PACKED UP HIS TOOLS AND PUT TWO 18-VOLT DEWALT batteries into the charger. The floor needed sweeping; he'd do that first thing in the morning. The sheetrockers would arrive after lunch, and he only had one more long wall to block for them. He turned to Casey, who sat on the floor writing something in her notebook. "Ready to go?"

Casey nodded and put her things away in her backpack.

"You finish your homework?"

Casey gave him a look. He could number those looks. Number one: *That was a stupid question to ask.*

"Of course, Dad."

Matt hung his bags on the nail by the front door and stepped outside. This far north the days were so short. Five-thirty and already dark as midnight. With the cloud cover, only the dim streetlights illuminated the neighborhood; the shadows they cast pooled light on the ground, like yellow puddles of water. The air smelled sweet—something blooming, mixed with salt spray. Matt breathed deeply, aware of his tired muscles and a weariness that sat on him like a big dog on his chest. He wiped off the bits of sawdust that clung to his eyelashes, then unlocked the truck door for Casey and got into the cab.

Thanksgiving was fast approaching. His sister Elaine wanted them to come down to San Diego for the holiday. His youngest sister, Jan, had offered to visit them in Breakers, bring her kids and cook a traditional dinner for them all. His mother kept leaving overly cheerful messages on his cell phone, saying how much she missed Casey and wanted to see her. He could easily picture the discomfort, the unspoken words, the looks of pity on their faces. They meant well; they loved him and Irene and Casey. But the thought of enduring even a day of their scrutiny and compassion twisted his gut.

Maybe he should just send Irene and Casey off on the plane. Maybe a few days alone would do him good—although his days were spent mostly alone as it was. And his nights in the house felt little different. He and Irene lived on distant shores. Even in bed, as she moved close to him to get warm, a chasm lay between them. They both knew they could fall into it at any time, and if that happened, could they ever get out? Matt sighed. Maybe they were already at the bottom of the chasm, just didn't know it.

He drove along Seawood, Casey quiet at his side.

Look number two: *I'm zoning out, so don't bother me.*

Even her nearness seemed an illusion, a deception. Something that looked like a daughter and acted like a daughter sat next to him. Someone he had helped create, taught to walk and read and tie her shoes. How could you invest so much time in children and not know them, not at all?

Only a month before graduation, Matt, fed up, had rummaged through Daniel's room one night. Daniel had said he was over at a friend's, but Matt checked up on him. The lying had gotten way out of hand. Whatever trust they'd had, Daniel destroyed it. Eleven o'clock on a school night and Daniel was untraceable. He hadn't answered his cell phone—he never answered it anymore, despite Matt's threats to cut off the service if he refused to take his calls.

Irene had told Matt to stop making such a big deal over it. What was *it*? Daniel's defiance, his dishonesty? What about his disrespect? Matt told Irene if Daniel didn't shape up and start looking for a job, he would kick him out of the house after graduation. Irene got furious and they argued. It was her fault, he told her, for letting Daniel behave this way. Kicking him out would make him take responsibility, get his life together, force him to set some goals for himself. Irene would have let him live at home forever, cooking for him and doing his laundry, never demanding he pull his own weight. He was spoiled—that was the problem.

When the argument escalated, Matt had stormed out of the den and up to Daniel's room. It didn't take him long to find the bottle of pills in Daniel's desk drawer. Such an obvious hiding place. Clearly, Daniel didn't care if he got found out. Maybe he even wanted to be caught.

Matt didn't bother confronting Daniel, just emptied the pills into the toilet and put the empty bottle in the trash. Daniel would figure it out. As if dumping those pills made a difference. No doubt there'd be more where those came from. Whatever they were.

The school counselor later told Matt it was a cry for help. Matt had scoffed at that.

Matt turned off Seawood and headed up the dirt lane. As he approached his house he stomped on the brakes. Through the sweeping windshield wipers, in the faint headlights' beam, Matt made out Thurber's truck—pulling out of his own driveway! The truck squeezed past his, tearing up gravel and nearly scraping metal. Matt saw only a tiny amber glow, the tip of a cigarette in the cab, but couldn't see the driver.

The thought of Thurber at his house set off alarms in Matt's head. What was he doing there? How had Thurber found out where they lived?

Was he looking for Casey?

That last thought sent him reeling. He shifted into Park and leaped out of the truck. Casey called after him in concern, but he ignored her.

He found Irene sitting on the sofa, her head in her hands. His heart pounded in fury. He yanked on Irene's arms and pulled her to her feet, reading distress in her face. Casey rushed into the house, slamming the door behind her.

"What happened—are you hurt?" Matt asked. His booming voice made Casey cower. Irene only shook her head.

"What was that jerk doing here? Did you let him into our house? Tell me!"

Irene looked at Matt's hand, still gripping her forearm. "Matt, let me go." She rubbed her face with her fingers. "What are you so worked up about?"

"Just tell me, Irene!"

Irene pulled out of Matt's grasp and walked toward the kitchen. Matt grabbed her arm again and spun her around. When he saw the anger in her eyes, he loosened his grip, lowered his voice.

"Please," he begged.

"I don't know what's the matter with you, Matt. He brought some firewood; didn't you see it outside?"

Matt's body rocked in place. He clenched his teeth. "I don't want that guy anywhere near our house. Or our daughter. He did some work for me a couple of weeks back. Until I saw the way he leered at Casey."

"Dad, he didn't *leer*," Casey said, pressed into a corner.

Matt turned and pointed a finger at her. "You—just shut up, okay? You are only fourteen and you have *no* idea what kind of trouble that boy is."

"And you do? You don't even know him."

"I said, shut up!"

Casey clamped her mouth tight and looked at her mother. Irene stood between her daughter and her husband, her face flushed.

Matt planted his feet. "The kid's a scumbag. Looking for trouble. If you had been there, you would understand. He shoved that lecherous look in my face, challenging me."

Irene sighed and went into the kitchen. Matt followed her. "You're not listening to me."

She opened the oven door and looked inside at a bubbling casserole. "I heard you. What else do you want me to say? I paid him his money and he left."

Matt paced. Maybe that was all there was to Thurber's little visit. But after hearing that motel owner's ranting in the market, Matt just knew more was going on. "I find it a little too coincidental that this kid who worked for me, and who'd do anything to get his hands on Casey, would show up on our doorstep."

"I'm sure he didn't know this was your house. Or Casey's. I never even told him our last name."

"Well, he sure knows now. He knows my truck."

Matt imagined a screwdriver in Thurber's hand, him prying open the truck tool box and taking out the hammer drill, his cordless saw. Smashing the window, just for the fun of it, with a rock. Rummaging through the truck cab, fingering the Swiss Army knife.

Easy to imagine.

He went back into the living room and added a log to the woodstove. Casey stayed in the corner, fuming.

Look number three: *eyes like darts*. If looks could kill.

Matt shut the metal door and faced her.

"And you—if he *ever* tries to talk to you, you tell me. You just walk away."

"Oh Dad, get real. I am not a naïve little girl—"

"No, you're a naïve teenager, with an attractive body that guys like Thurber just long to take advantage of."

"Dad!"

Matt shut his mouth and stared at Casey. His skin crawled. Thurber was written all over her face, the way he had seen it that day on the job site.

There was no number for this new look. Thurber had done something to her.

He stomped over to Casey and scrutinized her, saw guilt flit across her features. Her eyes avoided his. With his gaze he tried to translate the nuances in her face into some revealing story.

"Look at me!"

Irene came over. "That's enough, Matt. Why are you tormenting her? She hasn't done anything."

"How do you know? Look at her face—can't you see? She's been with him."

Irene looked at Casey, at her scared, pleading eyes. "Matt, you're getting carried away. Look how frightened she is! This has to stop."

"Yes." He pointed a finger at Casey. "It will stop. No more staying after school. I want you going home with your mother every day, you hear me?"

"Dad, that's not fair! You're putting me in a prison. No one lives out here. I have no social life at all. Why don't you trust me?"

"It's not you I don't trust. It's that creep. He's defiant, rebellious. Just like that lousy brother of yours—flaunting his disrespect and shoving his attitude in your face. And look where that got him!"

Casey and Irene gasped at the same time. Matt watched Casey's face cave in and her cheeks redden. "How dare you—" Casey said, then narrowed her eyes. "I hate you!"

She ran into her room and slammed the door.

Irene glared at him. She took a breath and shook her head. "How could you say that about Daniel? How *could* you?"

She looked at Casey's closed door, then swung around and strode into the kitchen. Matt stood in the middle of the living room. A tornado had just blown through, upending everything held tenuously in place. The fragile threads that linked him to Irene, to Casey, torn to bits.

Matt's burst of fury drained out. He collapsed onto the sofa, listening to Irene handling dishes and running water in the sink. All he'd wanted was to find the magic words that would keep his family safe.

For once.

That was supposed to be his job, wasn't it? To protect his family. The job assigned to men from the beginning of time. All his efforts, his sincere efforts, backfired again and again. Why? *Why?*

Only after Irene had finished cleaning all the counters in the kitchen and setting the table, only after Matt pounded on Casey's door for a full minute, only after he jimmied with the lock and finally pried the door open, only after they saw the window slightly ajar, did they realize Casey had left the house and fled into the darkness where all manner of calamity could befall her.

# Chapter 18

Sheriff Joe Huff squinted through the all-consuming blackness of night as he slowed into the town of Big Rock. Well, calling it a town was a far stretch. All those little pit stops along the Trinity River comprised a few struggling business ventures and the old splintery cottages those business owners lived in. Those folks catered to two sets of clientele: the summer rafters and passing-through travelers, and the off-season fishermen. So mostly what you saw along 299 for sixty miles were hamburger stands so dilapidated you wondered if the food was safe to eat, and some tiny markets with boxes of live crickets and racks of fishing lures near the front doors.

Huff turned the wheel of his old Jeep into the parking area outside the diner and pulled up next to the two other cars. This was one place he knew the food was good. Sally Bones—that really was her name—cooked up a great fish dinner. Friday night he could count on it, even if the half-pounders avoided every hook from Willow Creek to Weaverville. Sally had her ways.

The one lone porch light shone down on the entrance. Huff got out of the truck and sucked in the air. There was nothing like that river smell—rich and grassy. Smelled like lazy box turtles and algae on rocks. And all those dogwoods in brilliant fall colors alongside the road, and the maples. Seemed he just drank in that explosion of color.

You got tired of evergreens on the coast. Nothing ever changed; you couldn't tell one season from another. You saw green and more green. On the Res you got four seasons, could almost feel the earth spinning its way around the sun, the year waxing and waning.

Huff swung open the screen door and Sally's granddaughter welcomed him in. Wanda knew he'd be late, that he had some business in Big Rock. She'd save him some supper for a late-night snack. This place was only an hour or so out of his way, so why not nose about some?

If anyone had a story about Billy Thurber, Sally would. She knew the comings and goings of every person for a hundred miles around, could tell their lineage back to the gold rush days, who squatted where, the location of each family claim, how much gold they found. A walking genealogy chart.

Huff looked at the photographs crammed over every inch of wall. Most in black and white, dates and names scrawled in the corners with a black Sharpie pen. All those serious faces of mountain men and their families in front of hand-built cabins. Huff realized the only ones smiling were those in the more recent color photos—the guys holding up a big whopper of a fish. Well, life had been a whole lot harder way back when. You maybe didn't have time to smile much when dealing with hunger, disease, and freezing winters with only a leaky wood-stove and few hand tools.

Sally stuck her scarf-covered head through the little hole in the wall that separated the kitchen from the diner. "Hey, Joe. Long time no see." Her head disappeared and reappeared again. "Eddie brought some rockfish from the coast. You okay with snapper fillets?"

129

"Sure," Huff called over to her.

The wooden floor boards creaked as he walked across the room. A few other customers sat at the small tables. Sally's granddaughter came over to Huff and wiped down the plastic red-checkered tablecloth and laid out silverware and condiments. He smiled at her. "Joellen, right? My, you are sure growing like a weed. Not that you look like one."

The girl blushed with that preteen embarrassment sparked by older men's teasing. She hurried back to the kitchen.

After Hubble had made a stink about Thurber in the police station last Saturday, Huff had spotted the kid parked at Pelican Beach, sitting in his truck smoking a cigarette. He could see what ticked Hubble off about the guy. Kids like that loved to cop an attitude.

Huff had looked over his license and registration, his wood-cutting permit. He made Thurber wait in the truck while he called the information in. Nothing flagged, no record. Not even a traffic violation. The truck, however, was registered in the name of Nate Thurber, who, according to the kid, was his father. So, apart from a post office box in Big Rock, Huff knew nothing about Billy Thurber. He tried to pry bits and pieces out of the kid, but only got back an irritated, tight-lipped reply.

"I don't have to tell you anything," he had said. And he was right. Still, Huff couldn't resist doing a little more checking on this guy. And it gave him an excuse to go exploring in places he hadn't yet been.

A few minutes later, Sally waltzed out of the kitchen, pushing the swinging door open with her shoulder and carrying a stack of dinner plates. She deposited two at a far table, then came to Huff and set his before him. She always gave him extra portions, especially the mashed potatoes and gravy. No one made a creamier mashed potato—the kind that dissolved in your mouth on contact. And she made real gravy, not the powdery junk from those packets.

Sally leaned over and refilled his water and he scooted back to give her room. She wore her apron—the kind those chefs on TV wore. The pink polka-dotted scarf on her head didn't quite fit the look, but it kept her long silver hair from falling into the fish batter. That and the hairnet underneath. She wore the same knit pants as always, probably stretched to their limit around her ample stomach. Everything about Sally was ample.

Most particularly her enthusiasm for gossip.

She glanced around the room, sizing up the disposition of her customers. "You know that expression, 'happy wife, happy life'? Around here we say, 'happy sippers, happy tippers.'"

"How can anyone complain about your food or your service, Sal?"

Sally narrowed her eyes. "Don't try to pull one over on me, Joe. I know you didn't drive all this way just to eat my fish. Your woman's a fine cook, so you've told me, and you don't look like a fella that's cooling down from a marital spat." She scooted into the chair next to his. "Okay, let's hear it. Sally's all ears. Give me the *Reader's Digest* version, before someone needs something."

Huff chuckled and dug into his potatoes. She waited and watched him, the way women have watched men eat for all eternity—with that tickle of pleasure at seeing such a basic need satisfied, and being the one to satisfy it. "What do you know about a Nate Thurber and his son, Billy?" He watched her face as he swallowed a mouthful of juicy breaded snapper.

Her eyes filled with volumes of tales itching to get out. "Old Grizz," she muttered under her breath.

"Grizz. What's that?"

"The old fella, Nate. Been called Grizz as long as I can remember. If you saw him, you'd understand. Not too tall, but hairy. A kinda wild mop of gray hair, big fat beard and

131

moustache, real hairy arms. But mostly I reckon it's from his walk, the way he lumbers around." She got up and hunched over, and gave a good imitation of a bear plodding along. Huff laughed as she came and sat back down.

"Listen," she confided, "there're some strange stories; who knows what's true? A wife that disappeared. Word said she skipped out, oh, a whole lot of years ago. I never saw her, not even once. Most folks up that mountain said differently—that she was killed and buried somewhere. The sheriff looked, nothing turned up. Grizz raised that boy, way far back up the mountain. Eagle's Perch. Know the place?"

Huff shook his head. She patted his hand. "I'll draw you a map. Way away from civilization. Smack dab in the middle of nowhere. Ventured rarely into town, the closest being Weaverville. There're still a few left like him. Kinda reminds me of the old days, when fifty thousand logged and mined up here. Hard to imagine, when you hike up the north fork and there's nothing there. Thousands of camps, gold-hungry miners, mules and wagons and homesteads. Now you can't even tell they were ever there. A man'd come to town once a month for staples and a visit to the local whorehouse. More often, if he'd had a strike. Why, my granddad used to—"

Huff squeezed her hand. "Sal, I'd love to hear about your granddad some more, but one of your customers is trying to get your attention." He pointed at a couple getting up from their table.

"Oh, mercy me, my mouth off and running like a herd of buffalo. Be right back."

Huff ate his food, chewing thoughtfully. Eagle's Perch. Just the name of it poked his curiosity.

By the time he finished, Sally was on her way to him with a fat slice of apple pie topped with vanilla ice cream. She jiggled over and leaned close to his face.

"Listen, doll," she said, pulling a piece of paper from her apron pocket. "Here's a map up to the Thurber place. There's more I can tell you about Grizz, but I know that pretty wife of yours is waiting. When you coming back?"

"Sunday afternoon?"

"Good." She kept her voice down. "Before you do any snooping, you should hear some things. That man beat his wife—no mistaking. Probably beat that kid too. I only saw them a few times; always the man with the boy under his thumb. You know how that looks when you see it. That hardness in the eyes, and the way kids hold that fear inside, clamp down on it and keep it buried. That's Grizz and his kid."

The apple pie vanished in three huge bites. Huff spooned every bit of melted ice cream off the plate and into his mouth. Sally smiled, clearly appreciating a good hearty appetite when she saw one.

Huff stood and stretched the kinks from his back. He would have opened up his belt another notch, but it was already on the last one. He patted his belly. "Another great meal. See you on Sunday."

She gave him a peck on the cheek. "They say things turn up for the man who digs. Just watch you don't fall in the hole once ya dug it."

Huff put some bills on the table and found Joellen. She poured coffee into a disposable cup and snapped on a plastic lid, then handed it to him. All that food settling made him sleepy, and he had a lot of windy roads to go before he made it to the Res. One stretch was particularly bad where the road narrowed and twisted over the canyon, a really slippery spot. Too many drunk kids out for a good time ended up in the river. Playing cards and watching TV on the Res didn't qualify as a good time for most of them. But his daughters were raising those grandkids right. Getting them to appreciate the land, the outdoors. All the things you can do to entertain yourself in the middle of nowhere. You didn't need malls and theatres and bars.

He stood next to the Jeep, sipping his coffee and thinking about unraveling the mystery of Billy Thurber. He wondered just what old Grizz did to entertain himself out in the middle of nowhere. His curiosity was aroused. On Sunday he'd drive up to Eagle's Perch and take a look around, see who else lived up there. There were stories to be had; he just needed to do a bit of digging.

He marked Sally's words. He'd dig. But he'd watch he didn't fall in the hole.

# Chapter 19

CASEY KEPT HER EYES ON THE GRAVEL SHOULDER OF THE road as another car approached. She knew her dark clothes made her hard to see, so she pressed against the huckleberry bushes as the vehicle passed. The whoosh of the car splattered her with grit and water, but she just wiped her already wet face and continued her hard pace toward town. The rain had stopped but Casey shivered from the cold. She didn't expect to walk the whole five miles, didn't have a plan in mind. She just needed to get out of the house before she suffocated. Before she threw something at her father. At some point she'd go back.

More headlights cast her shadow on the ground. Without looking, she could tell the car was slowing down behind her. Relief rushed through her when she turned and saw the driver was one of the market checkers and not her father come to get her. When the older lady asked what on God's earth she was doing walking down Seawood in the dark, Casey told her she was going to a friend's house to do homework.

Casey had to listen to the lady the whole ride to town as she puzzled about parents who let their kids wander the roads at night all by themselves. Casey said nothing; she was in no mood to explain herself. She just leaned forward and let the heater blow on her, thaw her out.

The lady parked at the market and put on her name tag. She asked Casey if she would need a ride back home, as her shift finished at ten when the market closed up. Casey didn't think so, but thanked her for the offer—and the ride.

Casey walked across the parking lot, trying to look like someone with a specific destination. Her stomach rumbled, reminding her of the dinner she'd missed. She felt in her pants pocket and retrieved a five-dollar bill. That could buy her a sandwich.

She stopped and looked around at the buildings alongside the market—the realtor office, police station, the Laundromat. She could eat her sandwich in there, next to the heat of the rumbling clothes dryers. Read a magazine, pretend she was waiting for her wash to finish.

Her eyes traveled down to the far end of the lot, to a cluster of cars parked outside Alma's Restaurant.

Her breath caught in her throat.

There was something ethereal about Billy's truck positioned right under the lamppost, the beam of light like a beacon just for her, calling her. She nearly ran to the front door, then stopped. How did she expect Billy to find this mess attractive?

She took off her heavy coat and smoothed out her sweater, ran fingers through tangled hair, and wiped her face with her sleeve. She hoped all the mud splatter was gone. A mirror would be real nice right about now.

Trepidation filled her heart. What if he took one look at her and turned away? That would kill her. She just had to make Billy look past the outer flaws and see more, see *her*. Like the way he'd looked deeply into her that day on the beach. She pushed the fear away, refusing to let it stranglehold her. She wanted him, needed him, more than anything else.

After drawing a deep breath and relaxing her face, she opened the door to the restaurant and stepped inside.

The place was packed, so Casey found it easy to pretend she was looking for an empty seat. She scanned the room and found him alone at a table in the back. She could kiss the ground! The only vacant chair was the one across from Billy, a chair waiting for her.

As she started toward him, she hesitated. What if he had a date and the woman was in the restroom? Yet she couldn't afford to take the chance someone would snag the chair. She forced herself to walk over to him and was relieved when his eyes lit up at her approach.

"Well, here's a surprise," he said, his face flushed. "Casey Moore."

Casey almost melted into the floor when he said her name. *He remembered!*

He motioned her to the chair and she nearly fell into it; her knees were that weak. Her gaze took in the empty pitcher of beer and the basket of tortilla chips. Her stomach growled again but she ignored it, for another hunger grew in her gut, this one much more demanding. Fatigue hit her hard, along with a desperate despondency.

She pushed her father's angry voice from her mind. She pushed away her mother's overly worried concern.

She pushed everything out of her heart but Billy Thurber.

"Hi," she managed to say, cringing at the squeakiness of her voice.

Billy's head bobbed to the side and his eyes glassed over. Casey guessed he'd had a lot to drink. Well, maybe that was a good thing. She'd heard people were more easygoing when they were drunk. Open to suggestion.

"So what brings you to town?" His eyes narrowed onto hers. "You here alone, this late?"

Casey laughed and took a chance. She reached out and put her hand on his. Billy's eyes dropped to look at her fingers. "It's not late; it's only, like, six o'clock," she said.

"Feels late," he mumbled, playing with her fingers.

Casey's breath caught.

She watched the way his hand stroked hers and a rush of heat swept up her arm. Suddenly, the room seemed unbearably warm. Her head spun. When she raised her eyes, Billy was looking right into them. She drank in his face—his piercing green eyes, his soft wheat-colored hair that curled and fell over his forehead. The memory of his arms, so strong and sleek, as they held hers during that kiss. Her heart thumped hard against her chest.

His gaze dropped to her mouth, which hung open. In a second, he was leaning into her, inches from her face.

Casey exhaled. "Wow, it's really hot in here."

Billy scooted back his chair. "Yeah, how 'bout getting some air?"

They left their coats on the chairs and Casey followed Billy out the front door. The cold air caused him to open his eyes wide and suck in his breath. "Now that's refreshing." He turned to her. "How'd you get here? Walk all the way from your house?"

The line of questioning panicked her. The last thing she wanted was for Billy to grill her—or think about her parents worrying. She needed to get his mind on *her*.

"I got dropped off in town. It's Friday night; I can stay out a bit." She took his hand and pulled on it gently. "Come on, let's walk a little."

She led him around the back of the restaurant, to the footpath, away from the lights and into the shadows of the trees. Billy stumbled as he walked behind her. Yes, he was definitely drunk. Would he even remember she was here with him tonight? Well, she would do her best to help make it a memorable time.

Her dad's voice rang in her ears. *"You are only fourteen and you have no idea what kind of trouble that boy is."* And then she heard her dad make that mean comment about Daniel, how he'd gotten what he deserved. Anger overrode the passion she felt as she pulled Billy toward her and kissed him. She let the anger flow from every pore as she pressed her body against his, as he responded to her advances. She grew heated as she lost herself in his kiss. His hands on her shoulders sent electrical charges over her skin, making her wobble on her feet. She kept her mouth pinned on his, couldn't get enough of him.

Billy kissed her neck, rocking in place, reeking of beer. Casey stood there, willing to let him do anything he wanted. She kept hearing her dad call Daniel "that lousy brother of yours," the words growing in intensity in her mind. She tried to drown out her dad's voice by losing herself in the sweep of desire, but she found herself shaking all over, fear eating at her stomach, knowing she was treading on dangerous ground but steeling up her nerve to keep going.

Somewhere, on the periphery of her awareness, she saw movement, and then heard a man's voice. Someone was standing behind the restaurant, some guy she didn't recognize.

"Thurber," the man called out. "You back here?"

Casey quickly straightened her sweater as Billy disengaged his mouth from her skin. He swayed and listened. Casey pointed and Billy turned to look.

"Thurber," the voice called out again. "It's me, Zack. I saw your truck out there, man."

Billy looked back at Casey with a lopsided grin and wiped his mouth slowly with the back of his hand. Her body buzzed with electrical charge; she couldn't move if she wanted to. Billy grabbed her hair, pulled her close. "You," he whispered, "are really something ..."

And then he turned away and staggered back up the path toward Zack.

Casey's knees gave way and she sank to the ground, onto a bed of matted leaves. How could he do this to her? Leave her like this? She closed her eyes and lost herself in replaying their intimacy. She held her breath and waited. He would come back. He *had* to.

The chill of the night seeped into her bones. Noises from the restaurant carried on the air, bringing her back to her surroundings. She shivered and tried to stand. Slowly, the reservoir of passion drained away, leaving her shaky and weak. Billy and the other guy had gone around to the front of the restaurant. Billy hadn't returned.

Bitterness grew like brambles, twisting and entwining around her; she felt she could spit thorns. She stomped to the front of the restaurant, angry and needy.

Billy's truck was gone.

It was a knife driven into her heart.

After she went inside and retrieved her coat, she sat on the wooden bench on the sidewalk. She reminded herself that Billy was drunk. He wouldn't have just left like that. It was the beer; alcohol did things to your memory and concentration—she'd learned that in school. Why did that guy have to interrupt them? What did he want with Billy? When would she see him again? How would she find him?

Questions pummeled her, one after another. She was hungry and irritable. She wished she was older and could drive; she would go up and down all the streets in the county until she found him. Billy Thurber would come to his door and see her there, sweep her into his arms, and never let her go. She wouldn't have to go home to a house full of pain and blame and anger.

"Daniel," she muttered in anger, "why did you have to go and do such a stupid thing—to leave me like that ..."

Casey looked up when she heard a car door slam.

"Oh, thank God!" her mother said, rushing toward her. Irene grasped Casey's hands, the anger restrained in her voice. "Casey, we've been driving everywhere, looking for you. What are you doing here?"

Casey wiped her eyes. *Wouldn't you like to know?* "Sitting. What do you think?"

Casey saw her mother deliberating. Clearly, there was no point in chastising or gushing with emotion. Casey was safe, crisis averted. "Come," she said, taking Casey's hand. "Let's go home, all right? Have you had anything to eat?"

Casey looked at the car and saw her dad sitting in the driver's seat. She let her mother guide her to the back door as if she were blind and feeble. Irene opened the car door and Casey got into the backseat. Most fathers would say something, apologize for their outburst, or even dive right into a lecture.

Not her dad. He never said a word, like he didn't even care.

She sank back into the seat, and for the whole ride home no one said a thing. The car was filled to the brim with unspoken words—meaningless, powerless, empty words.

Filled to overflowing.


ZACK DIDN'T WANT TO GET INTO THURBER'S TRUCK. THE GUY was drunker than a skunk. As he slipped into the front seat next to Thurber, he kept one hand on the door handle. What if he drove off the cliff?

Thurber said nothing as he headed south on Seawood a few blocks, then pulled over and parked. Zack let out a long breath and relaxed his grip.

Thurber cut the headlights and turned to Zack. "Hey, Zack, buddy, where's your friend? On the boat?"

He laughed but Zack didn't get what was so funny. Was this jerk making fun of him? Zack was discomfited by the cynical tone in Thurber's chuckle. Like he had something up his sleeve.

Zack had purposely *not* told Randy where he was going. That bozo would have turned this little exchange into a buddy-bonding session. And with that big mouth, would have gotten them in even deeper than they were now.

"Well," Thurber said, "you have something for me?"

Zack had hoped to talk to Thurber, feel him out, confront him if necessary. Since that day on the beach, Zack's stomach had knotted with anxiety the moment he awoke each day. He was always looking over his shoulder with the feeling they were being watched. He didn't trust this guy Thurber, not one bit. And he couldn't take this constant worry and fear. So he had planned to offer Thurber a cut, if that was what it took.

But seeing him this smashed gave Zack pause. Thurber was in no shape to talk, so maybe he should wait for another time. At least he'd brought Thurber what he wanted. Maybe that would pacify him for now.

Zack pulled a baggie full of weed out of his pocket. Thurber fumbled with the plastic seal, unable to get it open.

"Here, man," Zack offered. He pulled the plastic tab, unzipping the bag. Thurber leaned over and stuck his nose inside, took a huge whiff.

"Wow," was all he said.

Zack picked at his cuticles. That bag wasn't cheap, but did he dare hint at Thurber to pay for it? Was he being paid with Thurber's silence? Zack swore under his breath. This is *exactly* what he hadn't wanted to have happen. Some stranger blowing into town and crossing paths with them—seeing an easy mark. You could trust the folks in town to have blinders on. This stuff went on around them year in and year out and no one paid any attention. But someone like Thurber, just *looking* for action—well, that was plain bad luck. And it wasn't like they could just park the boat somewhere else. They fished out of this harbor and their slip was paid through the year. Zack imagined trying to pull this off in the Eureka harbor, where all those fancy boats were moored. They'd be spotted in an instant over there.

Thurber turned and looked at Zack with glazed eyes. "Right nice of you, man. Hey, I'm gonna take a drive over to Pelican Beach, sit and enjoy the stars. Whadda ya say? Wanna share a joint?"

Zack felt the sweat working its way down his back. He pictured Thurber trying to take those curves in the dark, this wasted. Besides, he didn't want to spend one more minute with this creep. Zack could tell Thurber was toying with him, a cat with a cornered mouse. Probably would drive fast and try to scare him. Drop more hints about their little "fishing" venture. How in the world could he get himself out of this mess? One thing he knew about blackmail—it never stopped. Once someone got a hold of a good thing, why would they quit?

Zack's head throbbed. He had to think of something!

"Hey," he said, trying to smile in a friendly sort of way. "That would be great, but how 'bout a rain check? I told Randy I'd be right back and he kinda worries."

Thurber chuckled. "Doesn't seem like the mother-hen type to me."

Zack opened the car door. "But you go ahead," he said, getting out. "I can walk back from here. Need to stretch my legs, anyway." He shut the door and slapped the hood. "See ya."

The hairs on his neck tingled as he walked away from Thurber's truck. He didn't dare turn around and look back. After a minute, he heard the engine gun and the tires kick up gravel. Thurber had turned the truck around and was cruising by him. Zack gave a little wave.

Thurber looked through the window at him. He didn't wave back.

Zack's heart sank like an anchor. And like an anchor, his fear and anxiety lay there, on a dark ocean floor, tethered to him.

Pulling him down to its depths.

# Chapter 20

"TOMÁS, WHAT ARE YOU DOING?" ALMA ASKED. TOMÁS WAS kneeling in the corner of the restaurant's pantry. At first Alma thought he was praying. In such a strange place.

"Putting the cash in the safe."

Alma peeked her head inside the narrow room flanked with shelving. "What safe?"

Alma heard a quiet click and Tomás stood. "The one I just bought."

Alma made a little noise of surprise, then went into the dining room and shut off the lights. She still needed to mop the floor but she was dead tired. *Manaña*—it could wait till morning.

What a busy night at the restaurant. She wished Tomás would hire another waitress, but he said they couldn't afford it. Such a small profit margin when you had a restaurant. You had to get just the right amount of fresh produce and meat and cheese, and if you didn't figure right, you threw a lot of food out. A waste of money. Alma had no idea how Tomás calculated how much to buy. So often she'd take leftover beans and rice home to eat for breakfast. Miguel never minded what he ate, bless his little heart. He had his father's metabolism and energy. A little whirlwind.

Tomás put the last food container in the large refrigerator. "Ready?" he asked, removing his apron. He tossed it in a laundry hamper next to the sink.

Alma nodded. "So *qué pasa?* We never needed a safe before."

Tomás came over to her and smoothed her frizzy hair. "There's been talk, *rumores.* Some stealing in town, cars broken into. *Un caco*, maybe more than one thief. No sense being careless."

Alma lifted her sweater off the hook by the back door. "Tomás, what could happen up here? This place is quiet; you are still thinking you are back home."

"Well, they do have *pandillas* in Eureka, *verdad?*"

Gangs. Alma smiled and put a hand to Tomás's cheek. "You worry too much. Eureka is another world. Far away."

Tomás grunted and opened the back door. A cool breeze drifted in, cooling Alma's face. "Forty miles. Not so far away."

He stopped and went back inside the restaurant. "*Ven aquí.*" He motioned her over to one of the silverware drawers. Pulling it all the way out, he told her to reach back and feel around.

She eyed him curiously as she felt behind the tray of spoons. "*Ay*, what is that?" She withdrew her hand as if it burned. She whispered, "Tomás, are you crazy? What are you doing with a gun?"

He reached over and closed the drawer. "It's the same gun I had in San Jose. I had it packed, but now I will keep it here. Just in case."

"I thought you had gotten rid of it." Alma closed her eyes and mumbled a prayer. She knew he was thinking back to the day his cousin had been robbed at gunpoint in the minimart he managed. Even though he had cooperated and given the men what they demanded, they'd shot him anyway. He bled to death before the police arrived. Shortly after that, Tomás had bought his gun.

"Alma, pray all you like. But God expects me to protect my family and my interests. You know how I feel about that."

"*Claro que sí.*" She certainly did. Their own neighborhood back home had become dangerous to walk in, sometimes even in daylight. Tomás was fiercely protective of Miguel, wouldn't let him play in the park after he'd seen some of the Sureños in their blue gang attire hanging on the corner. It was only a matter of time, he said, before someone pulled a gun and a child was killed.

Tomás had admired Alma's *papá* for the after-school program he started and oversaw at the church, using the building as a safe haven to keep the youngsters off the streets and out of gangs. Luis had been a powerhouse in the community, helped so many troubled kids. But where her papá looked for the good inside, Tomás distrusted human nature. Luis trusted God would protect; he expected miracles. Tomás only expected trouble.

As he ushered Alma out the door and locked it behind her, he listened to the night, weighing each sound. "I'm thinking of putting an alarm in."

That was too much. "Tomás," she said, soothing with her voice, "I hope you are not getting paranoid. You need to trust God. He will watch over us."

Tomás made a face Alma was too familiar with. She clamped her mouth shut and followed him to the car. Let him have his safe and his alarm system, she thought. If that helped him sleep better at night, then *bueno*.

She looked over at Tomás as he drove, staring straight ahead with concentration. Everything he did just like that. Serious, focused. She was blessed, though, to have such a loving man. He spent every spare minute with Miguel and had so much patience with their mischievous boy. The two of them with their bound-less energy always found projects to do: sand castles to build on the beach, bricks to piece together in a pattern for the backyard patio, herbs to plant in the window boxes. They were two peas in the pod, if she remembered the saying right.

Tomás let the engine run while Alma went into her parent's house and retrieved the sleeping boy. As she carried him in her arms, she realized how heavy he was. Still skinny and small, but soon she wouldn't be able to lift him. The realization made her sad. Her *hijito* was growing up.

Tomás got out and took him from her arms. Carefully, he placed the boy onto the backseat and gently shut the door. Alma looked at Tomás's beaming face as they drove the six blocks to their house. How much he loved that child.

Each night, the same routine. Tomás would carry Miguel to his room and undress him, put pajamas on him, and tuck him under the covers. Only when he had kissed Miguel on the forehead and said a little prayer did he let Alma come in and check on him. There was nothing left for her to do but pick up the dirty clothes and turn on the night light.

Tonight, she sat on the edge of Miguel's bed, thinking how changed their lives were. Much less chaotic and fearful. But Tomás just couldn't let go of his paranoia. Too many years of street life had burned into his soul. In time, those fears, those memories would fade. Alma knew it took time. Some things were hard to let go of.

When her head hit the pillow, exhaustion overtook her. She draped an arm loosely around Tomás as he snored soundly beside her. In minutes, she too was fast asleep.

IRENE STARED OUT THE BEDROOM WINDOW EVEN THOUGH she saw nothing in the dark. How many nights would there be without stars? This perpetual darkness paralleled her own. The outer world mirroring her inner world. She pulled the covers up to her chin and rechecked the setting on the electric blanket. Even with her flannel nightgown and a thick pair of socks, she was still cold. All she wanted was to fall asleep, into a deep, forgetful sleep. A deathlike sleep.

Words to a poem came to her, one she had memorized in her English Lit class in college. Back in those happy, innocent days. Before.

*"Our birth is but a sleep and a forgetting."* Wordsworth. A poem about forgetting your true nature, that you originate from a divine bliss. By the time you grew up, any remembrance of that awareness had long dissipated. Like mindless sleepwalking, this life.

Luis's comments weighed on her mind. Ever since she'd spoken with him, they kept coming back to her. How people were put here on earth to learn compassion. She wanted a reason for all the suffering. He'd told her no one could learn compassion unless they themselves suffered. That suffering rounded you out.

At his house, Luis had shown her a Scripture. Something about how going through trials builds character, produces endurance, and eventually leads to hope. What would be the point, he asked, if this life was all there was? If nothing you did mattered at all? Then why not be as reckless and selfish as you wanted? Eat and drink, for tomorrow you died.

So many people took that fatalistic attitude, but were they happy? Why did it seem the only people who were truly happy were the ones immersed in compassion?

Why? Because humans were hardwired that way. Someday, Luis assured her, she would see that her suffering served a purpose. That something good would rise out of the ashes of despair.

She listened to the quiet. Not even a dripping on the roof. Casey would be long asleep. She had left Matt on the couch, where he lay reading a book on post-and-beam construction. He'd probably fallen asleep out there, with his glasses still perched on his nose.

She thought of Casey sitting on the bench outside the restaurant. How lost and alone she had looked.

When Casey was in the bathroom getting ready for bed, Irene had begged Matt to speak with her, to apologize. He said he would, at the right time. When Casey cooled down. She had held her tongue. Didn't he see he was pushing Casey away, keeping her at arm's length with his authoritative stance? She didn't dare point out the comparison—that he'd treated Daniel just the same way.

Tonight's blowup germinated dread in Irene's heart. The pattern was happening all over again. First the arguments and face-offs. Then the cold silence and suspicions.

Distrust. Anger. Blame.

An inevitable path that rushed them all headlong into misery. There had to be a way to break the pattern. She could not allow this to happen. She would find a way to stop the war, regardless of the consequences.

Because of the consequences.

Irene threw off the covers and got out of bed. She needed a glass of water. She felt for the doorknob, not wanting to turn on the light, not wanting a harsh delineation of her surroundings. There was something about switching on a light in a small room in the middle of the night that unsettled her. That, in such light, things seemed so flat and unimportant. So immediate, yet so useless.

She found Matt in a chair next to the woodstove, staring at the flames through the glass window.

Kneeling on the floor next to him, she spoke with hesitation. "Matt."

The flickering light illuminated his face in the dark room, exaggerating deep lines of worry. Irene could tell he'd been crying. She laid a tentative hand on his knee and was surprised when he grasped her hand tightly, a man flailing for a lifeline.

Was that what everyone did—strain for some *thing* to cling to, for one of those foam rings they tossed to you from the boat when you were drowning? *All of us*, she thought, *floating scared in a turbulent sea, depending on a job, a spouse, a child, drugs, alcohol, to fool us into feeling safe.*

Maybe safety was an illusion. *Maybe we're not supposed to feel safe.*

*Maybe if we just let go, stopped clinging, let it all drift away, we'd find our fear silly and irrational.*

*Then again, maybe we'd sink right to the bottom of the sea.*

She sat there with him for a long time, until the hard floor hurt her hips. "Come on, let's go to bed," she suggested.

Matt nodded.

She dismissed the glass of water and instead led him by the hand to the bedroom, where she lowered him down on the edge of the bed and removed his shoes and socks. There was something solemn and ceremonious about the way he sat there and let her undress him. He closed his eyes as Irene unbuttoned his shirt and lifted his arms.

She pulled down the bed covers and Matt eased himself under the layers of blankets. Irene scooted against his body, so cold it frightened her. She lay on her side and draped her arm and leg over his torso, ignoring her own need for heat. The warmth from the electric blanket radiated against her back while she shivered. Matt wrapped his arm around her and stroked her shoulder. He held her there, tightly, keeping her close, clinging.

She could almost feel the waves rocking them, pulling them farther from shore. From safety.

# Chapter 21

WHEN SHERIFF HUFF SLOWED AT THE INTERSECTION OF TWO dirt roads, he swore under his breath. There was that rusted water tower—again! He slammed the gear shift into Park and threw open the door to his Jeep. One look over his shoulder told him daylight was slipping quickly, and if he wasn't lost now, he surely would be in the dark.

He pulled out the piece of paper Sally'd given him and studied it for the millionth time. She'd warned him the logging roads intertwined and recrossed each other. That a goodly number of those wooden road markers were missing off the trees, shot off most likely by those living in the hills who didn't want to be found. People like Grizz Thurber.

There it was on her little map—the circle indicating the water tower. Exasperated, he walked around the Jeep, orienting himself, then got back in and headed up the road running along the right side of the tower, bouncing and swerving around the lumps and potholes and tire-sized boulders embedded in the dirt. Good thing he had a full tank of gas and his emergency box in the back. If he had to, he'd just pull out his sleeping bag, eat some granola bars, and drink water from the gallon jug. Then again, he could always hunt something, skin it, smoke it, and make moccasins while he was at it. Oh, he could manage for a long time on his own out here, if the mood suited him.

He mulled over the things Sally had told him this afternoon. She'd done a little digging for him, gotten some names of neighbors, where they hailed from, what they were doing up on their land. She also warned which ones were growers and likely to shoot off his head before asking questions if he came snooping around this time of year. Huff took heed of her warning. He was more than familiar with the guerilla-type tactics some of these folks used, all manner of sabotage and harassment. Everything from booby-trapped fence lines with wire-tripped grenades to vicious attack dogs programmed to kill. Over the years there'd been plenty of murders, all unsolved. People gone missing, their cars parked on some ridge and abandoned. Vendettas and blackmail. A whole nasty counterculture, as nearly invisible as some primitive tribe in the jungle. And that was just in *his* county.

The car leaped into the air when a tire caught on a rock Huff failed to notice. A stab of pain shot through his back when his rear end reconnected to the seat. He'd put off getting new shocks for some time, but when—if—he ever made it down the mountain to town, first thing tomorrow, that was on his to-do list.

He slowed and searched his memory. The road to the left forked in two directions. He was pretty sure he'd already tried the right arm. The map didn't show a Y, but Huff was fairly certain this was the correct place to turn. He jostled slowly along, wondering about the spare mounted under the chassis of the car, whether it had enough air in it should he need it.

A few miles later he saw the red-painted sign with the arrow at the base of a steep, smooth, paved drive. *Harrison,* the neatly written letters spelled out. Okay, he was finally on the right track. He stopped and redrew the map to show the Y, noted the distance from the intersection. Sally might be a first-rate cook, but her map-drawing skills needed some work.

He tried to remember what she'd said about Harrison. Were they the rich executives who came up from the Bay Area to fish and do some male bonding away from their wives? He thought so. Although he wondered why they needed to get *this* far away. They could just buy a riverfront lodge and not have to endure a grueling trip each time. But that must be part of the macho element—the remoteness filling some primal need to tackle the elements of nature, prove themselves outside the corporate world. Had to rough it when they got a little low on caviar and brie cheese, though. And wait a little longer for AAA to come change their flat tire. Huff chuckled. And, then again, this place was harder for some nosy wife to find, should one come up here sniffing for her errant husband. Huff imagined these guys probably brought a little female entertainment along to liven up the quiet nights.

He jotted down the odometer reading and continued. The road narrowed more; bushes scraped the sides of the Jeep as he jerked and bounced even harder. He shifted into First and tackled a steep hill. At one point the car was so vertical he hunched down over the steering wheel as if that would help keep the car from flipping on its back. He gunned his way through the tight rollercoaster twists until he reached a ridge that opened up to a stunning panorama, then kept going, enjoying the refreshing ease of a flat, wide fire road. This one was more kept up, probably connected down the backside of the mountain and used by CDF for fire control. To his right, the mountain fell abruptly, and way down below, glowing pink in the westering sun's light, was the snaky Trinity River. Huff watched an osprey glide on a downdraft toward the water, sun flashing off the white on its wings. He stopped the Jeep and got out, looked through his binoculars, and scanned the mountainside.

His sharp eyes picked out a few scattered dwellings, a glint of metal fencing barely noticeable under so many conifers. In under three minutes he counted six pot gardens, well camouflaged, but he knew what to look for. He spotted one large fancy home perched on a rocky outcropping. That must have been a monstrous task—hauling all those building materials up that rock face. Someone'd sure paid a pretty penny for that view.

Huff reminded himself of the time and resumed his trek. Ten minutes later he located the next road and turned onto it. Another eight minutes and he found himself parked in front of a seriously old cabin. He could tell hand tools had been used to cut and piece the rough-sawn boards for the siding and porch—decades ago. The wood looked to have been painted at one time; now the planking was gray and splintered. Two huge holes that a man could easily fall into and break a leg took up a good portion of the porch. The sheet metal roof had plenty of dings in it, and a chimney flue jutted up through the top. Just guessing, the cabin couldn't have been more than six hundred square feet in size. The usual assortment of scrap metal—rusted junked furnishings and such—littered the property around the cabin.

These were the things Huff noticed right away: the absence of a vehicle, for one. The kid had a truck; was there another somewhere? Two: no dogs, no smoke from the chimney, a whole lot of quiet. He liked to wait in his vehicle for a few minutes, just to be sure he wasn't going to be pinned down by someone's attack dog. Or the butt-end of a rifle. When Huff was satisfied he'd waited long enough, he walked toward the front door, which hung on broken hinges, wide open.

Before he even got within ten feet, the stench from inside the house assaulted his senses. He exhaled in relief once he sifted through the smells. There was nothing like the putrid stink of rotting human flesh, and he had half-expected to find Grizz Thurber decomposing in a chair, shot up with a round of bullets. Huff grimaced. It wouldn't be his first time, chancing upon a scene like that. Didn't mean it ruled out finding his body elsewhere on the property.

Upon venturing inside, he found other things almost as disturbing. The noise from the hordes of flies was as loud as a small engine, which got Huff to wondering. He pulled his bandana from his pocket and tied it around his nose, waving away the flies come to check him out. As he swung his arm around, the mass of insects lifted off the hewn oak table to reveal plates of maggoty food, half-eaten and left to rot in the recent warm fall weather. Dishes lay piled in the sink, unwashed and covered in more flies. Huff listened again and this time became aware of the absence of noise. To confirm his guess, he gingerly opened the refrigerator door. In the dim interior, he could tell everything had gone bad. There had to be a generator, but it wasn't running.

Huff went back outside, pulled the bandana down, took a deep breath, and cleared his throat. His eyes stung from the stench inside the cabin. He followed the extension cord to the small diesel generator around the back and, sure enough, it was drained dry. The switch was set to run, but the engine had shut itself off when the fuel ran out.

He tried to put a scenario together. Grizz could have run out of fuel and driven down the hill to town to get more, but for some reason didn't come back. Huff figured this disgusting mess had been simmering for at least a week or more. Or Grizz could have gone off into the woods, gotten hurt, fallen off a cliff. Something like that.

And then there was Billy.

Huff pondered Sally's words, how the father was abusive. What if there had been a struggle? He wandered past an open bin full of empty liquor bottles—*way* full. A drunken fight? On the front porch, he passed a smashed whiskey bottle. He bent over and checked the pieces of glass for blood and hair. Nothing.

Huff put the bandana back over his face and went inside again. This time he stood at the door and looked at the overall picture. A chair had been knocked over and rested on its side. He swiped at the flies and looked at the table while walking around its perimeter. He stopped at one corner of the four-inch-thick slab of wood. A dark brown stain marred the edge. His gaze dropped to the floor and he saw more brown stains. He knelt and touched the area, leaned closer and sniffed. This was blood, and not years old. More like weeks.

Could have been a fight. Huff imagined Billy and his father eating dinner one night ...

*Something happens. They fight. Grizz is drunk. Billy punches him? Grizz falls and hits his head on the edge of the table. Billy storms out and leaves his dad, not realizing he's badly hurt. Or maybe hoping he is.*

*Maybe Grizz finally comes around and goes to a hospital. Not likely—his type probably never set foot in a doctor's office. Or he wanders down to a neighbor to get help. Or—*Huff let his imagination go whole hog—*Billy kills his dad, been wanting to do it for a long time. He hurts him with something, a knife.*

Huff searched the table and saw only forks. There was no way to know if a knife was involved. What about a blunt instrument, or a gun? The blood was localized, in one spot. *Okay, so probably not a shotgun at least. Maybe Billy drags him out to the truck, finds a secluded spot, and dumps the body.*

Huff wandered into the only other room, a small bedroom in the back. There was just the one bed, but the couch in the front could serve as a second bed. The room was a mess, clothes everywhere, bedcovers in a shambles. Huff's eyebrows raised a little. The drawers of an old dresser had been pulled out and lay strewn about the floor, their contents thrown around. Someone searching for something in a frantic way.

He left the bedroom and checked the kitchen area, formulating a theory. Sure enough, every cupboard door was swung open, dishes and cans of food pushed aside, knocked to the counter. Not the kind of havoc a bear would have left. This had a thoroughness to it, and less destruction.

Who was looking, and what were they looking for?

What about a third person, an unknown?

He knelt and ran his fingers over the dusty floorboards just inside the door. Raccoon prints. Mice. By the look of things, even they'd high-tailed it once they caught a whiff of that mess inside.

"Well," Huff mumbled as he went back outside and took in the dusky light, "curiouser and curiouser." He studied the dirt, the porch. Found a couple drips of brown, no more. He sure would like to get to the bottom of this, but he'd done enough nosing around. This was Trinity County's jurisdiction, and he would report his observations to them. Maybe they already knew the whereabouts of Nate Thurber. He could be in a hospital or a morgue, or even just shacking up with someone in town, to be closer to a bar. Or his vehicle broke down somewhere. The possibilities were endless, and at this point proved nothing to make Billy Thurber a criminal.

Didn't rule it out either.

Getting down the mountain took a whole lot less time than going up. In under twenty minutes, Sheriff Joe Huff cruised along the river, enjoying the hum of the smooth asphalt and planning his Monday morning. First thing, he'd call the Weaverville sheriff and have a little talk about Grizz and Billy

Thurber. Then he'd take his Jeep in for a new set of shocks, before he forgot.

As he drove through Big Rock in the dark, he glanced at Sally's diner, the lone porch light off and the place closed up for the night. He thought of Wanda, probably making cookies for the passel of grandkids who spent Sunday evenings watching Disney movies at their place, stretched out on the rug and kicking their short legs in the air. He sure wished he could be there too, wrassling the little guys.

Huff let out a big sigh and turned the radio on low to the only channel his antenna could pick up—a staticky country station, which suited him just fine for background noise. In Willow Creek, he pulled into the gas station minimart and tanked up on some really bad coffee, dousing it with four tiny plastic containers of half-and-half and two packets of sugar. He pulled into his house in Breakers shortly after nine p.m., just in time to answer his ringing kitchen phone.

The dispatcher knew Huff was off duty for the weekend, but she thought he should know. A call had just come in not five minutes ago.

The Riptide Motel on Seawood Lane was in flames.

# *Chapter 22*

TWO FIRE TRUCKS BLOCKED HUFF'S ENTRANCE TO THE MOTEL. Nice that the CDF was only three miles away. Already they had their hoses aimed on the blaze, drawing water from the hydrant that hooked up to the motel's water tanks. Huff got out of his car and felt the shimmer of heat on his face. One entire building was engulfed in fire, the flames tickling the branches of the trees.

He scanned the parking lot and noticed it empty of other vehicles. Sunday night in November, after a solid week of rain, was as good a time as any to suffer a fire. Already one crew had the adjacent building completely soaked; another crew worked at containing the remaining conflagration. The trees weren't likely to catch, as wet as they were.

Huff found the chief and watched with him as the firefighters did their job. He waited until Gordon seemed satisfied with the progress of containment, then spoke.

"Where's the owner? Hubble."

"No one's seen him, or his car. Probably out for the evening. He'll have a surprise when he gets back."

Huff nodded. "That's for sure. Ironic, isn't it?"

"What is?"

"Him being a retired firefighter and all." Huff grunted. "Arson, you think?"

Gordon pursed his lips and turned his attention back to his men. "We should be able to figure it out; usually some evidence we can recover. But, first guess, I'd say so. We've had fires start in some of these dumps when guests have been careless: cigarettes, using a hot plate in their room, catching the curtains on fire — that kind of stuff. But it looks like no one is staying here right now. Maybe that's why the owner went out." Gordon shrugged and Huff could tell he wasn't going to lose sleep figuring this one out.

Behind Huff a crowd of neighbors gathered. "Excuse me," he said to the fire chief. He picked out Mrs. Waverly in the commotion, her head bobbing above most of the others. Her face showed distress, and when she spotted him, she hurried to his side.

"Oh, Sheriff Huff, oh my." With her dog clutched to her chest, she took his arm and squeezed it. "Is my house safe over there? How could such a thing happen? Should I evacuate and take Doodles someplace safe — "

Huff patted her hand and gave her his five-cent smile. "Now, now, Mrs. Waverly. Everything is under control and you don't need to worry."

Her eyes darted around, straining to make out the fire behind him. He led her away from the crowd and tried to get her to focus on him.

"Tell me, Mrs. Waverly, did you see anyone over here this evening? Any cars or trucks, anyone stop?"

She brought her eyes to rest on Huff. He could tell she was trying to remember. "I went outside a while ago, just when it got dark, to get a log for the fire. I don't like to keep the wood in the house, you see, because of the ants." She smiled at Huff, as if this information was important.

"And?"

"Oh, well, I saw that Mr. Hubble had turned off all the lights in the buildings. Now, that's not too odd; the motel owners do that when they're on vacation, or don't want any business. But I've never seen the lights shut off since he bought the motel."

"What about his car? Did you notice if it was there?"

Mrs. Waverly chewed her lip and thought. "I am sorry, Sheriff, I just can't recall. Maybe he went out for the night and didn't want any customers. He doesn't have a night manager, you see?"

Huff nodded. Hubble could have turned off all his lights, but, then again, someone wanting to cause trouble might have cut a power line or shut off the breaker if they didn't want to be seen. He had no idea if Hubble had left *before* the lights went out—or after. Or maybe the lights never came on in the first place.

After giving her more reassurances, Huff said good-bye to Mrs. Waverly. He circled back around the north side of the motel and looked around, using the small flashlight he kept in his pocket. Bits of ash and sparks floated through the air and settled on him. Thank goodness for a windless night. The smoke thickened from the onslaught of water spray, and Huff once more put his bandana over his nose. *This little piece of cloth is sure getting a lot of mileage today.*

At the end of the building he found a breaker box. All the switches for the lights were snapped to the Off position. He figured there was a similar box on the burning building, but didn't want to chance approaching it at present. He guessed, though, he would find the same thing.

The tiny box of a cottage had a dim light on. Huff walked over and looked in the window to see the bulb under the microwave shining down on the stove. He looked up when Gordon came lumbering over.

"We turned off the propane at the tank. He's still got electric inside."

"I noticed that." Huff pointed to the row of motel rooms to the north. "All the breakers to the lights on that building are off."

"Could be he shuts down some of the rooms this time of year. Most of 'em do that, to save on utilities. Although it makes for a lot of mold."

"Makes sense." So maybe there was nothing to it.

"I just asked those bystanders if they had seen anything suspicious, but no one had," Gordon said. "It could just be a short, an electrical fire. This place is pretty old."

"But?" Huff responded to the look on Gordon's face.

"When I got here I smelled burning fuel. I have a keen nose for that, and the fire hadn't spread far from that corner over there. And the grass nearby burned, just a circle of it. That's a sign of spilt fuel."

Huff grunted. "What about Hubble? Maybe he set the fire himself? Collecting on the insurance?"

"It's possible. The question is how long he's been gone; if the fire was set, how was it started—quickly, with a match, or slowly, with something smoldering close by? Would he be willing to risk his own place and all his stuff burning? Besides the felony charge—the risk of going to jail. I mean, he *is* a fireman and knows all this."

"Or maybe," Huff added, "this was a mean joke. Deliberate. To set fire to a fireman's property." He considered an idea that had tried to weasel into his head earlier. Now it faced him full on. Was it just a week or so ago that Hubble had burst into the police station complaining about Billy Thurber? Before Huff left for Eureka that morning, he had heard about the little scene in the market between Hubble and Thurber. One of the checkers told him how Thurber made some parting remark at the door, pointing a threatening finger at Hubble and saying he knew where he lived.

Was the answer that easy? Thurber getting back at Hubble?

Huff exhaled hard and turned to Gordon. "Call me. As soon as you have this figured out."

Gordon shook Huff's hand and went over to the smoldering building. Just a few flames licked the roof as a plume of smoke wound upward in the night sky. A handful of stars sparkled up there, but the moon was nowhere in sight. Huff grunted. A clear, cold night, no wind, no moon. If someone had wanted a perfect opportunity to set a fire that would stay small and manageable, say, contained to one specific property, well, this would be the night to choose. Did Hubble always go out on Sunday nights? Would he be able to prove when he left and where he went?

Huff didn't have to wait long to get answers to his questions.

Pulling up into the driveway of the motel was a dark, sleek car. A red Corvette.

"I'M GOING OUT FOR SOME AIR," LUIS SAID, RUBBING HIS full belly. Celia looked up from the sink full of dishes. "I feel like a stuffed tamale," he added.

Celia grinned. "You don't look like one."

Luis often took a short walk after such a day of eating. Sundays were like that. Starting after church with lunch around noon, then munching all day long as they enjoyed family time with Tomás, Alma, and Miguel. Today they'd all gone down to Drifter's Cove and helped Miguel build a fort out of driftwood. A big project that worked up another hearty appetite. Then another huge meal, followed by *postres*. Tonight he couldn't help himself. Flan was his favorite dessert and he had devoured three huge servings. With Miguel's help, *ciertamente*. When Celia wasn't looking, he had let Miguel lick the dish.

Luis walked at a steady pace, passing the shops and school, then turned down Huckleberry Lane. He reflected on the quiet conversation he'd had with Alma at the beach, her concern about Tomás. How Tomás now kept a gun at work and wanted to put in an alarm system. He understood Tomás's need to feel safe. Luis reminded her that her husband had spent a lifetime looking over his shoulder, expecting trouble. A hard habit to break. But *no te preocupes*, no worries, he told her, Tomás had never been reckless. Alma hadn't seemed mollified.

Luis thought about the trouble stirring in his community. Some of his parishioners had spoken with him about the recent robberies, which seemed to keep occurring. Two houses just south of town on the old highway had been broken into last week. People noticed the new police cruiser driving up and down the streets. Sheriff Huff seemed to have made light of it when Luis ran into him at the coffee shop and asked. You know how rumors spread, Huff had told him. Things get blown out of proportion. Just a few minor incidents; he would be sure to keep the town safe, he assured him.

But Luis sensed a growing climate of fear and unrest among his neighbors. Maybe the events over the last few years had made them shaky, what with the scandals in the local government. Some of these neighbors had lived here all their lives with little disturbance. Many were old and lived alone. They were locking their doors for the first time. More than one of them had mentioned the name of a young man who recently moved to town, a troublemaker who some felt was responsible for the recent crimes. Luis didn't know this man, but he admonished that one had to be careful and not judge without knowing the facts. Not listen to gossip and rumors.

Luis made the block and turned up Marionberry. Maybe he would change the sermon he had in mind for next week. Perhaps he would speak on fear and on putting trust in God.

Several Scriptures came to mind and he made a mental note to write them down when he got home.

He spotted the church on the next corner and the sight of it warmed his heart. He liked to think of it as a small beacon, like the lighthouse on Indian Rock. Signaling a safe haven for weary and lost travelers. Luis smiled at the mental image as he approached the church. He looked up at the canopy of stars, so many and so bright. To think that God knew the name of each one—how staggering a thought.

In the distance, Luis heard a faint siren, a rare occurrence in Breakers. As he stopped at the bank of tall beveled-glass windows that ran along the front of the church, a flash of movement in the dark recesses of the sanctuary caught his eye and hitched his breath. The two large candles set on the sides of the stage had been lit, and their soft glow showed the shape of a man—or woman—standing before the raised podium. Luis watched through the window as the person stood there, unmoving. He looked up and down the street, checking for a parked car to associate with this stranger, but there was none. Gently, he pressed on the door latch and it responded. Surely he had locked the front door this morning after service? Now he couldn't remember.

Whoever was in there did not seem bent on mischief. Celia would worry if he delayed too long, and something told him this person wanted to be alone—alone with God. He prayed by the door, asking God to help this one. Luis would come back in a while, to see if the person was still there. See if he could be of help.

Luis ducked out of view as the shadow inside moved away from the podium and sat in the front pew. He left the church and headed the three blocks toward his home. When he reached the front door, he stopped, catching a whiff of something in the air. His mind returned to the sound of the siren.

Smoke.

Something close by was on fire.

HUFF OBSERVED JERRY HUBBLE FROM THE OTHER SIDE OF the parking lot. He watched the way the man jumped out of his car and ran over to the fire chief, listened as he yelled and waved his arms emphatically. Eventually, the motel owner calmed down and stared at the last flames dying out on the charred and smoldering roof.

Huff knew that was mean of him, letting Gordon get the earful, but hey, he was wiped out. His morning had started early, taking the grandkids to the pancake breakfast at the Community Center, then hiking up Bear Creek with a picnic lunch, then helping Wanda fix the screen door and do some touch-up painting in the bathroom. Then there was all that driving up to Eagle's Perch, getting lost, the little tour of Thurber's pretty cabin, and the long drive home. Now, at eleven o'clock, Huff was in no mood to have Hubble mouth off in his face. In fact, he could just let Gordon talk to the guy, ask him all the questions. In the morning, he could come over here, fresh, showered, fed, and with a stomach full of coffee, and *then* deal with Hubble.

The idea was tempting, but a few questions gnawed at his mind. He knew he'd get little sleep if he didn't ask them.

Huff took in Gordon's look of relief as he came over to where the fire chief stood. As soon as Hubble spotted the sheriff, he became reanimated.

"You see this?" Hubble's face was flushed with color. His wild brown hair whipped at his cheeks in the light breeze. "This is Thurber's doing. That punk threatened me last week, probably watched my place, just waiting for the one night I decided to go to town."

"Where did you go, Hubble?" Huff asked.

"Like I told Gordon, I was at the KitKat Klub in Eureka. They can sure vouch for me there. Must've been over a hundred people in there. I usually go on Sunday nights."

Huff nodded, keeping his face blank. He could just picture Hubble in the front row of the strip club, watching the girls shake while he downed a few whiskeys. Huff smelled alcohol on Hubble's breath. "How much did you have to drink tonight?"

Hubble scowled. "Hey, that has nothing to do with what happened here. And F-Y-I, I only have one drink, early on, when I know I have to drive forty miles home. You can be sure of that!"

Gordon used this opportunity to bow out. He held up his hand. "I need to get these guys wrapped up. Joe, I'll call your office in the morning and we'll talk, all right?" Huff nodded, shook Gordon's hand, and the fire chief walked away.

"Tell me, Jerry," Huff said in a calming voice. "When you go out for the night, do you turn all the motel lights off, to discourage guests from stopping in?"

"What? Are you kidding? I never turn off the lights; it's just an invitation for someone to break in. You can see I have a note on the door that says we're closed for the night. And," he pointed toward the street, "the 'No Vacancy' sign is out there. Any idiot can read that."

"Do you keep a gas can somewhere?"

"Sure. I use it to fill the leaf blower and the lawnmower." Hubble paced back and forth, watching the firemen roll up their hoses.

"Can I see it?"

Mumbling under his breath, Hubble stomped off, his exasperation apparent. No doubt he half-expected someone to run off and arrest Billy Thurber before he got away.

Hubble led Huff over to a small shed behind his cottage. He opened the door, flicked on the light, and picked up the gas can from the dirt floor. "Here." He shook the metal can. "It's pretty empty."

"Well, how much was in it the last time you used it?"

"How should I know? You always remember how much fuel is left in *your* gas can? Come on."

Huff took the can from Hubble and smelled it. If any fuel had been poured out recently, dripped onto the can, it had already evaporated. He set the container down and walked back toward the burned-out motel. Hubble followed him to the breaker box mounted on the charred back wall. With a gloved finger, Huff popped open the door on the box. He shone the flashlight in, highlighting the flipped-off breaker switches.

Hubble leaned in over Huff's shoulder. "Son of a gun." With the potent exhale of alcohol alongside his face, Huff wondered about Hubble's one-drink declaration. Hubble looked Huff right in the eye. "I didn't do that. No way."

"Well, don't touch this; I want to get it dusted tomorrow."

Huff listened as Hubble ranted on about Thurber. Had anyone seen that truck over here tonight? Had anyone gone around to question the neighbors? His anger was genuine enough, Huff concluded, but could still be an act.

"I hope you have insurance," Huff said.

"Of course I do, fat lot of good that'll do. Couldn't purchase the place without proof of insurance; you should know that. Still, now who's going to stay here with the place looking like this? Do you realize how much income I'll lose while it gets rebuilt?"

Huff shrugged. "Most insurance policies have a loss-of-income coverage. Yours probably does."

"Yeah, well, with my luck, probably doesn't."

Huff felt his limbs weigh heavy, pulling him down. He needed sleep. He started to say good night, but Hubble, through his apparent alcoholic gaze, suddenly remembered something.

"Hey, listen, Huff, before I left for town—that was about seven or so—I got some phone calls on the motel line. I thought they were people looking for a room, you know. So every time I answered the phone, there was a pause and then someone hung up. Three times this happened. And don't tell me the same person kept getting a wrong number. It was that punk, I'm sure of it. Checking to see if I was home." As an apparent afterthought, he said, "Let's check the answer machine and see if there's more hang-ups."

Hubble hurried over to his cottage and unlocked the door. Huff followed him inside and watched him survey the room. "Nothing out of place, far as I can tell." He pressed Rewind on the ancient answering machine. One of those kind that still used tapes.

Huff met Hubble's eyes as the recording beeped, then clicked.

"See," Hubble declared triumphantly. "A hang-up!" There were two more, and no messages. He assumed a defiant stance. "Well, there you have it. Evidence. Someone shutting off the lights, calling to see if I'd left for the night. What more proof do you need?"

Huff gave the old-style phone a once-over. No caller ID. He made a mental note to check phone logs and see if those hang-ups could be traced. "We'll need a bit more than that, I'm afraid."

Huff walked outside with Hubble trailing at his heels. Hubble called after the sheriff as he walked toward his car. "Find out where that punk was tonight. I'll bet he has some alibi, but you can be sure it won't hold water. Huff!" he yelled.

Huff turned, wiping his tired eyes. He didn't bother to mask the fatigue in his voice. "What, Hubble?"

"This isn't the end of it, Huff. If you don't stop him now, who knows what'll happen next. Maybe next time it'll be your house."

Huff got into his car and started the engine. Memories of the cabin came to him. The flies all over the table, the blood on the floor, the cupboards ransacked.

He sighed and drove down Seawood Lane toward home.

He thought about snuggling up to Wanda in that big, four-poster bed up in Weitchpec.

He pictured the faces of those cute kids, crashed out on the rug in front of the TV.

He thought about all the things he had to do tomorrow and how he prayed someone, soon, would step forward and take over the job of Breakers' Chief of Police.

LUIS LOOKED UP AT THE CLOCK, THEN SET HIS BIBLE DOWN on the coffee table. He peeked in at Celia, her face pressed into her pillow as she slept on her side. She looked small and peaceful. Exhausted was more like it. Luis recalled Miguel tugging on her arm, *"Abuela, ven. See my fort!"* Miguel was always pulling on their sleeves, showing them this and that. So much enthusiasm for life, and always breathing so hard to enjoy every minute.

Luis and Celia kept a spare inhaler in their bathroom for Miguel. One time, down in San Jose while they were babysitting, they'd had to rush him to the hospital when he couldn't get enough air. But Luis could see a big difference, living up here. The fresh air was good for Miguel's asthma. They hadn't known about all the pollen, though, from the trees in the fall, when the cones burst open and yellow powder coated everything—including Miguel's aggravated lungs. *But that is seasonal and manageable.* Here, they didn't have to run an air purifier and humidifier around the clock.

He put on his coat and hat and gently closed the door behind him. The air still smelled faintly of smoke. Maybe just a backyard bonfire. A good night for one.

The chilly air made him pull his collar up. *Tonight must be the coldest night so far this year.* His breath came out in frosty steam, and by the time he arrived at the church, his hands were numb. He touched his cheeks and could barely feel them.

He quietly opened the door and stood listening for a moment. The two candles had burned low, the wax pooling in the metal trays. In that faint light, Luis walked down the aisle to the front, his sneakers silent on the carpeting.

His breath caught for a second when he saw something sticking out from the end of the first pew. A sweater or coat sleeve dangled. Luis let out a sigh; he thought he had seen an arm. All this talk about foul play in town was unleashing his imagination. Whoever had been here must have left their coat, although Luis couldn't figure how they didn't miss it the moment they stepped out into that freezing air.

As he reached the pew and bent to pick up the piece of clothing, he stopped abruptly. Someone lay on the bench, using their wadded-up coat as a pillow. Luis smiled as he studied the curled-up figure. He listened to the soft snores coming from the visitor's nose and wondered how anyone could sleep so soundly on such a hard bench. But then, there had been times during his sermons when he noticed someone nod off. He chuckled. He hoped it didn't happen too often.

Luis retreated to the front door, careful to not make a sound. He was glad this visitor felt safe enough to find shelter for the night in his church. That it served as a safe haven for this weary and possibly lost traveler. What better place than in God's house and under his protection. There had been many times, down south, when the temperature dropped and compelled strangers to seek out his church for warmth and comfort. He'd even had the benches closest to the heater upholstered with thick foam and heavy fabric coverings—for just that reason.

Luis gently closed the front door behind him and heard the latch click. He thought for a minute, then turned to the street, leaving the door unlocked.

# *Chapter 23*

OUT OF CURIOSITY, MATT DECIDED TO ATTEND THE TOWN
Hall meeting. Someone had put up posters around Breakers,
stating that, after the regular council session, anyone wanting
to address and discuss the "rash of crimes" should attend. Matt
had come an hour late, not interested in zoning ordinances and
holiday fundraisers. About fifty people filled the small room,
sitting on metal folding chairs. Four people, nicely dressed, sat
on the dais, with notebooks on the table in front of them. Matt
looked around the room and recognized some of the faces.

He had spent the last few days buried in his work—leaving
his house at the crack of dawn and not returning home until
nearly ten. It wasn't that he wanted to finish up this job and
move on to the next one; he just couldn't take the oppressive
climate in his home. Irene tried to cheer him up, but she was
trying too hard. He felt smothered. And Casey would leave the
room the moment she saw him. How was he supposed to talk
to her if she wouldn't even face him? Her anger was so palpable
he could nearly grasp it with his hands.

But he knew where she got that anger from. Such was the
downside of heredity.

As he sat in the back row, barely paying attention to the council discussion, he tried to remember Casey back when she was sweet and eager for his affection. How she used to climb into his lap and beg him to read to her. She liked big, thick books that took months to get through. He must have read her every Redwall book written. His friends had warned him about the turbulent teenage years, but he'd thought his children would be different. He had been a quiet, studious teen, never getting into trouble. But then, he'd had to be the man of the house as well, watching over his younger sisters while his mother worked as a bookkeeper for that construction company. His sisters had their wild moments, he recalled, but nothing that wreaked havoc in their lives. As far as he knew, they never did drugs or smoked. They participated in the church youth group, traveled to Mexico each spring to help build houses, and went to Vacation Bible School, just as he had. Sure, a lot of hormones raged in the house with all those women, but his sisters had also babied him — cooked for him, sewed patches on his jeans, even cut his hair ... with sometimes disastrous results. He'd drawn the line at their pleas to dye and curl his long dark locks.

So he had expected his experience raising his own children would be little different.

Matt had no idea that kids had treated Daniel badly after the accident with Jesse. He'd just assumed his son's friends would be compassionate and understanding. Yet Casey told Matt otherwise — that the kids shunned him, whispered behind his back, even called him a murderer. How could they do that, be so cruel?

He remembered Casey's pained look when she told him — and her chastisement. "Why couldn't Daniel transfer to another school, where kids would leave him alone?" she asked. Matt explained that running away was not an option. That, in time, things would settle down and his friends would come back around.

His words only made Casey angrier. Matt thought she was overreacting, being protective of Daniel. She didn't attend the high school, so she wasn't there to see these things firsthand. He even wondered if she had made some of it up, to find a way to spare Daniel from the pain and guilt he felt.

But in time Matt saw it with his own eyes. Friends stopped coming around, and when they did, Daniel was grumpy and argumentative with them.

Had Daniel brought this on himself? Pushing friends away because he felt guilty? Irene had insisted Daniel meet with the school counselor. The woman reported back, after a few after-school sessions, that Daniel isolated himself, withdrew from the other kids, refused to participate in group activities. She suggested he get some real therapy. But when Irene had made the suggestion to Daniel, he yelled at her. Did she, his own mother, think he was crazy, psychotic? *Just leave me alone*, Matt could still hear him say—pained, lashing words.

Matt realized he was gripping the seat of his chair. His attention drifted back to the podium where the chairwoman now tapped on the microphone. He hadn't even noticed the rumbling in the room. She hushed the crowd and Matt watched Jerry Hubble stomp up to the microphone.

Hubble wore the same dirty T-shirt and baggy sweatpants Matt had seen him in that day at the market. He wondered if the guy ever combed his hair or trimmed his moustache. He had that wild Einstein look to him.

"Okay, everyone, I'm not gonna take up your time, and I don't need to tell anyone what's been going on around town." His voice boomed through the speakers, and the chairwoman motioned for him to back off the microphone a bit.

"You've heard about the break-ins—the houses, the vehicles. It's our job as citizens to watch out for each other, like a neighborhood watch." Hubble searched the crowd and found Sheriff Huff, pointed at him. "Now, I've told Huff about this punk that's been hanging around in town—"

At that, a number of people yelled out, interrupting his speech. One woman in the front row stood and raised her voice above the others. "Now, Mr. Hubble, you cannot go around making accusations lightly. That is called *slander*, and you would do well—"

Jerry interrupted back. "Well, Miss hoity-toity lawyer, it's a free country and I know about the first amendment, so can it!"

His challenger stood stiffly, then with pursed lips dropped back down into her seat.

The chairwoman stood and touched Hubble on the shoulder, causing him to jump. "Please, you'll have to watch your mouth or we'll ask you to step down."

Hubble gave her a mean, puzzled look. "Whatever." He shut his eyes and gathered his thoughts. "Okay, where was I? For them that don't know it, my motel was set on fire last Sunday. No doubt you all have heard. I just want to know ..." He pointed again at the sheriff. " ... what the law is doing about it." A few shouts of agreement joined in. "Just sending a car to cruise around the streets a few times is *not* what we need here."

An older man in the middle of the room waved his hand in the air. "Well, being confrontational to that young fella is just going to add wood to the fire. You can't go around threatening people and expect them to not get angry."

Matt felt the rumble grow. People whispered to each other, nodding their heads. Sheriff Huff stood and spoke loudly from the back of the room.

"Mr. Hubble, I've told you this before. There is a process for this type of thing. It's called *law*. You need to let us do our jobs. We've noted your observations and complaints, and we're looking into the fire. We're doing everything we can."

Jerry nearly spit. "Oh, baloney. From where I stand, I don't see anything happening. Every place that punk has been, trouble's followed." More vocal objections. "Hey, all I'm asking of you," he said, gesturing to his neighbors, "is to keep an eye on this guy, this *Bil-ly Thur-ber*." He enunciated each syllable loudly. "Watch where he goes, see what he's up to." He locked his eyes on the woman in the front row. "*That's* not against the law, is it?"

Matt had heard enough. He yearned to stand under a hot shower for an hour, get the grime off his skin, and collapse in bed. He didn't feel like having dinner, although if he skipped eating, Irene'd be upset.

He slipped out the door as another outburst from the audience stirred the crowd once more.

JERRY STARED LONG AND HARD AT THE ROWS OF PEOPLE. HIS eyes searched out possible alliances and sympathetic faces. From the raised dais, he caught Mrs. Waverly's frightened expression. Right in front of her was that little Mexican guy, the one who had the restaurant. He seemed agitated and worried.

Across the room, Jerry recognized some of the local fishermen. They had their eyes glued on Jerry, especially the one with the red beard. That guy nodded in agreement.

Jerry spotted the quiet Chinese fella that ran the bait shop. Behind those thick glasses he read fear.

Then there were the dozens of old people, like Tim and Dottie Brody. Like Mrs. Waverly, they looked as scared as rats fleeing a sinking ship. Oh, these folks were plenty upset, and they needed a strong guy to lead the charge to keep the town safe. Shoot, everybody and their sister knew Huff spent most of his time up on the Klamath, that he was only filling in. No one could count on him to go the whole nine yards on this thing.

The chairwoman asked those in attendance if anyone else would like to step forward and comment. No one did. She pounded her gavel and closed the session.

Jerry grunted in satisfaction and stepped down. Pockets of people milled about, talking, and some even arguing. Good. The town was on his side; they knew he was right. All they had to do now was wait and they'd see. Thurber would make a move and that'd be his last one. He thought about his motel in flames and all the hassle it would take to get the place back in shape. Well, maybe it was all worth it, if it landed Billy Thurber in jail. That'd sure be a moment he'd like to see — the cuffs snapped onto Thurber's wrists.

As the room emptied out, he looked at Huff, standing in the corner, watching the meeting disperse. The sheriff narrowed his eyes and glared at him. Jerry snorted. He could tell Huff was warning him.

*Well, warn me all you like*, Jerry challenged back with his eyes. *I'm right, and you know it.* He walked over to the two fishermen gathering their things and introduced himself, feeling like a politician working the crowd, drumming up votes.

When Jerry finally left the building, he walked down the three blocks toward the library to where he'd parked his car. The sheriff was right behind him and it made his skin crawl. He was just about to turn around and tell Huff to back off when he stopped suddenly. His eyes widened as the horror of recognition set in.

A gush of profanity spewed from his mouth. His legs shook, and he froze right in the middle of First Street. Huff came alongside him and pinched his lips together at the sight.

They both stared at Jerry's beautiful red Corvette, parked headfirst against the library wall.

The back end of his car was smashed in, the bumper bent like a boomerang, and the rear glass window shattered. The trunk had folded up like an accordion.

"Well," Huff said with a big exhale. "If that doesn't take the cake."

Jerry reeled in his anger, then turned to Huff, his eyes burning like hot coals. His voice came out in a growl. "You better get that punk."

He looked back at his beautiful, expensive, violated car and under his breath added, "Or *I will*."

# Chapter 24

Joe Huff tapped his pen on the wooden desk in the police station, then stopped and looked closer at the surface and the spattering of small dings there. He smirked; he hadn't realized he had worn down the wood with all his tapping.

His brain was just as worn down—with all the heavy thinking he'd been engaged in.

Pressure came at him from all sides these days. Thinking of Hubble and the ruckus at the town meeting showed him there were some unhappy campers in town. He didn't like the mood forming—like bread fermenting with a noxious sour smell, rising and spreading a pall over the town. The city council members wanted this growing unrest controlled. The Humboldt County Sheriff's Department wanted Huff to make some headway on containing the escalating crime in Breakers, California. Wanda was pressuring him to take a week off for Thanksgiving break, as the grandkids were going to be out of school and would most likely be camping out at Paps's house. Now the Trinity County sheriff wanted Huff to drive up and discuss some things with him about the condition of Nate Thurber's cabin, and the hermit's totally unknown whereabouts.

A deputy named Chuck Warner had been sent to check out the scene up on Eagle's Perch ridge. He and a handful of men scoured the area with two hounds for a full day and found no trace of Grizz. DMV showed only one vehicle registered in Thurber's name—the 1985 Ford truck that Billy drove. The closest neighbor, the rich executive from Menlo Park, was not around and apparently hadn't been for some time. His house had already been winterized—the water valves shut off, generator disconnected, appliances unplugged. Vehicle tracks leading up to the asphalt driveway were weeks old, if not months. A thorough search determined Grizz Thurber was not occupying a bed in a hospital, and no one around Weaverville had seen him, let alone knew him.

Huff had asked Warner if any papers showed up during the search, mentioning any other relatives. Warner told him the only one they knew of was the one hanging out in Huff's part of the woods. So now the task fell on him to question the kid. Not that Billy was suspect to anything. He just might want to know his dad had gone missing, is all. Give the officers some suggestions on how they might find him if he'd landed into some trouble. A trail he liked to take, a friend's place he frequented. The usual.

Plus, Huff still hadn't questioned him yet about the night of the fire at the motel. Gordon said it was arson, no doubt. That some sort of fuel was used, ignited by a slow-activating substance sprinkled on the fuel. That left all manner of possibilities open—including Thurber and Hubble. But it also cornered neither and no one. Huff hadn't been surprised when Gordon failed to find any prints on the breaker box.

Just zooming ahead and getting nowhere fast.

Huff resumed tapping his pen. The clock on the wall ticked behind him. He looked at the four pale yellow walls of his office, the neat stacks of file folders, the manuals lining the table behind him. He closed his eyes and conjured up the smell of the river, the cry of an osprey swooping down, the taste of smoked salmon on his tongue.

The phone's harsh ring shook him from his reverie. He answered it, annoyed. He'd just settled into such a pleasant daydream.

Deputy Warner's voice came through the line in fits and starts. Huff made out every other word. *Cell phone*, he concluded. Where was Warner?

Deputy Warner told Huff where he was.

Standing on the bank of the Trinity River, six miles west of Big Rock, on a wide stretch of sandy beach just past mile marker eighteen.

Looking at a washed-up body of a partially decomposed white male, who had a mop of gray hair on what was left of his head.

# Chapter 25

IN LIEU OF A MORGUE OR CORONER'S OFFICE, BODIES REQUIR-ing autopsies in Trinity County came to the attention of the local funeral home director, who also doubled as the county's coroner. Sheriff Huff tried to remember if there was a proper title you addressed him with, like "Undertaker Smith." On the phone, the man had said his name was Russell, but Huff didn't know if that was a first or last name.

He looked in the rearview mirror at Billy Thurber, who sat in the backseat of the cruiser, deep in thought. Not much of a conversationalist, this one. The whole two-hour drive, Thurber had only answered Huff's friendly questions with a nod or a grunt, not a bit forthcoming with information.

When he'd spotted the old Ford truck yesterday at the gas station, he'd wondered if Thurber would have that nervous, guilty look on his face. But no, the kid was as cool as a cucumber. Only when Huff mentioned the body up on the Trinity River did Thurber's eyes widen — just a little. He had expected some resistance, but Thurber agreed to ID the body. Huff had plenty of questions he needed to ask, but decided to hold off until Thurber had a look at the corpse lying in the mortuary's cold storage. Plus, he wanted another deputy there when he interrogated Thurber, although he planned to call it a little "chat." Deputy Chuck Warner was supposed to meet them there.

All along the river, maples lined the road and punctuated the groves of tall conifers with their golden leaves. Huff kept his window down, enjoying the brisk fall air and the warm sun streaming into the car. What a waste of a glorious day. He knew he'd be stuck driving Thurber all the way back to the foggy, miserably damp coast and the day would be shot. Of course, he could have had Thurber meet him up here, but there'd have been no guarantee the kid would show. Well, at least he would have most of next week off for Thanksgiving. When he agreed to this sorry job, he'd informed the Breaker's city council he would not be around for any of the holidays; that's where he drew the line.

Huff slowed as he entered the town of Weaverville. "You grew up around here, right, Thurber?"

Another grunt. Huff watched his passenger in the mirror. "Quite a road getting up to your place. Must be a real pain in the winter, after a heavy rain." Huff watched it register on Thurber's face—that he'd taken a little trip to the old homestead. But the kid made no comment. Thurber probably assumed he'd gone up there after the body was found, not before. Huff didn't intend to clarify that point.

"When were you last up there, at your cabin?" Huff asked as he swung the car into the mortuary parking lot.

Thurber's voice was flat, unemotional. "A few weeks ago, I guess."

"You close to your father?"

Another grunt, this one clearly telling Huff to butt out.

Huff parked and Thurber followed him to the front door. Deputy Warner opened the door when Huff knocked.

"Hello, Sheriff," Warner said, then turned and sized up the kid. "And you're Mr. Thurber?"

"Billy." Thurber made a sour face. "Can we just get past the formalities and get this over with?"

Huff locked eyes with Warner for a moment. The deputy ushered them inside. "Sure thing," he said. "The coroner's in the back."

Huff had no real interest in seeing what was left of the waterlogged body. Russell had told him over the phone that he finished the report and it held some curious particulars. Because of the time spent in the water, he'd had difficulty determining how long the man had been dead. Probably between three and five weeks. In layman's terms, Russell explained how the condition of the victim's lungs were inconclusive regarding death by drowning. More likely from complications of advanced alcoholism. His liver revealed acute cirrhosis and inflammation—probably hepatitis, which the blood tests would confirm. And then, there was the crack on the front of his skull, which could have been from a blow to the head. Or he could have smacked his head on a rock when he landed in the river.

That one thing interested Huff—the possibility that Grizz hadn't drowned. If he died before he ended up in the river, just how did he get from his cabin way up on the ridge down to the Trinity, miles below? Maybe he should impound the Ford truck, to have the techs go over it for blood and hair— unless Thurber was willing to let them check it over. He just couldn't imagine an old drunk walking all that distance, but who knew? Maybe he did it all the time. Or someone gave him a ride down the mountain.

Still, that didn't explain how he got in the river. And what about the blood on the kitchen table and floor, and the ransacking? Huff hadn't seen anything that could have been used as a weapon, but, then again, he hadn't looked carefully. There could be a blood-encrusted pipe in the bushes three miles from the cabin. Like looking for a needle in a haystack.

Huff had to give it to the kid—he was only a little green around the gills when he came out of the back room, accompanied by the undertaker. Most people would have lost their breakfast instantly.

"He confirmed the identity," Russell said. "His father, Nate Thurber. I had him sign the paperwork."

Huff stood in front of Thurber. "Sorry, son. Not a pretty sight, seeing him like that."

Thurber raised his eyes and took a deep breath. "He's better off dead. Nothing to be sorry about." He pushed past Huff. "So, can we go now?"

Huff thanked the coroner and walked after Thurber, who threw open the front door and gulped fresh air. Huff gave him a moment to compose himself. Then they got in the car and followed Deputy Warner over to the Trinity County Sheriff's Department.

Now Huff noticed a change in Thurber's demeanor—the hands twitching, the nervous flickering in his eyes. When Thurber asked where they were *now* going, Huff told him that since he had ID'd his father, they had to ask him some other questions—for the record. Thurber swore under his breath, but he didn't seem at all upset over his father's death.

Warner took them into a small interrogation room. He explained to Thurber about the recording device.

"Aren't you supposed to read me my rights?"

Huff chuckled, aiming at setting Thurber at ease. "You're not under arrest. We just want to try to figure out what happened to your dad."

After Warner turned on the tape recorder and went through the legal litany and naming of those in the room, he asked

Thurber some questions. None of the kid's answers helped much. He last saw his dad a few weeks ago. No, the place wasn't in a shambles when he left, and he hadn't planned on returning anytime soon. He had lived there all his life with his father. His mother skipped town when he was small, about eight years old. They made their living cutting and selling firewood, besides his dad getting some veteran's aid. Sometimes they collected cans and bottles and took them to the recycling center in Weaverville. Huff remembered that big bin full of whiskey bottles, probably the source of most of their recycling revenue.

Thurber made a cynical face when Warner asked if Nate Thurber had any enemies. "My father was his own worst enemy. He drank like a fish and was pretty sick the last few months. He wouldn't go get help."

"Was he on any medication?" Huff asked.

"Just liquor. The cure-all for what ails you." Thurber fidgeted in his chair.

"Well, son, just how do you think your father ended up in the river?"

Thurber narrowed his eyes. "Beats me. It's a long ways away from the cabin."

Huff studied Thurber's face. There was something about it that bothered him.

"Billy, where were you Sunday night, November eighth— the night of the fire at the Riptide Motel?"

Thurber didn't even hesitate. "Does it matter what I tell you? You've already decided I did it—you and half the town."

"That's not how I work," Huff said.

"Well, I don't have any alibi. I wasn't anywhere I'd be seen, so believe what you like."

Huff didn't appreciate Thurber's snide attitude. The kid clearly knew there wasn't enough evidence to pin that fire on

anyone, not to mention the lack of eyewitnesses to the robberies around town, or the break-ins or thefts. Thurber had
that same cocky look he'd seen in a dozen criminals' eyes—
when they knew they were getting away scot-free. In this case,
Thurber could be literally getting away with murder.

Convenient that Thurber's truck was presently parked in
front of the Breaker's police station. Disliking the look on
Thurber's face, he decided he would have it impounded after
all.

"Where do you stay, over on the coast?"

Thurber did not like this question. After a beat, he answered. "Up in Fairhaven, off some dirt road."

"A house?"

"No, I have a camper parked on a friend's property."

Huff pushed a legal pad and pen across the table. "Draw
me a map."

He left Thurber in the room with Deputy Warner while he
went and made the phone call to have the truck impounded.
He also left a message with his former partner at the Eureka office to file for a search warrant—to search a camper
for any evidence of murder. He didn't have any specifics;
he doubted there'd be a murder weapon lying around. And
without specifics, the warrant would probably be refused.
Maybe Thurber had some papers—a will, title to property—
although that piece of mountain land wasn't worth killing
anyone over. In lieu of a will, Thurber would inherit all his
dad's belongings anyway. Huff doubted there would be any
way to tie Thurber to murdering his father—if that was what
had gone down.

He thought of Thurber's comment: "He's better off dead."
Thinking of Nate living alone in that decrepit cabin, suffering
from a destroyed liver and craving his next drink, made him
tend to agree with Thurber's words.

That didn't mean someone ought to have put him out of his misery, in any case.

Huff finished his calls and came back to fetch Thurber. On the drive to the coast, with his sullen passenger dozing off in the backseat, Huff wondered what Thurber would say when he arrived in Breakers and found his truck impounded. That was going to set him off.

Jerry Hubble had warned Huff after his motel burned down: "Maybe next time it'll be your house." Some people made a lot of empty verbal threats, Huff reminded himself. And then there were those who made good on their promises. You were either one or the other.

Time would tell which type Billy Thurber was.

# Chapter 26

THE AFTERNOON SUN WARMED CASEY'S BACK AS SHE SAT IN the small enclosed garden. School had let out early, just after lunch, for a teachers' in-service meeting. Meredith, with her notebook on her lap, sprawled out on a ratty couch, her leg dangling over the armrest. Casey thought it odd having a sofa in the middle of a flower garden, but Meredith's yard boasted an eclectic assortment of garage-sale conquests. The last time she had been at Meredith's to work on the science report, Sunny — Meredith's mother — brought out an old urn she found at the monthly flea market. Casey cringed when Sunny told her it still contained someone's ashes. Then her jaw dropped when Sunny opened the lid and started sprinkling the contents around the bushes and flower beds in the yard. Good nutrients for the plants, Sunny said. Meredith had only giggled.

A half-dozen cats stretched out on the brick patio. Sunny's garden was a tangled mass of vegetation, with prolific vines trailing over the ground and escaping over the short wooden fence. Cabbages and peas forced their way between clumps of foxglove and shrubby roses. Always an adventure looking for salad ingredients, Meredith said. Fortunately, she added, most of what grew in the yard was edible, so if she picked something unidentifiable, it probably wouldn't kill her to eat it. Sunny often came outside to dig, prune, trim, or gather something while Casey and Meredith worked. Wearing flowing gypsy-style skirts and dozens of clinking silver bracelets on each arm, she usually strolled in and out of the garden with platters of finger food and drinks, chatting about auras and the alignment of the planets. But Casey hadn't seen her today.

Casey liked coming over to Meredith's. She found Sunny's cheerful, carefree disposition refreshing, and Meredith entertained her with crazy stories of life in Breakers. Inside, the house was like a harem, with dozens of candles burning on long side tables under draping canopies of colorful fabric. Big poofy pillows covered the living room floor—every inch of it. To get to the bathroom, you had to step on them, like stepping on stones across a creek—barefoot, of course. Sunny burned incense, filling the house with a sweet, exotic aroma. Asian paintings and sculptures filled the nooks and walls. Such a different place than her own drab home.

Casey took off her sweatshirt and enjoyed the sun baking her skin. She lifted her face skyward and soaked up the warmth. Only one more paragraph to write on her tide pool observations and she'd be done until after Thanksgiving.

Strange Indian music floated out the back bedroom window. Casey frowned. That was not the only sound she heard coming from that room. Laughter, a man's voice. Sunny was "entertaining" again—Meredith's term for her mother's afternoon affairs.

Casey glanced at Meredith, over at the far end of the yard. Meredith chewed her pencil and twirled her long, chocolate-brown hair, concentrating on the paper resting in her lap. Casey sat in a plastic swivel chair under the lattice-covered patio right next to the house. Maybe Meredith couldn't hear what Casey heard—or maybe she was so accustomed to her mother's afternoon dalliances that she took no note. But the sounds drifting out the window set Casey on edge. Her face flushed hot as she forced herself to stare at her notebook.

She felt she would burst from the tension of the situation. She jumped up and dropped her notebook on the chair.

Meredith looked over at her. "Casey, are you okay?"

Casey managed a nod. "Just a cramp in my leg. Need to walk it out."

Meredith went back to chewing her pencil. Casey hobbled to the gate and opened it. After closing it behind her, she hurried around the corner of the house and collapsed behind a large bush next to the garage. She sat there, calming her breathing, willing herself to relax, but her body wouldn't listen. The sounds still rattled in her head, stirring up emotions, stirring up discomfort.

She lost track of how long she sat there, her mind drifting and blank. A film of depression swirled around her, hemmed her in. Maybe it was the carefree happiness Sunny exhibited, or Meredith's relaxed, unworried manner—Casey didn't know. But the unfairness of it all slapped her hard, caused anger to well up and overflow. She hated her life, her school, her inability to be like everyone else. Hated that she couldn't wake up happy every day like Molly or Debby, couldn't get excited over simple pleasures like manicures and new movie releases.

Hated her dad's silences, her mom's incessant worrying.

Hated not being able to hold Jesse or Daniel, tease them, laugh with them.

Her laughter had died with them and was buried six feet under damp, cold dirt, along with their bodies. Cold and rotting flesh, insects gnawing their bones.

Casey shuddered. Great racking sobs shook her chest. She wished she could smash something, like her dad had done the night after Daniel shot himself. He took one of his sledgehammers and destroyed the car. Just beat it over and over, swinging wildly at the windshield, the fenders, filling the void of night, the void in their lives, with a spray of pain. Glass and metal flying in all directions. Her mom somewhere in the house. Casey standing on the front lawn and watching him, feeling nothing at all. Barely noticing neighbors on the street, whispering.

A door opened nearby. Casey heard laughter and soft talking.

She took a breath and unclenched her fists. The scowl never left her face, not even when the footsteps came close, not even when she heard the door close and someone rounded the corner, buttoning the top of his shirt. Not even when Billy Thurber stopped suddenly, almost tripping over Casey, and took a hesitant step back, studying her tear-streaked face, her slumped figure on the concrete sidewalk.

Billy composed himself as Casey's eyes widened and the shock of seeing him *there* settled over her like dust from atomic fallout. Radioactive and deadly. She imagined the look in Othello's eyes as he gazed upon his beloved Desdemona sleeping, his seemingly traitorous wife, whom he would momentarily kill. *"Ah balmy breath, that dost almost persuade Justice to break her sword!"* Tortured that such beauty would have to end. *"Be thus when thou art dead, and I will kill thee, and love thee after."*

Oh *yes.*

Maybe it was the look in her eyes that caused Billy to back away without a word. He paused and chewed his lip, then brushed hair from his face, all the while keeping watch on her. Casey's mouth dropped open as Billy walked away, down the street to his parked truck. Anger rose and sparked; fury lifted her up and carried her like an errant wave. She reached Billy at the door to his truck, with his hand touching the door handle.

She spun him around and he grabbed her arm with brute force, digging his nails into her flesh.

Her voice seethed and hissed. "How could you?"

Billy dropped his head back, smiled at the sky.

Casey's voice grew in hysteria. "Why are you smiling?" She reached over and took hold of his shirt collar, scrunching it in her fist and pulling him inches from her face. He stared hard into her eyes, his green irises shimmering. She felt his heat, smelled his skin.

She made herself into a rock, a hard piece of iron. She emptied herself of every bit of softness. There was only this bitter anger; this cheated life; this miserable, unfair existence.

This living death.

Casey let go of Billy's shirt. She didn't think. Just walked around to the passenger door and got into his cab.

Back in Meredith's yard, her notebook and backpack lay on the bricks.

Back in that garden, Casey had left other things as well. Her childhood, with all its responsibilities and manners. Her place as a naïve, obedient daughter. Her task as a keeper of her brothers' memories. She left so much in that garden that all that remained sitting in the front seat of the Ford truck was a shell, a semblance of a living, breathing human being.

She waited until Billy climbed in. He sat behind the wheel and stared at her with confusion on his face.

Casey glared back at him. "Drive," she said.

# *Chapter 27*

WHEN THE DOOR OPENED, MATT DIDN'T BOTHER TO TURN around. He held a piece of crown molding up against the ceiling in one hand and the nail pinner in the other.

"Be right with you," he called out.

He was glad he stood on a short ladder, leaning his weight against the wall, for, when he turned and saw Casey standing in the entryway, he lost his balance and slipped off. In the flash of that moment, he not only registered her mussed-up clothes and hair; her dirty, bruised face; her slumped, shaking body; but saw Daniel all over again. The way Matt had found him that night, wandering the dark, rainy road—Daniel's shocked expression, his silent torment, his disorientation from the accident.

Matt struggled with separating the two superimposed events. The one with Daniel he tore from his mind and shoved back into its cage. Casey's stark presence signified something else.

His mind screamed *no,* no more horror. He hurried down the ladder toward Casey, reminding himself that she didn't drive, couldn't have flipped a car. He pounded his heart with reassurances. No one was lying dead on the ground; his daughter could still stand and walk. These were good things, he told himself.

Matt reached out his arms, to enfold her in them, but she pushed him away.

Her withdrawing confused him. Weren't daughters supposed to find comfort in their father's arms?

"Casey, what happened?" His heart raced in fear. *Don't do this to me*, he pleaded with his eyes. *Let me be here for you.*

Casey stood, shaking in place, as if a cold chill enveloped her in the heated room. Matt studied her more closely. A black eye was forming, puffy and discolored. Another bruise welled on her upper arm. Her sleeveless shirt was ripped at the shoulder and filthy, caked with dirt, under her arm. Matt looked into Casey's glazed-over, empty eyes and saw Daniel peeking out. He shook his head to fling away the vision.

"Talk to me, sweetie. You have to tell me what happened. Were you in an accident?"

Casey snorted and shot her dad a hateful look. Matt drew back. What did that mean, that look? Frantic impatience filled him. He fought to keep it out of his voice. "Casey." He searched for magic words. "Here, sit down."

He took her hand and made her sit on the carpeting, then went into the kitchen, eyeing her, worrying she might flee. He wet a rag, wrung it out, and brought it to her. This wall she'd erected tortured him; he needed to hold her more than she needed his comfort. There had to be a key to get into that fortress, just the right phrase, the correct behavior. He had no clue.

He watched her dab her face with the rag. She spoke to the floor. "I want to go home."

Matt nodded. "Okay." They both sat unmoving. Casey abruptly stood and looked toward the street.

"I fought him. He tried to rape me. He took me to that field behind the school." Casey shut her eyes tightly. Matt held his breath, afraid she would stop talking. Afraid she would keep talking. He had little doubt who Casey's attacker was.

"I did what they teach you to do. I pulled his hair and kicked him hard. He did things — " Tears gushed down her cheeks. She buried her face in her hands.

Matt leaped from where he sat and, before she could resist, wrapped his arms around her. She struggled and tried to escape his embrace. Stunned, Matt eased up, unlocked his protective circle and let her wiggle out.

"None of this would have happened," she said, spitting the words at him, "if you hadn't been so mean."

Matt gasped. What in the world was she saying?

She straightened, wiped hair from her mouth. "I was mad at you. I wanted someone to love me ..."

"Casey," he whispered, "you *know* I love you. How could you ever think — "

"Just shut up, Dad. You never hear me out. You're always the boss, always right. Always know what's best for everyone." She paced in measured steps, stomping the floor. Matt shut his mouth, forced himself to listen. *Let her vent some steam.*

"Billy made me feel special, different. I thought he really liked me."

Matt fought the urge to blurt out, *I told you so. I warned you not to talk to him.* Instead, he said. "Casey, you have to tell me." He waited until she stopped pacing and looked at him. "What did he do to you? Exactly. I need to know."

He could see her mind working, deliberating what to say and what to conceal.

"Just this." She gestured to her body, her appearance. "Isn't that enough?"

Of course it was. More than enough.

She added, with desperation lacing her voice, "You won't tell Mom, will you? She'll freak out." She added, "Please. Don't tell *anyone*."

"Of course not, baby." He ached with the need to hold and comfort her, but she stood with her arms wrapped around herself, bundling into a tight, untouchable package.

Hard as he tried, he couldn't get Casey to say more. He led her to the truck and opened the door for her, watching every move of her muscles, the way she winced as she got into the cab, the shake of her hands in her lap as he drove.

Matt willed his face to relax, presenting an impassive and calm mask that belied the raging maelstrom underneath. When he pulled up to the house, he asked if she wanted company. He could make her a sandwich, draw her a bath. She shook her head and said she wanted to be alone. Her eyes still threw daggers, sharp ones. The fortress was still barricaded and unassailable. But, for now, that was to his advantage.

He forced himself to wait until Casey went into the house and locked the door behind her. He waited a moment longer, hoping she wouldn't notice his desperate need to hurry. He didn't want her to know what he planned to do—which was nothing less than hunt down and confront Billy Thurber.

THERE WASN'T MUCH TO SALVAGE IN THE MOTEL ROOMS RAVaged by the fire. Six units to tear down and rebuild. Jerry had wasted the entire morning screaming at his insurance adjuster over the phone. Like he believed they were shorthanded and had to send for someone to come all the way up from Ukiah?

He kicked at a burnt headrest; it broke in pieces under his sneaker. Shaking his head, he looked up at what used to be a roof and saw clouds. He grunted, thinking how not long ago he had sucked the water out of this very carpet—carpet now soaked again, from the fire hoses. All that fuss and bother, repatching the roof. Wasting his deductible allowance.

Still, the insurance would pay for a new building. That would mean vinyl-wrapped insulated windows and doors that shut properly. At least his utility bills would go down.

He'd asked about loss of income and they'd had the nerve to require three years' worth of proof of occupancy percentages for the months he expected to lose money—receipts from guests, bank statements showing revenue deposits, a guest register. He explained he'd only bought the place a few months ago and the former owners now lived in Montana somewhere. They hadn't left him any records like that. You'd think the insurance company would have a brain. They actually expected him to track down those old fogies and retrieve said documents. Like he would do that!

Jerry reached for the glass he'd set down on the threshold and drank the rest of the scotch. After what he'd been through lately, he deserved a drink to calm his nerves. Who could blame him?

He stepped out of the charred room and into the freezing parking lot. The morning's warmth had been replaced by a cold front blasting down from Alaska that rubbed his face raw. He stared at the generic white rental car and fumed. His *other* insurance company had insisted on three repair estimates, which was more than a pain in the rump to acquire. It was not like he could just drive the 'Vette around to all these places in Eureka. That car was history; they should just give him a new one. But, *noooooo*, he hadn't made enough payments to warrant that. His beautiful ride was parked in the back of Mike's Body Shop, awaiting some slob from another shop to drive over on his lunch break to look at the car and write up an estimate. Just so the insurance company could tell him to pick whichever place he wanted anyway. He was drowning in bureaucracy. *Please, someone, send me a lifeboat!*

He turned when he heard tires kicking up gravel behind him. Jerry recognized that contractor, Matt Moore, as the truck came to an abrupt stop a few feet away. Jerry set the drinking glass on the hood of the rental car and walked over to him, pulling up his coat collar to keep the chill off his neck. Jerry wondered at the dour look, waited for Moore to get out, but he didn't. Instead Moore waved him over and lowered his window.

Jerry was about to make some catchy remark about the great roofing job and what a waste that had proven to be. Then he caught the agitation in Moore's face and it shut him right up. Was Moore angry with *him?* His mind leaped to the day in the market when Moore had all but ignored him. Was the guy carrying some kind of beef about him? Had he upset Moore that day he fixed the roof? Well, whatever it was, Jerry had more pressing things to concern himself with. *You think you have problems,* he wanted to tell Moore. *Hey buddy, just look around you.*

Then Moore spoke. Jerry had to get closer; he could barely make out what Moore was mumbling about.

"I'm looking for Thurber," he said. Jerry heard venom in the words. He was all ears.

Jerry leaned closer and grinned. "I know where that punk lives. You want me to show you?" His mind raced. Just what had that kid done now? Break into Moore's job site, steal more tools? He was antsy to hear the details. And what Moore had up his sleeve.

"I think he may still be in town," Matt said. Jerry watched a parade of emotions march across Moore's face—and none of them pretty. The alcohol warmed him, actually invigorated him. Jerry urged Moore to continue, sensing a plan forming, something that involved doing some damage to Billy Thurber. Something Jerry was just aching to be part of.

Jerry saw Matt hesitate—but not from indecisiveness. Jerry could tell the guy was struggling with involving another in his scheme. He had to make sure Moore knew he could count on him. "Hey, Moore, you don't want to take on that punk alone. I'll come with you. Two against one. He won't stand a chance."

Jerry didn't give him time to respond. He walked around the truck and got in the passenger seat. He felt a stirring of excitement, like the day he'd followed Thurber up that dirt road. This was way more fun than watching movie reruns all afternoon in his dump.

Moore spoke, his tone detached and businesslike. "Thurber tried to rape my fourteen-year-old daughter."

Jerry whistled and bit his tongue. *Oh, this is good.*

Moore continued. "I don't want to report it, since it would just make more heartache for Casey. And aside from a few visible bruises, there's not enough proof to put him in jail. Maybe just to interrogate him and let him go. So I don't want to go that route."

Jerry nodded. Smart choice. Thurber would get off and gloat. Then find his next victim. He needed to be taught a lesson. "I hear where you're going with this, Moore."

Moore stared intently at Jerry. "I'm going to make this kid understand he's never going to get anywhere near my daughter again. But *I'm* going to do this, okay? Threaten just enough to make a point. I don't want you adding to the situation. Just back me up, is all I'm asking."

Moore's plan made sense. "I'm in." Jerry turned his attention out the windshield. "Ready whenever you are." He tapped his foot against the floorboard. The door to his cottage was open, but what did he care? There was nothing in there worth stealing, and Jerry had a feeling they wouldn't be gone long.

He kept picturing the look on Thurber's face when he realized his goose was cooked. Sweet, too sweet!

Moore drove in silence, turning down First Street toward the harbor. Jerry didn't ask where they were going, but he strained to look out the windows, searching for the Ford truck or the figure he had so grown to despise. He guessed it to be around three o'clock. Still a couple hours of daylight left. Few cars were parked on the street. Traffic was light. They drove slowly up and down the neighborhood, and when they got to the end of Windswept Lane — the dead-end street that ran behind the school — they both saw the truck at the same time, parked in the cul-de-sac. To the left, cliffs tumbled down to a remote beach. To the right, the overgrown field stretched out for a few hundred yards before it met with the chain-link fence that enclosed the school's baseball field.

Moore pulled up beside the Ford and parked. Thurber wasn't sitting in the truck, but he had to be somewhere around — either down on the beach or cruising the neighborhood. Why park here if you were going to grab a cup of coffee at Shorelines? The beach was the likely choice, although the biting wind would be miserable.

Moore got out of the truck and looked down the hillside toward the beach.

"See anything?" Jerry asked as he tagged along, tightening his jacket around his neck.

Moore shook his head. Jerry could tell he was looking for a trail.

"Up here." Jerry pointed. Directly off the cul-de-sac was a small hill where the bushes had been trampled down over the years by tourists seeking an easy way to the beach. Jerry had taken it a dozen times but not all the way to the water. A wooden bench situated a few hundred yards in sported a great view of the sea stacks in the water. You could watch the surfers out there, dodging the sharks. Now *there* was an insane hobby.

Moore hoofed up the trail and Jerry followed. He grunted, thinking over Moore's words, the way he planned to *threaten* the punk. Yeah, right. Jerry knew what that implied. Moore carried nothing in his hands. Smart move. You carry a weapon—even just a piece of metal or a baseball bat—and it's aggravated assault or something with a deadly weapon. Better to just use your fists—a clean fight. You could always claim self-defense. Who would know? *Two against one*, Jerry reminded himself. No way this kid would go to the cops.

Jerry was just about to mention this to Moore when they rounded a corner on the hill, pushing through thick scratchy shrubs and emerging out on a ridge. Billy Thurber sat on the bench smoking a cigarette and looking out at the water. Thurber had little time to recognize them before Moore had the punk's collar in his grasp, his face bearing down on him.

Thurber struggled to pull back but Moore's grip held. "What's this about?"

Moore's voice rumbled. "As if you don't know."

Jerry watched a smirk rise on Thurber's face as the kid spoke the words: "Your daughter's a tease, you know that?"

Excitement surged through Jerry's veins. *You are dead meat*, he mouthed to Thurber, even though he knew the punk couldn't see him. His fingers twitched impatiently, awaiting Moore's next move.

Moore's fury lashed out in the wild swing of his arms, causing Jerry to back away, out of the fray. With one hand, Moore pinned Thurber against the bench, not letting him get up. His right fist smashed into Thurber's face again and again.

Jerry heard Billy yell and plead as he struggled and pushed against Moore. Just as he thought—the kid was a chicken full of hot air.

Thurber finally weaseled out from under Moore's grip and slid off the bench. Moore's fist connected with Thurber's gut, his kidney, with a knee to the groin following the punches. Thurber moaned and tried to swing, then pushed against Moore's thigh with his leg, knocking him backward.

Sweat poured down Jerry's forehead as he thrilled at the fight.

Thurber stomped on Moore's stomach, and Jerry heard him cry out in pain. He knew he had to step in, but just as he got up the nerve, Thurber turned and faced him, like a lion about to leap on his prey. Jerry shook, from his head to his feet, but then he thought of his car—his beautiful, shiny car, smashed and broken.

Jerry roared as he lunged for Thurber. He grabbed his legs and catapulted the both of them onto the hard bench. Thurber screamed when his back smacked hard on the wood slats. Moore got to his feet, holding his stomach, and reached over and yanked Billy up by his hair. Jerry scrambled out of the way, saw blood dripping down Thurber's nose. Thurber and Moore faced off as they stood between the bench and the bluff.

Jerry struggled to catch his breath. His gasps puffed in bursts of cold steam. A sharp pain jolted his neck. This was way more exercise than he anticipated.

Even though Moore had Thurber by the hair, the punk didn't flinch. Both were breathing hard on each other. Jerry held his own breath and watched, tensing up, ready for another go.

It came quickly and ended just as fast. Moore's knee connected swiftly with Thurber's abdomen, and it looked to Jerry like he stuffed all his anger and intent into that one focused act. Thurber screamed in pain.

Moore let go and Thurber dropped to the ground, doubled over.

Jerry could tell Moore wasn't done; maybe you were never done. But Thurber's face was a pulpy mess; his nose had to be broken, and Jerry wondered if Moore had cracked the kid's jaw and cheekbone as well. He knew Moore was reining in the urge to step on Thurber's face or strangle him. He was sure tempted himself, what with the punk so vulnerable lying there in the dirt. This just made his day, being here and being part of this.

Moore wiped his face, wiped his hands on his pants, pushed hair from his eyes. He straightened and glanced at Jerry, his look cold and distant.

Thurber rolled into a ball on the ground but managed to lift his head a few inches in Moore's direction. His voice trembled between short gasps. "You'll pay for this." He turned a shaky head to Jerry. "You too."

Jerry sneered. "Oh, make me scared—you stupid punk." He looked at the kid, beaten and defeated, blowing out a lot of hot air. But he also saw a fierceness in his eyes that gave him pause.

Jerry added, "If I were you, I'd leave this town and never come back. We're on to you. The whole town knows, and your number is up, punk. So take it to heart before you regret it."

Thurber stared at Jerry, then turned and spit out blood. When he closed his eyes in resignation, Moore turned and walked back toward the truck and Jerry followed.

As he watched Moore limp ahead of him, Jerry considered Thurber's threat. He laughed, reassured himself. Everyone in town *did* know about Thurber. And Jerry knew some of his angry neighbors were just as eager to stop him. If push came to shove, Jerry knew who he could call. He had made it a point, that night at the meeting, to memorize the faces in the crowd— the sympathetic ones.

And who did Thurber have on his side? No one but his lone self. One short punk who was dumber than a bucket of rocks.

Why, by sheer weight of numbers, they had him. A shoo-in, a done deal. Why couldn't Thurber see that and just leave?

When Moore dropped Jerry off back at his motel, he said nothing. Of course, Jerry would never tell anyone what had just gone down. Moore knew that. It was their little secret.

As the truck veered out of his parking lot, Jerry stared after it, thinking about Thurber probably driving to Emergency to get his nose fixed. If he could afford it. And if he could even see straight to drive. Jerry smiled at the thought of that smug, pretty-boy face all torn up. Make it hard to seduce another innocent, unsuspecting girl—for a while at least.

He picked up the shot glass from the hood of the rental car and headed back to his cottage. The afternoon light was fading and the temperature plummeting. Maybe they'd get some early snow up in the mountains. Jerry smirked. At least the day had ended a whole lot better than it started.

And that called for a drink.

# Chapter 28

FROM HER DESK, IRENE LOOKED OUT THE BANK OF WINDOWS and saw the playground—three swing sets and a metal jungle gym—all rusty, their colorful paint peeled off ages ago. They looked the way they might after some cataclysmic event, with the chilly wind pushing the swings erratically, as if by a restless ghost. Today, with the in-school teachers' meeting, the yard was empty and desolate. The staff and teachers had left an hour ago, but Irene lingered.

During recess and lunch, she often cracked the closest window just to listen to the happy squealing of the children as they played in the yard. Sometimes she let herself drift back to those years when those sounds had come from her own kids. She would sit at her desk and close her eyes and pretend. Pretend they were still small and safe.

Until Daniel was about eight, Irene had taken little note of the minor outbreaks and disputes. Didn't all kids fight over toys, pick on each other from time to time? She couldn't remember when it shifted from normal to excessive. Daniel was the eldest; he didn't want his younger siblings messing with his things. But that was no reason for him to go into Jesse's room and stomp on the intricately constructed castle Jesse had built out of Lego blocks. Jesse was six and worshipped his older brother, often following Daniel from room to room, talking at him, trying to get his attention. And too often he ended up sulking back to his bedroom and playing ponies with Casey instead.

No one had provoked Daniel to such behavior; later he said he just felt like smashing something. Irene tried to explain to him how he had hurt Jesse's feelings, how important it was to respect others' belongings. That was the first time Irene had seen that look on Daniel's face. A look that held no understanding, as if she had spoken gibberish to him.

A moral deficiency, Matt had called it.

Like they could pump him full of moral vitamins, through incessant lecturing and disciplining, and he'd recover.

But Daniel's unpredictable outbursts only grew more frequent. Casey and Jesse learned to spot the subtle warning signs and keep their distance. A turn of the head, the shifting tone in his voice, even the slump in his posture. Then they would coordinate a silent dance around Daniel, giving him extra room, as if he had blown up like a startled puffer fish hoping to scare off potential predators.

Irene stared out at the swings, soothed by their gentle rocking. The building felt like a museum, so eerily silent with everyone gone for the day. She tried to focus on the writing assignments in front of her, but the absence of children distracted her.

Only once had she gone into Daniel's room without knocking. Unlike Jesse, who wailed easily at a skinned knee or in a tired tantrum, Daniel had rarely cried. That one time, she could hear him sobbing, even through the solid wood door. How old was he? Maybe ten, eleven. She rushed to his side, thinking he was sick. Appendicitis? Stomach flu? Even physical pain hardly ever brought Daniel to tears. He'd fall down when he was a toddler, suck in his breath, clamp down on the water pooling in his eyes, and push on.

Irene's heart had melted at the sight of him on the bed, his face buried in his pillow. She wanted to wrap her arms around him, but he pushed her away. *"Leave me alone,"* he said. *"I want to be alone."*

Irene asked him: "What's wrong; how can I help?"

That was when he looked at her with those distraught eyes, as if he saw the path of his life unrolled like a carpet before him and knew he was powerless to change any of it.

His future was hurtling toward him and that was why he cried. He couldn't get out of the way.

She stood, aware of her achy limbs. Too many hours of sitting in a hard wooden chair with her knees banging up against the metal desktop. She put on her coat and draped her scarf around her neck, stalling the short, brisk walk to her car. The classroom was so warm and comforting; she didn't want to leave and resume her role as wife and mother. She didn't want to deal with the tension—so thick and oppressive—that crouched at the entrance to her house.

At the edge of her vision, she glimpsed a shape stumbling across the field, back by the baseball diamond. At first she thought she'd seen a bear, brown and wooly, bent over and ambling through the high grass. She had heard bears came into town, rummaged through trash cans and open garages. But when the bear stumbled and fell, the smile fled her face, and recognition startled her into action. Someone was hurt.

She grabbed her keys without thinking and ran out of the room, down the corridor, and out the back door onto the playground. The arctic air slammed her with shock, numbing her cheeks within seconds. Dark, fat clouds hovered, where hours earlier a blue sky radiated warmth. Irene was sure she smelled snow. She tried to place where the man had fallen, and then wondered if she'd imagined it. When she arrived at the edge of the field, she sifted through the thick brush with her arms, wading through a prickly ocean of thistles and brambles.

She found the man lying on his stomach, face down in the weeds. He moaned as she rolled him over and then she gasped. She recognized him, more from his coat and the curls of his hair than from his swollen face caked in blood. Billy Thurber lay there, straining to open an eye, trying to focusing on her.

"Here," she said, stripping off her coat. "You're shivering. My God, what happened to you?"

Billy moaned again as she helped him sit up. She felt his tight muscles through his flannel shirt, cold as marble. As she wrapped the coat around his shoulders, she looked at the daunting distance they needed to traverse to get him inside the warm building. Maybe she should just leave him here and call 911.

She reached for her purse to dig out her cell phone and then remembered it sat on the desk in her classroom.

A cold wind assailed her and she began shivering alongside Billy. How long would it take her to run to the classroom and call for help, then come back, keep him warm? She looked him over, wondering if he was in shock, or going into shock. She didn't know what you were supposed to do except keep someone warm. There were blankets in the closet cupboard, along with her first-aid kit—mostly Band-Aids and ointment. Stopgap necessities for minor injuries. The nurse's office had much more, but she didn't have a key to that room.

Just as she resolved to chance leaving him there, she felt a cold hand on her wrist. Billy tugged on her.

"Don't leave," he said through purple split lips. "It's not ... as bad as it looks."

Irene watched him spit blood off to the side, then turn to meet her eyes. One eye was swollen shut; the other opened halfway and locked onto hers, arresting her movement.

"I should get help. I can't carry you all that way." She pointed to the pale green building that seemed to recede as she stared at it.

"I can manage. Just help me up." He struggled to his feet.

Irene grasped his arm and felt him shake. "You're being stubborn."

He wobbled as he stood, not taking his eyes off her. "You." He chuckled, then coughed and winced in pain. "You're mothering me again."

Irene caught a quick glance of a fleeting emotion—something sad that made Billy look small and frightened. Every motherly instinct kicked in, forcing out Matt's warnings that ricocheted in her head.

What did she care if this young man turned out to be violent and mean? She had heard the talk in town—not just from Matt. From other people who said Billy had set fire to that motel, and had vandalized houses and cars, stolen things. At this moment she couldn't care less if Billy had even killed someone. All she saw in his bashed-up face was a lost boy, like Daniel.

Maybe if someone, even a stranger, had stopped once and just put their arms around Daniel, would it have made a difference? If a friend at school had noticed Daniel's mood that morning, tried to cheer him up or offered him a bite of a donut, would he have changed his mind and not put that gun to his head?

Suddenly, it became clear—that every little action had immeasurable potency, creating a hundred repercussions that could set off any number of events. Like breaking a rack on a billiard table, sending balls flying in all directions. If one word could be so hurtful—sticking like a knife in your heart for the rest of your life—couldn't a different word turn everything around?

"Let's go," he muttered. "My truck's that way." He pointed back toward the cliffs.

"No, I'm taking you to my classroom. I've got first aid there."

"Whatever." He swooned into her arms. She struggled with righting him, with ignoring the freezing cold besieging her bones, slowing her down. She had visions of the polar expeditions, men wrapped in furs and trudging through ice, clinging to one another, falling down and longing for sleep. She took three steps and stopped, then started again. *Off like a herd of turtles.* They would never make it to the building this way, doing this ludicrous stumble, like two drunks, like a potato sack race.

Irene stopped and let go of Billy, watching to see if he would fall down. "Stay here. I've got to get help."

Billy's face was a tint of blue. Her heart pounded as she rubbed her hands together. "Here," she said, reluctantly unwrapping the scarf from her neck.

Billy's eyes glazed over, but he kept them pinned on hers as she draped the scarf around his neck, wrapping it in a snug circle.

Billy clawed at his throat and screamed in panic, as if she had just put a noose around his neck. Irene jumped back, imagining snakes and spiders. She watched, stunned, unable to respond to such peculiar behavior. Billy gasped, a fish out of water, panting in erratic bursts, struggling for air. Literally unable to breathe.

Irene tore at the scarf, fighting Billy's own thrashing hands, and catching a clip to her jaw. She managed to pull it off, expecting to find him choking on something, on his own blood or who knows what. Instead, to compound her surprise, the moment she removed the scarf, he inhaled a desperate breath, like a swimmer surfacing after being trapped too long under water. Like a man buried in a collapsed mine, digging his way out and finding an ocean of air.

Billy fell back and collapsed on the ground, both hands gripping his throat, all his attention fixed on finding the next breath, sucking it into his lungs.

Irene knelt beside him and laid a hand on his chest. His wild eyes searched and found a connection between the hand pressed against his heart and the arm that led up to a woman's face.

Irene shut her eyes, willing her own heart to slow down. What a scare he'd given her. What was all that about?

She felt his heart slow into a steady beat. Like a bird trapped in a cage, his heart fluttered against the palm of her hand. She pictured flapping wings, birds settling down to roost, growing quiet, their eyes slowly closing. Soon, the heartbeat pulsing through her hand matched the pace of her own, synchronous and partnered.

She dared removing her hand and opened her eyes. Billy's entire body shook violently; his teeth chattered so loudly her own teeth ached in response. She hesitated when she picked up the scarf, worried her slight movement would set off another panic attack. But Billy's eyes were empty now and they followed hers without hint of emotion as she wrapped the scarf around her own neck and relished the token warmth it gave.

Irene was past being cold. She hoisted him up, linked her arm through his, and readjusted her coat around his shoulders. Without words, they moved slowly, Irene guiding his steps across the field, through the playground, and into the school hallway, where a blast of heat met them at the door. Time had a skewed quality to it; Irene had no idea what hour it was, or how much time had passed since she found him.

Trudging down the darkened hallway, Irene thought of
Dorothy in the land of Oz, walking down the corridor in the
Emerald City amid terrifying rumblings and flashes of light,
hoping the Great and Powerful Oz would grant her request.

When they entered her classroom, Irene sat Billy down in
one of the tiny chairs. She would rather have stood under the
blower that came out of the ceiling, letting the hot air defrost
her. Feeling returned to her fingers, pins and needles, as she ran
the water in the sink, urging the water to hurry and heat. She
wrung out a rag and went to Billy, who hung his head, hair falling over his face. She put a gentle hand under his chin and lifted
it, unsure where to start on this battered landscape of flesh.

She wiped the hair out of the way and cleaned his forehead,
falling into a familiar rhythm of tender strokes. There had
been many children over the years, sitting on chairs like these,
with Irene cleaning off a bloody knee or scraped elbow. And
there had been her own children, sitting on a stool, or on the
couch by the TV, or outside on the sidewalk — after tripping
from jump rope or Frisbee or just horseplay. How many boxes
of Band-Aids had she gone through in the last twenty years?

Billy winced as Irene cleaned dirt around his eyes, but he
let her continue, with a look of surrender and compliance, of
uncertainty and disorientation.

"Do you want me to take you to the hospital? I think you
might need stitches, and you may have suffered a concussion."

He tensed. "No hospital."

He started to stand but Irene stopped him with her hand.
"Okay. I'll get you cleaned up best I can. Just let me do that,
at least." She went to the sink and rinsed out the cloth, watching the water run from muddy red to clear. As she returned
and reached out to continue, he grabbed her wrist. The warm
room may have thawed out Billy's chilled limbs but his eyes
remained icy.

"Why are you doing this for me?"

Irene stepped back and looked at Billy's grip on her wrist. "I'd do this for anyone. You just can't turn your back on someone who needs help." She paused. "Can you?"

"Being a bleeding heart doesn't get you anywhere." He released his grip and took the cloth from her hand. She watched as he rubbed his face, cleaned the dirt and blood from his short beard, dabbed at his swollen eyes, with almost vicious intent.

"Here." He handed back the cloth. He stood and took her coat off his shoulders, then set it down on the small chair.

"Wait." Irene put her hand around the back of Billy's head to hold him there, then touched his cheek with the cloth. She felt him tremble under her touch. "You missed a spot here." With soft, short strokes, she continued, then startled when a drop of water splashed on her hand.

Billy's eyes were closed, but tears streamed down his face.

He held his breath and Irene held hers.

She was back in Daniel's room, late at night after the police and paramedics had all left, and her husband and Casey tossed in their beds, unable to sleep. Jesse, whisked away in an ambulance to the morgue, lay on a cold metal table with a sheet covering him. Daniel sat in his desk chair and let her touch him, the first time in oh, so long. She had taken a tissue and dabbed a smudge on Daniel's cheek and felt hot tears splatter her hand.

These two moments, alike and disparate, each overlapping and repelling the other.

A trembling sigh escaped her throat and snapped Billy from the spell she had woven.

He knocked her hand away. "What are you doing?" His head darted, taking in the room for the first time. "What is this, a school?"

Irene backed a few steps from him, gathering up the distance he pushed between them. He limped over to the door, one hand holding the side of his face. "Where's my truck? I parked it on that dead-end street."

"I'll drive you over there. It's too far for you to walk."

Billy snorted and straightened. Ripples of pain traveled over his face. Irene watched the way he shoved them aside—a mannerism that looked practiced and honed.

"Where is it? Just point me in the right direction." His tone was brusque and impatient. The "other" Billy was back from wherever he'd gone hiding.

Without a word, Irene walked down the hall to the back door and opened it.

"There," she said, pointing to the baseball field. "Your truck's behind that fence."

Standing at the threshold, she watched him as he stumbled across the playground, impervious to the wind chafing her face. When he reached the fence and passed the place where she had found him, he disappeared from view. She knew the street was just beyond there, the cul-de-sac where he'd left his truck.

After retrieving her things from the classroom, she shut off the lights and locked the door. As she walked down the dark corridor once more, she recalled how Dorothy had looked after the Great Oz had refused her request to go home and, instead, given her the impossible task of stealing the broomstick from the wicked witch.

Utterly devastated. Overwhelmed. Homesick.

When she had knelt beside Daniel in his room, in the swallowing silence and unbearable, smothering pain, the full weight of responsibility had crashed down on her. It fell on her to find a way to lead her family out of this pit—an impossible task. In all her searching, she never did find a yellow brick road, or a good witch like Glinda to wave a wand over her head and give her magic words to recite—words that would whisk her home.

No one warned her about the *other* path and how to get off it. Or hinted that once you were on it, you couldn't see where you were going for the obscurity of the trees. You knew that more danger lurked just around the bend, but what could you do? There was no turning back, and you weren't in Kansas.

There *was* no place like home—not anymore.

# Chapter 29

"ALMA!" CELIA CALLED OUT TO HER DAUGHTER COMING IN the front door of the coffee shop. "I am so glad you are here."

She waved Alma over to the counter, then turned her attention back to making a steamed milk. Alma walked around the small after-school crowd of students gathered in front of the glass display case as Celia handed a mug to a tall, lanky boy and brushed a wisp of hair from her perspiring face. "It's been crazy in here the last hour. You'd think it was summer."

Alma joined her mamá and cleared a few dirty dishes, making room on the counter. She shed her coat, hanging it on a hook behind her in the muggy shop. "It's the cold. I don't remember it being this freezing last Thanksgiving season. Everyone is dying for something hot to drink." She listened to the kids' requests for cookies and pastries, then gave them their treats in white paper bags. Celia worked at the coffee machine, making an espresso.

Alma put the change in the cash register drawer, then watched the last two customers sit down at a table. She turned to Celia. "Where's Miguel? With *Abuelo?*"

"No, he's in the back, playing with his toy logs."

Alma listened, along with her mamá, for the patter of noise and vocalizations that always characterized Miguel's play.

Silence.

"Miguel?"

Nothing. The kitchen was quiet. Too quiet.

They both reacted at the same time. Celia rushed to the back room with Alma behind her.

"*Ay, ay*!" Celia cried, wringing her hands. "Miguel!" She grabbed Alma when she caught sight of the back door, cracked opened and letting in a stream of cold wind. Miguel was nowhere in sight. Celia flung the door open.

"Mamá, you're supposed to keep this locked—with the key! You know he can open the deadbolt."

Celia looked ready to faint. Alma felt bad for attacking her mamá, but her fear clawed at her. "Look," she said, trying to calm her voice, "he must be somewhere close by. Go back inside; I will find him."

"No, I am calling your father. And Tomás."

"*Please*, Mamá, don't do that. You'll only alarm them. And Tomás will be hysterical. Let me look first." Alma saw the fear in her mamá's eyes.

"Hurry," Celia said. "And come back in five minutes if you don't see him anywhere. *Then* I will make those calls."

Alma watched Celia go back inside the shop, then started down the footpath. She shoved the panic down. Miguel had taken this path all the way to the beach many times with his family. But there were so many places he could veer off to.

She ran, oblivious to the biting wind, thinking how cold Miguel must be. Fear overtook her. "Miguel! Miguel!" she screamed. Her mind flooded with all the ways he could be hurt. What if he ran into the street and got hit by a car? What if he fell off a cliff? She pictured the path in her mind, where the dangers lay.

Minutes fled by as she searched—agonizing minutes. Each one meant Miguel was farther away, and colder. She thought of his small body, so lean and frail. Then she thought of his asthma and tears poured down her stinging cheeks. Her heart wanted to explode in her chest.

Breathless, she ran up the steps to the back of her father's house and pounded on the door. *Hurry,* she pleaded to the door, to God. Was he even home? Maybe, she hoped and prayed, Miguel was inside with him. But that couldn't be—her papá would have called Celia right away to tell her.

"What is it?" Luis said as he opened the door. His eyes widened at seeing Alma in such a state. She tugged on his shirt.

"It's Miguel. I can't find him."

Luis steadied her with his hands on her shoulders. "Wait— he is not with your mother?"

Alma shook her head. Luis looked at her chattering teeth. "*Espérate aquí*; I'll be right back."

Alma stamped her feet and called into the bushes for Miguel. She ran over to the gentle slope that tumbled to the beach and looked down the hill. Luis came running out, putting on his coat and carrying another. He handed her the coat, then flipped open his cell phone.

Alma put on the coat and buttoned it with shaky fingers. "Who are you calling?"

"The sheriff. And Tomás. We mustn't waste any time." He pulled Miguel's inhaler from his pocket. "I brought this—just in case."

Alma felt the blood drain from her cheeks, and he took her hands in his, drew in her attention. "Alma." His voice was quiet and calm. "Let us pray, and God will help us find him, all right? *He* knows where Miguel is."

Alma nodded and closed her eyes, letting her papá's strong, confident voice fill her with comfort and hope. When he finished, he gave her hands a little squeeze. "Now, where have you looked so far, and where is your mother?"

Alma told him.

"Okay, let's keep going toward the beach," he said.


As Alma kept calling out Miguel's name, Luis made his phone calls. Sheriff Huff answered on the first ring, thank God. He was already out the door, on his way to the coffee shop, where he would gather volunteers and search from there. Luis knew how fond Joe Huff was of little Miguel.

*Please, God, keep Miguel safe in your arms. Help us find him.* He punched in Tomás's number as he trotted after Alma. He knew how Tomás would respond and wondered if he should wait just a bit, hoping to find Miguel first, with little incident. But then he pictured how angry the boy's father would be if he learned Miguel had disappeared and he hadn't been told.

Tomás answered. "Yes, who is it?"

"It's me, Luis." There was no easy way to say this. "Tomás, Miguel wandered off from the coffee shop. We are looking for him now—"

Luis heard the hitch in Tomás's voice. "I'll be right there. Where are you?"

Luis told him. "Tomás, we will find him. We all need to stay calm and levelheaded. Sheriff Huff will be here in a minute."

"I'm leaving now."

Luis put his phone back in his pocket and stood on the steps. From there he saw Alma farther down, where the grove of alders thickened. She darted from one side of the path to the other, calling for Miguel. Luis joined in with his voice, looking into the yards of the nearby homes, the few that bordered the beach trail. Two of his neighbors came hurrying out when they heard the frantic calling. When they asked where they could help search, Luis pointed up the hill.

He kept praying, knowing God was in control, that he would help them. Luis trusted God, whatever the outcome. Sometimes God allowed bad things to happen for a purpose. King Solomon had written that time and unforeseen occurrence befall all men. Just because you had faith in God did not mean you were immune from the pain and sorrows of this life. No one escaped that. Otherwise, everyone would become a Christian just to gain immunity.

But faith acted as a comfort and a safety net from grief, because no matter what happened in life, God would make it all better in the end. *"All things work together for good for those who love God."*

He just prayed it was part of God's plan to keep Miguel safe and return him unharmed to those who loved him. Oh, how his heart ached for Miguel.

Luis turned when he heard shouting behind him. There was Sheriff Huff, plodding toward him — and Tomás following. A dozen or so neighbors spread out in different directions, calling for Miguel. Soon the cold air rang out with the boy's name, like bells in a church steeple.

Luis saw the frantic worry in Tomás's expression as his son-in-law grabbed at him, clawing his coat. "Luis," he said, "you haven't found him yet? Celia says he could have been gone now for an hour!"

"Let's keep looking, then. He has to be somewhere close."

"Luis, you know how fast he can run. He could be on the freeway by now!"

Luis spoke with a calmness he hoped would infect Tomás. "He's probably at the beach. You know how much he likes to go down there."

He suspected his words lacked comfort. The beach only presented more dangers: riptides, rocks, waves. He pushed away images of Miguel drowning, his arms thrashing in deep water, his head surfacing, gasping for air. He looked in Tomás's stricken face and knew his son-in-law pictured the same things.

Tomás took off in a frenzied run, down the rickety wooden steps. Luis watched Alma turn as Tomás came alongside her, as the two of them embraced in brief commiseration, then hurried for the beach.

Sheriff Huff came up to Luis. "We've got a couple dozen folks scouring the streets." He laid a hand on Luis's shoulder.

"Thank you, Sheriff Huff, for coming so quickly, and rounding up help."

"Your wife thinks he went down to the beach. Let's go."

Luis nodded. He thought of Miguel's driftwood fort and how much fun the boy had playing in it. When it was time to go home, that last Sunday, Miguel had cried. He didn't want to leave his fort. He was afraid the waves would wash it away. Tomás had assured his son that it would still be there the next time they came back to the beach, but Miguel didn't believe him. They would probably find Miguel there, sitting on the sand, trying to add pieces of wood to the structure, to reinforce it against the elements. Luis allowed himself a smile and a glimmer of hope. He hung onto that hope, keeping it flaring, like blowing on a smoldering coal that threatened to die out.

Halfway down to the beach, Luis heard Alma yell for him. Her voice sent a stab of pain through his heart. *Oh please, God.* He pictured Miguel's battered body lying lifeless on the beach. Instead, what he saw at the bottom of the steps confused him. The scene unfolded before him—a jumble of cries and flurried motion. He tried to sift through the onslaught of impressions coming at him full force.

There was Miguel, huddled into himself, screaming at the sky: "*Él me lastimó! Él me lastimó!* He is hurting me!" A strange man held Miguel's arm at length as the boy struggled to get away from him. In the commotion, Luis couldn't make out what the man was saying, as both Alma and Tomás were screaming at him.

Tomás grabbed the man and swung a fist into his face, which caused the man to ram sideways into Miguel, knocking him down. Miguel wailed as Alma scooped him up into her arms and ran to safety. Two men tried to pull Tomás off his target and got punched for their effort.

Miguel's cries carried on the wind, and more people came running down the steps. A crowd gathered, breathless and stunned. Pushing through the mass of people, Huff strode right into the melee, separating bodies with his strong arms, telling everyone to shut up.

Tomás saw the sheriff and pointed at the man who had held Miguel's arm. "He's hurt my son! Get him!"

The man yanked himself away from Tomás's grasp, pushed hair from his face, and readjusted his twisted shirt. He backed away from the hovering crowd and turned to the sheriff. Luis took a good look at the young man and a light of recognition flicked on; now he knew where he had seen this youth before.

JOE HUFF LET OUT A BREATH AND GAVE EVERYONE A FEW seconds to settle down.

"Mr. Thurber," he said. Now here was a volatile situation, and the implications were noteworthy.

Huff studied Thurber's bruised face, with its purple and green hues and swollen flesh. Someone had done a number on that face, he surmised, but not today. Huff shelved that thought and let his eyes wander across the faces in the crowd.

Tomás, however, was not one to wait for Huff's measured advice. He lunged again at Thurber. "You hurt my kid; I'll kill you!"

"Whoa!" Huff dove between the two men. With a firm grip, he pulled Tomás back, shushing him.

Tomás shook a finger at Thurber. "What do you think, Sheriff? This is the man causing all the trouble in town—this *monstruo*. And I get down here and he is trying to take Miguel and my son is screaming, 'He's hurting me!' "

Thurber rubbed his cheek where Tomás had struck him. "Oh, for crying out loud! I was just helping him. He caught his foot in that root." Thurber pointed to the base of the last step. "I told him to calm down, but he just squirmed and made it worse. I had to use some force to get it out."

Alma came over and gripped Tomás, who pulled his frightened, shivering son into his chest and stroked his hair. Alma took off her coat and wrapped it around the boy.

Luis stepped over to Thurber, motioning with his hands for everyone to calm down. He turned and looked in the eyes of his neighbors and clearly did not like what he saw. Judgment, anger, tempers about to explode. He spoke to the agitated group surrounding Thurber.

"Please, why don't all of you go home now? We appreciate your help, but Sheriff Huff is here, and Miguel is safe. Thank you so much for your concern." He waved them off and slowly the crowd thinned amid grumblings and accusations—spoken in loud voices.

Celia came pushing through the group, waving her hands in the air and praising God. "Oh, he's safe, *gracias a Dios*!" She ran over to Miguel and knelt down, tears pouring out of her eyes. She smothered the boy with hugs and kisses.

Huff looked at Thurber, who stood on the beach with a defiant air. He watched Alma bend down and examine Miguel's foot. The boy cried out when she touched the ankle. Alma looked at Huff. "It's pretty tender."

"See? I told you he hurt it," Thurber said.

"Well, what were you doing down here?" Huff asked.

"You're kidding me, right? So now it's against the law to sit on the beach, have a smoke?"

"I'm not saying that—"

Thurber cocked his head and glared. "What *are* you saying, Sheriff?" He stopped and looked in the eyes of his accusers and his eyebrows raised. "You really think I was trying to hurt him? What—kidnap him, and do what? Demand a ransom?"

Thurber laughed but Huff noticed Tomás did not find anything funny in Thurber's comments.

"Who knows what a pervert like you would do with a small, helpless boy—"

Huff saw Tomás coil up again, like a snake about to strike. He stepped in front of him.

"Okay, that's quite enough, Tomás."

Tomás leaned down to Miguel and mumbled some consoling words. Alma kept her arm around her son, tears of relief on her face. "Please," she said to her husband, "Miguel is safe. That man was only trying to help him. Look at Miguel's foot—he's telling the truth."

"You don't know that. That could have happened when that—man—tried to take him."

"Miguel." He turned to his son. "Did you come down to the beach alone?"

Miguel lifted his little head and nodded, his lips pressed together.

"Don't cry, *chiquito*," his father said, "just tell me what you were doing."

"I just wanted to play in my fort."

"That's okay." He pointed at Thurber. "Did that man hurt you?"

When Miguel nodded, Thurber blew up. "Huff, do something! Of course I hurt him. I had to, to get his foot free. I told you that."

Huff sighed. "Thurber, you see how this looks. Why don't you explain your side of the story?"

Thurber kicked at the step, clearly frustrated. "I was sitting on the beach, over there a ways, and I saw him come barreling full speed down those steps. He tripped and fell. I figured his parents were behind him, but when nobody showed up, I went over to him. Like I said, he tangled up his foot in that root and I tried to get it out. I would have carried him up the hill and brought him to the police station—"

Tomás cut in. "Oh, sure you would. Look at you, your face. You're the kind of guy asking for a fight, looking for trouble. I've known plenty of your kind. You really think we believe your lies?" Tomás spewed out a string of phrases in Spanish. Huff had a pretty good idea of the content, even though he didn't understand a word of it.

Thurber shook his head, disgusted. "You should keep a closer eye on your kid. What was he doing running off by himself? He's what, three? Four?"

This time Tomás slipped past Huff before the sheriff could grab him. Tomás had Thurber by the throat. "How dare you—"

Huff could tell by Thurber's expression that Tomás was going to get decked. And then, no doubt, the irate dad would press charges of assault. That was the last thing Huff wanted to deal with. He grabbed Tomás's shirt and nearly ripped it in an effort to pull him off Thurber. And just in time—Billy started swinging hard but only sliced up the air.

Alma and Celia backed away, joining Luis on the steps. Miguel had quieted down and hid in Celia's skirts.

"I want you to arrest him, Sheriff!" Tomás said.

"For what?" Huff watched Thurber out of the corner of his eye, just to make sure there'd be no more arms swinging in his vicinity.

"I don't know—"

"That's right, Tomás, you *don't* know. At this juncture, it's your word against Thurber's. And his side of things checks out."

Huff made sure Thurber caught his tone. Huff was *not* happy to find Billy Thurber at the crux of yet another odd happenstance. He just kept showing up like a bad penny. But, all things considered, was it really likely Thurber had harbored some malicious intent toward the boy? It wasn't as if Thurber even knew this family, had any grudge against them, like he may have for someone like Jerry Hubble. Even if— *if*—Thurber was a criminal, responsible for the thefts and the motel fire, and maybe even for Grizz's murder, what would he be doing kidnapping a kid? Was he the type to get his jollies from hurting a little boy?

He tried to picture Thurber down on the beach, seeing this boy all alone, so trusting and innocent. Deciding to take him into the bushes and do unmentionable things to him. Huff grunted. He could guess his way to New Jersey and back— that still didn't bring him any closer to the truth. You could think you had someone pegged and then be dead wrong. Look how many people went to the electric chair and only later were exonerated. A little late to apologize.

"Go on, then," he told the family. "Look, Miguel's none the worse for wear. Maybe now he'll think twice before wandering off. Just put some ice on his foot and give him one of those giant sugar cookies." Huff saw a twinkle in Miguel's eye and gave him a big smile.

If Thurber spoke the truth, then Tomás should be grateful. Here was a stranger who'd come to the aid of his son, and maybe would have brought him back in one piece. Maybe, Huff thought as he looked at the pastor, God had used Thurber to save that boy's life. What if no one had been down on the beach and Miguel decided to play in the waves? Or he wandered around the tide pools and slipped and hit his head on a rock?

A godsend, that's what it was called. Maybe that was Billy Thurber.

Huff chuckled. Wouldn't that be a hoot?

Joe Huff stayed on the beach until everyone had gone up the steps except Thurber. Huff scratched his forehead and breathed in the fresh ocean air. He turned to Billy. "Sorry about having your truck impounded last week. Hope it didn't inconvenience you any."

Thurber stared long at Huff. "You know they didn't find anything." He was about to say something else but stopped and shook his head.

"Clean as a whistle," Huff said. He waited. "Just doing my job, Thurber."

Thurber rolled his eyes. "Yeah. Sure." He waved Huff away and headed down the beach.

The sheriff watched him awhile, then turned and marched back up the steps to town. He thought about all the people mad at Billy Thurber. The numbers were growing daily. Thinking about Thurber's beat-up face made him wonder just what was keeping the kid here. He could go anywhere and sell his firewood. He thought about the remains of Grizz Thurber and what kind of life Billy must've had, living with such a drunk. An abusive drunk, according to Sally Bones. Oftentimes, people raised with violence tended toward violence themselves. And sometimes you had to use violence to protect yourself and those you loved. Only, society determined just which violence was acceptable and which wasn't. People didn't always agree with that determination.

And what if all that violence hardened you, turned you into a disagreeable, edgy person? As you went through life, people accused you and hated you, expected you to fail and to act mean. Why, you'd end up just the way they treated you, because no one wanted to look past the outer appearance. No one had given you a chance to be different.

Maybe under all that hard shell called Billy Thurber there was a soft, vulnerable boy. Just another victim.

If Huff really believed that about Billy Thurber, he didn't believe it for long. Because not ten minutes later, as he sat behind his desk enjoying the quiet ticking of his clock, he got another phone call from Deputy Chuck Warner up in Trinity County. It seemed the coroner had missed something in the autopsy, what with the decomposing condition of Nate Thurber's abdomen. Russell had gone in a second time when he realized that this wasn't like a normal body, where an entry wound would be easily seen.

Sure enough, he had fished around a bit and found, lodged behind Grizz's right kidney, an intrusive piece of metal—hidden in a mound of bloated tissue.

A bullet.

# *Chapter 30*

IRENE HESITATED AT THE BATHROOM DOOR, THEN KNOCKED softly. She heard water running in the sink and knew Casey had been crying—again.

"Casey, sweetie, I made you some pancakes. Please come out and eat." She put her ear to the door, hoping to hear an answer, but one wasn't forthcoming. "There's still time to drive down to your aunt's for Thanksgiving." A pause. "Maybe it would do us all good to get away for a bit, get into some warm sunshine. Aunt Elaine says it's been in the seventies."

Irene stepped back when the door opened. Casey had her hair bundled up in a towel and she was dressed in Jesse's tan corduroys—her favorite pants. She wore one of Daniel's hoodie sweatshirts—two sizes too big. Irene knew that when Casey felt insecure or unhappy she disappeared in mounds of her brothers' clothing.

After coming home late from school last Friday—after that strange encounter with Billy—Irene had found Casey buried under the covers of her bed. She finally coaxed Casey out and got a look at her face. Irene was befuddled, having gone from one injury to yet another. Her first thought was that Casey had been in a fight with Billy. Why else would the both of them have such bruises in the same afternoon? But when Irene posed that question, Casey was incredulous. She insisted she had been at Meredith's, working on her science project, and when she left, she tripped over a loose board that smacked her in the face.

At first Irene didn't believe her. Casey had displayed the nervous look that usually meant she was lying. But then, how likely was it that a small teenager like Casey could inflict the kind of damage she had seen on Billy Thurber's face? Maybe if Casey had martial arts' training, she could buy it. But her daughter was hardly athletic or coordinated enough to throw more than a few wayward punches. Yet the coincidence in timing disturbed her. And ever since that afternoon, Casey had been in a deep funk, speaking little, eating less, and spending all her free time in her bedroom. There was more to that story than just a loose board. Irene needed to break through the barrier and reach her daughter somehow.

"Well." Irene tried to sound light and cheerful. "What do you think? Do you want to go down to San Diego for the week?"

Casey stopped at the doorway of her bedroom. "Would Dad be going too?"

The question confused Irene. "Of course he would." She pursed her lips at Casey's scowl. "You don't want your dad to go?"

"Never mind." Casey headed into her bedroom. Irene followed but kept a considerate space between them.

"Honey, why don't you want to spend Thanksgiving with your dad? You can't still be angry with him — about that remark. He said he was sorry. Sometimes things just blurt out, you know — "

"I know, Mom." Irene waited while Casey searched for an explanation. "I'd rather stay here. I don't think I can take all those happy people, trying to feed me and cheer me up."

Irene sighed. She knew just how Casey felt. "No one expects you to pretend you're ... well, that everything's fine and normal. They know what you've gone through and that it takes time to heal."

Casey spun around. "Why does everyone think that time is such a cure-all?" She fell onto her bed and grabbed her red dinosaur. "Just wait a few years and you'll forget all that stuff ever happened, right?" She sobbed into the plush fabric of her toy. "I don't want to wait, and I *don't* want to forget. I just want Jesse and Daniel back."

Irene's heart ached. *That's all I want too.*

She sat on the bed next to Casey and laid her hand on her back. As Casey's sobs shook the bed, Irene said, "Let's just stay home, then. We can take some walks in the park or on the beach. Maybe make a bonfire and talk about your brothers. Keep the memories alive."

Casey lifted her head and gave her mom a sorrowful look. Tears spilled down her cheeks. "Thanksgiving was their favorite holiday." She sniffled. "I always made the stuffing with Jesse, remember? He'd hold the turkey open and I would punch it in with my fist."

Irene remembered. Ever since the kids were little, they had crowded into the kitchen early on Thanksgiving morning, perched on their stools, ready to help. They each had their tasks: crumbling bread and chopping walnuts in the glass chopper, mixing the sugar in with the fresh cranberries, whipping the cream for the pumpkin pie. Smells of food would make their mouths water as they sat in their pajamas all day, playing Clue and Boggle in front of the TV. They'd watch the parade and make comments about the crazy floats and costumes.

Last Thanksgiving, before Daniel's death, Irene had done all the cooking alone, and the day had been bitter and uncomfortable. They played no games and the TV remained off. Jesse's chair sat empty, but Casey still put a place setting in front of it. They went through the motions: saying grace, passing the food, eating a little of everything, then munching on leftovers for days afterward. Daniel had picked at his food, forcing every bite down.

This would be their first Thanksgiving without either of her sons.

The thought was unbearable.

"Maybe we should just skip it," Irene said. "I mean, it's just so painful knowing they're not here to share it with us."

"It's a family tradition, Mom. If we stop, it's like saying we don't have a family anymore." Casey added, her voice shaky, "We need to do it—for them."

Her words pierced Irene, making her think of what Pastor Luis had said: They were in a place of choiceless pain. They had no choice but to suffer it and use it to build more love and stronger bonds between them. As if pain were a kind of ointment you could spread over your life, and instead of burning you, eating through you like acid, it would redeem you, salvage whatever was left.

Irene looked at Casey's anguished face. She had love in her heart for three children, but only one remained.

She drew Casey into her arms and released that love, swelling and overflowing, a torrent of need. Her daughter fell into those arms, like falling from a burning building into a safety net.

For the first time in a very long while, Irene's arms did not feel empty or powerless. For a brief moment she stopped freefalling.

For a fleeting, treasured moment, she was a mother again.

"Hey, Matt, come take a look at this."

Matt walked over from where he stood picking out paint swatches. He had hoped to get the interior of the remodel painted this week, but Irene insisted he take off the rest of the week and spend it with Casey. *If she'd have him.*

Tim Brody got up from his stool and set the open newspaper on the counter. He sipped a cup of coffee and transferred his weight off his hip.

Dottie was weighing out a bag of eight-penny sinkers on the hanging scale for Matt. "What's it saying, hon?" she asked. She took the bag off the scale and scribbled the price on the brown paper.

Ever since that night Matt railed on Casey about Billy, she had avoided him. He trembled thinking about how she had looked, standing in the middle of the room, all beat up and her clothes ripped. And how her anger spewed out at him. He figured she was transferring that from Billy. The kid had hurt her badly—not just physically, but emotionally.

Matt felt his rage returning. How on earth could a grown man take advantage of a naïve fourteen-year-old girl? He hoped he had taught the creep a lesson, but wasn't sure. Didn't guys like him just brush off the dust and go back to their sick behaviors? Wouldn't he just find another young girl to abuse?

Tim pointed to the newspaper. "Listen, you know that fella that's been causing all the ruckus around town? Isn't this his name?"

Matt leaned over and scanned the short article on page three. A man had washed up along the Trinity River last week and the coroner now suspected murder. Matt's eyes widened at the name: Nate "Grizz" Thurber.

"That's him, isn't it—the young fella." He turned to Dottie. "You remember, Dot, that strange kid who knocked over the light bulbs that day?"

"Oh, him? He's dead? Didn't we just see that truck over at the market yesterday?"

"No, this guy in the paper—he's old. Says his son was brought in for questioning, but they don't have any charges against him at this point. They don't give any details, how he was killed or anything."

Dottie huffed and leaned over to read what it said. "So the dead guy's *son* is Billy Thurber. Says so right here. I told you that kid was neck-high in mischief." She turned and looked up at Matt, who was reading along with her. "I caught him stealing, that day he came into the store."

"Well," Tim said, "you didn't *catch* him. Just suspected, is all."

She grunted and walked around to the back of the counter. "Huh, I saw him plain enough. Had guilt written all over his face." She climbed up onto the stool, her face level with Matt's face. "I told Tim about all those robberies. You heard what happened to us, about the shed being busted into? Makes me want to just up and move, with all this hullabaloo."

Matt shook his head. It seemed everywhere he turned there was another break-in. But this news wasn't as disturbing as what he'd picked up on this morning, when he stopped in at Shorelines to get his coffee refilled.

Dottie must have been reading his mind. "Well, I think that fella is the one who tried to steal stuff out of the shed. And I heard just last night that the sheriff caught him on the beach, trying to kidnap that cute little Mexican boy—what's his name?"

Tim looked up at her. "Dottie, no one said anything about kidnapping. Some even say he was helping the boy, that he got hurt."

Dottie grunted. "Oh, fat chance."

"Well, you just can't believe everything you hear, Dot."

"I can if I want to." She gave Tim a sneering smile and he chuckled.

"Yeah, you'll do that anyway." Tim turned to Matt. "So what do you make of all this rigmarole?"

Matt tried to imagine Billy Thurber capable of shooting someone, maybe even his father. It took little imagining. Matt saw Billy's face before him, his mean eyes, his biting cynicism. Like he hated the whole world. He let his mind drift to images of Billy running his hands over Casey, her resisting and pushing at him, and him laughing at her as he tore at her clothes and forced himself on her.

Sweat broke out on his forehead and he took a deep breath. He hoped Billy Thurber *had* killed his father, and that he'd be arrested and thrown in jail for a very long time—like forever. It took every ounce of control not to run to the sheriff and tell him about the attempted rape. But he'd promised himself he would keep quiet, for Casey's sake. *There isn't enough proof. Thurber would deny ever touching her.*

Matt shook off his rage, wondering if he'd made the right choice.

Choices.

Keeping quiet about Casey's attack. Beating Billy's face in. Not doing even more damage to that creep. He didn't trust his own choices, not anymore. Now he second-guessed himself all the time.

Tim touched his arm. "You all right, Matt?"

"Yeah." He forced a smile. "Yeah, I'm okay."

Dottie stared him down. "You look peaked to me." She jumped off the stool. "Oh, I just remembered."

Matt watched her scurry to the back of the store. "I think that's all I need right now." He pointed to the bag of nails, then handed Tim a paint swatch. "Do you think you can mix me up ten gallons of this for next Monday?"

"You betcha." Tim gave Matt the receipt to sign. Dottie came trotting back toward the counter with a paper plate in her hand.

"Here," she said, handing it to him. Pumpkin-shaped cookies with orange icing lay piled in a pyramid. "I made these for you and your family—for Thanksgiving. They're gingerbread."

"She always makes these for our best customers." Tim pointed at the plate. "Watch out—they're addictive. The sugar'll make your toes curl."

Matt smiled and took the cookies. "Thanks. That's very kind of you. I'm sure we'll eat every one. Casey loves gingerbread." Matt watched Tim put an arm around Dottie. "Do you go anywhere for the holiday? Have any family?"

Matt saw a shadow cross Tim's eyes and Dottie looked away.

"Nope," Tim said. "It's just us now. Our son passed five years ago. Cancer." Tim stroked Dottie's hair mindlessly. Matt was sorry he brought it up.

"And Larry—that was his name—never had any kids. Had a wife once, for a bit. That didn't work out." Tim shut his mouth and Matt saw him fighting tears. Dottie remained unusually quiet. "It's hard," Tim choked out the words, "to outlive your kids. It just isn't right."

*Don't I know?*

Matt's throat closed up like a vise. He laid his hand on Tim's shoulder and pushed out the words. "No, it isn't."

He could think of a million things to say, but, in the end, there was nothing anyone could say that didn't sound forced, that didn't cheapen the hurt a person felt. Matt certainly knew that too well. Nothing and no words could fill that hole in your heart, and right now his own hole was a gaping crater.

There wasn't enough substance on God's green earth to fill a hole that big.

Matt thought about Tim and Dottie, sitting down to a turkey dinner. Feeling keenly their son's absence. Feeling a whole lot the way Matt would feel tomorrow, staring at his plate and trying to find solace in the ritual, trying to think of all the things he ought to be thankful for.

As he said good-bye and walked to his truck, he decided to ask Irene what she thought about inviting Tim and Dottie over for Thanksgiving dinner. It would be nice, for a change, to have some company. And he knew Irene would make way too much food. Having company might also distract them from the obvious: the empty places at the table, the missing faces.

*Misery loves company.*

He had forgotten that other people were suffering in their own cauldron of pain. That everyone went through loss sometime in this life.

That there was a whole *world* of pain.

# Chapter 31

BLACK AND WHITE. PLAIN AS DAY.

Jerry Hubble read and reread the article in the *Eureka Reporter* while hunched over in his ratty upholstered armchair in front of a small TV. He had the sound turned down low on the local five-o'clock news, hoping there'd be a report on the impending demise of that murderer, Billy Thurber. *See,* he told himself while twirling the amber whiskey in his glass full of ice. *You had him pegged from the outset.* He held the glass up to the lamp, letting the dim light catch the golden liquid, the nectar of the gods. That article was just another cause for celebration. There was nothing sweeter than seeing someone get their just desserts.

He tipped the glass and swallowed the rest of the whiskey. Then he pouted. Why wasn't anything on the evening news? And why did the article say they had questioned the runt but didn't arrest him? Well, it was just a matter of time, wasn't it?

Suddenly, Jerry felt a shiver go up his spine. In a hazy, blurred memory, he saw Thurber lying in the dirt, spitting blood. "You'll pay for this," Thurber had said, glaring at Jerry with those beady little eyes. He thought about Huff at the town hall, telling him how things had to be done according to procedure. The sheriff had tried to put him in his place, that morning at the police station. Telling him to let the law take care of this. "You gotta do things by the book. Just let me do my job."

Jerry snorted and jumped up out of his chair. If Huff was doing his job, that punk would be sitting on a hard bench behind cold bars right now. How in the world did they let him slip through their fingers? *Hello? The kid's dad washes up along the river and they think the old guy just threw himself in or something? Wasn't it obvious why Thurber had hightailed it to the coast right about the time his dad croaked? Get a clue, people!* You didn't need a degree to put two and two together.

Thurber's threat rattled around in Jerry's head as he unscrewed the bottle and poured himself another glass. His mood dropped like a boulder falling into a river. Deep in his gut he knew Thurber would weasel his way out of this, just like every other time. A travesty of justice—that's what it was.

As he plopped back down in his chair, he thought about Moore's daughter and how Thurber had tried to rape the poor kid. Then he thought about that little Mexican boy—how everyone was saying Thurber had grabbed the kid on the beach and was just about to take him off in his truck when the sheriff caught him. How everyone yelled for Huff to arrest Thurber, but he let him go. Just let him walk away.

What on earth was wrong with that sheriff?

Jerry could see it now—the cocky look of triumph on Thurber's face. He thought Moore had taught him a lesson, had wiped that smug expression from the punk's face. But now Jerry realized that little show of discipline had never even fazed Thurber. Just made him more bent on trouble. Obviously, Thurber was capable of all manner of evil.

It was high time he was stopped, once and for all. If they waited for the "law"—as Huff put it—to resolve matters, it would be too late. Way too late.

It was already too late.

An idea formed in Jerry's foggy brain as he set down his glass. An idea that had him trembling from his head to his toes. Pinpricks of excitement raced through his gut and made his heart pound fast and hard. He thought of Thurber, hiding out in that camper, up that dirt road, thinking no one knew where he lived. He thought of the looks of fear and anger on the faces of his neighbors at that town hall meeting. Well, there'd be another meeting. But this one wouldn't be announced. And Sheriff Joe Huff would *not* be invited.

With shaking hands, Jerry reached for the phone book and thumbed through the white pages. He made a list in his head but didn't write it down. Nothing would be put on paper that could give his plan away. He picked up his phone and punched in a number and listened to the rings.

*Justice would be served*, he told himself, humming a little tune as he waited. *A dish best served cold—just like revenge.* Nothing colder than lying at the bottom of the sea with a weight attached to your ankle, just shark bait.

And that's where he planned for Billy Thurber to end up— as soon as it could be conveniently arranged.

# Chapter 32

THE FRONT DOOR OF THE CAMPER SWUNG OPEN. FINALLY.

Joe Huff stood back a ways and let out a breath. Deputy Warner had knocked and announced himself plenty loud, and they'd all heard the rattling inside. The two deputies flanking Warner had their service revolvers drawn and aimed at the door. There was no telling if Thurber had that rifle or not. Or any other unregistered gun, for that matter.

If Thurber was flustered, he didn't show it. He took in the assembled group, his gaze coming to rest on Huff. "What's this about, Huff?" He rubbed sleep from his eyes. "It's not even seven a.m." He stood at the door to the camper and buttoned up his Levis in the frosty air. "And isn't this a holiday? Shouldn't you be off cooking a turkey somewhere?"

He stared at the weapons aimed at him and held out empty hands. He turned to Deputy Warner and gave him a scolding look. "Is this supposed to intimidate me?"

The deputy signaled his men and they holstered their guns.

Huff grunted. Yeah, it was Thanksgiving, and the sooner they got done with this search, the better. Wanda had not been happy when she got the phone call late last night, with Huff saying he'd be late. Wanda had the patience of a saint—unless his delays spilled into holidays with the grandkids. No matter that Thanksgiving was a "white man's" celebration, and one that oversimplified the role of Native Americans in the "founding" of this nation. Huff shook his head just thinking about it. Whites hadn't "founded" America; they pretty much annihilated the existing cultures with their imported diseases. But Huff still celebrated Thanksgiving. He and his family had plenty to be thankful for. Right now he would just be thankful if they could hurry this up so he could hit the road.

Huff watched Warner hand Thurber the search warrant and relaxed when Thurber went back inside the camper. The warrant specified the one rifle, a Winchester .30–06. They had no allowance to tear the place up looking for anything else. But—and that was a big "but"—Thurber could have other weapons, not just the one registered to his father. So he knew Thurber was not going to be happy when they asked him to step outside for a bit while they looked for any other rifles. Fortunately, the camper was pretty tiny. Huff looked around at the rusted car chassis and other junk in the yard. Maybe Thurber had thought to hide a rifle in that mess somewhere.

After the coroner had found that bullet lodged in Nate Thurber's gut, Deputy Warner had gone back up to the cabin and done a thorough search, inside and out, looking for guns, and for any signs that a weapon had been discharged anywhere on the premises. All he found was an unopened box of bullets, which he confiscated. If they did procure the rifle, they'd do a firing test on it with those bullets and see if they came up with a match. Guns of the same type tended to leave similar marks; you had to be sure you ruled out some other rifle.

And then again, different brands of bullets fired out of the same gun could take on different markings. Who's to say Billy had used his father's bullets? He could have bought a different brand. That is—if he *did* shoot his father with that particular weapon. An expert would need to compare the striations on the test bullets and the breech face markings and make a determination.

Huff wandered around the yard, nosing into the caches of rusted metal. When Thurber came out with the rifle, he snorted. *What a surprise.*

Warner took the rifle from the kid, then told him to step outside.

Thurber's jaw dropped. "You gotta be kidding. You asked for the rifle and I gave it to you." He looked over the warrant he held in his hand. "What are you saying now? That I shot my father? No one said anything about a gunshot wound."

"A further look at your dad's body revealed a bullet." Warner nodded at the rifle. "Shot from a .30–06."

Thurber chewed on that for a moment. He sure didn't seem to care much about that new bit of information. "So?" he said. "Probably the most common rifle out there. Just about everyone up in the hills has one." He reached inside his camper and pulled out a pack of smokes. As he lit one, he added, "Probably got shot trying to rob a liquor store."

Huff listened to the tone in Thurber's voice. He didn't sound worried or frantic, only annoyed. It'd be nice if they could bring Thurber in and hold him until they could rule out that Winchester had been used to shoot Nate Thurber. The coroner said the findings were inconclusive. Had that bullet killed Grizz or just wounded him? Regardless, the most they could legally do was detain Thurber for a few hours. The lab at the Department of Justice in Sacramento would take days to run tests, especially with the holiday. Maybe they'd have probable cause that Billy Thurber fired at his father.

But since it couldn't be proven that the bullet was the cause of death, what did they really have? A big nothing, that's what.

Assault with a deadly weapon? With no witnesses, no one to contradict Billy if he claimed self-defense? What if it *was* self-defense?

Huff could imagine a big strong guy like Grizz Thurber, drunk and feisty, getting mad at his kid and pulling the rifle on him. Billy grabbing the weapon, trying to yank it from his dad's hands. Flipping it around in a scuffle, Billy maybe trying to fire it off at the ceiling, unload the chamber. Accidentally hitting Grizz instead. Who was to say?

No one—that's who.

Huff's only option to insure Thurber didn't disappear was to set surveillance on him, but given the lack of direct evidence in this case he doubted the department would comply. And he, to be sure, was not going to give up his family time to play cat and mouse with Thurber.

He thought about the article in the paper—and how it would fan the suspicious mood in Breakers. Add that with the discovery of the bullet in Grizz's gut—which no doubt would worm its way into the next edition of *The Reporter*—and, well, that was a recipe for disaster.

While Warner and his men went inside the small camper, Thurber sat on a stump and finished his cigarette opposite Huff. He took a long drag and squinted at Huff in the crisp morning light coming up over the mountain. "You're loving this, aren't you?"

Huff smiled big. "Just doing my job."

Thurber scowled and spat on the ground. He said nothing more.

Ten minutes later Warner came out and stretched the kinks out of his back. His two deputies followed suit. Must have been a bit cramped in there.

"Okay," Warner said to Huff. "We're out of here." He turned to Thurber. "I'm trusting you to stick around."

Thurber laughed at that. "Like you really trust me. When do I get my rifle back?"

"When we're done with it. If it checks out clean. If not, well then, I guess we hang on to it a bit."

Huff could tell Thurber didn't like the way that sounded. "Whatever," was all he replied.

Huff stayed behind after he'd said his good-byes to Deputy Warner and watched the cruiser rumble down the narrow driveway, kicking up a whirlwind of dust. He thought of the great time ahead, pigging out on turkey and dressing and pecan pie, his wild grandkids tearing up the house, pumped up on sugar. Then he thought about Billy Thurber as he watched the kid smoke another cigarette, sitting on an old stump in front of a beat-up camper, alone without a friend in the world, for all Huff could tell. There had to be some pain in all that—not having any family to go through life with, to soften the hurts and be there to lift your spirits when they needed lifting. Could make you plenty ornery.

Huff tried to think how he'd feel—going through this life of hard knocks alone. He imagined how lonely he'd be, what that loneliness would drive him to do. He didn't even want to consider it and knew he was lucky he didn't have to.

But Billy Thurber had to. That was his life, his reality. Maybe his fault too. He could seek out friends, start his own family. If that's what he wanted. Maybe he liked being the loner, the outcast. He could pull off crimes at no risk to anyone other than himself. Doing what he wanted, when he wanted, answerable to no one.

But everyone was answerable for what they did.

You break the law, you answered for it, unless you were lucky enough to get away with your crimes. In the end, though, you were still answerable to God. Huff wasn't sure what he believed about God, but he knew in his gut that someone put that conscience in man and expected it to be listened to. That you felt guilt for a reason, that there were higher laws of right and wrong, and those laws were written in your heart. He only wished that if God existed and had given man a conscience, he would have given them a better model. One that really stopped people from doing bad things, hurting others. That was his only real beef with God—that he didn't make people just plain nicer. Why was being a decent and kind individual the exception instead of the rule? How hard would that have been for God to do?

Huff turned to Thurber, whose eyes questioned why the sheriff was still there, standing in the middle of his driveway.

"You doing anything for Thanksgiving?"

Thurber only grunted.

"Well, I'll come by on Sunday and bring you some leftovers. My wife bakes a mean turkey—and chocolate pecan pie."

Thurber narrowed his eyes. "And why would you go to all that trouble?"

Huff shrugged as he walked over to his Jeep and opened the door. "I guess 'cause I'm one of those rare nice guys."

Thurber stuffed his hands into his jeans pockets and said, "Whatever." Then headed into his tiny camper, shutting the door firmly behind him, leaving Huff standing outside, marveling at the beautiful Thanksgiving morning.

# Chapter 33

JERRY PACED ACROSS THE ROTTING PIER PLANKS. THE FRUMPY lady who worked at the smokehouse had told him yesterday how he could meet up with those fishermen. Saturday afternoons—that's when they often came back to harbor and brought in their catch. In the last two hours only one boat had puttered in, and that was a family out bottom fishing in the shallows along the coast. They couldn't tell him if there were any other boats out there—not in this sketchy fog.

Jerry reached the end of the pier and looked out over the railing—for the fiftieth time. Small waves lapped against the pilings. Seagulls swooped and pecked at each other, floated in the swells like decoys. A couple dozen boats tugged at their mooring lines, rocking back and forth in the murky green water.

Jerry caught that Chinese guy staring at him through thick glasses while leaning against the doorway of his bait shop. He remembered the small man's rapt attention during the town hall meeting. Maybe he should go and talk to him as well. Could he be trusted?

Jerry pursed his lips in aggravation. Well, could anyone be trusted?

He knew the answer to that one. As if on cue, the picture of his devious wife intruded into his awareness. How she'd drooled over that hotshot lawyer, with his fancy suit and polished shoes. How stupid did she think he was? He bet she'd paid for that grease bag's legal services with more than just cold hard cash.

Jerry forced his mind to concentrate on the matter at hand. There was nothing illegal about getting together with a few guys and having a little chat about things. Make a few suggestions, see how well they flew up the flagpole. Feel out the mood and maybe stir up some action.

He smiled thinking about the bit of action he'd had with Moore that day, when they trashed Thurber. You could get addicted to that thrill, that satisfaction of giving someone their due. Why, he should have gone into law enforcement instead of fire fighting. He sure would have been a lot tougher than Huff when it came to rounding up criminals.

Just as he planned to walk over to talk with the Chinese man, he saw a fishing trawler enter the harbor. He squinted and read the name on the boat as it punched through the bank of fog. *About time.* He dug his hands into his pockets and noticed their shakiness. As much as he'd wanted to start the day with a stiff one, he knew this business was serious, needing all his senses on full throttle. He'd nearly run out of his house as soon as he dressed and brushed his teeth, buying a cup of coffee along the way. He didn't trust himself to stand in the kitchen waiting for the coffeemaker to dribble out into his cup. Not when the machine sat under the cupboard that housed his whiskey.

He gave himself a figurative pat on the back. He was in control, on his game. His whiskey wasn't going anywhere, anyhow.

Already this morning he had spoken with that Mexican guy—Tomás. Boy, was he shook up from that incident on the beach with Thurber and his kid. Tomás had listened to Jerry's hints about needing to take some harsher measures against Thurber, and he was all for it. Just name the day and time, he said. And he offered to bring a couple of tough guys he knew that would "provide support." Perfect!

Jerry had left the restaurant feeling pumped. He'd made a few more stops at folks' he knew, reminding them how the old-timers were scared now, locking their doors. How these robberies were growing and nothing was being done about it. How his motel had been burned down. He saw the anger in their eyes—all of them. Folks who had lived in this sleepy town all their lives and were fed up with the unrest over the last two years. Fed up with Huff dragging his feet and making excuses. Yessiree, the time was ripe for action. Some of these guys were loggers, truck drivers. Big, strong, fearless NRA members who oozed patriotism. Who knew the Constitution guaranteed a man's right to defend his country, his town, and his family. Especially if the government failed to do so. He saw the admiration in their eyes for what he was trying to do.

So when the two young fishermen tied off their skiff and clambered up the steps to the pier, Jerry approached them with confidence. He took them aside and they listened while he gave his rehearsed speech.

He didn't have to say much before the redheaded guy named Zack interrupted him. "It's about time someone put that jerk in his place."

The other man, who said his name was Randy, hesitated. "I don't know what you guys are going on about. You're just asking for trouble." He looked over at Zack. "I thought you didn't want any trouble."

Jerry saw Zack cringe. "Listen," Zack said to his partner, "maybe you should just go get the truck, okay?"

Randy shrugged and headed toward the parking lot. Zack watched him leave, then turned to Jerry. "He doesn't get it.

That guy's a few bricks short of a wall." He lowered his voice. "I know some guys who might think Thurber is a problem. How many are you looking for?"

Jerry's eyebrows raised. Too many and this thing could get out of hand. But then again, the more involved, the more intimidation and the less likely anyone would talk. You rat and you have a whole lot of people coming after you. "We're just going to have a little talk. Anyone interested can come, but this is a *private* thing, if you get my drift."

Zack nodded, his eyes on the truck rattling up to the end of the pier and parking. Jerry told him the place and time. "I'll be there. You can count on it," Zack said.

Zack shook Jerry's hand and smiled. Once more, Jerry noted that look of relief—a look he'd seen on a lot of faces today. As he watched Zack climb up into his truck, he remembered how he'd felt all those years, fighting fires and saving people's homes. It felt good, doing his civic duty and risking his life to make a difference. What was he doing now? Running a dumpy motel. What service did that give to humanity? Zilch.

Now he had a chance to do something even better, something that could save more lives and heartache in the future. Yes, putting Billy Thurber out of commission was a kind of civic duty. Maybe he wouldn't win any medals or get a written commendation. He chuckled. Maybe his was a thankless job, in the end.

*But someone has to do it. May as well be me.*


"There're a lot of sand dollars on this beach, aren't there?"

Billy Thurber jerked up from his crouched position and shot Irene a hostile look. "You scared the daylights out of me. You shouldn't sneak up on a person like that."

"Sorry." She kicked at the sand with her shoe. "I didn't think I was sneaking. The surf is awfully loud."

Billy cocked his head and studied her. Irene studied back, noting the bruising had all but faded from his face. "You look a whole lot better than the last time I saw you."

Billy turned and gazed out at the horizon. "I guess I owe you one."

Irene gathered it was his way of saying thank you. "You're welcome." She came up alongside him. "What happened to you, that day?"

Billy kept his back turned, then started walking along the water's edge. Churning waves folded onto the beach, sending sheets of cold water up around his bare ankles. She interpreted his silence as a brush-off. Getting more than a few words from this boy was like pulling teeth.

"Isn't that water freezing? I don't know how you can wade in it like that."

Billy stopped and faced her. "What's with the small talk?"

"I'm just trying to be friendly. Is that a crime?"

She got a grunt for her answer.

Fog buried the cliffs behind her, but out over the water the gray clouds shredded into wisps, with sunshine rippling the surface of the sea as if draping it with a million diamonds. Matt was up on their roof, fixing the small leak, and Casey had retreated back to her room right after breakfast, reading *A Winter's Tale*. Irene had wished she had a place to hide out, to shut out the world. Instead, she cleaned the house, folded laundry, washed dishes, then found herself pacing the living room — wearing a proverbial hole in the carpet. Impulsively, she grabbed her heavy winter coat and drove down to the pier. Now that she had walked for an hour in the fresh air, she wondered why she didn't do this more often. The ocean had a way of chasing thoughts from her head, erasing her edginess and anxiety, even if it left her numb and empty.

She walked closer to the water and looked at the spattering of rocks and shells in the scribbles of sand. She noticed Billy had ventured up the beach and sat on a log that looked as if it had been tumbled in the ocean a few years and then spit out. He sat there, watching her, smoking a cigarette. When she approached him, he kept his eyes on her. Maybe trying to scare her away. Well, it wasn't going to work.

"Here." She handed him a sand dollar. He took it from her and looked at it. "I once saw a live one—on a trip to the Caribbean. Did you know they are funny creatures with little spines—like porcupines?"

"Thanks for the biology lecture."

Irene sighed. "Why are you so negative about everything? Isn't there anything that makes you smile? Don't you have a smile in there somewhere?"

Billy pinched his lips together. "What's to be happy about?"

*Good question.* Irene sat on the log beside him. "Someone once said to me: 'Gratitude is the best attitude.'"

Billy made a sour face. "You're kidding me, right? Didn't you tell me your son shot himself in the head? You grateful for that?"

A pain stabbed Irene's gut. She fumbled with her words. "I have other things to be grateful for. My husband, my daughter. My health."

"You lose those things in the end."

Irene turned and searched his eyes. "Of course you do."

"So what's the point?"

"Well, aren't you grateful for anything? I mean, maybe if you spent more time thinking about that, instead of how rotten things were, things you can't change, you'd be happier."

Billy turned to face her. His eyes bored into hers. "Listen, Irene." He spit out her name, like a bitterness in his mouth.

"Why don't you leave me alone?" He jumped up from the log and started walking away.

She followed after him. "Don't you want to be happy?"

"Do you? Is that what you do every day—try to find a way to feel happy? Like *happy* is the ultimate goal? Like *happy* will erase all your pain?"

"No, I think I spend each day trying to make sense of things that are inexplicable." She sighed. "Maybe that's just as futile as trying to find happiness."

"Ya think?" He snorted and picked up his pace, hurrying down along the water's edge. "Maybe you should just work on your gratitude."

Irene wished she could understand bitterness. Was it a disease? Why had it so afflicted Daniel, but not Jesse or Casey? Why did some kids find life manageable, if not easy, and others struggled like an animal trapped in quicksand? Jesse had seemed so content, so oblivious to the things that tormented Daniel. She was sure it had to do with temperament. Jesse hadn't cared if he fit in with a group of kids or worried if his friends liked him. His easy confidence had drawn admirers to him without any effort on his part. Conversely, the harder Daniel had tried to fit in and be accepted, the more he had been repelled.

Irene observed it even in the third-graders. How the boys vied for attention, horsing around, taking sides. She saw how their small cruelties caused pain. She thought of Corey, the chubby Yurok boy—a sweet, quiet child who loved to draw. The other boys picked on him relentlessly, especially at recess. One time Matt had come to visit her during lunch and saw what was going on in the yard. Three boys surrounded Corey, and even though Matt was a good fifty yards away, the moment he realized what was happening, he strode over to the leader of the little pack—a wiry blond boy—and lifted him two feet into the air by his shirt collar. He was petrified by Matt's fury and nearly crumbled when dropped back to the ground. Irene couldn't hear Matt's lecture, but she had a good idea what he was saying by his emphatic gestures. After that, the boys left Corey alone. Irene saw how he pretended to ignore his classmates' contemptuous looks, but no doubt Corey felt them keenly.

Irene caught up to Billy, breathing hard. She yanked on his shirtsleeve and he spun around and faced her. "Tell me—did you do those things—the break-ins, the fire? People are blaming you."

Billy tipped his head back and stared at the clouds. "What do you think?"

"I don't think you did."

Billy turned and scowled at her. "That's because you only want to see the good in people. That motel guy—he got what he deserved, having his place torched. You want to believe a 'nice young man' like me could never cross that line. Well, you're living in a dream."

He took the sand dollar out of his pocket and snapped it in half. "I'm broken—like this. Stop trying to fix me." He dropped the halves into her hand. "It's a waste of your time. And mine."

He pushed his hand hard against Irene's chest and knocked her backward onto the sand. The fall knocked the wind out of her. As she struggled to sit upright, she wondered at the flush in Billy's cheeks and his twitching hands. She watched him stomp off, then looked down at the broken shell.

Wasn't there a poem about the sand dollar? She shook out the halves and five ragged pieces of shell fell into her palm. A verse came to mind. *"Five white doves awaiting to spread good will and peace."* Something good comes out of something broken.

She looked closer. They did resemble small birds. But then again, it was all in how you saw them. Maybe to someone like Billy Thurber they'd just look like a bunch of broken, meaningless pieces.

Just like the fragments of life.

It was all a matter of perspective.

# *Chapter 34*

ALMA KEPT ONE EYE ON TOMÁS AS SHE CUT UP MIGUEL'S
food. All evening her husband had been acting strange: pacing, fidgeting, staring into space. Ever since that horrible day
when Miguel wandered off, a sullen mood had hung over him,
and he waved her away whenever she asked what was bother-
ing him. Even today, after church, he didn't want to have lunch
with her parents. Just wanted to go home and rest.

He did look exhausted. Maybe the restaurant was wearing
on him. He needed more help in the kitchen, and she could only
do so much, what with serving and clearing dishes. Maybe she
should suggest he close the restaurant two nights a week instead of one. They needed the money, *ciertamente,* but not at
the expense of Tomás's health.

She looked at her husband's plate. "Tomás, you've barely
touched your food. What is wrong, *mi amor?*"

"Nothing," he said, poking a fork into his rice. Alma watched
him take a few token bites, but she saw through his ruse. Something was definitely wrong when her husband lost his appetite.

"Miguel," she said, wiping sauce off her son's face, "go
get in your jammies, and then you can watch your cartoon."

Miguel scurried down from his chair and ran into the back bedroom. Alma leaned over and touched Tomás's hand. He put down his fork.

"Now," she said, "I want you to tell me what is *really* going on. Are you sick?" Her tone made it clear she would not settle for an excuse. Tomás knew that once she hooked her teeth into something, it was no good trying to hide from her. She would wear him down and pry it out of him one way or another.

"Alma, there are some things men need to do, and they don't need to involve their wives."

The edge in his voice set off alarms. She looked into eyes that were distant and brewing. "Tomás Antonio! You better spill those beans right now, or you will send me to an early grave. Just what are you planning?"

He slapped the table and pushed his chair back. "Alma! You don't understand. Do you have any idea what I felt when I saw little Miguel struggling in that monster's arms?"

"Tomás, watch what you say!" She tipped her head at Miguel, who had come back in the room and planted himself in front of the TV a few feet away. As she slipped a DVD into the machine, Miguel picked up the remote and pushed buttons. "Not so loud, Miguel."

She took a seat at the table. "I know how you felt. I felt it too. But Miguel was not hurt, and maybe that man was just doing a kindness."

Tomás grunted. "See, you are so blind and trusting, Alma. You want to believe that no evil can touch us, that God is watching out for us, our family. That we have some special protection. Well, there is a saying: 'God helps those who help themselves.' He expects us to do what is necessary."

"Yes, Tomás. But he also tells us to make room for God's wrath. Vengeance belongs to him. We are to love our enemies and pray for them. Not act as judges in his place."

Tomás pushed his chair back and stood. "Fine. You pray. But I am not going to sit on my rear and hope God will do something about evil people like that. Especially when they are threatening my family."

Alma threw up her hands. "No one is threatening us. You are so paranoid."

He leaned closer and gave her a stern look. "Well, you are hiding your head in the sand. And while you are there, this— dangerous person—is running around, free to do as he pleases. Tell me, Alma, how will you feel when you learn he has maybe killed some child—just like he killed his father?"

Alma's throat choked up. She buried her head in her hands, listening to Tomás walk across the living room. When she realized he had opened the door, she looked up. Tomás zipped up his coat and grabbed the car keys off the wall hook.

"Where are you going? Tomás, please tell me."

"Just a meeting. No one is *doing* anything. We're going to talk, that's all."

Alma had seen that look on her husband's face before. Back in their old neighborhood, when he and his friends learned who was stealing their cars. Alma had overheard Tomás on the phone, heard him discussing "plans" to fix the problem. A few days later, the paper ran an article about a mysterious death. This car thief had been discovered in a pool of blood in the alley behind her father's church. Shot five times with a handgun to the head and chest. No one was arrested; no one saw the crime. When she questioned Tomás, he said it must have been gangs. He shrugged it off, like he didn't care. But his eyes hid something. Just like now.

Alma put her hand to her heart and willed it to stop pounding so hard. She watched as Tomás kissed Miguel on the head and left the house, slamming the door behind him. Then she went over to the kitchen phone and punched in her father's number. When he answered, she tried to calm her voice, but it wavered in fear.

"What is it, Alma? Is Miguel all right?"

"*Sí*, Papá. But I need to speak with you about Tomás." Her voice caught in her throat. "Please, just come over. I am so frightened."

"I will be right there, *querida*."

Alma hung up the receiver. Why was it so hard for her husband to trust God? Seeing him like this broke her heart. He used to have such strong faith, kept his temper in check. And now—she didn't know what Tomás believed. He was letting fear take over. Trusting in his own strength and desire for justice, instead of waiting on God.

Tomás's words rang in her head. "*Fine. You pray.*"

Yes, that was what she would do—pray. A sense of helplessness washed over her. That was all she *could* do. Pray for Tomás to stay out of trouble. And pray for that young man. That God would protect him and deliver him from evil.

She lowered her head and squeezed her eyes shut.

*God help us.*

# Chapter 35

*WHAT'S THIS ABOUT?* MATT WONDERED AS HE DISCONNECTED the call. Jerry Hubble had sounded agitated, and his vague hints made no sense. *Drunk. Must be.*

He imagined Hubble sitting in his little box of a house, all alone, concocting schemes and letting his imagination run wild. He should never have taken Hubble with him that day. His business had been with Thurber alone. But Matt knew why he'd wanted Hubble along. He'd been afraid of what he would do with no one to keep his anger in check. He hadn't trusted himself and the force of his rage—like that really helped. It had been a wise choice at the time. Now he wasn't so sure.

"Who was that on the phone?" Irene asked. She sat on the sofa, leaning over a pair of Matt's jeans, stitching a patch. A fire crackled in the woodstove and rain pattered on the roof. Strains of classical guitar filtered out from Casey's room, where she lay on her bed reading. Matt stood at the kitchen counter, thinking how almost peaceful the house felt. Almost, if it weren't for the absence of Daniel and Jesse—an absence that screamed into every little corner of the house, of their lives.

Matt exhaled in frustration. Peace was that feeling you had when everything in your life clicked into place, when you woke up in the morning and couldn't wait to face the day. When all those you loved were safe and sound. Meaning, people rarely experienced that peace, even though they yearned for it with all their heart. You had pockets of it, single instances in time that were like gems in the dust. And even then, the gems were fleeting, slipping through your hands.

Maybe the only real peace lay in knowing that one day this horrid life would be over.

Matt thought about the strong faith he had once embraced. He had been taught that faith had to be tested to be of any value. That trials refined your faith, like gold put through the fire. And all the anguish would produce the outcome of faith, the salvation of your soul. That you had an inheritance waiting for you in heaven—imperishable, undefiled, and unfading. Now he wondered if he would ever get that faith back. What did he care about his own salvation? He only hoped the promises were true, and that Jesse and Daniel *were* in God's arms right now and that one day they might all be reunited. Right now that was just too much to believe, to hope for.

Matt pocketed his cell phone and went over to the woodstove, turning his hands in the rising heat. "That was Jerry Hubble—the motel owner down the way. He wants me to come over."

"Now?"

Matt nodded. "He sounded drunk. I guess I should go—see if he's okay."

Irene set her stitching in her lap. "That's odd, calling you. But maybe he's lonely. I heard he was recently divorced."

Matt thought about Hubble's volatile, abrasive personality and tried to imagine him married. It took some doing. "I'm sure I won't be long."

When he swung his truck into the motel parking lot five minutes later, he was surprised to see a half dozen vehicles parked in front of the bank of dark rooms untouched by the fire. Hadn't Hubble shut down his business until his repairs were completed? He stepped out of the cab and looked around in the dark, through the mist of light rain. Not even the motel sign was illuminated.

A door opened—one of the motel rooms—and Jerry Hubble stuck out his head. He waved Matt over and whispered. "In here, Moore." He heard hushed, angry voices on the other side of the door. The curtains were drawn closed.

Matt entered the dimly lit room and was surprised to see a group of men sitting on chairs in a loose circle. He recognized a few of them; some he had seen at that town hall meeting. They nodded at him or mumbled hellos, but the tone was serious and tense. Just what was Hubble up to?

"I didn't want to say anything over the phone," Hubble said, motioning Matt to an empty seat. "I wasn't sure if there'd be anyone else listening."

"So what's going on here?"

"Billy Thurber. We're trying to decide what to do about that punk. We're tired of Huff shuffling around and letting him get away with everything."

Murmurs traveled the room; Matt watched heads nod.

Matt saw seething hatred in the eyes of the Mexican man. "I caught Thurber grabbing my son, and I saw the look on his face. You can't tell me he wasn't planning something horrible."

"Well, here's something else you guys don't know." Hubble nodded toward Matt, a sly smile on his face. "Thurber tried to rape Moore's daughter. Beat her up pretty bad, but she got away—"

The group of men exploded into a heated argument. Matt glared at Hubble, who gloated over this private bit of information he'd just fed to the wolves. How dare he tell total strangers about Casey! He now understood what Hubble was up to: working these men into a fury that would demand action.

He sat quietly in his chair as the men argued. Some stood and faced each other in the middle of the room.

"We need to take this guy out."

"Whoa, nobody said anything about violence here!"

"Why not just teach him a lesson?"

Hubble jumped into the verbal melee. "We already tried that—me and Moore. Beat the daylights out of him. And then he just went after Tomás's little boy. It'll only rile him up and he'll do something even worse next time."

"I read how they found his father's body up on the river. Shot and killed with a rifle."

"Yeah, and Huff confiscated that rifle just the other day—from Billy Thurber," another said. "And they didn't even arrest him. It's obvious he murdered his own father."

"If he could do that, he could kill anyone," Jerry said.

"Well, if we're going to do something, I say no weapons and make it look like an accident." That from an older man with a weathered face.

Tomás pushed into the middle of the crowd. "We can all take this punk out. Let's tie him up and dump him up in the hills, far away. Where he'll never make it back alive."

A young man with red hair and a thick moustache spoke up. "Then you'd worry every night in your bed, wondering if Thurber was lurking outside your window. You want to live in that kind of fear for the rest of your life? I sure don't."

A big muscular man held out his hand to stop the talk. "We can wear masks or hoods. He wouldn't know who we were. It's dark out. We'll have flashlights shining in his eyes. He won't know what hit him."

The redhead groaned. "He'll figure out who did it. And then what?"

"Wait—you gotta hear my great idea!" Hubble said. "We knock him out and tie him up. Then we load him into Zack's boat and dump him out at sea."

The room got quiet as the men weighed the efficiency of the deed against the risks of getting caught. Hubble continued. "Look, a few of us go up to Thurber's place. I know where he lives. We bind and gag him and throw him in the back of Moore's truck—"

Suddenly, Matt realized what he was getting sucked into. These guys were really serious. It was one thing to beat someone up, another to take a life. How could these men even think of such a thing?

Matt stood and faced Hubble. "Hey, I don't want any part of this. You're not using my truck as an accessory to murder."

Hubble nearly spit the words at him. "What's wrong with you, Moore? That creep tried to rape your fourteen-year-old daughter. What if he tries again? What if he succeeds next time? You willing to take responsibility for your inaction?"

Hubble's words struck him hard. Ever since Casey had walked into that room, bruised and shaken, Matt had worried Thurber would try again. Especially after he had beaten him up. He knew he could only protect Casey to a point. And Thurber was out there, free to bide his time and wait for another opportunity to get back at him. What better way than to hurt Casey?

And the next time it would be worse—Matt believed that, deep in his soul.

So now what? Every fiber of his being wanted Thurber stopped. Did he trust the legal system enough to put Thurber away, so the kid couldn't hurt his daughter?

He knew the answer to that.

"There's got to be a way to threaten him, to make him stop. Something else we can do," Matt said. Even as he said it, he knew it sounded hollow. What in the world could scare Thurber enough to make him change? Nothing.

He looked in the faces of the men around him and saw they had arrived at the same conclusion. The redheaded man spoke again. "I say we go with Hubble's plan. I'll get my boat and bring it over to the end of the pier. You guys knock Thurber out and tie him up. You can drive all the way down the dock to the stairs. How long would it take to drag him out of a truck and haul him into the boat. A minute? Two?"

The big man chimed in, excitement in his voice. "Yeah, and once we're out to sea, there's no one around to witness it. No weapons or blood. Nothing. You can always wash down the boat. Make sure there's no hair or fingerprints."

Tomás added, "Just bind his hands behind his back. You won't get any prints."

The more Matt listened, the more surreal the discussion became. Soon, he was no longer hearing the men throwing around their ideas. He heard someone call Thurber "good-for-nothing." The words echoed in his head, causing an ache in his gut. Thurber's face intruded in his thoughts, hard-set and defiant.

Matt stood and the room spun. He grabbed the back of the chair and steadied himself. The air thickened and suddenly the mass of bodies crowded him, making him claustrophobic. Sweat dripped down his forehead and stung his eyes.

By the time he got to the door, the voices stilled. All eyes were upon him.

"Where are you going, Moore?" Hubble asked. "You can't leave now. We need your help."

Matt looked in the faces of men intent on murder. "I can't do this."

The big muscular man put his hand on the door, making sure it stayed closed. "Yeah, if you leave, who's to say you won't go fink to the sheriff?"

The older man spoke in a threatening tone. "You better come with us. Or meet us down at the pier."

Matt looked in the face of the man blocking his exit. "Let me leave."

The man turned and questioned Hubble with his eyes. Hubble scowled a moment, then waved his hand in dismissal. "Aw, let him go if he wants to." His eyes locked on Matt's. "I don't get it, Moore. You of all people should want to see that good-for-nothing punk get his just desserts."

Matt's heart raced as he stepped out into the fresh, cold air. Ground fog hovered around the parking lot and muffled the sounds in the room behind him. He heard the door click shut and it made him jump.

He got into the cab of his truck and noticed his hands trembled. Mindlessly, he drove slowly north toward home, but Hubble's words replayed over and over, like a skipping record.

He was back in Running Springs, on the front porch. On a night like this—foggy, misty, cold. Normally, June evenings were balmy and mild, but a front had whisked down from Alaska and temperatures had dropped. Earlier that evening, Irene had mentioned how they'd probably need to bring sweaters for the graduation party and for taking group photos outside the auditorium.

Matt sat on the porch swing with a heavy coat on, checking his watch from time to time, getting more and more worked up. This was the last straw. Daniel was supposed to come home two hours ago, and Irene and Casey had gone to bed. Matt told Irene he'd stay up and wait, to make sure Daniel was okay. But that wasn't the reason Matt stayed up. He had reached the end of his patience.

By the time Daniel showed up, dropped off by a carload of rowdy teenage boys, Matt's fury rumbled like a volcano threatening to erupt. He had spent years containing his anger and frustration, but no longer. Just like Thurber, Daniel had pushed everyone too far. And he'd gotten away with each over-step with just a little slap on the hand. Fat lot of good that did to alter his behavior. People like Thurber—like Daniel—needed to run up against a brick wall of authority. An impenetrable wall, one that didn't budge or fall to pieces at the first sign of attack.

Matt would be that wall.

Just seeing Daniel laughing in that clueless manner—not caring that he was past his curfew and causing his parents worry—made Matt want to wring his son's neck. All these years he had never laid a finger on any of his children. Never. But that night he snapped. When Daniel came up onto the porch, clearly high on something, Matt blocked his way to the door and slapped him hard in the face.

Daniel reeled backward in shock. "Why did you do that?"

"You have to ask?"

Daniel huffed and rubbed his cheek. "What? Because I'm a little late? Can't you cut me some slack, Dad? We were out celebrating the end of school."

"I don't care if it was the end of the world. We have rules in this house and you've broken them too many times. And you didn't call or answer your cell phone. You know we've told you again and again that you have to answer your phone."

Daniel kicked at the deck railing. "I was at a party, a *loud* party. No way I'd hear my phone ring."

"That's not the point and you know it." Matt felt anger surge through every pore in his body. He grabbed Daniel's chin and forced him to face him.

"Tomorrow, after graduation, I want you to pack your things and leave this house."

"What?" Daniel yanked away from his father's grip. "Where do you expect me to go?"

"I really don't care. Find some buddy to stay with, get a job, get an apartment. You're eighteen, for heaven's sake."

"And I suppose when Casey's my age, you'll throw her out as well?"

Matt read the panic in Daniel's face, but he didn't care. He was a solid, unmovable wall. "If she behaves the way you do. But she's not a good-for-nothing kid like you."

Daniel cringed as if Matt had struck him on the face again. Matt could tell tears were forming in Daniel's eyes, but his son pushed them back with sheer will. He watched a wave of emotion cross Daniel's face, watched his features harden into rock to match Matt's own stern expression.

"Fine. I'll be out of here by tomorrow night. You'll be rid of me."

"Good." Matt stared him down. "And don't go crying to your mother, because she won't change my mind."

Matt felt water on his face as he drove down the gravel road to his small cottage in Breakers. He touched his cheek and realized he was crying. When he pulled into his driveway, he cut the engine and shut off the headlights, then sat in the dark listening to the pinging of the engine as it cooled down. For a long time he watched light rain splatter the windshield, feeling the rip in his heart.

Irene startled him when she opened the passenger door. "Matt, are you all right?" She slid in and shut the door, sidling up to him in the dark.

Matt tried to swat the memory away, but it rushed at him anyway.

Daniel pushing past him and putting his hand on the doorknob.

The way he stopped and turned to Matt, his eyes brimming with pain.

His voice wavering. "You wish it had been me, don't you? Instead of Jesse—in the accident. That I had died instead."

Matt didn't stop to think. He just wanted to lash out and hurt him, to pierce through that concrete casing and make him bleed, the way he had made them all bleed for years.

"You're right." He stabbed Daniel with words as sharp as knives. "You should have died instead. Then we would never have had to suffer all this heartache."

In the cab of the truck, in the quiet of the dark, foggy night, Matt felt a crack, as if his heart had split in two. He buckled over the steering wheel and sobbed in great gasps, unable to catch his breath.

Irene wrapped her arm around him and leaned her head on his shoulder. "It's all right, Matt. Just let it out."

Matt tried to talk between gasps, searching for breath. "It was my fault, all my fault. How could I have done that to Daniel?"

Irene stroked Matt's face, wiped tears. He saw she cried too.

"The night before graduation ... I told him I wished he had died—instead of Jesse." He broke into a heaving sob. "I can't believe I told him that."

"You didn't mean it, Matt."

"I did. And then he went and—"

Matt's door opened and a rush of cold air hit him broadside. Casey put her hand on her dad's shoulder, her face frantic with worry. "Dad, Mom, what happened? What's wrong?"

Irene pulled Matt into her arms, cradling him. "It's okay, honey. We'll be inside in a minute." She gave a reassuring nod and Casey backed off, carefully shutting the door. Matt lifted his eyes and watched his daughter go back into the house.

He wiped his face with his sleeve. "Irene, I'm so sorry. So sorry. And I've hurt you and Casey so badly."

"Shush. Just let it go."

"How will you ever forgive me?" He raised his face to look into her eyes and expected harsh judgment. Instead, he only saw a shared pain, a shared loss.

"Matt, I don't blame you for Daniel's death. We're all to blame—and maybe not to blame. Oh, what's the point? We can't go back and change anything, make it different."

"No, but I can change things now. Stop being so hard on Casey. Criticizing her like I did Daniel. My poor baby—"

More tears gushed out, and Matt felt himself emptying like a raging river into a thirsting sea.

Irene spoke softly. "Casey loves you so much—"

"And I love her too." His throat clenched in pain. "More than she knows."

Irene patted his arm. "Well, then tell her. She needs to hear it from your own lips."

Matt turned and looked at Irene. Love poured from her eyes, love he didn't deserve.

She kissed his lips and wiped his hair off his forehead. "Come, let's go inside."

As she held his arm, the whole evening came back to him in a rush.

"Irene, Jerry Hubble and a bunch of other guys are going after that kid, Thurber. I think they plan to kill him."

"What! Where?"

Matt told her the details, as much as he could remember. She listened, horror-struck. "I should call the sheriff," he said.

Irene opened her door. "No, let me call. You go in and see Casey. I'm sure Sheriff Huff will be able to handle this without you."

Matt opened his door and stepped out, light-headed and weak. A soft rain tingled his skin and a wave of weariness engulfed him. "Okay."

As he stepped inside the house, Casey stood a few feet away, her face etched with concern.

"Oh, Casey." He walked toward her with outstretched arms. "I love you so much."

Casey let her father encircle her. She stiffened at the sound of his sobbing.

"I'm so sorry, baby, for everything," he said. "Please, just love me."

He heard her choke up. "Oh, Dad, you know I do."

Matt felt her soften, bury herself into his chest. He stroked her hair and cried, holding her there in the middle of the drab living room, feeling drained empty and utterly full at the same time.

The hard, impenetrable wall started to crumble.

One by one, rocks broke off and tumbled to the ground, kicking up dust, coating the two of them with debris. All those years of careful construction falling to ruin.

His handiwork, his fortress.

Matt shuddered and released a long pent-up sigh.

*About time.*


IRENE REACHED FOR MATT'S CELL PHONE THAT WAS CLIPPED to the dash, then hesitated. A powerful sense of urgency struck her. Matt's keys were still in the ignition. Without further thought, she turned the engine over and backed out of the driveway. She envisioned Billy's face, bruised and swollen, as she cleaned blood from his wounds. She thought about Matt, crying and sobbing over Daniel. It struck her hard—that Billy probably had no one to cry over him, to care about his fate.

What she'd told Billy was true; she didn't believe he had committed those crimes, or killed his father. She didn't know why she felt that way, but she did—with all of her heart. Maybe Billy was right, that she was just trying to see the good in him. Maybe she was naïve. But right now, the issue was moot. Right now, a group of crazed men were planning on killing him, guilty or not. It was too bizarre to comprehend.

She sped down Seawood Lane in the fog, straining to see out the windshield. The road appeared a few feet at a time. *Please God, let me get to the sheriff. Don't let them hurt Billy.*

She pulled the phone off its clip and dialed 911. The dispatcher came on and Irene told him she needed to speak to Sheriff Huff; it was an emergency. That she was on her way to town to see him. He took the cell number and said he'd have Huff call her. She set the phone down on the seat beside her and focused on getting to town.

She navigated the curves as fast as she could in the gray obscurity, hearing her tires spin on the graveled shoulder. *Calm down, slow down* she told herself, but urgency burned in her gut. As she made the last wrenching corner, the phone rang, startling her. She reached for it and knocked it off the seat to the floor. It kept ringing.

Irene slammed on her brakes and skidded to a stop. She threw the stick shift into Neutral and put on the emergency brake. By the time she found the phone and flipped the top open, the line was dead. *Unknown caller.* She swore under her breath and dialed 911 again. The dispatcher answered and she told him how she'd missed Huff's call.

"That's all right," the man told her. "The sheriff says he's on his way to the police station. You can meet him there."

Irene let out the breath she'd been holding. She disengaged the brake and continued down the road, pushing sixty on the straightaway.

When she pulled into the parking lot, she saw the sheriff standing at the front door to the police station with his keys in hand. He stood and watched her with a weary expression on his face, his rain hood pulled up over his head.

She jumped down from the cab and ran over to him, the cold rain pricking her face.

"Mrs. Moore." He offered his hand and she grasped it with both of hers. His eyes narrowed as he studied her. "What's happened?"

"Sheriff Huff, a group of men are after Billy Thurber. We have to stop them."

Huff's eyebrows raised. She knew he had questions, but they would have to wait. "We need to go *now*," she said.

"Hold on there. Why don't you tell me just what you've heard." He inserted the key into the door lock. "Let's go inside and talk—"

"Sheriff." Irene stopped him with her hand. "There's no time. I'll talk while you drive." She pointed to his cruiser.

"I can't take you to a possibly dangerous situation."

"I'll go there anyway. Better if I go *with* you."

Huff let out a big sigh. "Okay. You win. But you better start talking."

Irene hurried after Huff as he marched to his car in the now-steady rain.

"And you better call for backup," she said.

# Chapter 36

JERRY SAT IN THE BACKSEAT OF RALPH'S BIG DIESEL TRUCK, twisted around so he could keep his eyes on the bundle that jostled behind him in the truck bed. His heart raced with excitement as he replayed the last ten minutes in his head. Smooth! Everything was going without a hitch. Truth be told, he thought Thurber would have put up a fight, but they'd had the element of surprise on their side. He'd just loved the look of terror on Thurber's face when he saw three guys come at him. The little squirt had been asleep in his boxer shorts and come out when he heard pounding on the side of his camper. Didn't even yell out to see who was there. How dumb can you get?

Jerry had watched as Ralph, the big meaty guy, grabbed Thurber and restrained him while Tomás smacked him with a hefty piece of wood. He could tell that Mexican guy was used to roughing people up. Hit him just right and only once did the trick. The three of them bound Thurber's wrists behind him, and his ankles too. They gagged him with a rag and tossed him in the truck bed under a tarp. Now he was sleeping away, oblivious to his impending demise. Jerry giggled in delight.

That old guy, Dave, sat beside him, deep in thought. Jerry glanced over at Ralph, who concentrated on maneuvering the curves. Those two sure looked surly and mean. Just where had Tomás found them? Maybe, he told himself, it would be better not to ask. Whatever arrangement Tomás had made with them was none of his concern. But he was glad they'd shown up. He couldn't believe—after all the talk of support from those he queried in private—how few had put their muscle where their mouths were. Easy for his neighbors to complain and want to rid the town of that scum Thurber, but few were man enough to step forward. Well, five strong guys would be enough. And that's all that mattered.

To keep from leaning into Dave, Jerry braced himself against the front passenger seat, where Tomás sat in silence. Jerry could almost taste the heightened anticipation in the truck cab. Oh, what he would do for a drink right now! Every muscle in his body twitched. Their plan was foolproof; how could they fail?

Jerry gazed out the window at the thick fog and spattering of rain. He couldn't have picked better conditions. Once more, the gods were smiling. He let his imagination wander, picturing the weeks to come, with the town settled back to quiet and Thurber gone for good. How people would talk and speculate on what happened. And if someone did find out—or one of these guys talked, well, who would believe it?

Maybe Thurber's body would eventually wash up on some beach. But by then, would it even be recognizable? More likely, the sharks would devour every inch of him and there'd be nothing left. Plenty of great whites out there, as the surfers could attest. Just waiting for a yummy snack to come their way.

Ralph took a curve too sharply and the truck skidded out. "Sorry," he said. "How's our merchandise?"

Jerry looked out the rear window. "Rolling like a stone."

No one else spoke the whole way to town. When they slowed and followed First Street down the hill to the dock, Jerry broke the silence.

"Okay, you all know what you're doing, right? Dave, you go first, scope things out, see if anyone's out there."

Tomás objected. "This fog is perfect. I don't see why we need to waste time scouting. Let's just drive onto the pier and do it."

"No," Ralph said. "Jerry's right. Can't rush these things. Let's make sure no one's out there, walking on the beach or something."

Tomás threw his head back against the seat and muttered something in Spanish.

"Hey, just relax," Jerry said.

Ralph inched the truck closer to the pier, just before the bait shop. He parked and turned off the engine. After a moment, he opened his door and let Dave out of the backseat. Dave leaned in through the window. "I'll be just a minute."

Jerry's heart raced as he peered into the fog through the side window. Was that movement? He strained harder but couldn't make anything out. His imagination must be playing tricks on him.

*Breathe. Everything will be just fine.*

A dull ache attacked his stomach, growing worse every minute. This waiting was killing him! He spun back around and looked at the shape under the tarp, watching carefully for any sign of motion.

A quiet tap at the window made him jump. Dave pressed his face against the glass and signaled to them. All clear.

HUFF LISTENED TO IRENE WHILE HE DROVE THROUGH TOWN. She sure was worried over Thurber, which seemed odd. Did she know him? He recalled how Moore had given Thurber some work for a bit. Maybe she'd met him then. Or maybe her concern was more of a motherly nature.

She hadn't said why Matt had stayed home and sent her to come find him. No matter. If Hubble was really going through with this insane plan, he'd stop him—all of them. Two other squad cars were on their way from Eureka, but they wouldn't be here for maybe another twenty minutes. Huff grunted. A lot could happen in that time. A lot of *bad* business. Hopefully, he would diffuse the situation before it got ugly. He didn't think he was dealing with professionals here. Jerry, for one, was a complete loose cannon, but Huff expected he'd crumble at the first sign of a gun pointed at him.

Irene had mentioned the restaurant owner—Luis's son-in-law. Huff reflected on the incident at the beach, how hot-tempered he had been. But what father wouldn't have been upset? Huff knew the guy made great fish tacos, too, but that and a dollar would buy him a bus ticket. Apparently, Matt didn't get any other names at that gathering except for the fisherman, Zack. Huff didn't know him either, except by sight. So all in all it figured to be, at most, six or seven guys.

As Huff reached the bottom of the hill, a few hundred yards away from the dock, he shut off his windshield wipers and headlamps, then slowed to a crawl.

"How can you see anything? It's thick as soup out here," Irene said.

Huff noted the impatience in Irene's voice. He patted her hand, never taking his eyes of the road. "I don't see a thing. But I know this parking lot well enough."

Why'd Hubble have to go and plan something stupid like this? He had warned the guy, told him to let the law take care of things. So what if Thurber did burn down that motel? Was that enough reason to retaliate with murder? Some people were all kinds of stupid.

Asphalt turned into gravel, and Huff knew the crunching sound under the tires carried far on the night air. He stopped and lowered his window to listen. Irene sat still beside him. She met his eyes at the sound of a vehicle's door opening, then another.

Her voice punctured the silence. "That's them. Got to be."

Huff deliberated. How long should he stall? If he waited for backup, he might arrive at the pier and find everyone out to sea and Thurber at the bottom of it. He picked up his radio. The dispatcher answered.

"This is Sheriff Huff. Can you patch me through to the Coast Guard station here in Breakers?"

He felt Irene shuffle in her seat. When the Coast Guard captain came on the line, Huff told him about their situation and asked if they could get a patrol boat ready. When he finished his call, he turned and looked at Irene.

"See, we're going to drive down there, but because I have you with me in the car, I'm not going to get too close. I don't know who's out there and with what weapons. You need to stay in this car no matter what, okay?"

Irene nodded.

He let his gaze linger a moment on Irene's tearful face. "I mean it, Mrs. Moore. Don't get out of the car." The last thing he needed was for some emotional woman to try to help.

"Just save Billy Thurber." Then she added in a shaky voice, "If it's not already too late."

# *Chapter 37*

RALPH BACKED THE TRUCK ONTO THE DOCK AS JERRY AND Dave stood behind it, directing him. The old boards creaked loudly as the truck rolled over them and Jerry waved frantically, stopping Ralph. He ran over to the window and whispered. "Hey, this is making *way* too much noise. We'll wake everyone in town."

Ralph cut the engine. He and Tomás got out and followed Jerry to the back of the truck. Carefully, Jerry lowered the tailgate. "We'll just have to haul him from here."

Tomás let out a breath. "That's, like, a hundred yards from here." He looked around anxiously. "Okay."

Ralph nodded. "Then let's make this quick."

"I'm gonna go see if Zack is down below. He should be there by now." Jerry had told Zack to putter over to the dock as quietly as possible and just tie up and wait. The fewer people out in the open, the better.

He shivered in the damp fog and zipped up his coat. Whoa, it was cold—bone-snapping cold! The wood planking beneath his feet was slick from the heavy moisture in the air. He hurried down the pier, past the dark bait shop, careful with his footing. He heard the lapping of the water underneath him. Over the edge, the sea swelled inky black. No one would last long in that freezing water.

He looked back and barely made out the three men through the fog, hoisting Thurber's body out of the truck. If only his heart would stop pounding so hard!

Finally, he reached the end of the dock where the stairs led down to a small railed landing. Zack and his boat were not there! Jerry cursed in frustration. What if that kid had chickened out? They would be totally ruined. Panic pumped more blood through his heart and Jerry clutched at his chest. Was he having a heart attack? He looked down at the murky water churning around him, smacking the landing with small waves. The sight nauseated him.

Wait! He listened intently. There! A low motor coming toward him. It had to be Zack. Jerry hurried back up the steps to see how the others were progressing. Ralph and Tomás carried Thurber between them, moving slowly, with Dave flanking them. They were about halfway down the dock. *Okay,* Jerry told himself. *Still on schedule.*

As he ran back down the stairs, he slipped on the bottom step, twisting his ankle and landing in a thud on the hard wooden platform. A sharp pain smacked him from his shoulder blade down to his tailbone, making it difficult to catch his breath. He grimaced. *Great!* Just what he needed.

He stood, then took a few hesitant steps, and with each motion needles of pain skewered his back and his ankle. He steeled his determination and concentrated on the approaching motor sound.

A dull yellow light illuminated the fog around the dock. Abruptly, the engine noise stopped and a boat materialized out of the gray, floating slowly toward the landing. Jerry pushed against the prow, stopping it before it banged into the railing.

Zack climbed out and threw a line over the piling, then tied off the boat.

"How're we doing? Those guys up there yet?" Zack whispered, and Jerry read fear in his eyes.

"Almost. Had to park a ways down. The truck made too much noise on the planks."

Now Zack looked even more frightened.

"Just wait here. Don't move," Jerry said.

*Everything will be fine,* he told himself as he struggled up the steps, wincing in pain. His back locked up, making it nearly impossible to lift his legs onto the risers. Six grueling steps.

Finally, he made it to the top, winded and sweating hard. He was just about to head over and help Ralph, Dave, and Tomás with their burden when a bright light from the parking lot pierced the fog, exposing them for all the world to see.

*Oh no!*

"DAD, YOU HAVE TO GO FASTER." CASEY GRIPPED THE DASH as her father sped down Seawood Lane.

"I'm going as fast as I can, Case. I don't want to crash the car."

Matt chided himself for taking Casey along, but she had insisted, and they didn't have time to argue. When Matt realized Irene had taken off with his truck, he was struck with an inexplicable premonition of disaster. He told himself Irene was with the sheriff. But why didn't she answer his cell phone he left in the truck? What if she hadn't gone to meet Huff? What if she'd decided to go straight to the dock?

He knew his fears were unreasonable, but they ate at his gut. He'd had too much disaster in his life—more than his full share, more than most people. And something told him Irene was stepping blindly into trouble, although the hunch defied all reason.

"Dad, you haven't told me what's going on. Where'd Mom go in such a hurry?"

Matt hugged the car close to the center yellow line, which was all he could see of the road. "There are a bunch of men planning to hurt someone. I heard them talking." The last thing Matt intended was for Casey to know this trouble revolved around Billy Thurber. *If Casey sees him, what will she do?* Matt berated himself. No, he shouldn't have brought her along. "I'm just concerned that your Mom may have decided to get involved."

"But why?"

"I'm not sure, baby." Matt wondered that himself. Why would Irene concern herself with a stranger she bought firewood from? It made no sense. But, maybe like him, she had seen something of Daniel in that disturbed kid, something that tugged at her heart. "But she might just be down at the market. Maybe my cell phone went dead."

He startled at the touch of Casey's hand as she took his and squeezed it. "Dad, I get that way too."

"What way?"

"You know, expecting the worst. I hear a loud noise and think it's a gun. Or when a friend doesn't show up one day at school, I think they got hit by a car. That kind of stuff." She added, "It's just makes it worse, worrying like that."

Matt looked over at Casey and felt sad for her, for all that she had to bear at such a young age. It struck him that he wallowed so much in his own pain, he rarely thought of the anguish she must go through each day, the unbearable heartache of missing her brothers, how lonely she must feel. He ached to shield her from all that.

Matt pulled into the market lot and drove over to his truck, which sat parked in front of the police station. The sheriff's cruiser was nowhere in sight. Through the window, the office lay dark and vacant. Matt's hope sunk. He had to assume Irene and Huff were down at the beach — and only God knew what they'd find down there.

# Chapter 38

Z ACK STOMPED HIS FEET, MORE FROM NERVOUSNESS THAN cold. Hubble couldn't be serious—making those guys carry Thurber the length of the dock. Why, that would take them forever!

A loud thump above him made him nearly jump out of his skin.

"Hubble, are you okay?"

All he got in response was a tirade of cursing. Zack wiped the sweat from his forehead with his jacket sleeve. He had a bad feeling about all this, now that they were actually doing it. He tried to picture Thurber lying in his boat, bound and gagged. Then they'd troll out to sea and he'd watch Hubble and that big guy, Ralph, ease the young punk over the side and into the frigid water. He knew Thurber would come to and struggle. You could only last maybe five minutes in water this cold. He would die quickly.

Zack rubbed his cold hands. He wished now he had gone to town with Randy instead of this. Right now he could be sitting in that warm movie theater, eating popcorn. But no, he'd wanted to get that monkey, Thurber, off his back. Well,

Hubble was so gung-ho. Why hadn't he just let *him* do the dirty work? Why, oh why, had he volunteered his boat?

This was taking too long. He went up the steps, crouching low, hoping to see how close the others were. Fog buried everything in a thick shroud. He listened to the harbor buoy clanging in the distance. He thought he saw Jerry stumbling away from him but wasn't sure.

Suddenly, the fog lit up with an eerie yellow glow. Zack scurried back down the stairs, slipping and grabbing the railing as he looked back at bright headlights aimed directly at them. Zack gasped. They were caught!

IN THE HEADLIGHT'S BRIGHT GLARE, IRENE COULD SEE ONLY vague shapes. Somewhere, on that dock, or in a boat, was Billy Thurber. Was he still alive? How could these men—these neighbors of hers—lapse into such madness? And what about the sheriff? What if he started firing his gun and things went haywire?

Irene had to get out of the car. She had to do something.

Anger welled up, coupled with frustration. How many years had she hung back, not spoken up when Matt criticized Daniel? Not acted assertively when Daniel defied her? Her thoughts turned to her parents, the years of criticism she'd silently endured, never once telling them how cruel their words were. For forty years she'd smothered her voice, acquiesced to everyone around her, hated herself for being weak and not standing up for the things that smoldered in her heart.

She was sick to death of watching from the sidelines and seeing the terrible consequences of her constrictive fear.

Absolutely sick to death.

Irene threw the door open and ran. She heard Huff yell at her as she sprinted past him. From his crouched position around the side of the bait shop his voice boomed, although she didn't stop or slow down.

"Mrs. Moore—what in blazes are you doing? Get back here!"

She ran onto the dock, toward the men shrouded in fog and darkness. She could barely see in front of her, but she called out to them.

"I know you have Billy Thurber. Let him go!"

She nearly tumbled over a group of men who froze as she rammed into them. She got a quick glimpse of their frenzied expressions before they ran in frantic haste toward the end of the pier. Irene couldn't tell where they went; they vanished in a shroud of gray.

JERRY FROZE. HE HEARD A WOMAN YELLING. YARDS AWAY, Ralph, Dave, and Tomás jerked to a stop and dropped Thurber's body with a loud thump onto the dock. Jerry fell down and huddled over, his back screaming in pain. He covered his ears and buried his face into his coat, willing himself invisible. He knew he should try to get down the stairs and into the boat with Zack, but the pain paralyzed him. What should he do?

On the cold air of night, Huff's voice carried through a bullhorn.

"Hubble, I know you're out there."

Jerry sank even deeper into his coat, making himself as small as he could. Unless he wanted to jump into the icy water, there was no way out.

Moore! That idiot must have told the sheriff. Why? Why! Moore hated Thurber, didn't he? How could he turn traitor like that?

He should have *never* let Moore leave that meeting. But he'd trusted the guy—and look where that led him. Next time, he wouldn't trust anyone. Do what needed doing all by himself. If there was a next time.

Jerry groaned.

His simple, perfect plan had failed.

He was doomed.

# Chapter 39

A MOAN ROSE UP FROM IRENE'S FEET. SHE DROPPED DOWN TO the ground and startled at the tarp lying on the planking in front of her. Billy! She fumbled at the thick ropes that wound around the plastic. Huff's voice boomed again on the air.

"Mrs. Moore, I'm coming over. I want you to run back to me. Now!"

*No. I'm not leaving. I won't let them hurt you.*

Heavy mist settled around her, on her clothes and hair. Water dripped into her face. Her body shook uncontrollably. Somewhere in the dark were men bent on violence, and the only way to stop violence was with determination. Her cold, shaky hands worked at the ropes; the fibers rubbed her fingers raw. Any moment she expected to feel Huff grab her and yank her away, but she narrowed her vision and saw only Billy.

"Billy, can you hear me?"

Finally, the knots gave way and the rope fell loose. She found one end and untangled it, then unwrapped the tarp. She heard another moan. At least he was still alive, thank God!

She pulled the tarp off him, and even in the dark she could see blood in his hair and on his face. She steeled herself, knowing what strength she would have to muster to get him on his feet and walking. She certainly couldn't carry him. The strange sensation of dejá vu washed over her as she reached into her coat pocket and withdrew a handkerchief and dabbed at his face.

*God, help me get him to safety.*

For a slight moment, Billy's eyes opened, glazed and unfocused. They searched and found her face and a look of recognition lit them up. Through swollen, parched lips he said one word.

"Irene."

Hearing her name did something to her; it rattled around inside her and gave her strength. A strange feeling of peace permeated her, like a divine hand placed on her heart. She heard someone yell from the end of the pier. He sounded close, but she still couldn't see anyone.

"Huff, you better leave now, or someone will get hurt."

She heard Huff's voice boom back. "Someone's already hurt, Hubble. In a couple of minutes, this place will be full of police. We can do this the easy way or the hard way."

Irene heard arguing, and a scuffle. "What are you doing?" a man's deep voice cried out.

"Give me that gun!"

Irene froze. She guessed that was Hubble screaming.

"No!" Someone else, a higher voice.

Irene gasped. She had to get Billy away, *now*!

She pulled him to standing, like trying to heft a huge sack of grain, but somehow she managed it. He flopped against her as she got him to his feet. He looped his arms around her shoulders and laid his head against hers. She felt heat from his skin and heard his labored breathing. She stood there, getting her balance, aware of his heart beating against her arm.

In that fraction of a second, she remembered what it felt like, having Daniel in her arms. Feeling his lanky frame, his sinewy arms, smelling his scent. It all came to her in a heady rush.

The last time she had held him like that was the night before his death. She had woken suddenly, hearing the front door slam, then heard him clunk up the stairs. When she realized he paused at her door, she got up and opened to him. She remembered seeing the misery on his face and her own feeling of helplessness, unable to think of anything to say. But Daniel only reached out and draped his arms around her — like this. She held him for a minute, neither of them speaking, but she listened to his heartbeat.

And now, standing here in the damp mist, she realized Daniel had been listening to hers as well, just as he had in her womb eighteen years earlier.

One last time.

"Billy," she said, tears falling down her face, "we have to walk. Can you do that?"

She felt him nod and try to take a step, but at that moment two men came bursting out of the fog, running toward her. They struggled with each other as they ran, one man trying to grab something from the other's hand. Irene didn't realize the object was a gun until they were almost upon her.

All she could think of was the gun Daniel had held to his head. A small gray gun that he'd somehow acquired. How could something so small cause such destruction?

She stared at the gun shifting in her direction and, without a second thought, did the only possible thing she could do.

She pushed Billy behind her and body-blocked him.

This time there would be something between the gun and the head it was aimed at. This time she refused to be the observer. This time she would not fail to act.

She would not let another young man die because she kept her distance.

ZACK RAN TO THE PILING AND TRIED TO UNWIND THE LINE, but his hands shook so hard he got flustered. Above him, voices argued and yelled. He heard the sheriff again, warning Hubble. He couldn't make out the muffled words, soaked up in the thickness of the air, but he did catch one word. It stabbed through his heart.

*Gun*!

Zack gasped. Who in blazes had brought a gun? He attacked the rope with renewed fervor, finally freeing it and tossing it into the boat. He jumped aboard and turned the engine on. He wasn't hanging around, not one minute longer.

He pulled back on the throttle and eased the boat away from the dock, hoping he wouldn't hit anything. The fog swallowed up the harbor, erasing all but a few feet off his bow. He couldn't remember where the other boats were moored in the bay, but at this point he didn't care if he rammed a dozen of them. He just needed to get out of the harbor. *Fast*.

HUFF CURSED THE FOG. AND IRENE MOORE. HE SHOULD have listened to his instincts and refused to bring her along. What in the world was she doing out there? Didn't she understand the danger?

He crouched low and chased after her. The dock planking rumbled under his heavy boots, and he heard shouting. He yelled out again, warning Hubble.

The motel owner's voice sounded hysterical. "Huff, leave now or I'm shooting Thurber in the head."

*Oh great*! Did that imbecile have a gun? Or was he bluffing? Now he had to throw caution to the wind—with innocent people in harm's way.

Huff picked up his pace, careful not to slip. There! He could make out shapes ahead of him. With his gun braced and aimed, he strained to see what Irene was doing. She seemed to be helping Thurber to his feet. Just as he nearly reached her, he heard Hubble and Tomás running toward her, arguing with each other.

"Stop!" Huff yelled at them. "Drop that gun!"

Before Huff had a chance to get in front of Irene, the sound he dreaded exploded in the air. Irene dropped to the dock. He saw Hubble and Tomás trip up a few feet in front of Irene, then heard the gun clunk onto the wood dock. It skittered to a stop inches from Huff's feet. He grabbed it with his gloved hand and pocketed it. Then charged ahead and tackled both the men. He didn't see anyone else close by.

Huff had no idea how many men were on the dock, whether others would fire. He wished his backup would get here, now!

He threw Hubble over onto his stomach, then did the same to Tomás. Both men were whimpering and breathing hard. Hubble started to say something and lift his head, but Huff kicked him back down with his boot. Hubble screamed in pain.

"Shut up, Hubble." The guy was whining like a dog. "If either of you moves, you'll be sorry."

As he frisked them down, he looked over at Irene. She had fallen, and Thurber had her in his arms.

"Huff," Thurber said in a weak voice. "She's been shot. You gotta help her."

*Great!* He had to hope those two would just stay put; he didn't have time to cuff them or watch them.

Blood poured out of Irene's chest, near her collarbone. Huff heard her panting with a shallow, shaky breath. He knelt beside her and pulled out his radio, requesting an ambulance. Thurber took off his thin T-shirt and used it as a compress. Huff checked Irene over for other injuries but found none.

Then Huff looked Thurber over—bare-chested, shivering in his skivvies, with blood on his face and matted in his hair. Thurber seemed okay for now, if a bit shocked. He'd let the paramedics deal with him.

As Huff searched Irene's shoulder for the entry wound, he heard a voice call out to him, farther down the dock.

"Sheriff, we're coming over."

Huff crouched at the ready, his gun aimed into the gray soup. "Who are you? How many are out there?"

"I'm Dave, and this is Ralph. Just the two of us. Honest." An older man materialized out of the fog, walking slowly with his arms stretched high over his head, a withered look on his face. A larger burly man followed in like manner. "Don't shoot, please! There's nobody else and we're not armed."

Huff kept his revolver pointed at the men as he motioned for them to sit over next to Hubble and Tomás. "I hope to God you're telling me the truth."

The men nodded and sank down beside Tomás, hanging their heads.


MATT HEARD THE GUNSHOT THE MINUTE HE STEPPED OUT OF his car. His knees buckled under him. He had only heard one other real gunshot in his life and he winced at the memory of it.

Casey jumped out of the car. "Dad! We have to find Mom!"

He pulled himself together, forcing the violent, nauseating images from his mind. He spurred his feet to move and found himself in a sprint, with Casey gripping his hand, running alongside him. The scene unfolding before him was chaotic, but his eyes skimmed over the sheriff and the men huddled on the dock until they fell upon Irene.

His throat closed up and his breath caught. He barely noticed Billy Thurber, pushing him out of the way as he knelt down next to his wife. Casey fell at her mother's feet. Irene lay slumped on the damp planking, but she opened her eyes at the sound of Matt's voice.

Matt looked at the blood seeping from her shoulder, spreading down her gray sweater. He noticed the soaked T-shirt on the ground next to her and looked to his left, to where Thurber was limping, half-naked, back down the dock. The sight gave him pause, but he didn't give himself a moment to ponder Thurber's actions. He picked up the shirt and pressed it gently against the wound.

Irene groaned. Casey wept uncontrollably. "Dad, is she dying? We have to save her!"

"Honey, she'll be okay." He looked in Irene's face and saw she rallied a smile.

Her voice shook. "I'm all right. Just hurts." She closed her eyes.

Casey stroked her mother's hair, tears streaming down her face.

Matt searched Irene but didn't find any other injuries. He let out a trembling breath.

"Billy," Irene whispered. "See if he's okay ..."


HUFF FELT THE PIER VIBRATE WITH FOOTSTEPS. HE SPUN around. Two people were running in his direction. *Now what?* Moore and a teenage girl—probably her daughter—descended on Irene. *Wonderful. Let's have a party while we're at it.*

He watched Thurber get to his feet and stumble away. Huff was about to yell at him to stop, but the kid only made it to the bait shop before he collapsed in the doorway. Huff guessed Thurber was getting hypothermic. He should cover him up, but he needed to secure his perps first — although one look told him they had no plans to go anywhere. And he needed to make sure Irene didn't lose too much blood from that shoulder wound.

What he really needed was help.

And he heard it coming.

In the distance, the sirens' pitches grew louder and louder until the night seemed full of ear-piercing screeching capable of waking the dead. Three squad cars drove up onto the dock. Uniformed men spilled out and ran toward him, their weapons in hand. Huff stood in the bright headlights of the vehicles — one eye on the men huddled together on the dock — and put his hands on his hips.

"Took you long enough," he said.

# Chapter 40

MATT WONDERED AT IRENE'S WORDS. WONDERED WHY SHE was lying here, why Thurber'd had her in his arms.

"Please ..." Irene's eyes implored him, but just as he made to stand, he heard the sirens. In seconds, the pier was lit up as bright as day, and Matt heard men running onto the dock, yelling out to Huff.

Matt cradled Irene in his arms. Huff came over and told him the ambulance was on its way. He instructed Matt to keep the compress on her shoulder and to keep her calm and warm. Matt took off his coat and laid it over Irene. Around him, men called out to each other, cuffed and hauled off Hubble and three others whom Matt couldn't recognize from where he knelt. He looked over at the bait shop and saw Huff wrap a blanket around Thurber's shoulders, then help him walk over to the parking lot.

Flashing lights splashed red all around Matt. Mist fell onto his head and clothes as radios squawked like angry seagulls.

Instantly he was back at the "Trap," in the freezing hail, next to the flipped car, staring at Jesse's mangled body on the ground.

He fought the urge to throw up.

Irene opened her eyes again and started to speak. Matt shushed her and told her to rest. "The ambulance will be here in a minute. We'll get you to the hospital."

She lifted her hand and rested it on Matt's cheek. "... love you ..." She turned her head to see Casey. "Both ..."

"Oh, Mom," Casey said. "We love you too." She buried her face in her mother's hair and then Matt saw something he hadn't seen in many, many years.

Irene's face lit up with a beatific smile, radiating an aura of peace and calm. Matt felt something emanate from her face and soak deep into his own soul, as if the peace she generated held some mysterious power. Tears welled up in his eyes and relief washed over him, but he felt more than relief.

*Thank you, God*, he prayed, gratitude swelling inside and overflowing. *Thank you for saving Irene.*

He added under his breath, "And for saving me."

Time sifted slowly as he sat watching Irene, listening to her shallow breathing, making sure one breath came on the heels of another. A gentle tap on his shoulder startled him. Paramedics ushered him out of the way and tended to Irene, getting her on a gurney and taking her vitals.

"Dad, we can't leave her!" Casey clawed at his shirt as the medics rolled Irene's gurney toward the parking lot.

Matt took her into his arms. "Then go ride with her. I'll be right behind, in the car." He could tell Casey was torn between staying with him and going with her mother.

"Go," he urged. "I'll be okay."

Casey looked hard into his eyes and then ran after the medics. Huff walked over and laid a hand on his shoulder.

"What happened, Sheriff?"

Huff frowned. "I didn't see much. I don't know whether your wife is brave or just crazy. But she ran out there and made those guys drop Thurber. And somehow she got in the way, and got shot." He let out a breath and Matt noticed the strain and weariness weighing on his face. "Not sure who fired the gun, or who it belongs to."

Matt watched as the medics loaded Irene into the ambulance and helped Casey into the van to be with her mother. He watched until they closed the doors and drove off.

"You should go," Huff said.

Matt nodded. "How's Thurber?"

Huff grunted. "He'll have a nasty headache for a few days. But he's alive." Huff added, a perplexed expression on his face, "Thanks to your wife."

Matt looked over at Thurber, who was being attended to by one of the paramedics who had stayed behind.

Huff patted Matt on the shoulder. "I'll see you over at the hospital. I need to get a statement from your wife, when she's up to it. Looked like that bullet went in right under the collarbone. Missed her heart, and her bones. Went clean right through, from what I could tell. She's downright lucky."

Matt nodded numbly. He doubted luck had anything to do with it.

Irene's peaceful face returned to his thoughts. This was more than just a random set of circumstances. Something in his gut told him Irene's being here was no accident, that she was meant to show up and save Thurber's life.

He frowned. Maybe he was overreacting, reading into things, wanting to give Irene's bizarre behavior some deeper meaning.

And then again, maybe not.

ZACK'S HEART POUNDED SO HARD HE FELT THE BLOOD SURGE in his ears. As he rounded Indian Rock, he let out a breath and willed himself to calm down. He kept the running lights off and glided out of the harbor, the massive sea stack looming on his left as he cruised by. *Okay—now what?*

He could go to the Eureka Marina, tie up there, then hitch a ride to the mall. There he'd find Randy—and have an alibi. This *could* work.

Zack realized he was gripping the throttle so hard his knuckles were white. Behind him, in the dark, the pier drifted farther and farther back. He was edging his way closer to safety—and freedom. Relief washed over him. Even if those guys named him, what proof did they have he was ever there? Only Hubble had seen him, and who would believe *his* story?

He grabbed a towel from his lockbox and wiped down his face and hair. He didn't want to think about what was going down at that dock. Someone had been shot; he was sure of it. He'd heard a sharp report slice through the night, followed by screams and yelling. He only hoped it was Thurber and no one else. Then he remembered the sheriff, and a woman's voice. That *was* a woman he'd heard, wasn't it? Who in blazes would that be?

Well, he was just glad to be out of there. He was the lucky one, that was for sure. He must have had one more of those lucky coupons left. He made a promise to himself, right there, that he wouldn't do anything stupid like this, ever again. In fact, he was done with all the illegal deals for now. Just go back to fishing, lay low, keep clean.

Zack sighed. Enough worrying and looking over his shoulder, losing sleep, and waking up with a panic attack in the middle of the night. He was too young to spend his life living in fear each day. He'd had enough.

Suddenly, a boat appeared right in front of him. Zack yelped and yanked back on the throttle. A bright, blinding light shone down on him.

A loud bullhorn boomed. "Coast Guard. Turn off your engine and raise your hands."

Zack's jaw dropped open. What in blazes—

Men on the deck across from him tied rigging lines to his boat. *Tell me this isn't happening!*

A uniformed man stepped down into Zack's trawler. Reality hit him like a slap to the face. He was not going to make it to Eureka, or sit in that theater watching some corny adventure movie with Randy. He was probably headed to a jail cell, where he didn't even want to think of the terrors awaiting him there.

Slowly, he raised his trembling arms over his head while he watched the man talk into a handheld radio.

He should have quit while he was ahead.

He'd been wrong. He'd used up that last lucky coupon a long time ago.

# Chapter 41

CASEY SQUIRMED AROUND ON THE UNCOMFORTABLE PLASTIC chair. Her legs were cramped underneath her. Next to her, her dad thumbed through a magazine, not reading anything. How long had they been sitting in that emergency waiting room? An hour, two hours? By now she knew every corridor in this wing of the hospital, every vending machine. She was even getting to know some of the nurses by name.

"Dad, will we be able to take Mom home tonight, or will she have to stay over?"

"I don't know yet, baby."

Casey fumed and glanced at the faces of the other people in the room. They seemed worried too. In the last hour, Casey had watched a teenager come in with a cast on his arm and an old lady on some kind of breathing machine. The doctors would not let Casey go into the treatment room, so she could only imagine horrible things. She'd overheard the doctor explain to her dad how her mom had lost a lot of blood and needed a transfusion. But he *did* say she'd be fine. She hoped he wasn't just saying that to make them stop worrying. Seeing all that blood on her mom's sweater had nearly made her faint. Why wouldn't her dad tell her who'd shot her mom, and why?

*My mom could have died.* The thought shook her to her core. She didn't want to think of life without her mother, of standing by one more grave, of hearing one more funeral discourse. She would rather die herself.

And then—to have seen Billy Thurber holding her mother! Clearly, Billy had been trying to help her mom. That was his shirt her dad had used to stop the bleeding. Casey still could not fathom it. She hadn't seen him since that day she'd climbed into his truck. She'd only gotten a quick look at him on the pier, but there was blood in his hair and on his face. Was it his blood or her mom's blood? Was Billy the one they had been trying to hurt?

She had so many questions and no one to answer them for her. Her heart sank, thinking about Billy and what trouble he had gotten into. Thinking of her mom trying to help him— and him helping her.

A pang of guilt stabbed her. She knew what her dad must have felt—seeing Billy there on the dock. Probably wanting to kill him. Guessing, maybe, that Billy was the cause of all this, of her mom lying there, shot. She could picture what her dad would do with all that anger. All of it her fault.

Suddenly, she saw Emilia, learning in horror that Iago had accused her sweet mistress, Desdemona, of unfaithfulness. Yet it was to Casey that Emilia spoke those accusing words: *"You told a lie, an odious, damned lie. Upon my soul, a wicked lie."* A lie that resulted in Othello murdering his beloved wife.

An image of her dad with his hands gripping Billy's throat made her tremble and leap up from her chair. She tugged on her father's sleeve. He looked up from the magazine.

"What is it, Case?"

"I need to tell you something." She looked at the other people around her. Their eyes followed her. "Come out here." She gestured him into the hall.

When she got her dad to a secluded corner, she started to cry. He stroked her hair while he waited for her to catch her breath. She drummed up the nerve and spoke.

"I made it all up, Dad."

"Made what up?" He pulled back and searched her eyes.

"About Billy trying to rape me." Her dad looked confused; her words tumbled out. "I was mad at him—and at you. I wanted him to like me, but he laughed at me and told me I was just a kid. That I needed to grow up first ... and then maybe he'd give me the time of day. I wanted him to think I was older, but I guess I didn't fool him. His words hurt so much ..."

Her dad listened quietly while she sniffled and wiped her face.

"So I made it look like he hurt me. I even smacked myself in the eye with a stick to make it look bruised." She squeezed her eyes and more tears leaked out. "I can't believe I did that."

Casey dared a glance at her dad's expression, expecting harsh judgment. But, to her relief, he didn't even flinch. Why? She expected him to lash out, yell at her. Instead, he looked tired, sad. As though he was searching for words. Finally, he spoke as he reached over and stroked her cheek. His voice seemed to tremble.

"No, Case, I understand. It's horrible when you like someone and they reject you. It hurts so much you just want to strike out and hurt back."

Her dad fell quiet and stared past her.

Casey spoke to fill in the silence. "And I guess I was so mad at you, for saying mean things about Daniel. But when I saw Billy tonight, I knew you'd be angry." She frowned. "I didn't want you to think Billy was bad, that maybe it was his fault Mom got shot."

She felt her dad's hand shake as he rested it on her shoulder. "I don't blame him, Case. He was trying to help her; I know that." His face clouded over.

"What is it?" she asked.

He sighed. "Nothing, baby. Why don't you go back into the waiting room? I need to get a drink of water."


MATT WATCHED CASEY WALK DOWN THE HALL, THEN LET OUT a breath and clenched his eyes shut. He let the images come.

Pummeling Thurber with his fists, kicking him in the groin, breaking his nose.

He'd done what any protective father would have done, hadn't he? Still, guilt sat heavy in his heart. He could have just tried to *talk* with him, get his side of the story. Even bring the two kids together and hear them out. No, instead he'd had to be a champion, put the punk in his place. Maybe few would blame him for what he'd done, but he blamed himself. Anger, he now realized, accomplished nothing good. His unchecked anger had hurt one more innocent boy.

Matt's knees gave way. He sank down to the cold linoleum floor and poured out his heart, wondering if God was listening or even cared. *I know you say you forgive us, no matter what terrible things we do. I don't get how you can forgive me, when I can't even forgive myself. How do I go on from here?*

"Dad!" Casey waved at him from the waiting room door.

Standing, Matt wiped his eyes and hurried down the hall to find Irene sitting in a wheelchair in the waiting room. He saw bandages under her hospital gown. No doubt they had discarded her sweater.

She smiled at him as he ran up to her. "They won't let me walk out," she said.

Sheriff Huff came out from the swinging door next to the reception desk. "They say she's good to go." He patted Irene on her uninjured shoulder. "Won't be able to use that arm much for a while."

The doctor appeared and gave Matt a prescription slip. He told Matt how to care for the dressing and to be sure Irene got a lot of rest. Matt signed a release form and then turned to shake the sheriff's hand. "Thanks for everything, Sheriff."

Huff shrugged. "Just doing my job, Moore."

"I'll push," Casey said, getting behind the wheelchair.

Matt followed Casey as she steered the wheelchair down the hallway, around the corner, and out the automated glass doors leading to the parking lot. He helped get Irene out of the cold air and into the car. Casey curled up next to her mother in the backseat.

"Well, I think we've had enough excitement for one night," Irene said, her voice groggy from pain medication. "Let's go home and eat some ice cream."

On the drive home, Matt considered he'd have to talk with Casey at some point about the seriousness of her accusing Billy of rape. But not tonight. Then he thought about Billy Thurber. He owed the boy an apology. Tomorrow, he would see if he could find him. He imagined Thurber would just scowl at him, throw his words back in his face. But it was the right thing to do, regardless. And he needed to thank him for helping Irene.

Funny, all that anger he'd nurtured for Thurber — anger that had rumbled in his stomach every day — was gone. Maybe he'd had that kid all wrong. Maybe everyone did. Maybe he'd never know the truth about Billy Thurber, but one thing was for certain—he would think twice before casting blame on anyone ever again.


WHEN HUFF DROVE UP HIS DRIVEWAY, HE NOTICED SOME-one standing at his front door. He looked at his watch—eleven p.m. Who in the world would be out there in the cold this late? All he wanted was to get into the shower and let the hot water beat on him for a half hour. Was that too much to ask?

The man came and met him at his car. Huff recognized the pastor from the local church and from the beach that day. He put two and two together: Tomás was his son-in-law and he was probably there to make some sort of plea.

Huff got out, feeling stiff in every limb of his body. "Pastor Muñez, can't it wait until tomorrow?"

Luis's face showed his grief. "Yes, Sheriff. I am so sorry to bother you this late. But I can't sleep and I have to know—was it Tomás who fired that gun and shot Irene?"

Huff walked to the door with Luis following him.

"I didn't see what happened; I was too far away and the fog was pretty thick. But I will tell you this—all those men conspired to kill Thurber, and even if they didn't get away with it, there're still the charges of assault, battery, kidnapping, and intent. I can't tell you what the D.A. will do or who'll be charged with what."

"I know that, Sheriff."

Huff looked into the pastor's worried, tired eyes. "Look, I spoke with Irene," he continued. "She insists it was an ac-cident, that no one meant to fire the gun—it just went off in the scuffle." Relief washed over Luis's face and Huff placed a hand on the man's shoulder. "She refuses to press any charges, says she doesn't know who fired the weapon."

Huff recalled the look on Irene's face as she'd said all that. He didn't buy a word of it, but that was her business if she didn't want to pursue the matter.

Luis let out a long breath. "Okay, Sheriff Huff. That is all I need to know. I'm sorry to bother you."

"No problem."

"Oh," Luis said. "You know, I've been meaning to tell you. The night of that fire—at the motel? I saw someone in my church—around six o'clock. It was Billy Thurber. I recognized him down at the beach that day. I went back a little later and he was still there, asleep on the pew. I know people said he set that fire, but I don't see how he could have. Just thought you should know."

Huff raised his eyes at that little bit of information. Just two days ago Gordon—the fire chief—had told him the fire must have been set somewhere between seven and seven-thirty. And that traces of aluminum hydroxide were found on the grass— an over-the-counter compound that delays ignition. And those hang-ups on Hubble's answer machine that had been traced to the pay phone outside the Breakers Laundromat—those were logged in just after seven. Huff pursed his lips together. He had a hard time picturing Thurber in a church, unless he was hiding out.

He watched the pastor walk down the street toward his house a few blocks away. There were sad days ahead for that family, as Tomás would surely serve time in jail, along with all the others. Even if Thurber refused to press charges, the State wouldn't let it slide.

He thought about that little boy, Miguel, visiting his father in jail. He thought about Celia and Alma and all the tears they'd cry. And why? All because a few guys didn't like a young, troubled man who rubbed them the wrong way. Now, their lives would be the ruined ones, while Thurber would probably walk away, free as a bird. Made no sense, none at all.

He unlocked his front door and stepped inside the warm, quiet house. He thought of all the hullabaloo he'd have to go through tomorrow—statements, interrogations, reports, meeting with the D.A. Oh, it would be a whole bundle of fun.

He just couldn't wait.

# Chapter 42

BILLY THURBER STUFFED HIS HANDS INTO HIS POCKETS AS HE stood in front of Huff's desk.

"Well, if that's everything, then I guess we're done here," Huff said. He narrowed his eyes and scrutinized Billy one last time. "You sure you didn't see who fired that gun?"

Billy grunted. "Like I told you, Mrs. Moore pushed me back and stood in front of me. Besides, it was foggy—or didn't you notice?"

Huff ran a hand through his hair. "I just have to wonder why a fine, upstanding individual like Irene Moore would take a bullet for you."

"How should I know? Some people are hard to figure out."

*You should talk.* "Well, I don't know much about religious things, but I'd guess Irene turned out to be your guardian angel."

Another grunt.

"And that pastor at the church—he said he spotted you sleeping on a pew the night of the fire." Huff studied Billy, waiting for something. "Said you couldn't have set the blaze. Just what were you doing in there?" Huff wondered if the pastor had bothered to check to see if anything had gone missing—like some candelabra or cash out of the donation box.

Billy shook his head, his expression almost amused. "How do you know I wasn't asking God to send me that guardian angel?"

Huff chuckled—like he really believed that. "Right." He met Billy's eyes but found them empty of cynicism. "So, Thurber, where to now?"

Billy shrugged. "S'pose I'll go back up to the cabin, get some of my things. Maybe make a new start somewhere. Travel."

Huff offered his hand and Billy looked at it a moment, then shook it. "You'll need to contact me with an address, once you settle somewhere. I'm trusting you, Thurber, to do that. You'll be subpoenaed for trial."

"Yeah, I heard you the first time. I'll send you a Christmas card. And you know I want that rifle back, so you hang onto it for me." Billy gave him a semblance of a smile, and Huff almost sensed some friendliness in it.

"I'll have Wanda bake you a fruitcake."

Billy snorted and opened the front door. "Whatever."

Huff watched Billy through the glass window. Up until a moment ago, he'd had little doubt that rifle would test positive. But the way Billy spoke, with that look in his eye—a look that held a confident knowledge—planted a little seed of doubt. However, that meant someone else had shot Nate Thurber, and Huff realized he hadn't even considered that. Well, it was Trinity County's business, and they'd decide what to do if Billy's rifle didn't match the bullet.

As the kid got into his truck and drove away, Huff's fax machine whirred and spit out a piece of paper.

The letterhead indicated a Portland, Oregon police division. Huff read the message that explained how they'd arrested a couple—a man and woman in their thirties—busting into some cars at a state beach parking lot. The captain thought the Breakers Police Department would be interested, as some of the pilfered effects recovered from the trunk of the impounded vehicle matched items listed in the computer database, including a wallet and cell phone that belonged to the owner of one of the cars broken into at the local trailhead back in September. And they'd also found an assortment of power tools that could have come from Matt Moore's truck. They wanted the officials in Breakers to know the culprits had been apprehended and the items would be retained as evidence at trial.

*Well, well, well.* Huff reread the fax. It was just like he'd told Moore that day—these crafty-type folks breezed through town on occasion, working their way across the state. You saw it all the time. Scratch Thurber off that one too.

The phone rang and Huff answered it. He was surprised to hear one of the city council members on the line—a woman named Denise.

"Sheriff Huff, I've got good news for you."

Huff smirked. He just couldn't wait to hear what the Breakers City Council wanted from him now.

"You may not believe this, but we've found someone to fill the police chief position."

Huff nearly fell out of his chair. "Who?"

"He's a police captain from Oakland. Bringing his family here next week. But he'll be up for a visit in a few days. Are you willing to meet with him and show him around a bit?"

"Hey, I'll give him the royal twenty-five-cent tour."

"That's great. Well, we want you to know how much we all appreciate your dedication and hard work. Especially lately."

"How sure is this deal?" He didn't want to get his hopes up and then have them dashed.

"Oh, it's in the bag. He's already signed the contract and arranged for his house to be rented until it sells."

Huff breathed out a sigh of relief. This was the best news he'd heard all year. He pictured hammering that "For Sale" sign out in front of his own house, then packing up and moving to Weitchpec—for good. He saw himself net fishing on the Klamath, pulling in a monster salmon, helping the grandkids with their school projects, showing them how to polish rocks in the tumbler.

"Sheriff Huff? You still there?"

"Oh, sorry. Just daydreaming a bit."

"Okay. Well, gotta run. Just wanted you to know."

" 'Preciate that." He hung up.

*Well, what do you know?* Today had started out an ordinary day and was now ending with things he never expected. Getting to quit his job sooner rather than later. Finding out some habitual thieves were the ones who'd broken into those vehicles. And watching Billy Thurber leave Breakers—in his own truck, and not handcuffed in a patrol car.

Would wonders never cease?

# Chapter 43

"AND WITH MORE INFORMATION ON THE BIZARRE KIDNAPPING and murder attempt on the Breakers pier, here's news anchor—"

Jerry Hubble pressed the Mute button—once he located the remote—then threw the stupid thing at the dark screen looming at him in the dim light of his cottage. He upended the bottle of scotch and shook it over his empty glass, watching a few drips trickle out. He then threw both the glass and the bottle at the TV but missed by a mile. They struck the wood-paneled wall and shattered, sending glass flying in all directions.

After the ignominy of spending a week in the Humboldt County Jail, Hubble had been reduced to hitching a ride back to Breakers in his filthy, stinking clothes. The only person willing to give him a lift was a rancher who'd told him he could sit in the truck bed—along with two yappie Border Collies who ran back and forth across his legs the whole trip north.

He'd used every last penny of his savings to post bail. His lawyer had pressed hard to get him out on bail, but how could they have held him? This was a first offense, and no one had died—and did they really think he'd skip town? Just where in the world did they think he would run to without a dime in his pocket?

He looked around at the four ugly walls of his tiny cottage and realized with growing horror that soon he would likely be stuck in a cell a lot smaller, and with even uglier walls. His only shred of hope lay in the expertise of Aaron Stern, his new, expensive lawyer.

Jerry grumbled at the irony. He reached over to the coffee table and pulled the insurance check from the envelope. More than he had dreamed of getting from that fire, and now it would all go to some fancy lawyer who would bleed him dry for every cent of it. Wasn't that just like life? He could have opted for a State defense attorney, but he knew what would happen if he went in that direction. Something like five to ten—if he was lucky. With Stern—who was reportedly the best around—he had a chance of probation and community service—*a chance*. At worst, copping a misdemeanor and spending a year in County. Pulling weeds on the airport runway was a whole lot more appealing than staring out the bars of the county jail at the cars stuck in traffic on Fourth Street in downtown Eureka. But the way his luck had been running, he certainly wasn't getting his hopes up.

Jerry stared at the check, struggling to focus. He waved the piece of paper in the air and chuckled. All the trouble he'd gone to—beginning with singling out Thurber when the punk arrived in town. His golden opportunity to frame him for the fire he'd planned, giving him the perfect situation to cry arson instead of setting up an "accidental" fire in one of the rooms. Getting his neighbors to grow suspicious of the creep. Well, that hadn't been hard. Thurber probably *had* robbed those homes.

But why hadn't Huff arrested Thurber for the fire? Maybe the sheriff would have been more convinced if Jerry'd been able to coax Thurber into coming over that evening—so someone would have seen that truck parked on the premises. Even better if he'd had something that belonged to Thurber and left it at the scene of the "crime." He'd thought the plan was perfect, but that slippery weasel escaped that net—just as he had all the other nets.

And now, because of that fiasco at the pier, his beautiful Corvette was gone—repossessed. The giant sucking sound in the universe was his monthly car payment funneling into that lawyer's pocket. He'd have to buy some old, cheap car now—if he managed to stay out of jail.

He let the check drop from his shaky fingers and watched it fall to the coffee table. His head spun as he tried to stand, then he changed his mind and sat again. If only this merciless pounding would stop.

"Mr. Hubble, yoohoo, are you in there?"

Jerry strained his head around to the front door. That's where the pounding came from. He managed to get up, put one foot in front of the other, and arrive at the door where Mrs. Waverly stood, wrapped in a shawl and squeezing her dog to her chest.

His neighbor made a sour face when he leaned toward her and breathed hello. "Whatcha want, Mrs. Waverly?" Her dog growled and bared its teeth. Jerry backed up into the lamp in the entry. It fell with a thud to the carpeting.

"Well, Mr. Hubble, I can see this isn't a good time to disturb you ..." She huffed and cleared her throat. "But, really, Mr. Hubble, it's only ten in the morning. A bit early for liquor, don't you think?"

Hubble snapped at her. "Well, no one invited you over, did they? What do you want, anyway?"

Hubble took some enjoyment in seeing Mrs. Waverly's ruffled expression. "I thought you'd be interested to know," she said, stroking her dog, which did little to quiet its escalating growl. "As I was sweeping under my dresser, the necklace caught on the broom, you see."

Jerry shook his head, trying to remember something about a necklace. His neighbor continued: "Well, I hadn't lost it after all—it just slipped down the back of the dresser when I had taken it off one night. Silly me."

Jerry stood there, leaning against the threshold, wondering what in the world she was talking about.

Mrs. Waverly mumbled something and turned away. Jerry watched her walk in her stiff, shaky way as she crossed the street and disappeared into her house.

He shut the door and stood in the middle of his living room. The place was a mess, with clothing and dishes everywhere. He looked down at his grimy T-shirt and stained sweatpants and realized he still hadn't taken a shower since he arrived home.

A stack of bills sat on the kitchen counter—bills he had no intention of paying. Maybe they'd shut off his phone and electric. Maybe they'd foreclose on his trash-pit motel. What did he care? His lawyer had said something about an arraignment date and making sure he had some nice clothes to wear to court. Well, he didn't own any nice clothes, and he certainly wasn't going to go out and buy any. Without a car, he couldn't even get to the market for food unless he walked the three miles or thumbed a ride.

Jerry fell back into his big, stuffed chair. He thought about Billy Thurber and the first day he'd laid eyes on him at the market. How he'd sized that punk up, sensing trouble. How right he'd been. Because of that punk, his own life was now in the toilet. Then he thought of his ex-wife, living in his spacious house in Eureka.

Tears welled up in his eyes. Life just wasn't fair. All the rotten people got away with all their nasty deeds. And here he'd spent his entire life helping people, risking his life fighting fires, and trying to make his neighborhood safe. And where had it gotten him?

He wished he still had that gun. He remembered the surprise he'd felt, seeing it tucked behind Tomás's belt. At that moment he'd thought the gods had smiled on him, giving him the leverage he needed to make Huff leave. Instead, the idiot Mexican tried to yank it away from him. And then Moore's wife got shot. Worse, he lost his grip on the gun and it slid right to Huff's feet. Everything had gone south.

He should have taken that gun and put it to his own head. That would have been the smartest move. Now he knew better than to try to outsmart the gods. They'd toyed with him, tempted him, and teased him. Chewed him up and spit him out. He pictured them laughing at him, calling him a sucker. *Well, let 'em laugh.*

Jerry reached down and picked up a shard of glass from the carpet. He stared at the piece of label and ran his finger along the thick jagged edge. Maybe he should just end it all. Slit his wrists and erase his life. His ex was right—he was a loser. Always had been and always would be.

Jerry gripped the piece of glass in his hand as hot tears splashed onto his cheeks. He looked around his disheveled cottage. A year in the county jail might not be so bad. How could it be any worse than his miserable existence in this dumpy town of Breakers? And maybe, *maybe*, if that lawyer was worth his expensive hourly rate, Jerry'd be out in a year.

One thing he knew for sure—if he did get out, he'd leave Breakers for good. Go as far away as possible. Find a place to live where there were no more stupid, incompetent people— like that sheriff. Or jerks like Billy Thurber.

Jerry wiped the tears from his face with an angry swipe and got up to scrounge another bottle of scotch.

No, life just wasn't fair.

# Chapter 44

"HONEY, JUST WHAT *DID* THAT LADY SAY TO YOU?" DOTTIE asked for the third time.

Tim paid her no mind but watched the road instead. Driving took every bit of his concentration. When he got to the stop sign, he turned and looked at her. "She didn't say. Just wanted us to come in."

Tim had never met Mrs. Price, the elementary school principal. She sounded nice enough on the phone. Said some kid had something to tell them. What kid? They didn't know any of the kids in town—only some of their folks who shopped at their store.

"Well, remind me when we're done that I need to get a few groceries. Since we're out," Dottie said.

"As long as you don't dally. The note I put on the door said we'd be back by noon."

"Oh, I got the list here in my little old head. Between the two of us, we'll be done in a jiffy."

Tim parked in front of the school and walked with Dottie through the front doors and into the small office. A young, sturdily built woman with thick black hair noticed them through the little glass window in the next room. She looked like that Betty Crocker picture on the cake mix box. She stood and opened her door.

"Mr. Brody? Mrs. Brody?" She shook their hands and thanked them for coming. When she gestured for them to enter her office, Tim noticed a fat Indian boy with his head bowed, sitting in a chair next to the desk. He turned and saw Dottie's puzzled look.

"Corey," the principal said, "I want you to tell the Brodys what you told me."

The boy lifted his head and Tim heard Dottie make a little noise. He knew her heartstrings were tugged at the sight of this boy's anguished face. He'd clearly been crying.

The principal pulled over two small chairs and motioned to them to sit.

Dottie spoke in a quiet voice. "You don't need to be scared of us, Corey. Just talk and we'll hear you out."

Tim saw a spark of relief light up the boy's face. He sensed this poor child was often under someone's thumb.

The boy's words squeaked as he looked down at the floor. "I didn't want to do it. The other boys dared me."

"I told Corey it was brave of him to come forward. He's scared what the other kids will do to him," said Mrs. Price.

Corey raised his head and nodded.

"His teacher, Mrs. Moore, noticed he was bothered by something. He told her how some of the boys had coerced him to break into your shed behind your store."

Corey turned to Tim. "I didn't take anything—I swear."

Tim rested a hand on the boy's shoulder. "Of course you didn't, son." He met Dottie's eyes and saw her nod. She was ready to take that big cuddly boy into her bony arms and squeeze the daylights out of him.

His voice quivered. "One of the kids gave me an old army knife he found at the trailhead. Told me to use it to pry open the door. When I tripped, I made a noise, and then I heard someone come out and yell. The other kids ran but I hid inside. I think it was you who came out."

Tim nodded. "Go on." The story made sense, but he wanted to hear how it ended.

"I was ... so scared when I heard you come in there; I just pushed my way through and ran out as fast as I could."

Tim scrunched his face and tried to remember. Someone had brushed against him, throwing him off balance. No one had hit him with a board; he'd lost his footing and smacked his forehead against one of the metal shelves. Now he saw it clearly.

"Son," Tim said. "It's always best to get things off your chest. You feel better now?"

The boy exhaled and nodded. "Mrs. Price said you might want to tell the sheriff."

Tim saw the pleading in his eyes. He could picture how much aggravation those other boys would give this poor child if the sheriff was called in.

"Now, that surely won't be necessary," Tim said. "But, don't you agree those other boys shouldn't be allowed to get away with stuff like that? They'll just pull some other prank—and blame that on you or another innocent kid."

Corey nodded. Misery was written in big letters across his face.

Dottie leaned closer to Corey. "Hon, it'd be best if those kids got told off with their parents in the room with them. You don't need to be there. What do you think, Corey?"

Mrs. Price smiled. "And I will make sure their parents understand that if anything like this happens again, those boys will be suspended from school for a very long time."

Tim studied Corey's face. No matter how the matter was handled, Corey would be labeled a fink and more trouble was bound to follow.

Tim's heart went out to the kid. It sure was tough being young—almost as tough as being old.

LEE CHIN, THE OWNER OF THE HARBOR BAIT SHOP, drove slowly past the elementary school, leaning his head close to the windshield, straining to see out through his thick glasses. He allowed himself a glance at the library parking lot and felt the usual twinge of guilt. But he made himself look. A necessary reminder.

His old Rambler chugged down the street as it wound down the hill to the harbor. Things would be different, he told himself in his repetitive litany, if he had money. Anyone with such an expensive car would have plenty of insurance. It would cost them little to fix all that damage. But he couldn't afford insurance. If he had reported the accident, why, they would probably take his business away from him, maybe even deport him. Laws were changing. Everyone was scared about terrorists. Good thing he was Chinese and not Iranian. He snorted. Well, back in the early days of Eureka, they'd chased all the Chinese out of town. It could happen again. Look at what they did during World War II—how Americans put all the Japanese in internment camps—even citizens whose families had been in this country for generations.

No, better to keep quiet and lay low. He had a good thing here in America. His children were American citizens; his two daughters had married American men. He liked visiting his grandchildren. As bad as he felt about smashing that car, he felt worse about the possibility of being shipped back to China.

He parked his car and unlocked the bait shop. It would probably be prudent to have his eyes checked. His glasses were many years old, and scratched up. Maybe if he got a new pair with a better prescription, he would stop crashing into things.

He stopped in the doorway when something caught his eye. Next to the door handle, embedded in the wooden door frame, was a shiny piece of metal. Surely he would have noticed it before. He poked his small pinky into the hole and felt around. He'd seen plenty of bullet holes in the dock buildings in Shenzhen; plenty of gunfire, for that matter. But how strange for a bullet to be lodged in the wall of his bait shop, here in this sleepy town. And what was this? He looked closer at the planking at the base of his door. He stooped down and touched the stains, then smelled his fingers.

Blood! Was this a sign? What could it portend?

Chin hurried inside his shop and locked the door behind him. Maybe he should confess about smashing that beautiful red car the night he left the town meeting. Maybe the blood was symbolic of his guilt, creating a stain on his life. Maybe he'd better do something to counteract the bad karma he'd created.

Lee Chin hurried into the back room and knelt on his small rug. His little Buddha statue sat on the low table with a serene expression on its face. Surely he could just chant this bad karma away. That would do the trick. What did Buddha care about expensive American cars, anyway?

MATT SIPPED HIS COFFEE WHILE STANDING OUTSIDE THE PO-lice station. He had dropped by, hoping Sheriff Huff knew the whereabouts of Billy Thurber, and was surprised to learn the boy had left town for good. He couldn't blame him, could he? Matt grimaced. *Not after so many beatings.*

Huff wanted to know why Matt was looking for the kid. He told Huff he owed Billy an apology, and wanted to thank him for helping Irene on the pier that night. Billy could have run off once Irene was shot, but he stayed. And that implied more than stupidity or fear. Somewhere beneath that scowling, irritable demeanor lurked a person with feelings. Matt was sorry he hadn't gotten to talk with Billy; he'd been thinking about what to say now for days.

Huff said he'd get an address for him, that he could write him a letter. Well, that would have to do.

Next door at the realty office, a young brunette wobbled high up on a ladder, trying to secure Christmas lights to the little hooks protruding from the roof fascia. He cringed as he watched her.

"That's a pretty rickety ladder." He walked over and secured it with his hands. "You're not supposed to stand on the top step; you know that, don't you?"

The woman laughed and stepped down two rungs. "I guess I'm too lazy to keep moving the ladder."

"Better that than break your neck."

She pinched her lips into a guilty smile, then stepped down. "You're Matt Moore." The tone in her voice grew serious. "I am so sorry about what happened to your wife. Is she all right?"

Matt nodded.

"I'm Julie Driscoll." She shook his hand. "That sure was amazing, what your wife did."

This realtor wasn't the first person to say that to him over the last week, and Matt still didn't know how to answer. Did people think Irene was a hero or just reckless? He'd forgotten how well known teachers were in a small community. And a shoot-out on the local pier was big news for a place like Breakers.

"Well," Julie said, "this has been a strange year. Your family recently moved here, right?" Matt nodded again. "Were you here when all those break-ins started?"

He recalled how Jerry Hubble had pinned those on Thurber. "I heard that some of the houses on Bayview got hit."

"Oh, not only there, also ones up in Fairhaven and by the state park. Most of those were my rentals, and I was not happy, let me tell you."

"Was anyone ever caught?"

"Well, that's the reason I brought it up. I guess you didn't see this morning's paper. There was an article about a stakeout the Eureka Police did, after some anonymous tipster called in. They arrested two guys who own a carpet-cleaning business, and after they searched a storage unit the pair owned, they found it stocked to the gills with loot." She frowned. "North Coast Carpet Care. The very company I hired to clean all those homes at the end of the tourist season. You'd think I would have put two and two together."

"Sometimes we just don't see the obvious," Matt said, recalling a memory of a cleaning service hauling a carpet shampooer up some rickety steps.

Julie chuckled. "Yeah, you're right. We never seem to see things that are right under our noses — until it's too late."

Julie's word's stung Matt's heart. They sounded like an appropriate epitaph for his gravestone. He excused himself politely and climbed into his truck.

The little shopping center was decorated with strings of lights everywhere, even wrapping up the flagpole. A larger-than-life inflated plastic Santa and a team of reindeer sat out in front of the market. Christmas music played into the parking lot from speakers mounted on the corners of the building. Someone who sounded like Doris Day was singing "White Christmas," although he doubted it ever snowed here at sea level.

He thought back to a dozen Christmases past. He could almost taste Irene's eggnog and see the kids sneaking sips and giggling. A smile inched up his face and tears pooled in his eyes.

There was Jesse, so bright-eyed and sandy-haired. Standing on the stepladder just like that woman, Julie, had been doing—stretching his arms out to attach the star to the top of the tree. And Irene—sitting by the fireplace with Casey, teaching her how to thread her needle to make popcorn strings. Daniel's job was putting the metal hooks on the glass ornaments and helping Jesse hang them on the boughs.

When they finished decorating the tree, they would turn off all the lights in the room and wait breathlessly in the dark. Matt would plug in the string of lights and suddenly the room would be filled with color, with the tree sparkling with tinsel and the little bulbs blinking on and off. They'd all ooh and aah, and then run to get the presents they'd wrapped and pile them under the tree.

Matt sat behind the wheel, letting the good feelings from those memories feed his soul. Sure, they would never have another Christmas, all of them together, ever again. And that hurt, really hurt. If he could have one Christmas wish, it would be to hold his boys in his arms one more time. To tell them how much he loved them, how much he missed them.

As tears streamed down his cheeks, an unexpected feeling of comfort came over him. It started in one little place in his chest and spread across his whole body. It reminded him of the moment he'd held Irene in his arms as she lay bleeding on the pier with that peaceful look on her face.

*"Comfort, comfort my people, says God."*

Suddenly, he felt small, the little boy staring in wonderment at the huge, dazzling Christmas tree in his childhood home. He caught a whiff of pine. Felt the warmth of a crackling fire. He heard his mother recite the Twenty-third Psalm in her soothing voice.

*"The Lord is my shepherd, I shall not want. He makes me lie down in green pastures ..."*

Matt turned on the engine and drove out of the parking lot. He thought of Irene, now resting on the couch, wrapped in her electric blanket with Casey cuddled up next to her.

*"He leads me beside still waters; he restores my soul ..."*

He thought of Casey, her soft, sad eyes, missing her brothers. Trying to make Irene laugh, and baking giant oatmeal cookies that filled the house with the aroma of cinnamon and sugar.

*"Even though I walk through the darkest valley, I fear no evil; for you are with me ..."*

He saw Jesse's mangled body lying on the ground, hail falling around him in the biting wind, Daniel numb at his side.

*"You prepare a table before me ... my cup overflows ..."*

He thought of Tim and Dottie and how they'd joked and laughed around their table at Thanksgiving, reminding them all of their shared joy and suffering on this earth.

Then he thought of a young troubled man, just trying to get by, so misunderstood and mistreated. He saw Billy Thurber's eyes with their mean, challenging glare. He felt Daniel's hurt and anger condemning him. He let the hurt stake a claim in his heart, wondering if someday he would understand—no ... would *believe*—he was truly forgiven.

*"Surely goodness and mercy shall follow me all the days of my life, and I shall dwell in the house of the Lord forever."*

Matt wiped his wet face with his sleeve and felt the ache in his heart subside. He slowed as the hardware store came up on his left. Tim and Dottie were outside, pinning a wreath on the front door. They waved as he pulled into the parking lot.

"Hey, hon, how are you today?" Dottie called out, holding the wreath up for Tim to attach. Matt got out of the truck and walked toward them.

"Hi Matt," Tim said. "How's that wife of yours?"

"Good. She's recovering well."

"Bless her heart," Dottie said. "So whatcha need?"

Matt smiled, and for once it didn't feel pasted on his face. He actually felt something that reminded him of joy.

"Christmas lights, Dottie."

He smiled even bigger. "*Lots* of lights."

# *Chapter 45*

HUFF BALANCED THE STACK OF BOOKS ON HIS KNEE AS HE pressed the speaker phone button. "Sheriff Huff here." He dumped the load into the cardboard box perched on his desk chair.

"Huff." The voice sputtered through the speaker. "Deputy Warner. How're things going there? Seems you've had a little excitement in your town as of late."

"A little." He crammed one more book into the box and reached for the packing tape.

"I hear you've been replaced. Moving back to the Res?"

"You betcha. I'm packing even as we speak."

Warner chuckled. "I bet you can't wait to get out of there."

*You don't know the half.* "You get back the test fire results on that rifle?"

"Yep—that's one of the reasons I wanted to speak with you. Thurber's gun tested negative. Not his rifle."

Huff grunted. *So there you have it.* "You folks have any other ideas about who may have shot Nate Thurber?" No doubt this would get chalked up as another mountain mystery.

"Well, I finally tracked down Jonathan Harrison—he's the rich guy with the property about a mile below Thurber's. He told me about his encounter with Grizz."

Huff remembered the nicely paved asphalt driveway and the sign with Harrison's name on it. He was all ears.

"One evening in September, a few days after Billy Thurber showed up in your town—according to the information we gathered—Harrison's dogs started barking and ran down the driveway. At first, Harrison thought a bear was trying to break into his Hummer, since it was dusk and he was way up the top of the hill. Said the glare of the setting sun was in his eyes. He fired his shotgun a couple times into the air, hoping to scare the bear away. But then he recognized Thurber, drunk or crazed, trying to break into the vehicle. Harrison ran down and yelled at him. Said Thurber was nearly incoherent, mumbling about how his kid had taken off with his truck and he had to get to town." Warner added, "But he claims he didn't shoot him."

"You sure about that?" Huff could almost hear Warner shrug.

"The shotgun's the only weapon he owns."

Warner paused and Huff let the words sink in. They both knew that proved nothing. One of Harrison's buddies could have had a rifle.

They were grasping at straws. "Did he say anything about seeing Billy drive off in the truck?"

"No, but he did notice Grizz had blood on his face. Said he was ranting like a wild man. Scared him enough to pack up and leave for the season. Hasn't been up to his house since."

Huff chewed on the information a bit. "The kid could've driven off with his dad's rifle and truck, stranding him. Maybe they'd had a fight; that would account for the blood on the table and on Grizz's face."

"That's what I'm thinking. Not sure how Grizz made it from the top of the mountain all the way down to the river. That's about twelve miles. But he coulda been a tough old geezer, and his desperation for liquor may have greatly pressed him onward."

Huff grunted in agreement. "Well, any way you cut it, Billy didn't shoot his father. But someone did."

Warner's sigh made the speaker hiss. "Yeah, we're still working on that. But you know how it is up there. People defend their property and shoot first, ask questions later."

The front door to the station swung open and Huff looked up. "Gotta go, Warner. If you unravel any more of this story, I'd sure like to hear it."

"You bet. I know where you'll be—fishing on the Klamath. I'll find you."

A man entered the room and stood in front of Huff's desk. "Okay, thanks." Huff disconnected the call.

Huff thought Paul Kirby looked fine in his black police uniform. His rusty brown hair lay perfectly in place and even his shoes were spit polished. Very official. Breakers was getting a good man, from what he could tell. He'd spent half a day with Kirby last week, showing him around, hearing his stories of working on the force in Oakland. The man had seen his share of action over his ten years in the city, and those years appeared to have taken a hard toll—on both him and his family. Kirby had oozed with excitement over moving to such a pretty place and having a small, safe school for his two young sons to attend.

"Well, Kirby," Huff said. "You look eager to jump in and start policing this town." He motioned him over to the only chair not covered with stacks of stuff. "I should be out of here in the hour."

Kirby sat, posture perfect. "Oh, there's no rush."

"You settled into your new house?"

Kirby nodded. "My wife thinks everything has to be put away in one day. She's even hanging pictures on the wall already."

"Yeah, well, it's exciting to move." *It sure was.* Huff already had his moving van loaded, and Wanda was in town at the house, packing up all her trinkets and his jars of rocks. His hands were itching to grab hold of that steering wheel and head for the hills.

Wanda's family had a big party planned. Besides his daughters and all the grandkids, Huff figured half the reservation would be there at Wanda's brother's place, with the big barbecue set out under the back patio awning in case of inclement weather. Well, rain or snow, they'd have themselves a great time. Huff missed his grandkids so much. With all the craziness in Breakers, he hadn't been up to see them in weeks, aside from Thanksgiving. He planned to chase those little rascals until they—or he—fell from exhaustion.

He looked around at the bare walls of his office and taped up another box. He'd miss this place, sure, but the last few months had really worn him down—he could feel it in his old bones. He was glad to have served his town these two years, but it was way past time to leave. No more "retiring" from retirement.

"Sheriff Huff?" Kirby gave a look that made Huff realize his mind had wandered again. "I just came to tell you I'll be in later today with my things. Try to catch up on reading your reports."

Huff chuckled. "Well, be sure to make a big pot of coffee." He tapped a thick file on the desk. "There's a bit to wade through here."

Kirby's eyes shone. "I'm looking forward to it. Can't tell you how great it feels to be here in this quaint town, so peaceful and serene. Such a change from the insanity of the city."

Huff stifled the outburst of laughter wanting to escape. "Oh yes, we revel in peace and quiet up here." He shook Kirby's hand, then hoisted a box and stacked it with the others by the door. Time to go fetch Wanda and the U-Haul and swing around here for the last bit of loading.

He reached into the top desk drawer. "You'll need these." He handed Kirby a set of keys.

Kirby thanked him and shook his hand, then followed Huff outside. Huff watched Kirby get into the Breaker's police cruiser as he locked the front door and started walking back to his house. He chuckled, thinking about Kirby's idyllic view of his new town. It was just a matter of time. He'd lose that naïve opinion soon enough.

But, then again, maybe things would settle down for a while. Thurber was gone, Hubble and the others would go to jail. You could never predict it; crime seemed to come in waves, and they'd sure had some big rollers wash over this town lately. Maybe the storm had finally passed. Maybe they were in for a period of calm, until the next set of waves. Well, whatever happened, he was sure the new police chief could handle it. Besides, Breakers wasn't his concern anymore. He had better concerns—like hunting rocks with his grandkids and watching the grass grow.

# Chapter 46

*Three Months Earlier*

ON SEPTEMBER EIGHTEENTH, IN THE LATE AFTERNOON, Billy Thurber drove up the rutted driveway in his father's truck, then stopped and waited till the cloud of dust settled before opening his door. He reached over and grabbed the two bags of groceries and headed to the cabin. He stopped when he saw Grizz standing on the porch with his hands on his hips.

Billy felt disgust rise up in his throat, the way it did every time he got a good look at his father. He was sick to death of caring for the old man, sick of his screaming tirades and insane mumbling. For months he agonized over staying or leaving. The cabin that had been his home his whole life was now a prison of horrors. He was used to his father being drunk all the time, but now Grizz was impossible to handle. He'd cook food for him, but his father would throw the plate across the room. Billy'd find him heaving up his guts at all hours of the day. At night, Grizz would scream in terror from monsters that attacked him.

Billy'd had enough. He tried more than once to load his father into the truck and take him to the hospital. Each time, Grizz fought him, or jumped—more like *fell*—out of the truck. One time, while Billy was moving at a fast clip down the steep grade, Grizz came to and threw open his door and nearly rolled off the mountain—and Billy wished he had. Now, staring at his old man standing there, ready to kill for a drink, he knew he had to leave. *Today.* He was sick and tired of this losing battle.

Grizz pawed at him before Billy put even one step up on the porch. "Let me have it." More growl than voice.

Billy narrowed his eyes and braced himself for the blow that was sure to come. "Have what? I told you that's it—no more liquor."

He watched the demon take over his father's eyes. With potent fury, Grizz lunged at him and tried to wrap his hands around his son's throat. Grizz was only a couple of inches taller than Billy but weighed close to two hundred and fifty pounds. He threw all his weight at his son and landed face-first on the dirt as Billy sidestepped him.

Billy walked around him and went into the cabin. He put the grocery bags down on the counter and began shelving cans. He heard the roar in his father's throat and listened to him crash into the side of the cabin, then stumble into the small room that served as dining room and kitchen.

Billy turned and looked at his father's disheveled clothes, his wild, filthy hair falling into his face. His father stank. Billy had tried to get Grizz to take a bath but finally gave up. The stench was unbearable, even five feet away.

Billy knew in his heart that, if he left, his dad would probably die. No one was going to come and care for him, and Grizz wouldn't let anyone, anyway. Well, if his old man wanted to rot in this cabin, then fine. But he wasn't going to take any more of this. Not anymore.

He stormed into the back room and pulled open drawers. He stuffed clothes into a duffle while he listened to Grizz scream in the next room.

"Where'd you put it, you little twerp!"

Billy picked the rifle up off the dresser and pocketed one of the boxes of bullets. He heard the grocery bags crash to the floor. He came back into the kitchen and found Grizz on his hands and knees, feeling into the bags.

Billy felt like throwing up. He stepped around the bulk of his father and rummaged through the kitchen drawer, pulling cash out from under the utensil tray. He hesitated a moment, fingering the stack of bills, then stuffed all of them in the duffle. He searched the room, gathered up a few more things, then stomped out the front door to go hook up the camper shell.

He worked quickly, backing the truck into position under the camper, disengaging the metal supports, and latching everything into place. He threw the duffle and rifle in the back, checking to see if his emergency supplies were still in the cupboards. He found the water and canned goods, flashlight, matches. What he didn't have he could buy.

Once he found a place to set up the camper, he'd come back up to the mountains and get his first load of firewood. There were still at least twenty cords over on the south ridge waiting to be split and loaded. He could make enough money from that to hold him awhile. He recalled that his old high school buddy Jordan had some property in a place called Fairhaven — over on the coast. He'd stop by Jordan's house in Weaverville and see if he'd let him park the camper there for the fall while he sold the firewood.

Suddenly, a hand yanked him back from the camper door.

"Whadda ya think you're doing?" Grizz didn't give Billy a chance to answer, even if he had an answer coming. He smashed Billy's face with a backhanded blow that sent him reeling across the yard.

As Billy lay there on the dirt, his head spinning, with Grizz barreling toward him, he thought of all the years he'd let his father beat him. Never once had he lifted a hand in return. He knew the day he did that, his father would kill him. Maybe not at that moment, but while he slept or when his back was turned. Grizz had threatened him plenty.

What he didn't understand was why he'd stayed with this crazy tyrant this long. What did Billy owe him? Nothing, that's what. There were earlier years when Grizz had been a decent father to him, before the drinking got out of hand. Ever since his mother abandoned them both—when Billy was about eight—there'd just been the two of them. They'd taken care of each other and made the best of it.

But those days were long past—and best forgotten.

Billy rubbed his back where he'd landed on a rock. He got up just in time to avoid Grizz's pathetic lunge. Hurried to the truck before he could change his mind, and got in. He rolled up the windows so he didn't have to hear his father scream at him.

As he backed up, he felt Grizz pound on the side of the truck with his fists. He tuned out the cries that turned to whimpers and swung the wheel, cramming the gearshift into First, then sped down the driveway, bouncing over potholes and kicking up a cloud of dust behind him.

In the side mirror he caught a last glimpse of his father stumbling down the driveway in a futile attempt to catch up with the truck.

Billy turned his head and locked his gaze on the road before him, telling himself he was finally free. His heart thumped in harsh judgment, berating him. He had longed for this moment for years, but the taste was bitter.

Somehow, freedom felt just like another prison.

FOR THREE DAYS GRIZZ HAD TURNED THE HOUSE UPSIDE down, and after realizing in his misery that there was no liquor to be found, he took off down the road. Surely the store was just down the way—wasn't it? He didn't have any money, but he'd think of something.

His need drove him, clouding out everything else. Without a coat, carrying no water, his boots untied, he tripped his way along and eventually found himself at the base of a steep hill in the warm, waning fall afternoon. His head throbbed from when he'd slipped and smacked it on the kitchen table. He could tell his face was streaked with blood; flies settled on his eyes and cheeks, drawn to the moisture.

He paused, his eyes riveted on the huge, shiny bulk of the yellow Hummer that appeared out of nowhere. Salvation was at hand! He fell against the vehicle and felt his way along until he found a door handle. Never mind that he hadn't driven in years, that his hands and legs shook so badly he could barely walk, or that his vision was blurry and he could barely see more than a few feet in front of him. The car was his ticket and his only hope. He squeezed the door handle and yanked with all his strength. Nothing.

Suddenly, wolves came at him—big, snarling creatures, foaming at the mouth. He screeched in fear and cowered, curling himself into a ball. The air around him filled with horrendous barking.

He wasn't sure if they were real or not. Slowly, he raised up and inched along to the other side of the car, trying to put the wolves out of his mind. That door was locked too. In frustration and despair, he pounded his fists on the window. Maybe if he got a rock, he could smash the glass and get in. Surely the keys would be in the ignition, waiting for him.

He felt the wolves snap at his clothing, felt their hot breath on his arms. He batted them away but they kept coming. Somewhere in the distance he heard a man yelling, and then the air ripped apart with gunshot.

Grizz tore off down the dirt road, expecting that any second the wolves would tear him to shreds. But they fell back and abandoned their chase, and Grizz stumbled on, his mouth dry and clothes dripping with sweat.

Hours went by. He lost all concept of time. The road was a treadmill that kept going on and on, but he never got anywhere. In the dark, by the light of a rising half-moon, he trudged down, down, the cold chill coming up from the river making his bones ache. He fell often and struggled back up. He pushed the gnawing need for water from his mind, forgetting why he was even on this road in the middle of the night. Where was his cabin? Where was Billy?

Disoriented, he wandered off the main road and onto a narrower one that veered south at the water tower. Something glinted in the distance, but he had no idea what it was until his fingers touched the metal mesh of the tall chain-link fencing. He couldn't recall a fence like this near the liquor store.

He fingered the mesh with both hands the way a blind man would feel his way along. When he reached the gate, he fumbled with the metal latch until it popped up and the gate swung wide open across the width of the driveway.

A BUZZING SOUNDED IN A SMALL HOUSE BURIED IN A GROVE of firs. A man with thick dreadlocks jerked his head up as he sat by the fireplace trimming marijuana buds. He glanced

at his partner, who listened in a stupor to the muffled ringing of the gate alarm. Dreadlocks pushed aside the pile of
*cannabis* and found the remote control. He clicked on the
TV and watched the live cam at the gate. His friend—with
long, stringy dark hair and a Grateful Dead T-shirt—stood,
wobbled for a moment to get his bearings, then stooped in
front of the TV set.

"Who is that?"

Dreadlocks answered. "Great. Someone nosing around in
the dark." He took a long toke off the joint smoldering in the
ashtray and got up.

"Let's go," his buddy said.

They grabbed their rifles as they left the house in their bare
feet.

As they trudged down the dirt road, Dreadlocks strained to
see a shape in the dim light. At first he thought it was a bear,
but then the shape spoke. Incoherent mumblings came from
the shaggy man's mouth; he was drooling, as if he had rabies.
Rather than slow down, the crazy man started running toward
him—stumbling and yelling, almost hysterical.

Dreadlocks didn't hesitate. He lifted his rifle, took aim, and
shot.

"What did you do that for?" the guy with the stringy hair
asked.

Dreadlocks shrugged. "He was trespassing."

"Great." Stringy Hair grabbed his friend's sleeve and studied the man on the ground, who lay unmoving. "Is he dead?"

Dreadlocks dropped to the ground next to the old filthy
man. "Phew, he stinks."

"Well?"

"Well, what?" Dreadlocks asked.

"Is he dead?"

"I can't tell."

Stringy Hair sighed as if his plans for the evening were now interrupted by this inconvenience. "Wait here."

Dreadlocks stood in the road, staring at the strange hairy guy on his driveway who seemed oddly out of place. Soon, two headlights came his way, causing him to squint. Stringy Hair got out of the truck.

"Help me throw him in the back."

"Where are we taking him?" Dreadlocks asked.

His friend thought for a moment. "The rest area. Someone'll be by in the morning to empty the trash cans. They'll take care of him."

Dreadlocks reached down and hefted the man's legs. His friend grabbed the man by the shoulders. "Dude, this guy weighs a ton." He scrunched his face at the smell. "Come on, let's hurry and get him out of here."

They didn't speak the whole trip down to Highway 299. Stringy Hair drove slowly while Dreadlocks tried to remember where they were going. At the stop sign, he looked both ways. The road was dark, void of cars. They turned east and continued a few miles until they approached the turnout for the day use rest area. The place looked deserted.

Stringy Hair stopped the truck at the farthest picnic table and they listened to the night with the windows rolled down. The river rumbled a couple dozen yards away, the only sound Dreadlocks could make out.

They got out and hoisted the old man, then dumped him onto the picnic table.

"There. They can't miss him like that," Stringy Hair said.

"Yeah. Let's go."

Stringy Hair looked down at his chest. "Oh, man!"

"What?"

"Look at my shirt. It's got blood on it." He sighed. "My favorite shirt."

"I hear vinegar will get that out."

"Really?" Stringy Hair's reddened eyes brightened. "I think I saw a bottle of the stuff under the sink."

They got in the truck and drove away.


THE NEXT MORNING, IN THE DIM PREDAWN LIGHT, GRIZZ Thurber awoke with a screeching pain in his gut. He managed to sit up, puzzled by the wooden table beneath him. He heard the sound of water and fell to the ground. As he crawled along on his knees, he looked back and noticed a trail of blood on the pavement, wondered where it came from. His throat screamed for something to drink, so he followed the sound until he reached damp sand.

By the time he found the water's edge, he felt faint and faded in and out of consciousness. Sunlight eased up over the ridge of mountains before him, lighting up the sky with a soft glow, but it provided no warmth. He shivered uncontrollably.

He dunked his head in the cold water and the shock made him yelp. Even though his thirst raged, he couldn't seem to swallow. He no longer had any feeling in his hands or legs, and he collapsed on the beach of the river and rested his cheek on the cool sand.

He was a worm or a turtle.

He was tired, so tired.

But then—he heard wolves again and panic struck his heart. Somehow they had followed him here! He crawled into the water. Wolves hated water, didn't they? He moved farther into the current on his hands and knees until the sand disappeared beneath him.

Suddenly, he felt light as a feather. The cold wrapped around him like a cocoon, and the water swayed and rocked him as he drifted. All his aches and pains disappeared, and he closed his eyes in relief. He heard someone call out. As he drifted, a man's muffled words filled his ears.

*Billy, is that you?* he thought, as the swift water carried him downstream.

Without waiting for an answer, he slowly sank beneath the surface of the river.

"HEY, WHY'D YOU FELLAS RUN OFF?" DEREK SAID TO HIS TWO black Labrador retrievers. "What're you barking at?"

Derek looked around but saw nothing on the beach. He figured they must have smelled a rabbit or a raccoon. He watched as the two dogs sniffed at the ground, then peed on some bushes. He picked up a stick and tossed it in the slow-moving water.

"Go fetch," he said.

As the dogs splashed into the river and fought over the piece of wood, Derek noticed something large and dark floating downstream. At first he thought it was a body, but then dismissed the idea as ludicrous. It had to be a log. He was nearing the end of his California vacation and his eyes must be tired from all the driving. California sure was a big state. Tomorrow he would head home to Arizona.

He squinted and looked again, but whatever floated downstream tumbled over the rapids and disappeared from view around the bend.

"Let's go, fellas."

The dogs ran back to him, fighting playfully over the stick. He lifted the hatchback of his car and patted the carpeting.

"Time to hit the road."

# Chapter 47

BILLY THURBER STOOD BACK FROM THE CABIN, TAKING A good look. Mean, dark clouds threatened to release a torrent of rain any minute. The wind blew in spurts from the north with a bitter cold. Billy zipped up his coat. Huff had warned him of the vile condition of the cabin, but Billy had no plans to go inside. He just wanted to see it one last time. Maybe lightning would strike it and burn it down. Or maybe, after a few decades, it would rot away, end up looking like so many of the abandoned mining homesteads up on the North Fork. A skeleton of forgotten memories. Good riddance.

All the way up here, Billy had thought of Irene Moore. He was still thinking of her. Sweat ran down his face even though the day was cool. He was a wreck of nerves and he couldn't get his hands to stop twitching. Why? As he walked onto the porch, he kicked hard at the cabin siding, fighting the urge to punch his fist through the wood. He had left Irene and Breakers behind him. His father was dead; he was free to go wherever he wished. No strings, no entanglements, no obligations. No guilt. So why this agitation?

He walked to the back of the cabin and unhooked the generator. He looked around and tried to think of anything else he could use. He sat on a flat boulder a few feet behind the cabin and his breath caught in his throat.

He tried to force the images from his mind, but they rushed at him mercilessly. He watched himself in Irene's arms, lying on the playground at that school. He shook violently from the cold—a day like this, with the wind whistling across the open field. She took off her coat and wrapped it around him, and he saw her shiver and her lips turn blue. Why did she do that for him? Billy sat there, shaking uncontrollably. He watched Irene take the scarf off her shoulders and drape it around his neck.

Instantly, Billy grabbed at his throat, unable to breathe. He jumped to his feet. Was he losing his mind?

He looked around, reminded himself where he was. He was alone, up in the mountains. Irene was not there.

But his mother was.

Billy held his breath and watched.

Winter. Cold. A staccato of harsh words. That was Grizz, screaming at his mother. Again. A rush of memories assaulted him. Grizz drunk, knocking his mother across the cabin. A crow bar gripped in his fist, poised. Her cheek swollen and black, bruises on her arms and legs. Billy cowering in his room, listening to her screams of fear.

Billy breathed hard while the images tumbled out of a secret cache in the back of his mind. Some cage door had flung open and those memories all escaped, fleeing for their lives. He saw his mother, studied her delicate face, her wavy blonde hair falling down her back. The pale blue blouse she wore rolled up at the cuffs. A sliver of a bracelet jangling at her wrist. He noticed her long, weathered fingers, dirty from pulling weeds in the garden. He recalled a patch of snap peas, tall stalks of corn, a bowl of ripe strawberries nestled between the rows of fragrant onions, their heavy white blooms bent over.

Billy lifted his eyes and saw the remnants of a chicken wire fence a dozen yards down the hill, on a flat ledge below him. He had forgotten that as well.

He saw his mother cooking in the kitchen, stirring stew in the big cast iron pot, the tendrils of steam twisting toward the ceiling. Spreading snow-white icing across the top of a cake and handing him the wooden spoon to lick. And sitting beside him on the couch, denting the mattress, reading him stories, stroking his hair.

Billy batted at the images, trying to push them away. That was not his mother! She was mean and cruel, never loved him, walked out on him when he was eight. In his mind he heard his father's angry voice, griping and cursing her year after year, for up and leaving them. For twelve years those words had been drilled into him, festered hatred, pounded down his earlier memories, burying them in a deep, deceitful grave.

But the truth wiggled its way to the forefront of Billy's consciousness, whether or not he wanted it to.

He saw himself huddled behind the bed, pressed into the corner. Cupping his hands over his ears so he didn't have to hear her scream. When she ran out of the house with Grizz after her, Billy had to follow. His mother rushed around the back with Grizz at her heels. Billy saw she had on her coat and scarf. She was leaving and Grizz had no intention of letting her go.

Billy looked at his own clothes and saw he had on his coat and cowboy boots. Suddenly, he remembered. His mother had come into the bedroom earlier, while Grizz snored on the couch. As she stuffed some of his things in a pillowcase, she whispered, *Hurry, get dressed. We're leaving.*

Billy gasped at her words, sounding so clear as if she now spoke them in his ear. He touched his cheek where he'd felt her warm breath. His mind shifted to the other Irene, who'd held him on the playground, her soft breath grazing his cheek as he lay in her arms. The stark realization slammed him. His mother was taking him along. They were sneaking out, getting away from Grizz. She wasn't abandoning him—she was *taking* him!

Billy chased after his mother and Grizz, crying and pleading. He grabbed a piece of Grizz's sleeve, but his father batted him away, a pesky mosquito. He fell and hit his head on this boulder. This one, here. Then he cowered behind it, his head swimming in a swirl of shadow, and watched in horror.

Billy whimpered. Grizz grabbed his wife and spun her around. She clawed at his face, struck him with her small fists, but Grizz laughed in drunken, vicious victory. Billy's jaw went slack as Grizz grabbed her by the shoulders and took hold of her scarf. His heart stopped beating as he yearned to tear his gaze away, but morbid curiosity compelled him to watch.

Grizz knotted the scarf around his wife's throat, tighter and tighter. She flailed her arms, tried to gouge his eyes with her fingers, but he just laughed and gritted his teeth while tightening the noose around her neck. She threw her head back and Billy heard her try to suck air. Stumbling out from behind the rock, he lunged at his father, a pathetic, poorly aimed attempt that Grizz aborted with a kick to Billy's groin. As Billy wrenched over and vomited, he managed to turn his head and in that instant caught the flash in his mother's eye, a match flaring, then dying out.

After an unbearable eternity of struggling, she went limp, with Grizz holding her up like a rag doll, shaking her a bit, seeing if she was finished with all her fussing.

Grizz hauled her up the hill behind the cabin, tossed over his shoulder like a sack of feed, unaware of Billy trotting behind, crying in great sobs. He hid behind a manzanita bush while Grizz threw her to the ground and went back to get a shovel. In the freezing cold afternoon, Billy crouched behind that bush and watched Grizz dig a hole and throw his mother into it. Grizz covered up the grave, then stomped the dirt down, kicked rocks over it.

Billy stayed by her grave long after Grizz had wiped dirt off his hands and stumbled back down to the cabin. Fat tears poured down his cheeks as he laid his hand on the dirt, trying to feel his mother there. He kept vigil into the night, his limbs as numb as his heart, and finally, fitfully, curled up in a ball and fell asleep on the loamy ground.

A crack of lightning shook Billy out of his memory and back to the present. He pulled the hood over his head as rain beat down on him. He felt as if all the blood had drained from his body. Raising himself up off the rock to stand took effort. He walked in a daze to the small shed and grabbed a shovel from the splintered wood wall.

As he trudged up the ridge behind the cabin, his rain-soaked pants stuck to his legs. He put on his gloves, crested the small hill, and looked around. Twelve years had swallowed up the grave, leaving an unmarred hillside of tall grass and blackberry brambles. Billy wandered around, stepped behind a bush, then squatted down. He peered out behind the twisted manzanita— and knew.

By the time he had dug through the matted top layer and made inroads into the softer dirt below, Billy was soaked with rain and sweat. He pulled down his hood and wiped the dripping hair out of his tearful eyes, then kept at his task until he reached his goal.

Billy moaned at the sight of it.

The decomposed clothing in shreds, eaten through by countless insects, the wisps of dirt-encrusted hair, now turning blonde as the rain fell down on it, exposing it to light once more. And the ivory bones, all in place, strangely perfect and at rest.

Billy watched as water fell in a deluge from the heavens, a flood washing away obscurity and deception and all things hidden. Bringing into daylight what had long lain in darkness, buried in the recesses of Billy's own heart.

He took one long last look, then reached for the shovel, his hands now strangely relaxed, the twitching gone.

*Mom*, he said in a small, faraway voice.

He dug into the soggy mound of mud and tossed a shovelful over the bones.

*I miss you.*

# Chapter 48

RAYMOND FERGUSON PEERED THROUGH THE FRONT WINdow at the truck pulling up into his RV park. He set down his mug of coffee and turned the volume low on the small TV perched on the ice cream cooler. Behind him, in the house, he heard his wife rattling around in the kitchen, preparing dinner. His mouth watered at the smell of fried chicken crackling on the stove.

Raymond stood and laced his boots, then put on his wool coat. He swung open the door to the cramped office, letting in a flurry of fat snowflakes. He glanced up the snow-powdered road to the handful of trailers and campers nestled in for the winter. A few had little lights on. Those were his regulars — the ones who lived here year-round. Drop-ins were rare after Thanksgiving, so he was curious. Well, more than curious, since the paper had printed that article about the hold-up at the local 7-Eleven in Etna. Imagine — someone coming in wearing a mask, of all things, in their quiet Scott Valley. He'd lived in the valley all his life and never heard of such a thing. Oh sure, over in Yreka maybe, where all kinds of weirdos got off the freeway. But few people traveled the back road over the Trinities, where there were limited services. It was like he'd told George yesterday—the world was slowly going to hell in a handbasket.

Raymond narrowed his eyes as the truck ground to a stop in front of the office porch. He smelled bad brakes. He wondered if the driver had just come down the I–5 grade with them smoking like that. Well, he would send the guy over to George's shop to get 'em looked at. George could use the business this time of year. So could they all, the economy being what it was.

Raymond took pride in his small park. In the summer, lots of people vacationed around here—backpackers exploring the Marbles, fishermen angling after fat trout, rafters eager to tackle the rapids. He practically acted as a tour guide during the busy hot months. He kept all the little lawns mowed and the flower beds along the driveway weeded nice and pretty. But things shut down tight and quiet right around Halloween. He hoped the savings he stocked away from the summer would carry them through a slow winter—again.

A young man stepped down from the truck cab. Raymond sized him up. The first thing he noticed about the boy was how filthy he was—like he'd been playing in the dirt all day. All right, maybe he was a laborer—no shame in that. Then he noticed the strange, dark expression on the boy's face. Raymond walked over and extended his hand, leaving it hanging in the air as the young man ignored him and looked away.

*Not very friendly, this kid.* Ferguson dropped his hand and cleared his throat.

"Name's Ferguson." He waited, noticed the boy's hands fidget. Caught his darting glance at the office door. Raymond tensed. His cash box was in there, sitting on top of the cooler beside the TV.

"You have any spaces open?" the boy asked.

Well, if that wasn't a stupid question. All the kid had to do was look around—the place was nearly empty. "Sure do. You fixing to stay the night or longer?"

His visitor pursed his lips together. "Longer."

Ferguson nodded. "So what's your name? Where you from?"

The young man frowned. "Why don't you just tell me where to park and when you want your money, okay?"

Ferguson stepped back. "Sure thing. Don't need to get snappy."

He pulled a folded piece of paper from his shirt pocket and circled number sixteen on the photocopied map. "Up there," he pointed. "The bathrooms and showers are behind number twenty. You can pay in the morning, if that suits you."

As the kid studied the map, Ferguson looked him over more closely. Hadn't that article described that robber as young, kind of lean, not too tall? He searched his memory, trying to remember.

The kid caught him looking at him. "What are you staring at? You got a problem?"

*No, you do.* "Well," he said, trying to lighten the mood. "You go on and get settled, all right?" His stomach grumbled, and he was getting cold standing out there with the snow falling.

The young man grunted. "Whatever." He turned and walked back to his truck.

Ferguson watched the young man with narrowed eyes. He needed the money, but he had second thoughts of renting a space to this kid. There was something about him he didn't like, that spelled trouble. Maybe in the morning he would encourage him to move on. Find a place up in Yreka or Weed. Now that he thought about it, that kid surely matched the description in the paper. Just what he needed—some thief hiding out in his RV park.

The young man startled him out of his thoughts by turning to face him. Ferguson watched in curiosity as the hard lines softened around the kid's mean eyes and tears pooled up and spilled onto his cheeks. For an awkward moment, neither said a word. Ferguson took a chance and caught the young man's gaze. The eyes had lost their edge, reminding him of the look he'd seen countless times in deer he'd shot, as they lay dying.

"You all right?"

The young man nodded and wiped his face with his shirtsleeve, streaking dirt across his cheek. His voice broke as he spoke. "Name's Thurber. Billy Thurber." He reached out to Ferguson. Ferguson pulled his own hand out of his coat pocket and shook the young man's hand. Those eyes had a story to tell, no doubt. But he wasn't one to pry. Still, something tugged at his heart.

"You hungry?" he asked Thurber, who stood stiffly, with snow dusting his hair and piling up on the shoulders of his coat. "My wife's cooked a mess of fried chicken. Be pleased to have you join us."

Billy Thurber hesitated, then nodded. Ferguson thought he heard the kid mumble thanks. He led him over to the office and swung open the door. A warm wave of heat blew out, and the aroma of dinner set Ferguson's mouth watering.

He ushered Thurber inside. "Yessiree, my wife makes the best fried chicken in the county. Take off your coat and toss it over there." He pointed to the upholstered chair next to his desk. He stole a glance at the kid and looked harder. No, this guy, Thurber, had blond hair, not brown. And the article in the paper said the thief was tan. This kid was pale, clearly not the one the police were after.

He cleared his throat and smiled, glad to have a little company.

"Betty," he called out, tossing his coat on the chair alongside Thurber's. "Set another place at the table. We've got a guest for dinner."

# Chapter 49

"THERE'S STILL TIME TO CHANGE YOUR MIND, IF YOU'D rather stay home."

Matt closed the latches on Casey's suitcase and carried it to the front door.

"Dad," Casey said, "We're supposed to get away for a few days, give Mom a rest, remember?"

Irene folded another sweater, moving slowly. Her shoulder twinged, but the pain was manageable. The doctor said not to lift anything heavy, but she should try to give her arm some motion. "No, I want to go," she called out from her bedroom.

"And Dad, Aunt Elaine loves to cook. We can have some *real* food for a change. I'm tired of microwave taquitos."

"What? I make real food. What about that chicken last night?"

Casey brought her backpack over to the door and set it down by the suitcase. She sneered playfully at her dad. "No comment."

"You ready, hon?" Matt asked, coming into the bedroom and lifting the suitcase from the bed. Irene nodded. He leaned over and gently kissed her. "How are you feeling?"

Irene smiled. "You ask me that, like, every ten minutes."

Matt chuckled at her imitation of Casey's speech. "Sorry, force of habit."

She stroked his hair. "It's a good habit."

Matt turned off the bedroom light. "Then I'll load the truck. We should have plenty of time to grab lunch at the airport before we have to board."

As Matt and Casey carried the luggage outside, Irene checked her purse to make sure she had her medicine. She knew they were doing this for her, taking her down to San Diego for the holidays to get her mind off things. But the vacation would be good for all of them. Casey would immerse herself in playing games with her cousins, and Matt's mother and sisters would smother him with food and attention. He'd complain, but Irene knew he loved their teasing. And she figured they'd put her to work helping in the kitchen. She could manage that.

They agreed to not bring up any of the recent troubles. Better to leave all that behind them. Maybe Matt's family would notice her shoulder was a bit stiff, but she didn't have to tell them she'd gotten shot in a crazy attempt to protect a young man she barely knew.

Irene closed her eyes and sighed. She thought she'd blank out the events of that night, but the opposite was true. She recalled the seconds as if they had unfolded in slow motion. She clearly saw those two men and the looks on their faces as they ran toward her. Saw the gun lift and the deliberate look in that man's eye as he aimed at her. Even though she'd told the sheriff it was an accident, it wasn't. The man who wielded the gun had locked eyes with hers in defiant rage. She had stood in the way of his target—Billy Thurber.

What struck her most was the hatred in that man's face. Rather than frighten her, a strange pity had welled in her heart.

That hatred was a kind of suffering, just like anger. It roiled under the surface, like a restless sea.

The image reminded her of a Scripture. *"The wicked are like the tossing sea that cannot keep still. There is no peace, says my God, for the wicked."*

Few times in her life had she experienced true peace. She'd felt it so strongly that night, as Billy hung in her arms.

She thought peace would be a gentle, soft feeling, but it was much the opposite. Peace was powerful and tremendous, forceful and consuming. It flattened everything around into submission, like an atomic explosion blasting out in all directions and leveling the ground for miles around. That was what she had felt, she now realized—empowered. When she had shed her fear and worry over her own life, she allowed room for God's spirit to step in. And who could successfully oppose the power that created a million galaxies? She doubted she would ever forget that sweeping sensation of peace.

*Thank you, God, for that gift. For using me to save Billy.*

Casey ran back inside the house. "Ready, Mom?"

She let Casey take her hand and lead her to the truck. Matt opened the door for her and helped her up. "You guys are babying me. I can manage."

"Oh, Mom, stop complaining. We're supposed to baby you."

She chuckled as Casey clicked her seat belt for her and said, "There, all nice and safe."

*Safe.*

She thought of that image—of a whole world of people floating in the ocean, desperately grasping for a lifeline—yearning for safety. Yet the world was a dangerous, uncertain place. There was nothing on earth that could guarantee your safety, your unhindered passage through the hidden icebergs lurking under the surface.

That you wouldn't suffer loss.

That someone you loved wouldn't get ill or meet with a horrible accident.

That you wouldn't find yourself freefalling.

Like Billy had told her on the beach that day, "You lose those things in the end."

"Yes," she had answered. "Of course you do."

So do you just give up on life, be afraid to risk love? Maybe Tennyson said it best in that famous poem: "'Tis better to have loved and lost, than never to have loved at all." Hurt would always accompany love — sooner or later. But how could you live life without love? What kind of life would that be?

She thought of Pastor Luis's words as Matt backed out of the driveway and headed down the gravel road. How we were put on earth to learn compassion, so we would grow beyond our selfish concerns and understand the way God loved us. Be more like him. Compassion was what counteracted the sorrow.

That, and trust — trust that God would make all things better, in the end.

As she stared out the truck window at the turbulent green water beyond the road's edge, she thought about her strange encounters with Billy Thurber. How he had stumbled into her life. She believed deep in her heart that there must have been some purpose in it, but she would probably never discover what part she played.

She just had to trust, was all.

# Acknowledgments

A BIG HUG OF GRATITUDE FOR MY READERS, ENCOURAGERS, and prayer partners. I couldn't walk this path without holding your hands and having your shoulders to cry on. Your prayers lift and buoy me on the journey. I am especially indebted to Kathy Ide, Renae Brumbaugh, Catherine Leggitt, and Ann Miller—you are each a godsend—my four legs of support. Your tough-love critiques are cherished and always challenge me.

Thanks, also, to the Trinity County and Plumas County Sheriffs' departments for information on forensics, firearms, and jurisdictions.

And thanks to so many others who read, advise, and uplift me in my writing journey: Jim Bell, Stephanie Morris, Jessica Dotta, Pola Muzyka, Jeanette Morris, Cindy Coloma, Rachel Williams, Kimberly Bass, Cheryl Ricker, Nick Harrison, Tina Dee, my agents Nancy Ellis and Susan Schulman, Elisabeth Pajara, and my friends in the San Jose Christian Writers' Group and the Santa Cruz Writers' Group. Sometimes just a kind word at the right moment was all it took.

And most of all, thanks to my husband, Lee Miller, who is a constant support and fountain of encouragement. I love you beyond words and am so grateful to God for you. Thank you for the gift of time you give me to write and pursue my dream. And thanks to my daughters, Megan and Amara. You are so amazing and inspiring. My books cannot be written without all your great ideas, input, tough criticisms, and reassuring hugs. You are God's greatest gift to me in this world.

The author welcomes all comments and thoughts on this book. Please visit her at www.cslakin.com.

## Share Your Thoughts

**With the Author:** Your comments will be forwarded to the author when you send them to *zauthor@zondervan.com*.

**With Zondervan:** Submit your review of this book by writing to *zreview@zondervan.com*.

## Free Online Resources at
## www.zondervan.com

**Zondervan AuthorTracker:** Be notified whenever your favorite authors publish new books, go on tour, or post an update about what's happening in their lives at www.zondervan.com/authortracker.

**Daily Bible Verses and Devotions:** Enrich your life with daily Bible verses or devotions that help you start every morning focused on God. Visit www.zondervan.com/newsletters.

**Free Email Publications:** Sign up for newsletters on Christian living, academic resources, church ministry, fiction, children's resources, and more. Visit www.zondervan.com/newsletters.

**Zondervan Bible Search:** Find and compare Bible passages in a variety of translations at www.zondervanbiblesearch.com.

**Other Benefits:** Register yourself to receive online benefits like coupons and special offers, or to participate in research.

**ZONDERVAN.com/**
**AUTHORTRACKER**
*follow your favorite authors*